IN
THE
WIND

ALSO BY BARBARA FISTER

On Edge

IN

BARBARA

THE

FISTER

WIND

ST. MARTIN'S MINOTAUR ⚒ NEW YORK

IN THE WIND. Copyright © 2008 by Barbara Fister. All rights reserved. Printed in the United States of America. No part of this book may be used or reproduced in any manner whatsoever without written permission, except in the case of brief quotations embodied in critical articles or reviews. For information, address St. Martin's Press, 175 Fifth Avenue, New York, N.Y. 10010.

www.minotaurbooks.com

Design by Dylan Rosal Greif

Library of Congress Cataloging-in-Publication Data (TK)

ISBN-13: 978-0-312-37491-4
ISBN-10: 0-312-37491-7

First Edition: June 2008

10 9 8 7 6 5 4 3 2 1

For Tim

ACKNOWLEDGMENTS

This story grew out of feeling an unnerving sense of déja vu as the counterintelligence practices of the Vietnam War era were revived under the PATRIOT Act. I'm grateful to those "radical militant librarians" and booksellers who have made a point of refusing to trade our civil liberties for a false sense of security. On a more personal note, I'd like to thank Dan Mandel, the Patron Saint of Persistence, Gina Scarpa, who has an uncanny ability to put her finger on what isn't working, and all the folks at St. Martin's. Finally, I owe a round to my friends at 4MA who keep teaching me how to read.

IN THE WIND

ONE

*I*t starts, as always, in the crowded cooler of the old Cook County medical examiner's office. A worker in coveralls and a mask loads the rough wooden boxes stacked against the wall onto a dolly and trundles them, three at a time, down the hallway to the loading dock, where a truck is waiting. He hums to himself, steadying the topmost box with one hand, and doesn't notice the fluid that looks like antifreeze dripping from the corner of one of the boxes.

I follow the unmarked panel truck through South Side neighborhoods, into the suburbs, and to the cemetery, where a long trench is open near the back fence. The grass here is brown and sparse. Broken roots reach like bony fingers through the newly dug earth, and a cracked drain pipe drips rusty water. Two men unload the boxes and lower them in, nudging them close together to save space. Each box has a round brass tag nailed to one end—no names, just numbers.

When the last one is in place, lying unevenly because it barely fits, an old black man in a suit clasps his hands and mumbles a prayer before scattering a handful of dirt, which patters down on the plywood with the sound of rain. There's a moment of quiet, just the rustle of the wind and the hum of traffic on a distant highway. Then he turns away and the backhoe starts up, making a shrill, insistent racket.

Only it wasn't a backhoe, it was the phone. I picked it up, feeling the familiar knot of sorrow in the center of my chest that always came with that dream. "Hello?"

"Anni? Is that you?"

"Yeah."

"You sound funny."

I recognized that low rumble: Father Sikora, the priest at St. Larry's, the Catholic church and community center four blocks from my house.

"I was asleep." I picked up my watch and squinted at it. Not quite 6:00 A.M. "What's wrong? Is Sophie—"

"Not Sophie. It's someone else. She needs help. You got a car now, right?"

"In a manner of speaking."

"What does that mean?"

"It runs most of the time."

"Oh. Well, listen . . ." I heard him take a breath. "Take care of her, okay? I'm counting on you." *Click.*

I stared at the phone for a moment before I put it down. Father Sikora wasn't much for small talk, but this was cryptic even for him. I met him ten years ago, when I was a rookie police officer assigned to the Wood District, where his church was an anchor for the community. When I needed some insight into why there was a spike in vandalism or how residents would respond to a new policing initiative, he had the answers. He was in his late sixties, now, a barrel-chested Pole with a bald head, a boxer's mashed nose, a rolling gait from an arthritic hip, and gnarled hands that could wield a nail gun for hours of hard manual labor or cup the head of a newborn with immense gentleness. The sole priest in a busy parish, he offered three Masses on the weekends, one each in English, Polish, and Spanish. He'd never asked for my help before. Maybe another troubled teen had gotten lost in the big bad city. That seemed to be my specialty these days.

Between that dream and the strange conversation, I felt disoriented and in sore need of coffee. I pulled on a pair of cutoffs and ran water into the old stove-top percolator, scooping in some of the Puerto Rican coffee that I buy at the local corner grocery. I filled a bowl with Little Friskies, went out on the porch, and left it at the bottom of the steps for the three-legged stray cat who lived in the alley. He crouched by the trash cans, pretending indifference, but one ragged ear swiveled toward the sound. For reasons of feline pride, he preferred to think he stole the food when my back was turned. I knew he wouldn't make his move until I went back upstairs and shut the door behind me.

The early-morning sun flooded the room with light from unexpected angles these days. I finally had time to work on the classic Chicago two-flat that I'd bought a year ago. I rented the downstairs flat to a young family and lived on the second floor, in an apartment that had been a poky, dark warren of small rooms until I'd knocked out walls, opened the ceiling to expose the rafters, and ripped up carpet and layers of old linoleum to uncover the hardwood underneath. My brother, Martin, helped me install some old windows with rippled glass that I'd found at a junk shop, rigging them with old-fashioned sash weights hidden behind the casings so they opened and shut with buttery smoothness. They were thrown wide open now, the streets playing their morning music: cars, city buses wheezing away from their stops, neighbors calling out to one another as they headed to work—something I didn't do anymore, which meant I had plenty of time and more than enough energy to make some renovations.

From an early age, I had known exactly what I wanted to do with my life. I would join the police force and become a detective based at Area 4 headquarters, finding the bad guys, helping their victims. No one who died on the streets would be buried without a name or a story, not if I was working the case. Things had gone according to plan—until I saw a cop named Hank Cravic lose his temper with a cocky teenager, leaving the kid with permanent brain damage. The boy's family filed a civil suit against the city and, when it finally made its way through the courts, I was called as a witness. The city settled with the family for an undisclosed sum without ever admitting responsibility, but after I testified against Cravic, everything changed.

It took a few months before I finally admitted to myself that I couldn't do the job anymore, not without the support of my fellow officers. I turned in my shield, filled out the paperwork to get a PI's license, then borrowed a sledgehammer and went to work remodeling my apartment. I have a gift for anger management.

The percolator started to burble, and just as I turned the flame down, I heard tapping at the door. Since no one was visible through the peephole, I assumed it was one of the kids who lived downstairs. They were always up at the crack of dawn, and in mid-June, dawn cracked early. But it wasn't a child; it was a short, fat woman in a blue jumper and orthopedic shoes, her face hidden under the bill of a baseball cap. When she took it off, I recognized her as one of the workers at St. Larry's.

"Can I help you?"

"I'm Rosa." She gave me an uncertain smile. "Father Sikora sent me?" She added, as if she wasn't sure herself.

So it wasn't a runaway in trouble; it was a middle-aged woman who dressed like a nun—a nun who was a Cubs fan. "Oh, right. Come on in." I suddenly felt awkward about the skimpy tank top I'd worn to bed, the paint-spattered cutoffs, even conscious of the tattoo on my shoulder. It was a tasteful little diamond in a traditional Hmong design, but I doubted middle-aged church workers approved of women with tattoos.

"Sorry about the mess. Been doing some remodeling." I wiped dust from a kitchen chair with a dish towel, then wiped the table for good measure. "Have a seat." I ducked into the bathroom to brush my teeth, run a comb through my hair, and change into a T-shirt and a pair of jeans.

When I returned, Rosa was sitting at the kitchen table, dimpled and plump and so short, her feet dangled above the floor. Her hair, once dark but now threaded with silver, fell in a thick braid down her back, and her eyes were bright and curious as she tilted her head to read the address off a pile of mail in a basket on the table. "Koski-nen," she said thoughtfully. "Isn't that a Finnish name?"

"Right," I said, taking two mugs out of a cupboard. I braced myself for the usual reaction, a variation on "Funny, you don't look Jewish." With my dark hair and brown skin, I wasn't your typical Scandina-vian. But she surprised me.

"You must have Saami ancestry."

"Maybe. I don't know anything about my ancestors, just that the name is common in Finland." Not many people knew about the Saami, indigenous nomads who herd reindeer in northern Finland. She could be right. Or the genes that gave me my looks were Filipino, or Lebanese, or Puerto Rican, some multiethnic gumbo. It didn't matter to me where they came from; I knew who I was.

But I didn't know much about Rosa. I'd seen her working at the bustling community center next to the church. The old rectory housed a soup kitchen, a food shelf, and programs for families, teens, and the homeless, all of it run on ridiculous optimism and a loaves and fishes approach to budgeting. Rosa was usually somewhere in the background, holding a baby or talking softly in Spanish to a glower-ing teenager who was upset because of some slight or other.

"Is that your family?" she asked, nodding at a framed photo propped next to the basket of mail.

I brought over mugs of coffee and sat across from her, glancing at the photo taken the day I graduated from the Academy, me in a hat that looked too big, dwarfed by my brother and grandfather, who stood on either side. I realized I should have put it away somewhere until I'd finished taping and sanding the drywall; the glass was coated with fine white powder, like frost. "Yup. I'm the one in the uniform."

"Father Sikora told me you're a private investigator now, that you work for Sophie Tilquist's parents."

"They asked me to help find her when she ran away. I would have done it anyway, I've known the family for years." Jim and Nancy

Tilquist were my oldest and best friends. Their lives had been thrown into disarray when their daughter Sophie was diagnosed with bipolar disorder at age fourteen. In the three years since, during manic episodes, she would disappear from home, looking for excitement in the city. Most recently, I'd found her at St. Larry's, communing with archangels among the flickering votive candles in the sanctuary.

With the first sip of coffee, my hand automatically started looking for a cigarette, and I gave it a mental smack. I'd quit that, too, but the urge was still there. It was time to get down to business. "So, I understand you need help."

She nodded at me over her mug, her dark eyes solemn. "I have to go somewhere and I don't have a car."

I had to struggle to keep a straight face. The old priest knew I'd just gotten my PI's license, but apparently that hadn't impressed him as much as the news that I'd finally bought a battered car from one of his parishioners. He'd been ragging me about using my bike to get around town since the Cougar I'd driven for years died of old age. He thought it was dangerous, that the city was no place for bikes. I hadn't paid any attention to him, enjoying a brief holiday from the daily hunt for street parking. But I finally realized I could get a phone call in the middle of the night and have to prowl the city in search of Sophie, and that meant I'd have to have a car.

"Sure, I can give you a lift. Where do you need to go?"

"Bemidji."

I wondered if I heard her right. "You mean, Bemidji, Minnesota?"

"Actually, it's a little north of there. You've never heard of it."

I drank some coffee. That would take, what, ten hours? Fifteen? A couple of days shot, going there and back again. I thought about offering her a ride to the bus station, and the bus fare if necessary, but Father Sikora would have done that, if that was all she needed. Something was going on, something neither one of them wanted to explain.

I liked the old priest. When I used to stop by St. Larry's with questions and a badge, he would look me in the eye and answer without messing around. True, there were times I could tell he was holding something back, but I'd learned through experience he always had good reason. And he'd been kind to Sophie, who had mistaken the bright, clamoring excitement that filled her mind for a divinely inspired mystical experience. She'd been stable since the last episode, though. I could afford to be out of town for a few days.

Besides, for reasons I couldn't guess, Father Sikora was counting on me.

I looked over at the woman, her eyes on me as she sipped from her mug. "So," I said to her, "what's the best way to get to Bemidji?"

I threw a change of clothes, my cell phone and a couple of paperbacks into a knapsack, and checked my wallet, realizing I'd better hit up an ATM before we left town. At only 6:30, it was too early to call my brother, Martin. He was planning come over after work the next day to help me replace the bathroom sink. I'd give him a ring after we got on the road, explain the change of plans.

The feral tomcat, who was pretending someone else had cleaned out the bowl of Friskies, watched us suspiciously as we came stairs, then darted off in his lopsided way when we got too close. Though it was early, the sky was already hazy and bright, the stagnant air as hot as if it were coming from an open oven. For the second week in a row, temperatures were predicted to reach the upper nineties by afternoon. As we came through the narrow gangway between my house and the next, I caught the pungent scent of stale tobacco and sweat, and stopped short, causing Rosa to step on my heels.

"Morning, ladies." He was leaning back on his elbows, surveying the street as if he owned it. He took a slow toke on his cigarette to show how comfortable he was. "Gonna be another hot one."

"Get off my porch, Tyler."

"Just resting my feet."

"Rest them somewhere else."

He shrugged and gave Rosa a roguish wink as he stood. I was afraid he'd ask if she could spare a few bucks, so I gave him a "Get lost" glare and pointed her toward my car. As I circled around to the driver's side, I looked back. Tyler was ambling away down the sidewalk, flicking ash off his cigarette, a cell phone pressed to his ear, probably setting up his next score.

"Who was that?" Rosa asked.

"Just a guy I arrested a couple times. For some reason, that makes him think we're buddies." Tyler was a country boy from the southernmost end of the state. He had a drug habit, a soft accent, cornflower blue eyes, and shoulder-length wavy locks and a wispy beard that made him look like a picture of Jesus, except Jesus never had so many tattoos on his arms. He made a specialty of charming his way into old ladies' homes and, while they made him some sandwiches, pocketing anything he thought he could sell. He was a master at talking his way out of trouble, becoming a confidential informant for more than one cop, as adept at playing them as his old ladies.

"He sometimes comes by for supper at St. Larry's." Her eyes were fixed on the rearview mirror. "Always complains about the food."

"How long have you worked there?" I asked as I coaxed the Corolla's engine to a rough start.

"A little over a year. So, you're the one who bought Laronda's car. I thought she'd never find a buyer."

The Corolla chugged loudly as I pulled out into the street. It needed a new muffler, among other things. "Yeah, I was in the market and . . . I don't know, I felt sorry for her." Laronda, the previous owner, had launched a campaign of stopping me on the sidewalk or in the market, patting my arm, telling me what a good little car she had—a little dented up was all—how she needed the money so she could pay off some hospital bills, buy the medicine the doctors told her to take. She'd almost looked disappointed when I finally said yes, okay, I'd buy the car. Like it had been too easy. Rosa didn't say anything, but I got the feeling she felt sorry for *me*, suckered into buying such a piece of junk.

"Father Sikora's a good guy to have on your side." I said.

"Yes, he is." She looked placidly out the window, not taking the invitation to explain why she had to leave town suddenly.

"Don't you think you should tell me what this is about?"

"It's better if I don't. You were at the Temple last month, weren't you?" If she was trying to change the subject, it worked. I looked at her, surprised. "One of our regulars was on the list this year. I wanted to be there for him. What brought you to the service? Someone you knew?"

"I go every year," I said, not really answering her question. It was an annual memorial service, held at the Chicago Temple, that strange neo-Gothic skyscraper in the Loop that combines Methodist ministry and fifteen floors of office space. A few dozen people would gather there at the end of May to remember those buried by the county at public expense. Not that much was expended—embalming performed by students of mortuary science who needed the practice, a forty-dollar pine box, and a few square feet of a trench in the Homewood cemetery, where they were interred, a dozen at a time, as soon as investigators in the morgue detail were certain no one else would foot the bill. Fifteen or twenty of the three hundred or so buried by the county each year didn't even have a name. My mother was buried there, identified only by a number until Jim Tilquist had helped me track her down. I had only the vaguest memories of her, and never found out how she died, but I went to the service every spring, and sometimes took the trip with her to Homewood in my dreams.

I waited for traffic to clear and pulled onto Western, swerving around an old woman pushing a grocery cart filled with her belongings. She traveled up and down the street every day, always pushing the same load, always with that look of fierce purpose, never seeming to get to wherever the destination was.

There was an ATM machine in the front entrance of a pharmacy just up the block. I pulled into an open spot in front of an unmarked car where a plainclothes cop was drinking coffee in a go-cup, the *Sun-Times* spread out across his steering wheel. It wasn't just the shoulder rig bulging under his jacket that told me he was a cop, but the look on his face, a tense kind of patience earned from hours of surveillance. If some lowlifes were giving Rosa trouble, finding a parking spot right in front of an armed police officer seemed a piece of luck. I put it in neutral and pulled the hand brake, leaving the engine running, thinking the fewer times I had to deal with that balky ignition, the better. "I need to get some cash. Why don't you figure out our route."

I reached across, opened up the glove compartment to pull out the pocket road atlas, and saw an ugly snub-nosed .38 with a taped grip that I had forgotten was in there. I glanced at Rosa, pulling the map book out from under it, but she didn't seem to notice the gun, or politely ignored it at least.

"Just take the Kennedy outbound," she said, settling the atlas in her lap. "I'll get some change together for the tolls." She started to burrow in her purse.

As I headed toward the pharmacy, I glanced back. The cop was focused on his newspaper, not interested in me or the illegal handgun in my glove compartment. There were a couple of newspaper boxes on the sidewalk. I put in two quarters and pulled out the morning *Trib*. The usual: a headline about the latest crisis in Iraq, concern that the power grid might fail again as temperatures rose. Protests held at police headquarters over the second shooting of an unarmed black youth by police in a matter of weeks. I wondered, not for the first time, why they bothered to call it news.

It was too early for the pharmacy to be open, but the door to the lobby with the ATM was unlocked, monitored by a pair of security cameras. I slipped in my card, punched in the numbers, and tucked the bills into my wallet. That gun was bothering me. Chicago has some of the strictest handgun laws in the country. It's not a good place to be caught with an unregistered weapon. I'd found it during Sophie's most recent manic escapade, in a squat where she had been staying. It hadn't been fired recently, but just in case, I had wiped it down thoroughly and stuck it in my glove compartment, not mentioning it to her parents, who were already frantic enough. When I'd finally found Sophie, she was in no state to explain where it had come from, and in the turmoil of getting her hospitalized, I forgot all about it. I knew I should turn it in at one of the districts, but it would lead to hours of paperwork and questions. It would have to wait until I returned from Minnesota.

As I pushed out to the sidewalk, two men approached. My first thought was that they had been watching the ATM and had picked an easy target—a woman, yet, all of five foot three, slight of build. The sensible thing would be to play it safe and hand over my wallet. But they weren't muggers; they were wearing suits and ties. And when I glanced over at Rosa, I saw her face was stiff with dread.

Operating on pure instinct, I tossed my newspaper at the bigger of the two men to distract him and then turned to the one approaching close behind me and kneed him hard in the groin, causing enough of a jolt that he dropped the SIG Sauer he was holding out of sight behind his right leg. It clattered to the sidewalk, and we both dived for it. The big man, batting at the paper that fanned around him, tripped over our legs and crashed down hard. I head-butted the other one and got my palm on the grip of his pistol. By this time, the assault on his *cojones* had got the better of him; he was hunched over, gasping, face screwed up in pain.

The plainclothes cop was out of his car now, identifying himself

in a bellow loud enough to be heard within three blocks, his service
weapon extended. I rose to my knees and sent the SIG spinning toward him across the sidewalk, showing him my palms. He stopped it
with his foot and pointed his gun at its owner, whose hand was moving into his jacket.

"Fiske, FBI." The man took out a badge case and let it fall open.
He dabbed his split lip with the back of his other hand and frowned
at the stain. The bigger man lumbered to his feet, breathing hard. He
held his right arm tenderly to his chest, wincing as he scanned the
street. "God*damn* it!"

Fiske got up to retrieve his weapon, then ordered me to lie facedown on the sidewalk. He cuffed my wrists behind me and gave them
an extra tug to show who was boss. The early rush-hour traffic had
slowed to a crawl as people gawked. The homeless woman pushing
the grocery cart had made it this far in her daily trek and was
doggedly trying to steer through it all, her eyes wide with panic, a
driver hanging out his window, yelling angrily after she clipped his
car with her cart.

Fiske patted me down thoroughly, then bent close enough that I
could feel the heat of his breath, smell the coppery tang of the blood
that stained his teeth. "Verna Basswood," he said intimately, his voice
vibrating with tension. "Where'd she go?"

"Who?"

He spat, a red glob landing near my face on the sidewalk. "You're
going to regret wasting my time."

Cruisers were drawing up, sirens whooping as he grabbed my arms
and hauled me to my feet. I couldn't make out the questions people
were asking me over all the racket, but I could guess what they were
about. The spot where I'd left my Corolla idling was now vacant.

TWO

spent the next eight hours in a small windowless room in the Dirksen Federal Building, with Fiske and a parade of other agents asking me questions about how I knew Rosa Saenz, about my political leanings, and how much involvement I had with leftist organizations. I thought the answer to that one was easy—none—but Fiske pounced as if he'd caught me in a major omission. Apparently, the community center at St. Larry's qualified in his book, and witnesses had seen me there on more than one occasion. I wasn't going to let them know about Father Sikora's phone call, not until I had a chance to talk to him, so I stuck to the bare truth: I only went there to canvass during investigations—oh, and once when they had a bake sale. I'd bought a dozen oatmeal cookies, if I remembered correctly. Fiske exhaled wearily and massaged the skin between his eyes, body language for "You're lying," but I stuck with my impression of an honest citizen doing her duty.

Two hours into it, I asked if I could make a call—not to a lawyer, just to check in with my brother. I wasn't sure what I had gotten myself into, but if there was any chance my name was going to end up in the news, I didn't want him to hear about it secondhand. Fiske took me to another room, pointed to the phone on the desk, and pretended to read some notices pinned to the wall as I dialed the number of the cell phone Martin always carried in a holder clipped to his belt. I told him I was at the Federal Building, answering some questions, but that was nothing to be concerned about. I reminded him about our plans for the next day—that after work he was going to take the

rain into town and help me replace the bathroom sink. Maybe we
could order out a pizza for dinner. It was a short conversation, but at
least I had made sure he wouldn't worry if he heard I'd been taken
off the street in handcuffs.

Fiske escorted me back to the small room and he and his colleagues dragged me over the same territory several more times, digging for details. It was getting tiresome, so I mentioned casually that
one of the times I'd stopped by St. Larry's, I was looking for Jim
Tilquist's daughter. I left out the fact that Sophie was in a psychotic
state at the time, and that her parents were my clients, the first and
only clients since getting my PI's license. I simply explained that I had
known Sophie's stepfather since I was a child. When I went on the
job she'd been my mentor and friend, and I'd even introduced him to
the woman he married. It wasn't surprising that when his oldest
daughter ran off to spend some time in the city, as teenagers will
from time to time, the family asked me personally to find her and
bring her home. She wasn't gone long enough to make it official police business, and Jim liked to keep his personal life private, given he
was the FBI's senior agent on the Chicago Terrorist Task Force.

Introducing Special Agent Tilquist's name into the conversation had
an interesting effect. There were three suits in the room at that point.
They all used different techniques to avoid looking at one another:
scratching an ear, examining a loose thread on a sleeve. Fiske fingered
his swollen lip and asked if I wanted some more coffee. Even though I
said I didn't, he rose, the others following him out. I sat by myself for
nearly two hours. I'd wanted them to know I had friends there in the
Dirksen Building, but I hadn't expected so strong a reaction.

With all that time to think it over, I retraced everything they'd
asked me, trying to figure out what was going on. When Fiske had
cuffed me, he'd asked about . . . Vera? Verna? It had sounded strangely
familiar, but I couldn't think why. The authorities seemed to think

Rosa was mixed up in something political; that much was clear. Though nobody had used the phrase "national security," their questions pointed in the direction of a terrorist investigation. But they had declined to explain, and I couldn't imagine any connection Rosa might have to their usual suspects—fundamentalist Islamic organizations or eco-activists who spiked trees and burned SUVs.

When Fiske came back, he was alone. He went over his original questions again, adding a few more for good measure, but his tone had changed from hostile to strictly professional. When he asked what connections I had with the Native American community, I was puzzled, but I dredged up every name I could think of, from a community-relations officer who claimed to be part Cherokee to a homeless Menominee who panhandled in Grant Park.

Fiske kept coming back to Thea Adelman, a lawyer who showed up on television whenever Native American issues were in the news. I'd been up against her in court and knew she was a talented defense lawyer and an effective muckraker—and no friend of the police. She had been profiled in the *Trib* earlier in the week, complaining about how ineffectual the Office of Professional Standards was in dealing with the systemic racism in the department. The photographer had posed her in front of police headquarters, using as a backdrop the resentful sidelong, glares of the cops going in and out.

When that line of inquiry was exhausted, Fiske went back to basics. "Where is Rosa Saenz? Why did she come to you? When are you going to stop stonewalling?" He began to salt his questions with bits of personal information about cases I'd worked, friends and enemies I'd made along the way, why I'd resigned so abruptly and whether it was connected to that lawsuit against the city. His tone was sympathetic, but he was letting me know he knew enough about me that he could tighten the screws whenever he wanted. "That brother of yours," he said casually, "I hear he's . . . what's the phrase they use these days, 'special needs'? Wouldn't be good for him if you got in trouble for withholding information, would it?"

I seethed inside, but kept my answers simple: I didn't know why she came to me; I didn't know where she was.

It was 3:00 P.M. when they finally cut me loose. I stepped outside and took a deep breath. Even though there was a full day's worth of scorching heat trapped in the concrete box of Federal Plaza, I felt myself start to shake. It was partly exhaustion from all those hours of weighing each word, monitoring my facial expressions, avoiding the small traps that Fiske and his colleagues kept setting for me. But it was also the residual emotion from an experience I hadn't totally understood before. Though I'd conducted my share of hardball interrogations, I never really knew what it was like to be on the other side. I felt used and dirty, as if I'd been stripped and prodded in front of an audience. All I wanted was to go home and take a shower.

But as I started across the plaza, headed for the nearest El station, I found myself flanked by a couple of friendly CPD detectives, who offered to take me to Area 4 headquarters to file a report on my stolen car. Having had enough of small windowless rooms for one day, I declined, but they wouldn't take no for an answer. It turned out they had a few questions, too.

ou want to run that by me again?"

"Not really." I glanced at my watch—5:30 already. I figured the simplest way to get through this was to act cooperative and wait them out, but my patience was growing frayed. Across the table from me, a beefy middle-aged detective named Alvin Prochaska massaged the side of his face as if it ached. I knew him from working at Area 4. He was one of those overweight guys with bad feet who worked the phones and typed reports with two fingers, collected his paycheck, and counted the days to retirement, which would be spent in a rustic cabin in Wisconsin, where shellacked fish decorated the knotty-pine walls.

"Let's start with the woman showing up at your door this morning. It's not like I got anything else to do." One watery blue eye regarded me; the other one was hidden behind the hand that was propping his head up.

"This is stupid."

"That's the only part of your statement I'm willing to believe." I slumped back in my chair and closed my eyes. "So this woman shows up at your door this morning," Prochaska prompted me in a bored voice, going through the motions one more time. "How'd you know her, exactly?"

"I'd seen her a few times over at St. Larry's, that's all. I have no idea why she took off in my car."

"If you didn't know this woman that well, why were you going to drive her all the way to Duluth?"

"Bemidji."

"Whatever."

"Like I said, she seemed like . . . a good person. Like a nun or something."

The watery blue eye blinked slowly, a reptilelike look of skepticism. "You'd drive a nun you hardly know to Brainerd at the drop of a hat?"

"Bemidji. Listen, it's hard to explain, but . . . did you go to a Catholic school, by chance?"

"St. Mary of the Angels." He pointed over his shoulder with his thumb, knowing exactly where it was, one of his cardinal points.

"Then you know what I'm talking about. A nun asks you to do something, you don't mess around. You do it."

He tipped his head in grudging agreement. "Fine, but you didn't ask what it's about? Do you know how far away Bemidji is?"

I noticed this time he knew the destination. "Not exactly. It's, like, north of Minneapolis, right?"

"It's, like, north of everything." He gave me a sleepy one-eyed glare and then with a thick forefinger flipped through a little notebook lying on the table in front of him. "No luggage?" he asked, knowing the answer.

"Just a little handbag."

"So, what you're telling me, you barely knew this Rosa Saenz." He peered at me, as if I were wearing a sign he was trying to read in a foreign language that he didn't know. "And out of the blue, she shows up at your door. And you were going to drive her hundreds of miles. . . ." His translation skills failed him. "You want another cup of coffee?"

"No thanks. What's this is all about anyway?"

He didn't answer, just let his face slide back into his palm and propped it there. We looked at each other for a while. Then he sighed heavily and we sat there some more.

"Am I going to be charged with something?"

"Well, you did assault two federal officers."

"I didn't know those guys were Feebs. They didn't announce. Looked like a robbery, okay? It's not the safest neighborhood."

"I realize that. I work here, remember? Which— Listen, just out of curiosity . . ." He leaned across the table. "When you figure you're being mugged by two guys who weigh two, three times as much as you, and they're armed and you're not . . . you think it's wise to take 'em on?"

"They pissed me off." He rolled his eyes. "All right, maybe it wasn't too smart, but—"

"You got that right." Having dispensed his personal-safety tip of the day, he went back to paging listlessly through his notebook, blinking so slowly, I thought he was falling asleep. The door opened and his partner, Dugan, came in. He was a rangy, restless six-footer with a crooked tie, a crooked nose, and an air of private amusement, as if there was some cosmic joke out there that nobody else appreciated. "We found your car, Ms. Koskinen," he said. "Abandoned up by Humboldt Park."

Prochaska hauled himself to his feet, turned his back to me so he could mutter privately to Dugan. "So, what's the deal?"

I could barely make out the answer. "Boss just held a press conference. Unis are on double shifts until the fugitive's apprehended."

It seemed unreal suddenly, the word *fugitive* colliding with the image of the woman sitting peacefully in my kitchen. Whatever Rosa was accused of, whoever she really was, it was big enough to make the evening news. What had Father Sikora gotten me into?

Prochaska sighed. "Aw shit. Like we need this now. Look, I gotta . . ." He glanced over at me, then down at his watch. "There's this thing my wife's got on tonight. I'm already late. She's gonna chew my ass."

"Go on home, Al. I'll wrap this up." After he left, Dugan turned back to me. "You're not planning to leave town, Ms. Koskinen?" he said, enjoying the cliché.

"Well, I was really looking forward to seeing that famous Paul Bunyan statue, but . . . no, I'm not going anywhere. We're through?"

He looked around the dingy room. "Hey, if you want to stick around, fine, but I'm outta here. Give me a minute, and I'll run you up to your car."

He ushered me out into the squad room. It was all eerily familiar: phones trilling, rough laughter, an irate mother looking for news of a child who had been picked up for questioning. The handful of detectives working late fell silent and glanced at me with the same hostile indifference they reserved for cons and defense lawyers, then turned back to their work. That attitude had grown pretty familiar, too, in my last months on the job.

Dugan flipped through a pile of "While you were out" slips at his messy desk; then we headed down the stairs and through the lobby of the uniform division downstairs. A crumpled sheet of paper scuttled across the tile as Dugan pulled the door open for me. Rosa's round, smiling face was on it. Apparently, it was a flyer distributed to the patrol officers sent out to find her.

When we stepped through the glass doors, the air wrapped around us like a muggy, warm blanket. Clouds lowered over the city, ripe with rain, but there was no hint of a cooling breeze. "Why don't I just catch a bus?" I nodded toward the stop on the corner. "The fifty-two goes right by the park."

"Nah, it's on my way. Let's go." Dugan gave me a smile, but there was something in his tone that told me it wasn't optional. We crossed the street to the parking lot, where employees' personal cars were parked inside a chain-link fence topped with barbed wire, got into his Jeep, and headed out into the clogged arteries of the rush hour.

He was a casually aggressive driver; either that or something was wrong with his depth perception, given the way he wove in and out of traffic, always a hairsbreadth from disaster. "Must have been a little weird, being in the box, huh?" he said, cutting in front of a van with only a few inches to spare. "Given you used to interview suspects there not so long ago."

"How long you been at Harrison?" I asked attempting to change the subject.

"Six weeks. Not that I'm new at this. Sixteen years in. Patrol in Shakespeare, then narcotics, five years in Belmont Violent Crimes. Don't laugh, we actually had some, though I have to admit there were times we were tempted to go out and commit a few, just to stay awake. A stint at headquarters before a transfer to Harrison."

"Who'd you piss off?"

"Whaddya talking about? It was at my request. And hey, they had a sudden resignation. Guess I owe you one."

I wasn't sure about that. Belmont, covering the city's wealthy

North Side, had the lowest crime rate of Chicago's five areas. Area 4, often called Harrison, after the street its headquarters was on, had hot spots seething with gang violence, racial friction, and all the usual outcomes of joblessness, drugs, and poverty. "You're doing this all backward. Most people use seniority to move to a quieter gig."

"One thing I've noticed over the years: Most people are idiots."

I held my breath as he took advantage of a slowly accelerating truck to switch lanes and gain several inches.

"You know what I dealt with the last couple of years?" he went on. "Not criminals, not victims. Data. Mountains of data. We got everything so automated, so tied together with mapping systems and court records and rap sheets. Seven million offender records, nine million incidents, all the numbers you need to run the PD with maximum efficiency. Like 'How many arrests did this officer make last month? Is he earning his salary?' It was bullshit. I wanted to do something real for a change."

"Harrison's real all right."

"That's for sure. My mom's still mad at me for transferring. She calls me regularly to give me a lecture about why she isn't talking to me anymore."

"She worries."

"We got a lot of cops in the family. You think she'd be used to it."

"I don't think it works that way. How'd you get Prochaska for a partner?"

"Hey, he's all right," he said defensively, sensing criticism. "Little slow on his feet, maybe, but he's been around forever, knows a lot."

"Could be. I never worked that closely with him. Our investigative styles weren't real compatible."

"Somehow, that doesn't surprise me." We inched forward. Dugan tapped his fingers restlessly against the steering wheel, nervous energy radiating from him like the heat rising in waves from a sidewalk. "How big of a hurry are you in?"

"No hurry at all," I said quickly, thinking he was about to throw a bubble light on the roof and show me more of his exceptional driving skills.

"Great. Let's get something to eat." He was already turning down a side street. "There's a barbecue joint a few blocks from here. They have this amazing habanero sauce, guaranteed to clear your sinuses." He glanced at me. "No?"

"My stomach's kind of touchy tonight. Drank too much bad coffee at the Federal Building. Out of that pot labeled 'for suspects only.'"

He nodded sympathetically. "The one they spike with lye. Hey, I know just what you need." Inspired, he turned abruptly into an alley, barely missing a fence post, and parked behind a row of storefronts that held a Laundromat, a corner grocery, and a store with no name other than Ropas Usadas.

He led me through a back door, past a kitchen, and into a tiny dining room, five of the six tables occupied by Asians sitting over steaming bowls of noodle soup, the only item on the menu. A hand-lettered sign on the wall gave our options in Vietnamese and English: beef, shrimp, or chicken *pho*, with a choice of two sizes, huge and enormous. A small television on the counter was tuned to a soccer game. I studied the banner scrolling at the bottom of the screen, hoping to catch news about Rosa, but it was only giving scores. Dugan pulled out a chair for me at the one open table, saw the seat was mended with tape, and suddenly looked unsure of himself. "Should have warned you. It's kind of . . . We can go somewhere else."

"This is fine. The food smells great."

An old man who looked like a stump of weathered wood with a towel tied around it took our orders, which Dugan gave, once again in take-charge mode. Before waddling away, the old man gave me a smile that showed three or four pegs of yellow teeth. "They know me here," Dugan said. "I like to grab a bite in the neighborhood before

I head home. I rent a garden apartment from one of my aunts in Hyde Park. The restaurants there are trendy, full of ferns and shit, catering to the university crowd."

"So it's not on your way after all."

He winced, caught out. "Humboldt Park's not that far."

"It's miles in the wrong direction. What's this really about?"

"I just want to talk, but not in an interrogation room. Got a call couple of months ago, when I was still at headquarters. From Jim Tilquist."

Tilquist again. I searched my memory. Had he ever mentioned Rosa Saenz? Not that I could remember.

"We worked together on a few things in the past. He wasn't too happy about your resignation. Wanted to be sure that you weren't being pressured or anything."

"Christ." I hadn't talked to him before handing in my shield, hadn't realized how disappointed he must have felt when he heard about it. "It was my decision. Hope he didn't give you a hard time."

"He was just watching your back. You know him pretty well, huh?"

"Since I was a kid. He worked at Harrison then. Got me interested in police work." He'd been my mentor, coaching me patiently through the cultural politics of the district where I'd first been assigned, putting a good word in all the right places so I'd make detective in record time. After he married my friend Nancy and became a father, he left behind the gang shootings and raw violence of the West Side to earn a law degree. He worked for a couple of years in the Northern District on federal prosecutions before joining the FBI. He handled public corruption investigations for the local field office, then was appointed to lead the Terrorist Task Force, where his connections with the CPD were especially valuable. I tried to remember when I'd last spoken to him. It had been a short conversation in their kitchen one evening. He'd come in late, looking tired and drawn, and poured himself a stiff drink before even saying hello. His daughter was the only subject of conversation that night.

"He said you were trying to solve his cases when you were ten years old. What was that about?"

"I was eleven. And it was a case that was never solved. Well, unless you count it as a missing person's."

"Who was missing?"

Raindrops chased down the window, turning the neon signs of a bar across the street into a canvas of runny paint. "My mother. She couldn't take care of my brother and me, so when I was two years old, we went into foster care. It wasn't working out, especially for my brother, Martin, who . . . Well, it was only going to get worse. So I figured, hey, I knew a few things about our mother, and I had a photograph of her. I thought there might be some relatives we could move in with, so I went to Area Four and asked to talk to a detective. People there were being kind and stuff, but Jim Tilquist was the only one who actually listened to me."

He had seemed so old, though he was only thirty-five at the time. I remembered him offering me a cup of coffee as if I were a grown-up, making it half milk and sweetening it with three packets of sugar, knowing somehow I was too proud to say I wasn't used to the bitter taste. He paid attention as I talked, and his fingers were gentle as he took the photograph from me and studied it, holding it carefully by the edges, like evidence. He seemed to understand without being told that it was the only thing I had to go on.

The old man brought two big bowls of soup and set them in front of us, then returned with a heaping platter of fresh basil, bean sprouts, and sliced peppers. I picked up a plastic spoon decorated with blue dragons and tried the broth. "This is excellent."

"Better skip the peppers; these suckers are hot," Dugan said, scooping most of them into his bowl. "So, Tilquist helped you find your mom?"

I nodded. "Took awhile. Turned out she had died four years earlier. Undetermined causes, decomp pretty advanced. No ID on her,
nothing."

He winced. "That must have been tough."

"I barely remember her, tell you the truth. We did find a relative,
though, my grandfather. He adopted us, gave us a good home, which
was the main thing."

Dugan watched me eat for a minute, then took up his chopsticks
and went to work slurping noodles. "You're a PI now, huh?" he asked,
dabbing splashes of broth off his shirtfront with a napkin.

"Maybe. I mean, I got the license, but I'm not planning to join a
firm or anything. I'm thinking about law school, actually."

"You want to be a lawyer?"

No, I wanted to be a cop, but that was no longer an option. I felt a
spurt of irritation. "You ever going to tell me what all that was about
today?"

"All what?"

"Getting jumped by the FBI, cuffed, questioned for hours. Why
are they after Rosa Saenz? What the hell's going on?"

He poked around in his bowl for a moment before looking up at
me. "All right, even trade. You tell me what happened—no bullshit
this time—and I'll give you what I got."

"What bullshit?"

"You were lying to us."

"I wasn't. . . . Okay, maybe I left out a detail or two."

"So let's fill in the blanks. Why did Saenz go to you?"

"Look, off the record?"

"Depends."

"On what?"

"How criminal off the record turns out to be."

"Nothing criminal. Somebody sent her to me."

"Who?"

"A friend I don't want jammed up. I'll find out what the story is, let you know what I can. Hey, it's more than I gave the Feebs."

"You'll get back to me, though, right? And soon. The feds are being strong, silent types, as usual. If we're supposed to tear the city apart to find this woman, I want to have a better idea what I'm dealing with."

"I understand. And I really don't know why Rosa wanted to go to Bemidji. She didn't say. Actually, now that I think of it, she said it was north of Bemidji, a place I wouldn't have heard of. I figured she was running from someone, maybe witnessed something that would put her in danger. I can't see her doing anything criminal, though."

"Lot of people seem to feel that way. Fiske, the one in charge—you have some history with him?"

"First time I ever laid eyes on him was this morning."

"When you thought he was trying to rob you. Most muggers don't wear suits like that."

"Neither do most cops," I shot back.

Dugan snorted. "That's what our guy said. Got to be in the Outfit to afford an outfit like that. Or just be willing to pay top dollar to look good. Fiske is ambitious and takes himself mighty seriously. You made him look stupid, disarming him in front of an audience."

"I didn't exactly go looking for this."

"I know, but trust me, he's not the kind of guy you want as an enemy. How'd he know Rosa went to you for help?"

Good question. I was pretty sure, given the line of questioning, that Fiske didn't know about Father Sikora's call. But somewhere along the line . . . "Tyler," I said, realizing suddenly he must have been the one. He's a hype, feeds his habit with petty crime and selling intel to the cops. He saw us together this morning. Must have known the feds were looking for her, phoned in the tip."

"A one-man neighborhood watch, huh?"

"A neighborhood pest."

"That community center where she worked—it's near where you live, right? What's it like?"

"It's a busy place. They have a soup kitchen, English lessons for immigrants, youth programs—" I cut myself off, picturing my last visit to the teen center, but he was watching me closely, sensing more. "Jim Tilquist has a seventeen-year-old daughter who's attracted to the streets, doesn't realize what kind of trouble she could get into. I've tracked her down a few times for the family. Last month, I found her at St. Larry's. A lot of kids her age hang out there." Though on that particular night, she was the only one having religious visions.

"She knows Saenz then?"

"I don't know. She never mentioned her. Look, what does Tilquist have to do with this? And why do they want Saenz anyway?"

"You really don't know?"

"I told you that already. Come on, it's your turn."

He delayed by slurping up some more noodles, then hunted around for his napkin, wiped his fingers. "Fiske believes she's a fugitive they've been after for over thirty years," he finally said.

"Vera something, or Verna?" Dugan looked up sharply. "He asked me where she was. They think Saenz is this person?"

"Apparently."

"What's the charge?"

"Homicide." He produced the word after a slight pause, and then he seemed to come to some decision. "Someone shot and killed a federal agent here in Chicago back in the seventies. It was a big deal." He spoke softly, fixing his eyes on mine with a look that said, Put it together.

"You're talking about . . ."

"Special Agent Arne Tilquist. Your friend's father, killed in the line of duty."

"But that means . . ." My head was swimming. I helped the woman accused of shooting Jim's father escape capture. What had

Father Sikora been thinking, sending her to me? He knew I was a friend of the Tilquists.

"Verna Basswood was a person of interest, but she was never apprehended," Dugan said. "The feds believe Rosa Saenz is Basswood."

I stared out the window, going back over Fiske's interrogation. No wonder they took notice when Jim Tilquist's name came up. I knew that his father had preceded him at the FBI, that he was killed on the job when Jim was young, presumably assassinated by members of a radical group he had pursued in the early seventies. I'd read up on the case years ago, but Jim never talked about it. Thirty-five years was a long time to evade capture. And I couldn't wrap my head around the notion that the woman who had asked me for a ride was a desperate fugitive. A violent radical. A killer.

Dugan was studying me. "You must be feeling lousy about this."

"I just don't understand. She seemed so . . ."

"Like a nun? Or so you said. For what it's worth, the community reaction is on her side, one hundred percent. You weren't the only taken in."

"The person who sent her to me—you better believe I'm going to talk to him."

"You seem distraught. Am I going to have to put you on homicide watch?" He made a face so goofy, I couldn't help laughing. But if he was trying to make me feel better, it didn't work for long.

"What am I going to tell him?"

"Jim Tilquist? The truth. Sounds like he's been a good friend for a long time. He'll understand."

"I wish *I* did. This woman—she's a church worker, a grandmother to the neighborhood kids, their *abuelita*. Maybe the feds are acting on a bad tip." But I flashed on her expression as she spotted the two agents. She'd known who they were, and what they were after. And, with a sinking feeling, I remembered there was a loaded firearm in my car when she took off in it.

"I don't know. There's stuff going on with this case I don't understand at all. One thing I *do* know—" Dugan was suddenly leaning forward, giving me a hard look, the kind you use on suspects.

"What?"

"You've barely touched your food. That's considered a sign of disrespect. This culturally insensitive behavior could upset my friends." He wagged a chopstick at me. "So if you don't finish that soup, Koskinen, I may just have to do it for you."

THREE

t was nearly 8:00 P.M. before I got back to my apartment. I had finished the soup, to Dugan's mock disappointment. Then we drove to Humboldt Park and circled it until I spotted my Corolla parked beside a fire hydrant. He pulled up beside it. "Shit. She totaled it."

"Actually, the previous owner did that." I plucked a parking ticket from under the window wiper. "You have friends at headquarters. Want to fix this for me?"

"No. Does this thing actually run?"

"Sure. Most of the time."

He prowled around it, frowning. "Doesn't look very safe."

"Dugan, jeez. It's fine. Needs some body work and a tune-up is all."

I was anxious to check out the contents of the glove compartment, but he hovered, waiting to see if it would start, hoping to prove me wrong. I tried the ignition and got a hiccup and a cough. I pumped the gas pedal, turned the key again, and, after some judicious nudging on the accelerator, the engine caught and idled roughly.

"Call me," he said, scrabbling for his wallet at the last minute and handing me a card after jotting on it. "Anytime. Cell's on the back."

"Okay." I tucked it into my pocket, wondering why he was so interested in a case that wasn't even his.

"The city's a tinderbox," he said, sensing my unspoken question. He rested an arm on the roof the car, leaned down to be at eye level with me. "Two black kids have been shot by cops in the past month.

There's a lot of anger out there. And it's hot, way too hot for June. Given the crime she's charged with, we have to proceed as if Saenz is armed and dangerous. There's going to be a massive law-enforcement presence on the streets, and it'll set people off. The sooner she's in custody, the better. For everyone."

"I'm with you on that. Thanks for dinner."

"My pleasure. Let's do it again sometime."

"Ah, no. I don't think so." His face went blank, and I realized he thought I was giving him the brush-off. "Look, I enjoyed it, but you're new at Harrison. You don't want to get off on the wrong foot."

"Hell are you talking about?"

He wasn't making this easy. "*You're* the detective; figure it out."

"What, that brutality lawsuit? You did the right thing."

"That's what I thought at the time, but you testify against a fellow cop, you may as well turn in your tin right away, get it over with. I could handle the crap they gave me, the pranks and the ugly phone calls, but sometimes you need backup, and I wasn't getting it. You saw how everybody was looking at me at the shop. Most people—"

"Are idiots, like I said." He planted his hands on my window frame, as if holding the car in place by force until he had his say. "I come from a cop family. I know how cops think, but I'm not going to stand up for assholes just because they wear a uniform."

"I'm just saying—"

"Thanks for the warning, but I can handle myself. Besides, you're supposed to get back to me soon as you talk to Rosa's friend, remember? And don't kill him; I'll want a chance to interrogate him first." He straightened up and gave my Corolla two thumps on the roof, like a cowboy patting a horse.

I was impatient to check the glove compartment, but he kept watching me chug down the street, hands in his pockets, shaking his head, amused by the spectacle. As soon as I was safely out of his sight,

I reached over and opened the glove compartment. The road atlas was still there. The .38 snub-nosed revolver wasn't.

found a parking place two blocks from my house. There was a rustling in the weeds by the trash cans as the cat disappeared into the undergrowth. Pilar, my downstairs tenant, came out onto her back porch, her baby riding on her hip. "Hey, I heard you got arrested."

Someone must have seen me cuffed on the sidewalk this morning and had spread the word. "The authorities just wanted to ask me some questions."

"You were gone the whole day."

"They had a lot of questions."

"Was it about Rosa Saenz? They hassling people about her, knocking on everybody's door. It's all over TV that she killed a FBI agent a long time ago. Only that don't make sense. Everyone says she's a nice old lady, wouldn't shoot nobody." I hope Pilar was right about that, I thought as I climbed the steps to my flat. Given I'd inadvertently supplied that nice old lady with a weapon.

What the hell was I going to say to Jim?

Inside, I switched on a lamp, then took out my cell phone and dialed Jim's office number. His voice told me he was on another line and invited me to leave a message. I couldn't come up with one.

There were several messages waiting on my voice mail. A reporter on the cops and courts beat of the *Chicago Tribune* who knew me from the old days wanted a comment. There were three hang-up calls, one after a barely audible sigh that somehow sounded like Father Sikora. Another message from the reporter, wheedling, reminding me he had a deadline, and then Nancy Tilquist, asking me to give her a ring. I deleted them all and called her.

"Oh, good. I was wondering when we'd hear from you."

"Have you talked to Jim?"

"Briefly. He's still at work; I don't know when he'll get away."

"How's he doing? Did he tell you—"

"He didn't say much. Just that they'd spotted the woman who was wanted for his father's murder, but that she'd escaped. Listen, there's something I need to talk to you about, but it's . . . complicated, too hard to explain over the phone."

"Is it—"

"Not Sophie. She's doing fine. In fact, she's spending the evening in the city with friends. I'm in town, too, not that far from you. I know you've had a long day, but could you come over? It's important."

"Where are you?" She gave me an address in Bucktown. I put the phone down, wondering what she wanted to talk about. I'd known her for years, almost as long as I'd known Jim, and I usually could guess her state of mind from the tone of her voice. But this time, there was something tense and complicated going on behind her cryptic words that I couldn't tease out.

She and Jim made an odd pair. Nancy was a British-born anthropologist who taught at Stony Cliff, the college where my grandfather had been chair of her department. He'd always had a habit of taking people under his wing, and Nancy, a young single mother with a rambunctious toddler, had become practically a member of our household. She had the left-leaning skepticism of law enforcement typical of academics. Jim came from a long line of career cops and was ten years older than Nancy, and a hundred years more jaded about the human condition. But I didn't care about their differences. Apart from my brother and grandfather, they were the most important people in my life. My adolescent scheming to bring them together had been so transparent, they began their courtship as a kind of joke, as if I'd written an amateurish sitcom script and they were humoring me by acting their parts, playing it with broad comedy. But little Sophie quickly grew attached to Jim, and it wasn't long before something genuine sparked between the two of them.

They'd been married fifteen years now, adding two more daughters to the family, a surrogate family for Martin and me since our grandfather's death. But in the last year or two, the strain of Sophie's illness was beginning to wear on their relationship, and the long hours Jim was putting in at work didn't help.

The last remnant of twilight was fading from the sky as got in my car. I passed roving packs of kids having noisy, aimless fun, hookers gearing up for a long night's work, a group of old people sitting in lawn chairs in a driveway, drinking beer and laughing, a radio playing *rancheros* while one of them tended bratwursts on a grill. Not far behind me, a silver Cavalier followed at a discreet distance, making the same turns I did. Apparently, all those hours spent answering questions at the Federal Building hadn't satisfied the authorities. I had a tail.

After crossing an invisible border, I drove along streets that could have been in another city altogether. Gentrified, artsy, hip, and a little rough around the edges, although too well-off and settled to be as cutting edge as it wanted to be, Bucktown was less than two miles from my neighborhood, but in an alternate universe, one where most of the residents were white and college-educated, the children went to private schools, and a cup of coffee cost over three dollars.

I found the address and parked as close as I could, my battered Corolla looking ashamed of itself among the luxury cars on the street. Behind me, the Cavalier disappeared discreetly down a side street. The house was a well-preserved two-story brownstone with arched windows glowing in the night. I let myself through the wrought-iron gate and followed the flagstone path to the porch.

"Ms. Koskinen? Come in." The woman who opened the door was tall and slim, her face framed by hair that fell to her waist and looked like black silk. I recognized her—Thea Adelman, the Native American lawyer whose name had piqued Fiske's interest. I hesitated before climbing the front steps, trying to fit this new information into the picture, but she didn't appear to remember me.

She pointed me toward the living room. Nancy rose from the couch and gave me a quick hug. Her wiry shoulder-length, hair was thickly threaded with gray, and she seemed even thinner than when I'd last seen her, her skin drawn taut across her cheekbones. In the three years since Sophie was first diagnosed with bipolar disorder, Nancy always seemed poised for bad news, bracing herself. "Thanks for coming, Anni."

"What's going on?"

"We'll explain. This is Thea." The woman put out a narrow hand, which felt cold in mine.

"We've met, actually," I said. "The Yellow Medicine case, six years ago."

Her welcoming smile faltered. "Of course. I thought your name sounded familiar."

"I'm Harvey," the man said, stretching out a hand. Harvey Adelman, her husband and partner at law. He had nice crinkly eyes and a warm smile. Apparently, he hadn't picked up on his wife's reservations about me. "Would you like something to drink? Coffee, or—"

"No thanks."

"What case was this?" Nancy asked.

"Ray Yellow Medicine," Thea said before I could answer. "He was a homeless man who was picked up on an assault charge. The police coerced a confession out of him while he was under the influence of alcohol. Once he'd had a chance to sober up, he recanted, but the state's attorney pursued it is unfortunately."

"Ray got mad at the owner of a corner store who wouldn't let him use the facilities," I explained. "So he tried to drown him in the toilet."

"My client had an alibi."

"His girlfriend? She couldn't even keep her story straight."

"That confession was coerced." Thea smiled tightly.

"We could hardly shut him up long enough to Mirandize him, much less coerce anything out of him. Lucky for him he had a good lawyer," I added generously, though it didn't seem to help. "Look, if you got me here to ask me what I know about Rosa Saenz or Verna Basswood, or whatever her name is, it won't take long. I don't know anything."

The Adelmans exchanged startled glances, then looked at Nancy, who shook her head. "I didn't mention any names on the phone."

"What makes you think this is about Rosa Saenz?" Thea asked me.

I looked at Nancy, but she was studying her hands, avoiding my eyes. "When the feds were grilling me, they wanted to know about any connections I had with the Native American community. I mentioned we'd been up against each other in court. They got real interested."

"Did you tell them where to find Rosa?" Thea asked, a subzero chill in her voice.

"I couldn't have even if I'd wanted to. I don't know where she is. Do you?"

"No, we don't, either," Harvey said mildly. "So what exactly did you tell them?"

My first impulse was to say it was none of their damned business, but I swallowed my anger and kept it simple. "Saenz came by early this morning and asked me to give her a ride out of town. I said okay. When I stopped at an ATM, two guys moved in on me. Looked like I was being robbed. I resisted. In the confusion, she took off in my car. That's it. The feds wouldn't even tell me why they're after her, so I was the last to learn that I'd helped a fugitive escape. A fugitive wanted for killing my best friend's father."

"That's what they're saying, but it's bollocks," Nancy said firmly.

"I've met her. She talked to us the night you found Sophie at the church. I don't believe for an instant she could have killed anyone."

"Let me give you the details as we know them." Thea spoke formally, as if she were making an opening statement in court. "The FBI believes Rosa Saenz is Verna Basswood, an activist who was indicted in 1973 for the murder of Special Agent Arne Tilquist. He was trying to eliminate a small radical splinter group of the American Indian Movement operating in Chicago under the leadership of Logan Hall. Tilquist led a team of FBI agents in a raid against the group. It was a fiasco. An agent was seriously injured—hit in the spine, ended up a paraplegic." She looked at me challengingly, expecting a response, but I didn't say anything.

"Days later, members of the group were spotted at a farmhouse in southwestern Wisconsin," she went on. "Agents stormed the place. It was a bloodbath. Everyone there was killed, including Logan Hall. A week after that, Arne Tilquist was found dead in a basement in North Lawndale, shot in the head. The investigation focused on Verna Basswood, the only member of the group who hadn't been present in the farmhouse. They concocted enough circumstantial evidence for an arrest warrant, but Basswood disappeared into the underground."

"And now they think they've found her," I said.

"They haven't found her."

"Okay, counselor, I'll rephrase. Are Rosa Saenz and Verna Basswood one and the same?"

"Whether or not that's the case, Rosa Saenz is innocent until proven guilty. You need to understand that during the seventies, the FBI went after anyone they felt was a threat, using any means necessary. If violent confrontations weren't an option, they would coax informants to lie and then manufacture enough corroborating evidence to put their enemies away. It wasn't legal, but it was an essential tactic in a wider program to intimidate the public and discourage dissent. If that sounds familiar, that's because it's exactly what they're doing today."

"You've heard Jim complain about it," Nancy said, appealing to me. "Nobody's more devoted to the job than he is, but this isn't the organization he joined. The fact Rosa Saenz is accused of murdering a federal agent in an FBI family—you can imagine what they'll make of that. She doesn't have a hope of a fair trial, not the way things are now."

"We want to take on Rosa's defense," Harvey said, leaning forward earnestly. "Her case can expose how badly our civil liberties have been eroded since nine/eleven, but we'll need an experienced investigator. Nancy has been working with us on another matter. She thinks you could help us."

"You know as well as anyone how the system can get things wrong," Nancy said to me. "And Jim has always said you're the best he ever worked with."

I turned to her, my voice low, keeping the conversation between the two of us. "Yeah? What would he say about me working for the woman accused of murdering his father?"

"I told you: She couldn't have murdered anyone. It's impossible."

"But what would he say?"

"It's the right thing to do." Her eyes were fixed on mine, daring me. And while I sensed she was speaking for herself, it sounded like the kind of thing Jim would say. The right thing. Simple as that. But it never was that simple.

"We're getting ahead of ourselves," Thea interjected, cool and firm, all business. "Before we go any further, I need to ask a few questions. Just so we're all on the same page. Ms. Koskinen, how long were you employed by the Chicago Police Department?" She drew a yellow legal pad over and picked up a pen.

"Ten years. Two in uniform, eight at detective rank."

"That was a quick promotion."

"I'm good. I'm also a woman."

"Is that relevant?"

"It's accurate. I was fast-tracked because it helped the numbers at headquarters. Lots of qualified men wait longer for promotion."

That wasn't the answer she wanted. "During those ten years, were there any civilian complaints filed against you?"

"Three." I had a feeling I knew where this was going.

"Substantiated?"

"One was."

"Any penalty?"

"Couple of weeks without pay."

"That sounds serious. Who filed the complaint?"

"It was the Rebecca Garza case," I said, anger flickering like heat lightning inside my head.

"You haven't answered my question."

"Jonathan Garza filed the complaint. Her husband, the guy who beat her to death and tried to palm it off as a home invasion. He cracked a joke at the wrong time. I hit him; I was taken off the case. He was convicted anyway."

"I see. What about the other complaints?"

"Thea, you've got the wrong end of the stick," Nancy said. "She was cleared on those, and besides—"

"Nancy, come on. You know how it works. The Office of Professional Standards finds fault only when the offense is so egregious and so public that they have no choice."

"One was a guy I had some history with," I said before Nancy could intervene again. "Things got rough during an arrest. He used it to jam me up."

"The other complainant?" she asked, our eyes locked.

"Similar situation. Except she was a woman."

"Do you lose your temper often?"

"Only when I want to."

Thea studied me with that hint of uncertainty I'm used to seeing when people are trying to figure out if I'm a light-skinned black, a Latina, or maybe just Italian. "Ms. Koskinen, please don't take this the wrong way, but Rosa's case is one that will involve racial sensitivities, an area in which the CPD has a particularly poor record. These two complainants—"

"Amazing coincidence. Both of them were black."

She set her pen down, aligning it neatly with the notepad. "Surely you can understand why I have some concerns. We'll be defending a Native American accused of a capital offense in a racially charged case. This assignment will require speaking with witnesses who have no reason to trust an ex-cop. And now we find out you've had a number of civilian complaints on your record, all filed by people of color."

"No. Garza was white."

"Latino. It's a pattern. Every one of your complainants was a member of a minority."

"He was a chiropractor. He lived in Lincoln Park, drove a Jaguar. I don't believe this."

"I'm sure you have had a lot of experience investigating homicides, and I appreciate that being a woman in that profession must have been challenging—"

"Not to me."

"—but given the political nature of this case and the current climate in this city, I don't feel it would be in my client's best interests to involve you in this investigation."

"Then we're both happy, since I wasn't planning to take the job." I rose. "See you later, Nancy."

"Wait." She followed me to the door and blocked my way. "Anni, this is my fault. I didn't explain things to Thea. She just—"

"I tried to help a woman this morning, right? Only she didn't let me know I was betraying a friend in the process. She took off in my car and I was the one who got handcuffed, stuck in an interrogation room, told I was a lying piece of shit for hours on end by an arrogant smart-ass in a suit. Then you bring me out here to help this woman *again,* and I get the same damned treatment. I don't need this."

"Anni, listen—" she began, but I'd had enough. I pushed past her and left.

FOUR

Out on the sidewalk, I paused to take a breath and get my anger under control. A couple in their twenties, dressed in matching black leather, jewelry glinting from odd places, passed, casting sidelong glances my way. Probably members of the Bucktown Neighborhood Watch, ready to report anyone acting suspiciously unhip. They were walking a designer dog on a leash that jingled rhythmically, or maybe the jingling was from the metal hanging from their pierced body parts. The dog cringed close to his master's legs as they passed. They say dogs can smell fear. Maybe they can smell pissed off, too.

I headed down the sidewalk to my car. As I fished keys out of my pocket, Nancy Tilquist came out, slinging her bag over shoulder as she hurried down the flagstone walk. "Anni? Hang on." I waited as she fumbled with the latch on the cast-iron gate and then clanged it shut behind her. "Thea was caught off guard, realizing you two had been adversaries on a case. Don't make your decision hastily."

"*My* decision? It's her call, not mine." I looked around the street. No sign of the Cavalier that had been following me.

"You could do this job, probably better than anyone else. And given the current political climate, a dissident accused of murdering a federal agent? Rosa Saenz is going to need all the help she can get."

"I'm not talking about this without first hearing how Jim feels."

"You need his permission, do you?"

"I need his friendship. Nancy, don't you think there's enough on everyone's plate right now? Why are you pushing this so hard?"

"Because this woman is going to get railroaded. You could help her."

"We're not talking about just any case; it's Jim's father."

"So what? Arne Tilquist was part of an organization that suppressed dissent through surveillance and intimidation. And it's happening all over again. Sometimes you have to take a stand."

There was more going on here than the murder of an agent thirty-five years ago. I'd sensed the friction in the air between Nancy and Jim about his work lately. She had long ago come to terms with the fact he wore a gun to work, that she could get a phone call one day that he'd been injured or killed because of what he did. She'd put up with the long hours and the phone calls that took precedence over the school play or the soccer game without complaining. This was different, the hardened silence that fell between them when the news was playing on the kitchen radio, reporting on a speech by the attorney general or a judicial decision about detentions, while Nancy chopped vegetables with a jittery efficiency. I knew Jim was frustrated by the gung ho impulses of some of his colleagues, and he was offended by legal arguments that justified torture or surveillance of dissidents. But while he was getting the reputation of being cranky and overcautious at work, at home he was simply working for the wrong side.

"Jim was there for me when nobody else was. I can't do this to him."

"Do what? He'd be the first to say she deserves a fair trial, and she's not going to get it. Not in this climate."

"It's a moot point. Thea doesn't want to hire me. Look, it's late and there's stuff I still have to do tonight. I'll see you around." As I walked over to get into my car, Nancy glanced at her watch and swore. She got out her cell phone and had a short conversation as I coaxed the engine to life. I leaned over and rolled down the window on the passenger side as she slipped it back into her bag. "Problem?"

"I'm late for the baby-sitter, that's all."

"Where's your car?"

"Sophie has it. I'll take a cab."

"Around here?"

"I can pick something up on Milwaukee."

"Get in." I reached over and opened the door.

She hesitated. "Just drop me at the station."

"I can—"

"I'll take the train," she said firmly.

We drove in chilly silence for a few minutes. "Who's watching the girls tonight?" I finally asked.

"Chandra Patel. Lives down the block. Alice says she's too old for a sitter, but in the evening I like having someone older about the house, and Chandra's very responsible."

I thought back to the days when I'd filled that role. Martin and I were living in our grandfather's little bungalow then, just down the street from Nancy's house. Sophie had been an easy child to take care of. Bright and curious, a sunny disposition with, apart from her stubborn opposition to bedtime. She would try to stay awake as I read aloud, her head heavy against my shoulder, eyelids drooping, always wanting one more story. I had held her younger sisters in my lap, too, but I couldn't remember their specific weight and shape the way I could Sophie's. There was a hole inside my chest, a cavity that filled up with sadness whenever I thought about what was happening to her and what it was doing to her family.

As we drove along, I automatically checked the rearview mirror. Nancy finally noticed and twisted around to look. "Are we being followed?"

"Not at the moment. Someone tailed me to Bucktown, though."

"FBI?"

"That's my guess. How'd you meet Thea Adelman anyway?"

"Dem bones. I told you we figured out which tribe to send them to, didn't I?"

I nodded. A year before, an old eccentric had willed her North Shore home and all of its contents to Stony Cliff College. It was a big shambling house stuffed with shabby Victorian furniture, worn Oriental rugs, old pottery and flintlock rifles, and oddities like stuffed owls and dried snake skins, curiosities that the donor was certain were of museum quality. The land the house sat on would probably fetch millions, but neither the building nor its contents had seemed of any value—until the staff taking an inventory came across a glass case full of bones.

That's when Nancy was called in. She contacted the county coroner to confirm that the bones were human and likely very old. Papers found in the house said they'd been excavated from an Indian mound in Ohio over a hundred years ago and had been purchased from a traveling show by the donor's father in 1915. Jim was the one who'd started humming the old song when they told me about it one night over dinner, and ever since we'd referred to them as "dem bones."

"Thea's representing the tribe?" I asked.

"Right. She's handled NAGPRA claims before."

"NAGPRA?"

"The Native American Graves Protection and Repatriation Act, a law passed in 1990 to get human remains and funerary artifacts returned to native groups for reburial. We were following the regs to the letter, and I thought it was finally wrapped up. But a couple of weeks ago, just when we thought everything was settled, this lunatic group filed a counterclaim. They call themselves the Nordic League and say European explorers got here before the Indians, and that the remains are Caucasian and must be those of their ancestors."

"Sounds bizarre. Think the courts will take their claim seriously?"

"There was a similar suit out west awhile ago, and it dragged on for years. I suppose Thea won't have time to work on it anymore if she's going to defend Rosa Saenz. It's going to be a big case. You know, you really should think about working on it."

"I'm not doing anything without talking to Jim first. Besides, Adelman thinks I'm a racist."

"But—"

"And I think she's a jerk, so either way, it's not going to happen."

Nancy sighed. "I worry about you," she said softly, almost to herself.

I looked over at her. We were angling down Milwaukee, but even though it was a well-lighted street, her face was in shadow, half-hidden by her thick, curly hair. "Why?"

"It's been almost two months since you resigned, and you haven't done anything except tear up your house."

"I found Sophie that time."

"That's not a real job."

"Technically, it is." I didn't want them to pay me for something I'd have done anyway, but they had insisted we formalize the arrangement with a contract. Jim even scrutinized the invoice to make sure I hadn't underbilled them. I had, but not to the point it was obvious. I didn't want to bruise his pride.

"When Thea told me she wanted to take on Rosa's case, I thought, Anni. This would be a brilliant job for her," Nancy said. "It's always been your passion, finding things out, setting the record straight. Ever since you were a kid."

"Since I met Jim."

"Even before. The way he tells it, you were like that when you walked into his office. Wouldn't take 'I don't know' for an answer." She laughed. "You and Martin, what a pair. Everyone thought Golly was mad, adopting you. But you were good for him. He was awfully lonely until you two came along to complicate his life."

Gerasim Golovkin—"Golly" for short—had given up on finding his long-missing daughter, when he found us instead. He was a chain-smoker, overweight, and permanently rumpled, with the melancholy face of a basset hound and a deep, rumbling laugh. He'd married late in life, unwisely, and his wife had divorced him soon after their child was born. He'd had occasional contact with his daughter during her childhood, until she ran away at age fourteen, joining the countercultural youth migration of those turbulent times. Though he'd had little practical experience with children, he somehow knew exactly what we both needed.

We moved in with Golly when I was eleven and Martin was thirteen, and at first I thought we had it made. He never raised his voice or his hand, and he was infinitely patient with Martin, whose quirks and oddities were finally given a name: autism. But the learning I had to do that first year was the hardest of my life. I had to learn to tell the truth, to leave the food in the cupboards, instead of stashing some under my bed just in case, to find words for what I felt, instead of finding revenge. He was understanding and unflappable, but he hadn't let me get away with anything. It had been five years since the decades of smoking and a careless diet caught up with him in the form of a massive stroke, but I still thought about him every day. Lately, his memory was entangled with my yearning for a cigarette. The smell of fresh tobacco always reminded me of his hugs; when he'd wrapped his arms around me, my nose would press against the pack of Chesterfields he always kept in his shirt pocket.

When we reached Union Station, Nancy opened the door, then hesitated. "You're not doing this for Sophie, are you?"

"Doing what?"

"Putting your life on hold so you can sail to the rescue whenever she decides to be crazy. Because it's causing enough damage without messing up your life, too."

"No. Of course not. Look, there was only one career I ever considered. Now . . . I have some decisions to make, that's all, and I don't want to rush into anything."

"Okay. Just had to be sure." She looked down at her hands, which lay twisted in her lap. "I know it's not her fault, but sometimes I get angry at her. For what it's doing to her sisters, to all of us."

"I know. I get frustrated, too."

"Though she's doing better lately. Her doctor says once they find the right balance of medications, things will settle down." She said it dutifully, but the strained smile she gave me as she left was not very convincing.

I had one more person to see before heading home, but the Cavalier that had tailed me earlier made me uneasy. I headed uptown, in a deliberately misleading direction, and pulled into the parking lot of a busy restaurant on Armitage. I felt foolish, crouching down to look under my car—until I saw the rectangular box fixed under my rear bumper with a strong magnet. I gave the GPS tracker a sharp tug to pull it loose and looked at the cars nearby. The Cadillac with a Bush—Cheney bumper sticker and Nebraska plates would do. I attached the piece of government property to its undercarriage and drove to St. Larry's. Father Sikora had some explaining to do.

It was nearly midnight when I arrived. The stained-glass windows of the church glimmered faintly in the dark. Next door, the community center had closed for the night, but the front stoop held a cluster of kids talking and smoking—not just tobacco, to go by the sweet and acrid scent in the air. One of them bounced a handball off the steps, catching it with an easy snap against his raised palm. I parked and crossed the street to the apartment block where the old priest lived in a small studio.

He came to the door barefoot, wearing shorts and a T-shirt that strained over his chest. "You shouldn't be here," he said, his eyes flickering up and down the hallway.

"I wasn't followed. We need to talk." But it was clear from the way he blocked the door, his expression as blank as a brick wall, that he wasn't going to explain anything, not then anyway. "Okay, I'll keep this short. I'm pissed off that you sent Rosa to me when you know Jim Tilquist is my friend."

"She didn't kill anyone."

"If you're so sure of that, see that she gets this message. Thea Adelman is going to take her case. I've seen her work; she's good. This is the best break Rosa's going to get. She should turn herself in before anybody gets hurt. Do you have any idea where she is?"

"No."

"Well . . . put the word out anyway. She needs to get in touch with her lawyer."

He closed his door. I headed for the front entrance, my keys in my hand. I'm not sure what it was—perhaps the movement of one of the small muscles around his mouth, a flick of his eyes to one side. Whatever it was, I knew that in that single syllable he had just lied to me. It isn't always so easy to tell when someone's lying, but he wasn't very good at it. Maybe he hadn't had enough practice, given his line of work.

Outside, a ball came bouncing erratically down the sidewalk as I reached my car. It thunked against the hood of the Corolla, and a short, chubby boy in baggy shorts skidded after it, catching it on the rebound. "Sorry. Got away from me."

"No harm done."

He added in an undertone, "You looking for that white chick? The crazy one?"

"Why?"

"She was here with Lucas, that raggedy-ass tagger. You know who I'm talking about?"

I knew Lucas, a skinny teen with shoulder-length black hair, evasive dark eyes, a shy smile, and no fixed address. He'd been on the streets for three or four years, shoplifting and hustling to get by, known to police for creating some of the most inventive graffiti on the West Side. Sophie could be in worse company, and often had been. At least Lucas wouldn't take advantage of her in a vulnerable moment. If anything, it would be the other way around, Sophie dragging him into one of her reckless schemes. And he didn't have parents who could pull strings with the police or hire a lawyer to get him out of trouble.

"When was this?" I asked.

"Little while ago, right before the center closed. There was a bunch of people here, having a meeting about Rosa getting arrested. That girl, she was into it, getting all 'cited."

"Excited like how?"

"Like all political and shit. Saying the government was screwed up. Bad-mouthing the president. Hey, you ain't going to pay me? You did before."

"But I'm not looking for her this time."

"Damn. Give me a few bucks to buy some smokes anyways."

"What are you, fourteen? They'll stunt your growth."

He scowled and bounced his ball hard against the sidewalk, then slouched back to his friends, but I could tell he was secretly pleased; he was still shy of his thirteenth birthday, so he took my words as a compliment. I drove around the block, keeping an eye out for Nancy's old Volvo, but I didn't see it anywhere. Sophie had probably driven it home by now. At least I hoped so.

was sound asleep when the phone jerked me awake. I snatched it up.

"Anni? It's Jim."

"Hey, how're you doing?" I switched on a lamp. It was nearly 2:00 A.M., according to the alarm clock beside my bed.

"Ah, you know . . . could be better." He spoke carefully, as if holding his words so they wouldn't spill. "Nancy said she talked to you today. About a job."

"Did she tell you what it was?"

"Oh, yes. She gave me an earful, in fact. Afraid I wasn't too receptive. She went to bed a couple of hours ago, still mad."

"I tried to call you earlier today. I'm sorry I let that woman talk me into—"

"Don't. You didn't do anything wrong." There was a clink as a bottle hit the edge of a glass clumsily, the sound of sloshing as he poured. I guessed he'd had a drink or two already. Maybe more. "Oh, wow, it's later than I thought. Hope I didn't wake you up."

"That's okay."

"Sorry. And after all those hours you spent in the box today with Fiske. Bet that was fun. Don't know if you noticed, but he's kind of an asshole."

"I noticed."

"This is going to be a big case, his chance to make a name for himself." I heard him take a swallow. "People kept coming into my office all day to congratulate me, for some reason. I was having a hard time taking it in. Nothing all these years, nothing at all, and then this tip comes out of the blue. . . ."

"This can't be easy for you."

"Brings back a lot of memories, that's for sure. Those were strange times. So much anger about the war. About civil rights, about authority, you name it. Every night, the evening news would show battle scenes in Vietnam, and then the ones in our streets—people smashing windows, getting teargassed. The country was unraveling. And my father was in the middle of all that. Fighting the good fight. Keeping the nation safe."

His last words sounded as if they were set off in quotes. There was a complex crosscurrent there, a mix of sarcasm, regret, and something I couldn't name. "You never told me much about him."

He didn't speak for a moment. "We didn't get along that well, tell you the truth. He was old school, strict. I wanted more than anything to make him proud, but I thought I'd never measure up. And after I got back from the war—did you know I enlisted?"

"I thought you were drafted."

"No. Dropped out of college and signed up. Thought it would impress the old man." He laughed. "By the time I got back, I didn't give a shit what he thought. And then . . ." He took a deep breath. "He was gone. In an instant."

He sounded so bleak, I had to say something, however inadequate. "I'm sorry."

I heard him let a breath out shakily. "Hell, it was so long ago, I don't know why I'm . . ." He cleared his throat. "Thing is, we had an argument the day he was killed. I always regretted that the last words I said to him were in anger. Maybe that's why I hate it so much when Nancy and me don't patch things up before bed. I worry I won't get another chance."

"Of course you will. Things will look better in the morning."

He suppressed a sigh. His ice cubes rattled as he swirled his drink, took a gulp. "We met her that night," he murmured, his words slurring a little.

"Who?"

"Rosa Saenz, when Sophie was hospitalized. I'm having a hard time picturing that woman killing anyone, much less my father. I mean, he was a big guy, imposing, powerful. She's so . . . gentle."

"People change. She was involved in a political movement that advocated violence back then. Like you said, they were strange times."

"They're pretty strange now, stranger than you realize. I admit, when Nancy told me she'd been talking to the Adelmans, I felt . . . you know, betrayed, I guess."

"I don't know why Nancy is acting like this."

"I do. It's a matter of conscience. She says Saenz doesn't have a chance at a fair trial, and she's probably right. Things are so fucked-up at work these days. They treat me like a dinosaur, a creature from another era. Fiske fits right in, though. He would arrest his grandmother on terrorist charges if he thought it would get him a headline and a promotion. I've been sitting here the past couple of hours, thinking . . . I don't know. Maybe Nancy's right. Maybe it's not such a bad idea, you working with the Adelmans on this."

"Come on, Jim. I couldn't help anyone who harmed your family."

"I understand, but think about it. Fiske says he'll close this case, he'll see justice done, blah blah, the usual bullshit, but he doesn't care about any of that. Rosa Saenz is his ticket to the big time. He gets a conviction, I'll never be sure if it's real or if he just found a way to make a name for himself."

"Maybe we should talk about this tomorrow."

"This matters to me," he insisted truculently. "It's my father we're talking about. I don't want to wonder for the rest of my life if the wrong person was put away for his murder. And listen, here's another thing I've been thinking about: Why did Saenz go to you?"

I sighed. "I didn't tell this to Fiske, okay? Father Sikora called and asked me to help her. I didn't know she was wanted. I'm not sure he did, either."

"But why *you*? She helped out with Sophie that night, so she has to know we're friends. She could have gotten a ride out of town with someone else, but she chose you. Do you have any idea why?"

"No. She didn't tell me anything."

"Doesn't it strike you as strange?"

"Maybe, but there's nothing I can do about it, I wasn't offered the job. Besides, I signed up to take the LSAT later this month. I could start school in September."

"What do you . . . *School?* What are you talking about?"

"Law school. Would you write me a letter of recommendation? If I pass, I mean."

"Where'd you come up with this bullshit?"

"You went to law school."

"Oh, Anni." He laughed, couldn't stop until he had a coughing fit. "Jesus. Why would you want to make all the same mistakes I did?"

"I just thought . . ."

"Forget school. You should take this case," he said with the stubborn certainty that comes with too much alcohol. "Fiske has always criticized the way I run the task force, thinks I'm too careful, too soft. He's just waiting to show me how to do things right, be a tough guy. He'll screw this up, and he has an excuse to leave me out of the loop, given that I'm personally involved. If you were working on it, at least I'd know what's going on."

"But Adelman made it pretty clear she doesn't want me on her team."

"She could change her mind. Will you think about it anyway? I don't want to fight with Nancy anymore. I want us to be on the same side."

"Okay," I said gently, feeling sad. "Say, I had dinner with someone you know," I added, trying to distract him. "A CPD detective named Dugan. Said you called him a couple of months ago, gave him a hard time about my resignation."

"Dugan?" It took Jim a moment to change gears and focus. "Oh, right, from the task force."

"*Your* task force? The CTTF? He's assigned to that?"

"Used to be. I heard he transferred out of headquarters. Seems like a nice guy. You seeing each other?"

"No, he just . . . It was just dinner." I found myself going over our conversation in the little noodle shop. So, Dugan had been involved with the Chicago Terrorist Task Force, working on national security issues. Was his interest in Rosa Saenz a little more complicated than he'd made out? I'd told him a lot more than I'd told Fiske. Was he sharing that information with someone at the FBI?

"I kind of chewed his head off that day, come to think of it." I heard a gurgle as he refilled his glass. "Caught me by surprise, hearing you'd resigned."

"I'm sorry I didn't talk to you first. There was a lot going on. It just didn't seem like a good time."

"You can always talk to me, Anni. I like giving you advice. Like about this job. Can't say it was my idea, but it's growing on me. It's getting late. I suppose I should let you go."

"You should go to bed yourself."

"Soon. Just need to unwind a little. Been kind of a rough day."

"Don't unwind too much, or you'll wake up with a hangover. Hey, did Sophie get home okay?"

"She's staying overnight at a friend's apartment. Didn't want to drive home in the dark after the reading."

"Reading?"

"Yeah, some . . . I'm not sure. Some open-mike poetry thing at a café in Old Town."

"Did you talk to her?"

"No, I got home too late. Sophie's fine, Anni. At the moment." There was dull resignation in his tone, a sense of inevitability. Fine until the next time. "Get back to sleep. I'll head to bed myself in a minute."

"Take care."

I put the phone down, troubled, wondering why Sophie had lied to her parents, trying to decide if I should go out to look for her. But both Jim and Nancy had said she was all right, and they knew the signs. Whatever she was up to, it wasn't being guided by delusional voices. In the end, I just made sure the alarm was set, then lay back down to catch a few hours of sleep.

FIVE

The alarm went off at four 4:00 A.M. I crept down my back steps in the predawn shadows and slipped down the alley. I'd made arrangements the night before to borrow a pickup truck from a neighbor. He let me use his Ranger to haul materials from Home Depot in exchange for filling his tank.

This time, I wasn't getting remodeling supplies, though. I just wanted to take precautions in case the feds had followed their tracer's signal halfway to Omaha and realized I'd misled them. They might be watching my Toyota. And I had a feeling Fiske wasn't one to take a joke.

Father Sikora had lied to me the night before. I was pretty sure he knew where Rosa was, and with any luck he might lead me to her. I drove to an all-night gas station to top off the tank and buy a *Trib* and a small surveillance-size coffee, knowing bathroom breaks weren't likely to be an option, then found a spot to park near the alley where I could keep watch on Father Sikora's big old Impala, which was parked behind his apartment building. But first there was something I had to check. Even though I'd taken care not to bring up his name while I was being interrogated, Rosa had worked at St. Larry's. The FBI were likely to take an interest in her boss. I made my way to his car, hugging the shadows, and ducked low to shine a penlight across the undercarriage. No tracer. Apparently, he wasn't as suspicious a character as I was. Either that or they were confident they had other ways to keep tabs on him, using informants like Tyler.

I went back to the Ranger and settled in to wait, slumping low in the seat. When it got light enough to read, I propped the paper in front of me and scanned the front page. There was a short article on the hunt for Rosa Saenz, a k a Verna Basswood, skimpy on the details. Special Agent Arne Tilquist stared out of an official photograph from the sixties, blond hair combed back over a bullet head, square jaw grim and determined. He didn't look anything like his son. It wasn't just the difference in physical features and coloring; Arne looked utterly sure of himself. Lately, Jim didn't seem sure of anything.

There were two more photos with the story: a recent picture of Rosa that looked saintly enough for a holy card, paired with a blurry photo of a young woman, her face in profile as she looked over her shoulder, long hair streaming in the wind, a clenched fist raised, Verna Basswood at an antiwar demonstration in 1969.

I kept the paper open in front of me, turning pages occasionally, as if I were catching up on the news before heading to the office, and let that old trance descend, the one you fall into while doing surveillance. The trick is to let most of your body go into a state of suspension, breathing slowly, every muscle relaxed, nothing having to work except your eyes and a small receiver in your brain that's tuned to what they're seeing, ready to alert the rest of you when necessary.

Two hours passed before Father Sikora came out his back door carrying a thermos and paper sack. He scanned the street warily as he pretended to tighten the lid on the thermos. I was parked so that I sat on the far side of the truck and in shadow, far enough away that his gaze moved past without any reaction. Apparently reassured, he headed down the steps toward his car with that rolling, uneven gait of his.

It was now nearly seven o'clock, and though the traffic was heavy, I was able to keep his Impala in my sights without getting too close, making sure while I was at it that nobody else was following him. We drove south on Western, past small *panaderías* and storefront Pentecostal churches, crossing the Sanitary and Ship canal into the South

Side. When the Impala turned off onto a side street, I followed at a distance through a residential area of modest houses on small lots. A woman sat drinking coffee on her stoop, sleepily fanning herself as she watched two little girls chalk a hopscotch game onto the sidewalk. Ahead, the priest took a corner. I let a panel truck and a couple of cars pass by first before following.

The Impala made more turns. I wasn't sure if Father Sikora was being devious or simply had gotten lost, but I stayed as far back as I dared, always keeping a vehicle or two between us, constantly scanning for cars that didn't belong, nondescript sedans like the Cavalier that had tailed me the previous day.

We entered a semi-industrial area that looked as if it had gone through a war a long time ago and had never been rebuilt, old buildings settling into decay, pieces having been carried away by scavengers over the years, weeds growing up through the rubble. There were a few businesses, the kind that you don't find in more prosperous neighborhoods: a sheet-metal shop, a foundry. One of the lots we passed held piles of odd-colored sand that had eroded and left vivid streaks and dried puddles on the ground that looked toxic.

The Impala turned into an unpaved alley that seemed to dead-end into a jungle of weeds and scrub. I continued past and parked at the end of the next block behind a closed filling station. I checked to make sure the cell phone in my pocket was turned off, then walked back to the dead-end alley, my senses on high alert. The priest's car was nosed up against a smaller vehicle, one I hadn't seen because it was completely concealed by the big Impala. I wanted it to be a bizarre coincidence, a clone of Nancy's car, but the Stony Cliff College parking sticker on the rear bumper of the old Volvo clinched it.

I could see the headlines now: FBI AGENT'S DAUGHTER AIDS GRANDFATHER'S ALLEGED MURDERER. Sophie had a knack for creating family conflict, but this took the prize.

The alley ran beside a run-down building that had once housed an electrical-supply wholesaler, according to faded letters barely visible against the brick. Its windows and front entrance were boarded up with weathered plywood. Though the property was surrounded by a fence topped with coils of razor wire, and placards warned it was protected by a security company, the signs were piebald with rust and the lot was overgrown with brambles. Just past the parked cars there was an opening where the chain link had been cut with wire cutters and bent aside. The snipped ends weren't shiny, and I could make out a faint path worn through the weeds leading to the rear.

I slipped through the gap into the overgrown strip of land behind the brick building, where leggy cottonwood trees leaned over a still stretch of dusky olive green water that smelled of corpses. I realized it had to be Bubbly Creek, the southernmost fork of the Chicago River. Years ago, the stockyards had treated it as an open sewer for carcasses and offal. Bubbles still percolated through the stagnant water. Circles dimpled the water like raindrops, though it wasn't raining. I heard a splash from the bank and watched a V-shaped dent crease the water until whatever it was ducked under and disappeared. Developers were beginning to colonize the upper reaches of Bubbly Creek as a waterfront location with a view of downtown. Condos would probably go up here before long, replacing the brambles and cottonwoods with a tastefully landscaped parking lot. It seemed a shame. There was something secret and peaceful about this place where nature had fought its way back to reclaim what been a bleak industrial nightmare.

The tumbledown brick building turned a blind eye to the river, its windows boarded up. A Dumpster, tilted on broken wheels and overrun with bindweed, stood at an angle near a lean-to tacked onto the rear of the building, a rickety structure made of rusted sheet metal and plywood. The rear door was closed, but there was a splintered gash where the hardware that had secured it had been pried off. I could hear the grinding of truck gears and the rumble of traffic crossing a bridge upstream, but the building itself seemed heavy with silence.

I walked toward the lean-to, my jeans making a swishing sound through the weeds. As I reached to push the door open, I heard a noise behind me and turned just in time to see a metal bar swinging toward my head. I ducked instinctively and the rebar smacked against the plywood door. I grabbed my assailant, but the momentum of his swing unbalanced us both. As we fell together, my head hit the corner of the Dumpster. Sparks went off behind my eyes, but I managed to wrench the piece of rusted rebar out of his grip and fling it out of reach under the Dumpster. Then I trapped him facedown under me, twisting his arm up until he grunted with pain and stopped struggling.

It was Sophie's friend Lucas. He was taller than I was, but didn't have the skill to use it to his advantage. He was just a skinny kid, better at running away than putting up a fight. With one cheek pressed to the ground, he peered up at me apprehensively through a tangle of shoulder-length dark hair speckled with spray paint.

"Let him go."

She stood over us, her face so pale that it looked translucent, shadows like bruises under eyes that were jittering with excitement. She held a gun clutched in her trembling hands. It had a stubby barrel, and though I couldn't see the taped grip, I suspected it was the snub-nosed revolver that had been in my car when Rosa took off in it. "Take it easy, Sophie," I said, showing her my palms and easing my weight off the boy. "I need to talk to Rosa Saenz."

"No. She's not here. Why can't you just leave us alone, Anni?" Sophie's gaze flickered around the yard. "Did you bring them with you?"

"Who?"

The barrel wavered in front of my eyes, her grip tight but her arms shaking with tension. "You know who. The pigs, the *federales*. Your pals."

"I'm alone. You need to put that gun down."

She just frowned, but a sound behind her made her shoulders twitch. Father Sikora stood in the open door of the lean-to, in the shadows. "She followed you here," Sophie said to the priest, sounding hurt and betrayed.

He tilted his head toward the darkness inside. Sophie hesitated, but then she lowered the pistol and went in. He wrapped his hand around the barrel of the gun, and after a moment's resistance, she let go of it, scowling. Lucas rose and brushed off his clothes, giving me a sidelong look that was half-wary, half-ashamed. I followed him into the lean-to, a shadowy space Illuminated only by the chinks in the wall. A jumble of broken office furniture was piled against the wall.

"Go on," the priest said, nodding toward an inner door. "I brought some breakfast." Sophie shot me one more resentful glare before she and Lucas passed through and closed the inner door behind them.

"Is she here?" I asked the priest when we were alone.

He didn't answer, just looked at the pistol, embarrassed, and put it in his pocket. "Anybody follow you?" he asked.

"No."

"You're sure?"

"I was more careful than you were."

He gave a small sigh. Enough light leaked into the lean-to from gaps between the metal siding that I could see the worry etched in his face. A radio was muttering in the next room, the WBBM traffic report: things moving slowly on the Dan Ryan; a truck jackknifed on the Stevenson. The search for a fugitive was holding things up at toll plazas. E-ZPass lanes were delayed as police visually inspected vehicles. I explored the sore place on the back of my head with two fingers. The skin wasn't broken, but it was tender and already starting to swell. "Banged my head on the Dumpster," I explained.

"Let me see." He took my head in his hands and tipped it toward his chest as he gently probed the spot with his fingertips. "Hmm. Feeling sick? Dizzy?"

"It's just a bump." I pushed his hands away. "Listen, the police are out in force. Rosa's not going to escape this time. She should turn herself in before someone gets hurt."

"She says she didn't kill that man."

"If that's true, it will make it easier for Thea Adelman to defend her. She'll arrange a surrender and get started clearing her name. The sooner we do this, the better. There's a lot of cops out there, and they're under a lot of pressure. They see Sophie waving a pistol around like that, she could get killed."

"The kids are only trying to help."

"They're putting themselves at risk. Give me the gun at least."

"I can't do that."

"It's loaded. Sophie doesn't have good judgment. If she got hold of it again—"

"She won't."

"Rosa has to put an end to this. She should turn herself in."

"That's her decision, not mine."

"They'll find her. That's the reality. At least with a lawyer—"

He held up a hand, signaling he'd heard enough. He glared up at the ceiling, where birds had built nests in a niche between the roof and the wall, and probed his cheek with his tongue, frowning as if he had a toothache. My ears hummed in the quiet, as if the bang on the head had left something vibrating inside.

"Father—"

"What?" he asked, irritated, not wanting to be rushed into a decision.

"Can I sit down? I don't feel so good after all."

Sophie spun in the column of light, enjoying my stunned reaction, reaching one arm above her head as if she were conjuring it all from the air by magic. "Amazing, isn't it?"

The walls of the high, narrow room bloomed with shapes that jostled together, a jumble of angular words and leering faces, birds, skulls, angels, flames, a riot of billowing color that flowed up the broken plaster, framing the places where chunks had fallen away, as if they were masterpieces in a museum of ruin. The windows were boarded up, but light poured into the space through a hole in the roof.

"You did all this?" I asked Lucas. He ducked his head and shrugged, embarrassed and pleased. I'd seen his work before, on bridges and walls, street art created in minutes as he glanced over his shoulder, on the lookout for cops or business owners. Sometimes they were hasty throw-ups, bold lines of color slashed across brick or concrete, oddly elegant, like a line of poetry in a foreign script. Other times, he used stencils to spray-paint delicate arabesques, the same images springing up all around the city in a day or two, blossoming on walls and underpasses temporarily, until they were painted over or sandblasted into oblivion. Here, where he could take his time, he'd created a complex interior world in a building that would face demolition soon, if it didn't fall down by itself first.

Lucas had made an encampment in the section that still had a roof. Plastic milk crates held gallon jugs of water and canned goods; clothes hung on nails driven into the wall. Tools of his trade were neatly laid out on a wooden plank raised on cinder blocks: cans of spray paint, sheets of clear acrylic, craft knives, along with a pile of tattered books and issues of *ArtNews* and *Aperture* rescued from someone's trash. It was a cozy, sad imitation of a home, with a Mexican blanket laid out on the old linoleum like a rug, the backseat of a junked car dragged in to serve as a couch. Rosa sat beside me next to a milk crate that held the thermos, cups, and pastries that Father Sikora had brought with him. He sat on a backless office chair, refusing a softer spot on the car seat, saying he'd never be able to climb out of it.

Lucas squatted on his heels and reached for an empanada from the flattened bag extended by Rosa. He gave her his shy smile. "*Megwich.*" She rewarded him with a small nod. "She's been teaching me—" Lucas started to say to me, excited, then flushed, as if he'd said too much. He took a bite of the empanada and brushed crumbs off his chest.

"Coffee?" Rosa asked politely. I shook my head, then wished I hadn't as a headache sloshed from one side of my skull to the other, making bile rise in my throat. Her eyes flickered toward Sophie, who was pacing the room restlessly. "I heard a commotion. Did you get hurt?"

"Bumped my head is all. So, what do I call you, Rosa or Verna?"

She gave me a patient little smile. "My name's Rosa."

"All right, then. This isn't a good situation, Rosa. You're going to have to decide what to do, soon. You know Thea Adelman, the lawyer?"

"Why do you ask?" All those years underground, she had grown accustomed to dodging questions like mine.

"She wants to take your case. I've seen her work; she's good. If anyone can straighten this out, she can. But you need to put yourself in her hands as soon as possible."

"Don't listen to her," Sophie said over her shoulder. She was wearing a skimpy silk chemise and a scrap of a red satin skirt over leggings, clothes that could have been provocative but, instead, made her look younger than she was, a kid playing dress-up. Her hair was a ragged fringe, growing out unevenly after she'd hacked it off with scissors during her last manic episode. Somehow it looked good, as if she'd invented her own street-urchin style. But I didn't like the way her fingers twitched, plucking compulsively at the hem of her skirt as she paced.

"When it gets dark, we'll go," Lucas said. "Like we planned. We'll get you out, Rosa. There's lots of places to hide." He was trying to sound confident, but it came out wistful.

"They'll be here before that," I said. "You don't have that kind of time."

Sophie's tension was like an electrical field humming in the air. "Whose side are you on anyway? Just shut up."

"Take it easy." Father Sikora took a pastry and broke it two, then put the pieces down untasted. He gave a little sigh.

"The streets are full of cops," I said. "People's tempers get short. Someone's going to get hurt."

Rosa filled a cup and took a sip. "This is good coffee, Father."

"It's Guatemalan. I grind the beans myself." He rubbed his palms together and frowned.

"Look, I can only imagine what it's been like for you," I said, leaning closer and touching Rosa's arm, trying to get her to look at me. "Your friends gunned down in that farmhouse. All these years wondering when it might happen, waiting for that knock on the door. I don't blame you for wanting to run. But with a good lawyer on your side, it's different. You can fight this."

Her eyes met mine for a moment, intelligent and wary. She pressed her lips together and made her face blank.

"Call her. She wants to help, and she knows what she's doing. You can use my phone." I pulled the cell phone from my pocket. Still in one piece, I was relieved to see, in spite of the scuffle outside.

"No," Rosa said softly, but without any doubt in her tone. I glanced at Father Sikora. He was studying his hands, unwilling to take sides.

"Okay, then I'll do it." I opened the phone, but before I could switch it on, Sophie lunged to snatch it out of my hand. She threw it so hard against the wall, it broke, plastic and electronics flying. "Are you nuts? They can trace you. They can tell where you are."

Lucas picked up the shell and examined it. The screen was cracked, the keypad dangling loose. "Busted," he said apologetically, showing it to me.

The priest and Rosa stared at Sophie, who shook with tension, visibly frustrated. "I'm not crazy. It was in the paper."

"It's true," I said. "Cell phones send a global-positioning signal to the nearest tower, and, theoretically, you could locate someone that way. It's been done in criminal cases before. But my phone hasn't been switched on since I left my house, and anyway, they wouldn't have any legal grounds to be monitoring it."

"Like that matters? Don't you know what's going on?" She roamed back and forth, full of unfocused, dangerous energy, like a downed power line lashing across the pavement, spitting sparks. "They can watch every move you make, and nobody's doing anything about it. People should take a stand, like they did before." She looked at Rosa, seeking approval. "They should be out in the streets, protesting."

"Fine, but this situation—" I started to say.

"Just shut *up*!"

"Sophie? Calm down." The old priest stared at her until she slowed her pacing, coming to rest her shoulders against the painted wall resentfully, arms folded across her skinny chest, digging the toe of her shoe against a crack in the tiled floor. "And Anni, that's enough from you."

"But you don't—"

"*Not another word.*" He knuckled the armrest of his broken chair for emphasis. I could suddenly see the strain in the old man, the exhaustion, the toll of uncertainty.

There was silence except for the patter of the radio, the sound of occasional traffic passing on the street outside. My head pulsed with dull pain. "So . . . like, what do we do now?" Lucas asked finally. "What if she starts yelling or something? People might hear."

"We could put her in the basement," Sophie said. "The walls are thick."

It felt as if my skin were shrinking, growing tight around me. "Hey, if I wanted to lead the cops to you, they'd be here already. I just want all of you to get out of here safely."

"Yeah, out of here and right into jail." Sophie's foot was jiggling now, as if it was trying to get away from her and resume pacing. "You shouldn't have come here. It's your own fault, whatever happens." She turned to the priest. "If we let her go, she'll head straight to the cops. But we can't just let her sit here with us. She'll hear everything we have to say."

"Like what?" he said.

"Our strategy."

"Oh. We have a strategy?"

Impatience shook Sophie again like a fever. "We have to plan what we're going to do when it gets dark."

The priest looked at Rosa for guidance, but she didn't say anything. "Anni stays here with us," he said finally.

"Great. Fine. This is so totally stupid. I'm going outside. Someone needs to keep watch." Sophie held out her hand, her chin defiant. "Give me the gun."

"Don't be ridiculous."

Sophie headed for the door, muttering, "This is bullshit." The priest gave Lucas a meaningful look, and he grabbed another pastry and followed her out.

Father Sikora offered me a cigarette, which I refused, then lit up himself, triggering an old itch that plucked at my nerves. The radio was on low, muttering the news. I glanced sidelong at Rosa when her name was spoken, but she kept her face blank, as if they were talking about someone else.

"You're angry with me," Rosa said after a few minutes.

"You didn't mention you were wanted for murdering my best friend's father. If you thought I could get you past police barricades because I had connections—"

"That's not it at all. I came to you *because* you're Jim Tilquist's friend. If we'd had time, I would have explained. I met him that night Sophie was so confused. He's a good man, a decent man. He's not like the others. It's important the truth about what happened to his father comes out. The FBI has covered it up long enough."

"Spare me the conspiracy theories. Right now, all I want is for this to end without violence. How'd Sophie and Lucas get involved anyway?"

"They know me from St. Larry's," Rosa said with a sigh. "Lucas is a regular, and Sophie's been coming by since that night you found her in the sanctuary. She's upset with you right now, Anni, but she's a lovely child. Kind and courageous and concerned for others."

"She's not looking so good at the moment."

"I don't think she slept at all last night. Lucas, either. If anything happens to them—" She bit her words off.

"They want to help," Father Sikora said. "We all do."

She gave him a pained smile. "Lucas has a place near the park," she told me. "The basement of an apartment building. The manager goes to our church; she doesn't mind him sleeping there. I knew the police would be looking for your car, so I parked it and went to him. I wish I hadn't gotten him mixed up in this, but I didn't know where else to go. During the night, they decided to bring me here instead. It's more private."

"Not private enough. I understand the kids were at a meeting at St. Larry's last night."

"Lucas went to find out what he could. That's where he ran into Sophie. They told me there was quite a crowd." She seemed puzzled by it.

"You've touched so many lives," the priest murmured. "You have a lot of supporters, Rosa."

"Somebody there might have seen where the kids went afterward," I pointed out. "Might have noted the car, be able to provide a description."

"They wouldn't talk to the police," Father Sikora said confidently. "Everyone in the community is on Rosa's side. *Everyone.*"

Anger flushed through me, making my head pound. "Like that matters?" I turned to Rosa. "Let me explain how this works. If you're a cop, if you're doing your job right, you get friendly with street kids who use a little smack to make things easier. You joke around, show them you're not a hard-ass. But when you need information, you take them in and cuff them to a bench, leave them there with nothing to do. Trust me, it works. Before long, they start to feel it, that sickness, and they know it's just going to get worse if they can't score soon. They don't want to talk, they think they won't, but give them a few hours and they do."

Rosa's face was blank, but I could sense tension in her folded hands, the fingers tightened around one another.

"Or women who work the streets and feel like garbage because that's how everyone treats them. You get to know their names and the names of their kids, talk to them like they're human beings, and that's sort of confusing, because they know if you need something from them, you're not going to be nice anymore. So you pick one of them up, one who you know has kids waiting for her in a room where there's nothing to eat, kids who worry every night that maybe this time she won't make it home. You put her in a holding cell and tell her she can go home soon as she's willing to answer a few simple questions. You think she isn't going to talk?"

"Anni? That's enough." Father Sikora's voice rumbled with quiet anger, but I kept my eyes on Rosa. She was keeping her face turned away, but she knew these people as well as I did, and from the tremor in her cheek, I knew my words were having an effect.

"Or how about those guys who look like they're eighty-five but they actually just turned forty? You know the ones. The drinking life, it's like cat years—you get old fast. Most people look right past them, pretend they aren't there, but not cops. You find one you can work with, buy him a meal now and then, act friendly, encourage him to get his shit together, even though you know he won't." I saw her

mouth tighten. I leaned a little closer. "And when you need something, you bring him in and make him feel ashamed and worthless
and guilty as hell for letting you down, and then what do you do? You
show him a little folding money, just enough to buy himself a bottle,
and tell him he can have it soon as he answers your questions. And
he'll talk. They always talk."

"I thought you were different," she whispered. "But you're not.
You're a monster."

"I did my job, that's all. These people may love you, they may
think you're the best person in the world, but they're sitting in interview rooms right now, facing up to the fact they're not strong enough
to protect you."

She still refused look at me, but as she raised her eyes to the
priests', I saw a sudden spasm of pain cross her face. She got up and
went through the door into the lean-to. "Should have put you in the
damned basement," the priest muttered.

"She needs to know how easy it will be to find her."

He pushed himself up from the chair, wincing at the stiffness of
his hip. "Didn't have to be so mean about it."

I did, actually, but it didn't make me feel any better about it, or
about the times I'd done what it took to get information I needed for
a case. I heard the murmur of voices coming from the next room.
Then Sophie stormed in, Lucas hovering close behind her, his eyes
darting anxiously between us. She stared down at me, her eyes glitter-
ing, as if someone were holding a flickering match behind them. "Why
are you being like this? Everything was fine until you came along."

"It wasn't fine. You're not safe here."

"You want her to get caught."

"No, she *will* get caught. Sophie, you've been up all night; you're
not thinking straight. And I'll bet you haven't—" I cut the words off,
knowing it what I had to say would only make her angrier. And it
did, even though I hadn't finished the sentence.

"Taken my pills, that's what you were about to say, right? You're always asking me if I took my damn pills. I have them with me, okay?" She took an amber prescription bottle out of her pocket, rattled it. "See? I have my fucking pills."

"You just seem a little agitated, that's all."

"I'm *agitated* because the police are after us and you want to turn us in."

"No, I don't." I kept my voice low and calm. "Face facts. If she goes in with a lawyer—"

"Stop! Just *stop!*" She turned as Rosa came in, followed by the priest. "We can get you out. I promise. We'll make a plan; we'll use my mother's car. I know we can do it." Her voice was too loud, echoing up through the two-story space, her words jumbling together like the paint on the walls, bright and confused.

"Sophie—" Rosa reached for her.

"Don't listen to her. She's lying about everything. She's on their side. This is going to work. It *will.*"

"We'll talk, all right?" Rosa said to her softly, her voice soothing. "We'll make a plan."

"Not with her sitting there! She's not my friend anymore. She'll turn us in. She wants to—" Something made Sophie suddenly go still, her head raised. It took me a moment to identify it. A siren, wailing in the distance. She wrapped her arms around her chest. "You told them," she whispered, her eyes filling with tears. I shook my head, but she looked as if she was teetering on the edge of a cliff and I had tried to shove her over. The siren grew louder, then receded, on its way to some other trouble in another place.

Rosa rested a palm on her shoulder. Sophie closed her eyes, her face going slack, all the tension draining out of it. She sank down into a crouch, sighing with relief. Rosa ran her fingers gently through the girl's raggedly cut hair. "Anni, would you give us ten minutes?" she said quietly. "You won't have to be down there very long. Please?"

Her eyes flickered to Sophie. For her sake, she seemed to say, and though my heart hammered at the thought of being shut in a dark basement, I knew that she was right.

t was much smaller than the rest of the building, just a square box of rough-cut stone, barely big enough to hold the big old-fashioned boiler that had once fed steam heat through a complicated jumble of pipes. I caught only a glimpse of the hulking rusted shape before Lucas shut the heavy door, but I could smell it, a damp, metallic musk. I sat at the top of a wobbly set of metal steps bolted to the wall and listened to the murmur of voices on the other side of the door.

"What's she using?" Father Sikora's voice, was pitched low.

"Using?" Lucas's voice had that evasive sound you hear so often in interview rooms, trapped and stalling for time.

"Come on. I'm not blind."

"She just . . . Okay, we did a little crank. Just to stay awake."

"Speed? That's just great. You know she's on medication." A pause. "She's not taking it, is she?"

"That stuff makes her sleepy. I said we could take turns watching, but she didn't want to. What do you think we should we do? It won't be dark for hours and hours." His worried voice faded as they moved away from the door, and I couldn't make out their words anymore.

I never liked being enclosed in small places. This one reminded me of a basement at one of our foster placements, a damp, dark cellar, smelly and full of spiders, a place I'd had to go when I needed a time-out. I knew this was different, I was a grown-up now; I wasn't being punished. But knowing didn't help much. After twenty minutes, the door opened a crack and Rosa said, "I'm sorry this is taking so much time. It won't be much longer. I promise." When she closed the door,

I couldn't help myself: I thumped my shoulder against it, hard, and it swung open. Lucas leaped up to force it shut again. I heard a bolt shoot home, then something being shifted across the floor to prop against the door for good measure.

I put my aching head in my hands and tried to breathe slowly. Get a grip, Koskinen. Calm down. I tried to focus on their words, making out some of the louder ones in the murmuring stream of unintelligible patter. *Lawyer. Cops.* Sophie's voice, jagged and loud: "The gun. We have the gun. Why not?"

Then a sudden change in the atmosphere, the sound of voices calling outside, dogs barking. Someone hissing a warning to be quiet. A moment of dead silence before a quiet shuffling of feet. The forgotten radio muttered on until it, too, stopped, the batteries exhausted, leaving me alone in the dark.

fter awhile, I eased myself cautiously down the metal staircase. The rusted bolts that held it to the wall were loose, and
every time I shifted position, it wobbled ominously. I was
worried the whole thing would come crashing down at any
minute. But I stayed several steps up from the bottom because I could hear small animals scuttling around in the dark.

I was leaning against the wall, the stone cool under my cheek, when
a noise from above penetrated my fugue state. It took me a moment to
identify the sound: the lean-to door scraping the floor as it was forced
open. My head throbbed and my legs felt leaden and stiff, but when
someone called my name out, I yelled an answer and started up the
steps. They shuddered and rattled against the loose and rusted bolts as
I pounded the door with my palm, the steps tilting under my feet, but
I wasn't concerned about falling anymore; I just didn't want to be left
behind again. When the door opened suddenly, I tumbled through,
Dugan barely catching me by the shoulders before I fell headlong.

"Anni? Christ, what happened to you?" Dugan steadied me,
peered down at my face. "Al?" he called out over his shoulder. "Give
me a hand."

Dugan led me to the broken-backed chair. Gray twilight leaked
through the hole in the roof, the painted walls looming over us,
strange and menacing in the twilight. Dugan crouched in front of me
and made soothing patter as he surreptitiously checked out the state
of my clothes. My T-shirt and jeans were streaked with dirt and rust,
but I knew he was looking for unfastened zippers, torn clothing—any

sign of sexual assault. Feeling suddenly self-conscious, I brushed cobwebs off my shirt and wrapped my arms tight around my chest.
"How'd you find me here?"

"We got a tip a couple hours ago," Dugan said. "Some guy phoned
Area Four from a pay phone, said you were in trouble. Wouldn't give
his name. Too bad he hung up before he told us exactly which building you were in, or we'd have found you a lot sooner. What's this
about? Who put you in that basement?"

"I don't . . . Last thing I remember . . ." Confusion seemed as
good a strategy as any. I should have been ready with a story, but the
last few hours hadn't been good for clearheaded planning. I still felt
shaky and strange, as if part of me remained trapped in that damp
subterranean cell. "I just don't know." Some of the weirdness wobbled into my voice.

"Got a thump on the noggin," Prochaska said, poking the back of
my head, which made me gasp. I felt the tender knot gingerly. It was
a good-size goose egg.

"Is this connected to Rosa Saenz?" Dugan asked.

That wasn't a question I wanted to answer, so I gave a little groan
instead. "Man, my head hurts. Feels like it's going to explode."

Dugan exchanged a worried glance with his partner, then took my
chin gently and stared into my eyes. "Can't tell in this light," he muttered. "How many fingers am I holding up?"

I looked at the two fingers. "Uh, four, right?"

He stood, looking grim. "Al? Get the car."

Al Prochaska waited beside me on a plastic chair, jiggling the heel of
a wing tip while Dugan strode off on a mission. He'd been flashing his shield at everyone, demanding that they take a look at me,
but even a veteran detective can't jump the ER queue, not when there

are two bloody car wrecks, a walk-in gunshot wound being routed to Trauma, and a toddler having convulsions in his grandma's arms.

I noticed Prochaska glance at his watch for the third time. "I'm sorry this is taking so long. I'm not sure I even need to see a doctor."

He didn't seem all that convinced, either, but he said, "You'd better. Just in case."

"I appreciate you guys taking the time to follow up on that tip, especially with all the heat on about the fugitive."

"Thank Bulldog Dugan. He wouldn't quit."

"So, whatever happened with the search? They find her yet?"

Before he could answer, his partner returned with a harried doctor in tow. "Headache, nausea, double vision. I think one of her pupils may be enlarged, but I can't be sure."

The doctor peered into my eyes, frowned, then prodded my head with her fingers, making me wince when she found the bump. "Let's run some films," she said, suddenly in a big hurry, calling for an orderly.

"Is Saenz in custody? Wait. What—"

"Shut up, Koskinen," Dugan snapped as a gurney was wheeled up. "Get on the damn cart already."

Prochaska was edging away, tapping his watch. "Hey, Dugan? I got to get going."

"Yeah, fine. I'll take a cab." He tossed him a set of keys. "What's the situation?" His voice was jagged as he trotted along the gurney.

"Wait here," someone told him as the walls rolled past, wheels jittering under me.

Even parked out in the hall, you could hear the hum and *kachunk* of an MRI. A uniformed cop was watching through the doorway, head tipped to one shoulder to talk into his radio. "Kid's got two broken legs. The mom's in surgery, probably going to croak.

What's that?" He glanced over at me, his eyes wandering past without interest. "No, he's all right, the son of a bitch. Few stitches. I'm waiting on the dad. If he's able to talk, I'll get a statement."

He switched it off, flexed his arms, and yawned.

"Bad accident?" I asked.

"Drunk driver. Broadside, big mess." He ran a tongue over his teeth, frowning.

"Too bad. Hey, the Rosa Saenz thing, what happened with that?" He looked at me, his face a careful blank. "I used to be on the job, worked out of Harrison. Name's Anni."

The caution left his eyes. "Pete Fletcher, Marquette District. You ain't been watching the news? They been running all this live coverage."

My imagination played a fevered news clip: a hostage situation, a siege, Father Sikora holding the gun and wondering what to do with it. "No, I was too busy getting my head busted. Has she been caught?" It came out too vehemently. "Sorry, I got a monster headache."

He gave me a sympathetic wince. "Not yet, but we will. That lawyer, the Indian broad with the Jewish husband, you know the one? Always on TV, talking about police brutality and shit? She's making a big photo op out of it, a chance to make more speeches about what jerks we are. Un-fucking-believable. A woman who put one cop in a wheelchair for life, shot another one dead, and they're talking about her like she's some kind of saint." A couple of orderlies maneuvered a gurney through the door. "I hope they fry the bitch. Good luck in there. Say, guys? Think I can have a word with your patient now? . . . Sir, I just need to ask a few questions. . . ."

don't think this is wise," Dugan said, paying off the cabdriver at the curb in front of my house.

"Drop it, Dugan. There's nothing wrong with me," I said. Except

for the thudding headache, which wasn't improved by him giving me
the same advice so many times.

"You should have stayed overnight, like they said."

"I already told you. I'm fine," I said over my shoulder, heading
down the narrow gangway toward the rear of the two-flat. All the
windows were dark. Pilar and her boyfriend, Joey, must have gone
somewhere with the kids.

"You're fine, but you still can't remember anything that happened?"
Dugan was practically breathing in my ear, following so closely. "You
have no idea how you got there?"

"Would you quit with the questions?"

"Come on, try. Did you drive there, or was someone else driving?
Was it a man or a woman? How'd your phone get broken?"

"I don't know."

"Sounds like a concussion to me. You have anyone to stay with you
at least?"

"No need."

"You heard what the doctor said. Every two hours, somebody
should check, make sure you're all right." He stepped back, startled,
when something dark zigzagged past his feet. "Fuck! What was that?"

"A cat."

He stared into the shadowy yard. "You sure?"

"Is that a comment on my neighborhood?" The gratitude I'd felt
for him finding me had long since been replaced by irritation. I just
wanted to get out of my dirty clothes, take a shower, and fall into
bed—not to be fussed over by an interfering cop. I turned to face
him at the bottom of the stairs. "Listen, I appreciate what you did,
but now . . . would you go away? Please?"

"See, this is why I'm concerned. You're not acting rational," he
said, his overly patient tone of voice making a squiggle of pain dart
through my head, like fingernails on a chalkboard.

At the same moment we both became aware of a dark shape rising at the top of the stairs. Dugan went into defensive mode, pushing me back while reaching for the grip of his pistol.

"It's okay," I called out to both of them, my voice taut. "It's my brother."

Dugan let his hand fall away from the butt of his weapon, his breath going out in a little gust like a sigh. I left him there and climbed the steps. "It's all right," I said softly to Martin, feeling sick that I'd forgotten all about him coming over to work on the house. "He's a cop, a friend. This neighborhood makes him jumpy, that's all. How long have you been waiting here?"

I wasn't sure he was processing my words, but after a moment Martin gave a one-shouldered shrug. A long time, I guessed, waiting for me to come while the light faded from the sky.

"I'm sorry I wasn't here. I got a bump on the head. I'm okay, though. I'm fine. Let's go inside."

I switched on lamps, introduced them to each other. Martin kept his hands pushed deep in his pockets and stared at the wall as Dugan studied him. Brother? I could imagine him asking himself. Martin's nearly a foot taller than I am, with fair skin and sandy hair that's always tousled, as if he's just gotten out of bed, a scruff of beard, eyes the same shape as mine but a lighter shade of brown, the color of maple syrup. "I forgot he was coming after work to help me work on this place."

"Yeah, your sister was kind of busy, what with getting knocked out and locked in the cellar of an abandoned building," Dugan explained. "We just came from the hospital. The doctor thinks she might have a concussion."

"I'm fine," I said firmly. "He's exaggerating."

"You think you could keep an eye on her tonight?" Dugan asked. "Make sure she's okay?"

"He's making a big fuss about nothing," I said. "But tell you what—I'm really thirsty. Could you run down to the market on the corner and get something cold and fizzy? Root beer would be good, or Coke if they're out. You have money?" He checked in his pockets, found a couple of bills and a handful of loose change. He showed them to me. "That should be enough." He folded the bills carefully, pocketed the change, and left.

As soon as he was out of earshot, I rounded on Dugan. "What are you trying to do, scare him to death?"

"I'm sorry. I didn't realize. Is he . . ." He searched for the politically correct word for it.

"He's not retarded." I heard it come out too loud, too angry, an echo of school-yard battles fought long ago, even the same words. I stumbled over to the couch and sat down, drawing my knees up, suddenly feeling light-headed. I closed my eyes and rubbed them. I heard the faucet run, felt the couch dip as Dugan sat beside me. But I didn't want to open my eyes, not until the heat and prickly feeling went away. I was damned if I was going to get all emotional in front of Dugan.

"He's different, that's all," I said finally, choosing the words as I took the glass from him. Chicago tap water never tasted so good. I pressed the cool glass against my forehead. "He doesn't talk much, and he gets anxious when his routine is messed up. But he's not stupid. It's just words he has trouble with. Words, and people like you who frighten the shit out of him for no reason."

"I didn't mean—"

"You were about to draw on him."

"I wasn't. I thought . . ." He raised his palms, dropped them on his knees. "Never mind. More water?" I handed him the empty glass, and he went to refill it. His trousers, I noticed, were muddy at the cuffs and speckled with burrs that must have come from the weeds growing around the buildings where they'd looked for me.

"Remodeling, huh?" he asked, making conversation. He handed me the glass and wandered around the room, taking off his jacket and pulling at his tie. Sweat had made half-moon stains under his arms.

"I bought the building awhile ago, rent out the downstairs. I'm finally getting around to fixing this flat the way I want it, now that I have the time." He paused beside the front windows, peering out at the street. "Martin's doing a lot of work. He made that bookcase."

"Nice." Dugan ran a hand across the silky wood finish. "He's a carpenter?"

"A lab technician at Stony Cliff College. Keeps equipment running, fixes things."

Dugan prowled on, pausing at a Mission-style oak table that held my laptop and stacks of papers. "Did he make this, too?"

"No, that belonged to our grandfather."

"The relative you found after you met Jim Tilquist?"

"Yeah. Well . . . more or less."

"What does that mean?"

"We went to live with him, but it turned out we weren't actually related."

"Yeah? How'd that happen?"

A slight breeze, not much cooler than the room temperature, stirred through the open windows, carrying the usual night sounds, which were comforting in their ordinariness: a boom box, cars moving on the street, voices from the corner, where kids hung out. I felt drowsy. "I told you how Jim Tilquist helped me look for my mother's family. There were a lot of people with our last name, but none of them knew who she was. The only person we found with her name and birth year had died in infancy. My mother must have picked it out of the obituaries, or off a grave marker. So Jim pulled hundreds of missing person's reports. There was a guy on the North Shore whose daughter left home at fourteen, just like our mom. We arranged to meet, and some of the things he said . . . well, it could have been her."

"You lied to him," Dugan said.

I'd forgotten for a minute I was talking to a cop, someone trained to pick up on what wasn't said. "I didn't say anything he didn't want to hear."

He laughed. "Incredible. You let him believe—"

"We needed a place to live."

"Hey, I'm not judging you."

"He knew anyway. I found out later that he knew all along, but he took us in just the same."

Suddenly, I was embarrassingly close to tears. It had to be the bang on the head, or those hours in that basement. I never acted like this. I felt my cheeks burn. Dugan glanced away, giving me a chance to compose myself.

"He died five years ago, left us everything he had. I kept his desk, and a few of his books, sold the house. We made enough on the sale to set up a trust fund for Martin in case anything happened to me."

"Like getting knocked out and locked in a basement?"

"Like getting shot. I had to be sure he'd be taken care of. Jim and Nancy Tilquist agreed to administer the trust if they had to." I rolled the empty glass between my palms. "You served with Jim on the Chicago Terrorist Task Force, right?"

"Uh-huh, when I was at headquarters."

The headache jabbed a thin, sharp needle of pain just behind my ear. "Funny you didn't mention that before, being on the CTTF."

"It wasn't a big part of my job. I sat in on meetings, ran some numbers when they asked for them. What's the problem?"

"No problem. Only it explains why you're so interested in what I know about Rosa Saenz."

He laughed in disbelief. "The CTTF doesn't have anything to do with that case. Anyway, I work Violent Crimes now. And yes, I do have an interest. You know what's been happening in the past twenty-four hours? We're going door-to-door, stopping cars, talking to people on the street, and, in the process, turning up illegal weapons and drugs and people with outstanding warrants who figure they've got nothing to lose. Officers have been bitten by dogs, we got kids pushing crap off rooftops onto our heads, and, on top of that, the press is dumping on us for being storm troopers. But you go off and decide you're going to find this fugitive all by yourself."

"She came to me. I didn't ask to be part of this."

"At first, maybe, but that doesn't explain how you ended up in that basement. You trying to be a hero, redeem your tarnished reputation? That's just plain stupid, going into a situation like that by yourself, no backup."

The headache was back, pounding with my sudden fury. "Like I had backup when I was on the job? Christ, Dugan. Why do you think I quit?"

"You got tired, fed up," he muttered, suddenly embarrassed. "How would I know?" He scratched the back of his neck.

"What are they telling you?"

"There was some situation, a crazy guy with a knife," he said with a shrug, dismissing it. "You'd had enough. It happens."

"They're saying I lost my nerve?"

"Look, nobody blames you if—"

"Unbelievable. You want to know what really happened? I'm canvassing not six blocks from Harrison headquarters, trying to trace a gun some asshole used in a robbery, and this girl comes running up, scared out of her mind. Her mom's boyfriend flipped out, said he was going to kill everyone. So okay, I call it in and head to their apartment, where this guy's waving a knife around, room full of crying kids. Anybody else, there would have been half a dozen squad cars there in minutes. But I was the one who responded, and that meant we were on our own. Me and that terrified woman and her kids. We weren't going to get *any* help, not until it was too late."

"You're saying—"

"I talked the guy down, got the knife away from him. Nobody got hurt. But it was too damned close. Soon as I finished the paperwork, I put in my resignation."

He gave that some thought. "This is because—"

"Because I testified against Hank Cravic. After that, I couldn't get backup when I needed it. And I decided then and there I was never going to put people at risk like that again."

He looked at his shoes for a minute, then rallied. "Okay, fine, I get it. But that doesn't explain what you were thinking, going after a fugitive wanted for murder without anyone to watch your back. You just said that's why you quit—you didn't want to be in a dangerous situation on your own."

"Weren't you *listening*?" I wanted to throw something at him, imagined hurling the empty glass, hearing it shatter. I set the glass down carefully, reining in my temper. "I didn't need backup. That family did. This is totally different. I'm not putting other people in danger. It's just me."

"Just you, huh?" Dugan was looking past me. Martin was in the doorway, cradling a paper bag in his arms. "I hear you're a pretty smart guy," Dugan said to him. "Maybe you can make your sister see sense, 'cause I'm not getting anywhere. She seems to think she's some kind of Lone Ranger, out to set things straight all by herself. Not bothering to tell anyone where she's going or what she's up to. That's pretty damned dangerous."

"Don't, Dugan." I didn't like the way Martin was staring at a spot near his feet; he looked alert, as if he were listening, but I knew he was disconnecting, going into that private place of his.

Dugan turned. "You lied to me," he said quietly, but his voice was vibrating with anger.

"When?"

" 'I don't remember anything. My head's going to explode.' " He mocked my voice savagely. "Oh, you had me going, made sure I quit asking questions. Pretty dumb, huh? I actually felt responsible, asking you to talk to whoever sent Rosa Saenz to you, telling you to get back to me. I made my partner spend hours out there, busting into empty buildings, talking to everyone we could find. I was goddamned worried, all right?"

"Like I said, I appreciate—"

"Well, listen: You may think you're responsible to no one but yourself, but when things get fucked up, it's cops who have to clean it up. And we have enough problems in this city right now. Use your head next time."

He slung his jacket over his shoulder and headed for the door, rigid with anger. But then he paused, turned, and, after a moment's hesitation, said in a calmer tone to Martin, "Hey . . . could you stay the night? Wake her up every two hours, make sure she's tracking? Chances are she's faking it, part of the act, but she could have a concussion. Better not take chances."

Martin nodded, and Dugan raised a hand as if to give him a pat on the shoulder, but something made him think better of it. He glanced back at me, then left.

"It's not true," I said in the stillness after Dugan had clattered down the stairs. "This thing I got into? It was nothing dangerous, really, just a mix-up. Don't worry about it, okay?" Martin looked at the floor, making no sign he heard my words.

Dugan was a cop, and cops were bullies, just like the boys who scented weakness on the air, signaling the pack to surround the new kid in the school yard, a boy dressed in all the wrong clothes, different from the others, vulnerable. And gradually the grins would grow broader, hands would reach out to shove and poke, knowing almost by instinct that he hated to be touched, that he couldn't speak in his own defense. After that, they'd known how to make him curl up in a defensive crouch and make weird noises anytime they wanted, as predictable as prodding a mealybug with a stick, only more fun. I wanted to fly down the stairs after Dugan, knock him down and rub his face in the dirt, wreak some school-yard vengeance. Instead, my headache felt like a clenched fist, pounding.

"Look, when I said it was 'just me,' I was talking about my job, about the way things were at the end. Not about us. You know that, right?" But he still looked distant, locked away in some remote and lonely place. I closed my eyes, pressed my thumbs against the lids, wishing I knew how to make things better.

I don't have many memories of our mother. A hand taking mine to cross a street. A crinkly blouse, a necklace of blue glass beads. The spicy smell of her red-and-yellow Indian block-print skirt. Martin is two years older than I am; he remembers more, I'm sure. When she left us, it was the first betrayal of many. New foster families, new schools and neighborhoods every year or two, all of them with rules that nobody explained, punishments that came out of nowhere. And in time, the naturally trusting, sweet nature he'd had in his early years retreated somewhere deep inside, leaving him silent, untouchable.

Not me. I fought back. The way I figured it, one of us had to.

I heard the rustle of paper, the *phht* as a bottle top was twisted off. Martin put ice in two glasses and poured carefully, pausing to let the bubbles subside, making them even-Steven, like always. He gave me my glass, then sat at the other end of the couch and I told him about everything that had happened over the past twenty-four hours, making it simple and clean, an orderly chain of events, even though he wasn't paying much attention; he was busy moving his glass around, working out how he could make his ice cubes fall in a certain predictable pattern. But as I talked, things began to sort themselves out and the knot of pain in my head began to ease.

I borrowed Martin's cell phone to make some calls. Sophie had come home much later than expected, Nancy told me, all wound up by staying up too late with friends after the poetry reading and forgetting to take her pills until she got home. They'd had words, but things had settled down; in fact, she was playing a board game with her youngest sister, being nice to make up for the earlier argument. Nancy couldn't hide the thread of tired despair in her brisk, practical tone, but at least I knew Sophie was safe at home and not speeding on drugs or her own inner chemistry.

"By the way, that friend of mine," Nancy added, "she wants a word."

"Friend?" The headache was crouched just over my eyes, getting in the way, making it hard to think.

"About that job. You know . . . the job? We sorted it. She wants to go ahead."

It took me a moment to figure out what she meant; she was avoiding saying Thea Adelman's name over the phone. I made a vague response that seemed to satisfy Nancy, even if I wasn't sure what it meant.

Two more calls, one to a local pizza joint and another to a towing firm to get my neighbor's pickup truck hauled back from where I'd parked it near Bubbly Creek. Then I showered and pulled on clean clothes. After eating a slice and drinking another glass of pop to settle my queasy stomach, I fell into bed. As I drifted off to sleep I saw Martin sitting on the couch, the lamp catching gold threads in his hair as he munched pizza and listened to the radio on low volume, every few minutes checking his watch so he'd know when exactly two hours had passed.

SEVEN

When I woke, Martin was sound asleep, one arm cocked under his head for a pillow. He'd stayed up most of the night, rousing me every two hours. Around 5:00 A.M., I convinced him he'd done his duty and he could get some sleep. Now his long frame was folded up on the couch and he was breathing softly and evenly, like a little kid, his mouth slightly open. I stood over him for a moment, then reached down and ran my fingers lightly through the fringes of his hair, feeling a twinge of guilty pleasure. He didn't like me touching him when he was awake.

The headache was gone and the knot of swelling where I'd banged my head had gone down, though it still smarted. I started a pot of coffee, filled a bowl with Little Friskies, and went out on the porch. The air was a few degrees cooler outside, but I could tell from the way the sun suffused the humid haze with a hard white glare that it would be in the upper nineties again. The three-legged stray peered out of the weeds with a pissed-off look. I set the bowl on the bottom step, but he stubbornly refused to approach it until he had the yard to himself.

Pilar came to her back door holding the baby, her three-year-old daughter hovering by her legs. The little girl's round cheeks were streaked and dirty with tears, and two fingers were stuffed in her mouth like a plug to hold in sobs. "Hey, can I talk to you?" Pilar said. The front door slammed and she rolled her eyes. "Sorry, I got to get Ryan. Can you come in a minute?"

She headed through the apartment to the front door. I took the three-year-old's hand and followed Pilar onto the front porch, where a suitcase and a clutter of other bags and belongings were stacked up beside the door. "What's going on?"

"Look, I know I signed a lease and everything, but— Ryan! I tole you to stay close." Her five-year-old son halted at the end of the block, as if attached to an elastic string that had stretched as far as it would go. Then he turned and zigzagged back. "We're going to go stay with my sister for a while. I called for a cab, like, hours ago. Put that down!" she bellowed. Her son had found a broken car antenna in the gutter and was waving it over his head. "That kid's wearing me out."

Ryan tossed the antenna aside and ran to the porch, butted his hard little head against my leg in greeting, then careened off again, arms flapping. "He's pretty wound up," I agreed.

"Been acting like that ever since Joey moved out."

"Oh, Pilar, I'm so sorry. I didn't know you were having problems. When did this happen?"

"Yesterday. Thing is— Ryan! You come back here." I caught the kinetic little boy in my arms as he came galloping past, wrapped him in a big hug to keep him still. "I don't know what's going to happen now, and I can't afford the rent, so I gotta get out of that lease."

"Don't worry about that. Take some time to work things out."

"It was those police coming by all the time—Joey said he couldn't risk it. And I just can't do this by myself, you know? Three kids, it's too much."

I couldn't figure it out. Joey seemed like a quiet, dependable guy. He worked construction jobs whenever they were available, did yard work or plowed snow when they weren't. Only the baby was his, but he treated all the children as if they were his own. I knew he had grown up in a tough neighborhood and guessed that he'd flirted with gang life, given the roughened skin on his shoulders where he'd had tattoos removed. A defensive reaction to police showing up at his door wouldn't have surprised me. But this was something else, something much more serious. "Does Joey have a problem with a warrant, or—"

"He's undocumented."

"But—he grew up here. He's lived in Chicago all his life."

"Since he was two. His parents were illegal. He never got naturalized. What's he going to do if they deport him? He don't know anybody in Mexico." She spotted a cab nosing its way up the street, looking for the address. "Finally." She took the little girl's hand. "Listen, my brother-in-law, he's going to get the furniture—next weekend, maybe. I'll have everything out for sure by the end of the month."

Ryan wriggled, trying to slide under my arms like an eel, but I held him tightly. "Pilar, those people who came here to ask questions, they weren't from Immigration."

"So? That one, Mr. Fancy Clothes? He knew Joey was illegal."

"Fiske. He was bluffing. Trying to throw a scare into you."

"Guess it worked, huh?"

"Pilar, listen—"

"I gotta go. That meter's running."

I helped the driver load up their luggage while Pilar settled the kids. Ryan was bouncing on his knees in the backseat, trying to convert all the fear he sensed in his mother into giddy goofiness. "Don't worry about the rent," I said before closing the cab door. "The apartment's yours until this is straightened out. If Joey needs a lawyer—"

"We don't got that kind of money."

"I know people who might be able to help for free. What's your sister's number?" Pilar smoothed the baby's hair, her mouth tight, and I kicked myself. She thought I would just get her family deeper in trouble if I knew where they were staying, but she was too polite to point it out. "Never mind. Just don't worry about moving your stuff out. Take whatever time you need." I stood in the street, watching the cab drive away, Ryan clowning like a desperately cheerful bobble head in the back window.

I climbed the steps to my flat, anger and frustration churning in my chest. Martin was still snoozing on the couch. When Pilar and her children first moved in, I found the constant noise below distracting; now the quiet hung as heavily as the hot, humid air.

Settling at my grandfather's desk with a mug of coffee, I switched on my laptop and checked the news. Rosa Saenz was still at large. The intense manhunt had led to vocal criticism of the police. One community activist called for calm; another one called for action. A spokesman for the Fraternal Order of Police defended the officers who were trying to apprehend a woman wanted for a vicious act of terrorism. Parishioners at St. Larry's, unshakably certain of Rosa's innocence, were organizing a defense fund. I downloaded a podcast of an interview with Thea Adelman from a local NPR station. She provided an overview of the American Indian Movement and the government's historical and recent attempts to stifle lawful dissent. She was articulate and compelling, but something about her precise and slightly superior voice set my teeth on edge.

This wouldn't be an easy working relationship, but if I there was any chance I was going to take the job, I knew I'd better be prepared. I sent a message to a contact who worked at the Cook County medical examiner's office, then brought up a database of the *Chicago Tribune*'s historical archives, pulled over a notepad, and set to work.

Three hours passed quickly. I compiled pages of notes and a stack of printouts, then checked my E-mail. My contact had already come through with a scanned copy of Arne Tilquist's autopsy report, dated December 28, 1972. It was expensive, getting the document this way, but if I went through official channels, it could take weeks. I made the payment through an Internet account, then printed out a copy and started to read. Tilquist had been shot in the face, a single .22-caliber bullet entering through his left eye. There had been tattooing close to the wound, traces of burned gunpowder that suggested the shot had been delivered within a foot of him, probably only inches from his face. That seemed odd. Tilquist had known the last remaining member of the radical group had threatened retaliation after the raid in Wisconsin. Why would he have let his guard down enough to let her get so close? But even more surprising was the wound path. "Holy shit," I said out loud.

Martin stirred, blinked, brought his wrist out from behind his head so he could see his watch. He sat up suddenly, bare feet thumping on the floor, panic in his eyes. "Don't worry, it's Saturday," I reminded him. "It's okay to sleep late on Saturdays."

Martin scratched his chest, still uneasy. His routine was out of whack, and that always made him uncomfortable.

"My head's better," I told him, touching the spot on my scalp where the skin was still tender. "There're eggs and cheese and a package of tortillas in the fridge. Feel like cooking?"

"Okay," he said, two flat syllables, then got up and padded sleepily into the bathroom. As usual when Martin said something out loud, I was struck speechless with surprise.

I looked back at the autopsy report, double-checking the diagram, and even doing a few calculations on a scrap of paper. Tilquist had been over six feet tall, Rosa less than five. The angle of the path the bullet had followed in Arne Tilquist's brain was all wrong, given an assailant more than a foot shorter. I couldn't be sure, of course, without knowing the details of the crime scene. He'd been found dead in a basement. Maybe she'd been standing on the stairs when she shot him. Maybe she'd caught him by surprise, threatened him, forced him to his knees. But still, it was an anomaly that made my pulse quicken.

I finished reading the report, then started another pot of coffee while Martin worked on breakfast. He didn't have a kitchen of his own. It was easier for him to have his ID card swiped in the college canteen, the cost of meals automatically deducted from his paycheck, than to have to deal with grocery shopping and handling cash. But the canteen didn't serve *migas,* his personal specialty. He lined up the ingredients on the counter, tested the knife's edge with his thumb, aligned the cutting board, then started chopping onions and peppers, his hands sure, his motions precise. It was important to get all the pieces the same size. By the time the coffee was ready, the kitchen was fragrant with the smell of sautéed onions and garlic, peppers and cilantro.

After we finished heaping platters of eggs and cheese and tortillas, we spent a couple of hours replacing the ugly seventies-era vanity in the bathroom with an elegant old pedestal sink. Then I drove Martin home. On the way, we stopped at the Best Buy on North Avenue, where I bought a couple of cheap prepaid cell phones, figuring that using disposables and changing them out every week or so would frustrate any attempts to tap or trace my calls. While still in the parking lot, I tapped the number of one of them into Martin's cell phone, putting it first in his short list of contacts. He'd never called in the past, but I wanted to know he could reach me in case of emergencies.

It was 3:00 P.M. and the heat had been building all day, making the cars on the expressway shimmer in front of us. When we took the exit for Stony Cliff, the deep shade cast by the big trees lining the streets was a welcome respite from the sun. I dropped Martin off near the science building, surprised by the number of cars in the parking lot. The college didn't have a summer session, so it was usually quiet and sleepy, apart from hosting a handful of conferences and Elder-hostel programs. Martin didn't notice. He loped off, intent of getting back to his routine, which on Saturday afternoon meant playing chess and watching videos with his nerdy pal Josh, a physics major who was on campus to do summer research with a faculty member.

I drove the short distance to Jim and Nancy's house. I wanted to get more details from Nancy before approaching Thea Adelman— and, more importantly, make sure Jim really wanted me to take the job. When we'd talked on the phone, the news that his father's al-leged killer had been found was still raw, and he'd had a few drinks under his belt; I wouldn't be comfortable until I could speak to him face-to-face. But when Alice, their middle daughter, came to the door, she told me they weren't home. They had gone to a demonstra-tion.

"What demonstration?" I asked.

She shrugged. "Some wing nut's giving a speech at the college, so I'm stuck here baby-sitting. As always." Her voice was heavy with adolescent ennui. Just a few months ago, Alice had been a cheerful child with a quirky sense of humor, but hormones were working their usual mischief, turning a nice kid into a surly changeling.

I walked the two blocks to campus and followed one of the foot-paths to the big open lawn at the center of campus. About fifty peo-ple were gathered in front of Old Main, a handsome sandstone relic that dated back to the founding of the college. Most of them were college age, with a handful of older people, including a clutch of knobby-kneed Elderhostelers in shorts and floppy hats. Standing alone at the top of the broad steps of Old Main, a man stared over the heads of the crowd, his hands folded in front of him. He was dressed like a Mormon missionary in dark slacks, white shirt, and a tie, and he seemed both nervous and resolute. Half a dozen men wearing matching black T-shirts with some sort of logo were hand-ing out leaflets at the bottom of the steps. They were a contrast to the student crowd, with their hair shorn close to their skulls, their faces tight with hostility. Nancy was at the foot of the stairs, deep in conversation with her boss, the provost of the college. I spotted Jim standing apart from the crowd, leaning against a pillar in the shade of the library's portico, so I crossed the lawn to join him. "What's going on?"

"Dem bones, dem bones. You hear about the nutcase organization that filed a counterclaim?" He pulled a crumpled flyer out of his pocket and handed it to me. "They're holding a press conference."

"Yeah? I don't see any press."

"Allegedly, a television crew will be here any minute. Maybe they need it for a lighthearted segment: 'Your Crazy Chicagoland Neighbors.'"

I unfolded the pamphlet. It was printed in an archaic runic font and featured the same logo as on the T-shirts, the letters NL flanked by dragons that looked as if they'd been scanned off the cover of a Dungeons & Dragons book. It laid out in stodgy prose the principles of the Nordic League, an organization that believed the truth about the genetic superiority of northern Europeans was under assault in the United States, thanks to ignorance and political correctness. The League's claim to the remains housed at the college was based on a scientific study that determined the bones in question were Caucasian and very ancient. This was important proof that Norse explorers had settled in North America centuries ago, making those of European ancestry the true Native Americans. Supporting documents could be found on the group's Web site; donations to their legal fund could be made through PayPal.

"Old-fashioned white supremacists," I said. "They must be feeling a little outnumbered in this crowd."

"All according to plan. It's not easy for a handful of kooks to get the attention of the press, so they put up posters at local universities to guarantee some newsworthy conflict. Pretty savvy move, actually."

"This is a private college. Can't Safety and Security tell these guys to get lost?"

"Legally, I suppose so. But they'd be accused of suppressing unpopular opinions. Better to let these nuts make fools of themselves publicly. That's the provost's theory anyway." Jim must have been interrupted in the middle of yard work. He was dressed in a T-shirt and grass-stained jeans, and he looked relaxed as he leaned against the pillar. But I followed his gaze and realized he wanted to be at Nancy's side but was holding back. Maybe she'd made it clear to him she didn't want to have an FBI agent hovering over her in public.

Anticipation rippled through the small crowd as a team from Channel 7 arrived. At the same time, we both became aware of the sound of a vehicle with a bad muffler, growling and wheezing as it grew closer, an unusual sound in this North Shore neighborhood. We watched as an ancient green school bus chugged along a side street. "This is going to get interesting," I muttered. Jim looked at me. "That's the St. Larry's church bus. I have a feeling this demonstration is about to be hijacked for another cause." The bus disappeared behind a building, then came around a corner and pulled into the circular drive across from Old Main, wheezing to stop. The doors folded back and people poured off. New and volatile energy rippled through the crowd. "I'll go keep Nancy company," I said, and Jim nodded gratefully.

I worked my way through the crowd. A woman handed me a flyer with Rosa's image on it. WE KNOW THE TRUTH, it said in English and Spanish over her picture, with the bilingual text claiming she was being framed in the name of national security, linking her persecution to other racist acts by law enforcement.

One of the men who'd climbed off the bus with a stack of posters under an arm looked familiar. Someone called out to him, "Hey, Ramon. Got more of those signs?" When he turned, I got a good look at his profile. Not Ramon, I thought. *Daniel.* Detective Daniel Huerta, an undercover officer who had been assigned to Area 4 Narcotics last time I worked with him. What was he doing here? If he recognized me, he showed no sign.

The provost huddled with the news crew, then sprinted up the steps of Old Main, heading toward the man in the missionary getup. He started to extend a hand automatically, then seemed to think better of shaking hands with a white supremacist in front of television cameras, so he scratched his nose awkwardly instead. He muttered a few words to the man, then turned and raised a palm to call things to order. As he started to speak, I finally reached Nancy, who gave me a quick nervous smile.

"Good afternoon," he boomed in a lecturer's voice, and waited for the noise to subside. "As you all no doubt have heard, the college recently received the bequest of an estate that included human remains excavated from a burial mound over a hundred years ago. We recognize the extreme distress this causes the descendents of these, uh, deceased persons. It is the intent of the college to repatriate these remains to their descendants as soon as possible. As it happens, two competing claims have been filed in court. We ask for your patience as we work through the legal process." He paused. "Mr. Brian Folkstone of the Nordic League, who's one of the claimants, wants to make a *brief* statement." The provost raised his eyebrows at the man as he stressed the word *brief*. "After which we will adjourn to enjoy the rest of this rather warm summer day." He beamed a benign smile.

"Why not do the right thing now and turn the remains over to the tribe?" someone yelled from the crowd.

The provost tried his patented smile again. "As you can imagine, this process is complicated. I won't bore you with the details, but the short answer to your question is, we can't. The courts—"

"Have you read this crap?" The man I recognized as an undercover cop held up one of the flyers. "Why is this college providing a forum for a right-wing hate group?" He looked around for support, and a rumble of agreement came from the protestors. The provost opened his mouth to respond, but Folkstone interrupted.

"That's not true. We're not a hate group." His voice was high-pitched and a little jittery with earnestness. "On the contrary, we applaud the efforts of native peoples who struggle to maintain their identity in the face of one-world globalism. All we're asking for is the same right to our racial identity. It's the law that is racist. Repatriation rights are limited to non-Europeans." That caused an irritated reaction from the crowd, and he seemed to gain momentum from it. "The fact is, Europeans reached these shores long before Columbus. Those bones have been identified by scientists as being of Caucasian ancestry. The government wants to deny the historical facts by burying the evidence. This is a pattern—" He was drowned out by boos.

"How are these remains being handled?" a woman called out, her voice angry and accusatory. "Are they being treated as objects of study, pawed over by scientists?"

The provost looked at Nancy, who seemed to shrink for a moment before she climbed up two steps and announced firmly, "No on both counts. We've handled them with the respect they deserve. Until we receive the court's decision, they are being kept under lock and key."

"What about the research that proves the bones are Caucasian?" The question came from the front of the crowd, probably from one of the men wearing a black shirt.

Nancy shook her head, exasperated. "That article you're referring to was published seventy-five years ago. There have been advances in paleoanthropology since then. Its findings are not valid." She paused, and the air filled with an urgent clamor of questions and angry yells. "Look, I'm sorry," she blurted a little desperately. "We're doing the best we can."

The provost raised his arms for attention. As the hubbub quieted, the undercover detective jabbed a finger at the man on the steps. "We're sick of all these racist lies."

A woman nearby shouted, "Two black kids shot by cops in the last
few weeks, Rosa Saenz being hunted down on trumped-up charges.
And now these white supremacists want to claim the bones of Native
American ancestors. We know the truth."

The crowd took up the chant. "We know the truth!" People held
signs up, Rosa's face bobbing over their heads. The crowd was rau-
cous and giddy, not sure what to do with its new energy. The reporter
directed the cameraman to turn around and scan the scene. The protesters seemed upbeat, even festive, as they chanted. A man I recognized as the head of Campus Safety and Security went up the steps to
mutter something to the provost, who had his hands up again, inef-
fectually patting the air. Campus security officers and a handful of
Stony Cliff police were moving through the crowd, trying to disperse
it peacefully. But a few yards away from where I stood at the bottom
of the steps, Detective Daniel Huerta was standing close to a burly
Latino who was chest-to-chest with one of the black shirts, a man
with a small head, a thick neck, and close-set eyes full of fury. Huerta
leaned close to them, saying something I couldn't make out, but it
didn't calm them down; in fact, it looked as if they were about to
start throwing punches. I elbowed my way through. "Hey, easy." I
pointed out the security officers who were heading toward us. "What
are trying to do, start a riot?" I looked at Huerta as I spoke. His
mouth tightened, but he didn't respond.

The young Latino was belligerent. "What, I'm supposed to just
put up with their bullshit?"

"You take a swing at one of these redneck losers, you're the one
who goes to jail."

Another young man bumped his shoulder. "Hey, I got my kids
here, man. They don't need to see no violence." The Latino huffed
and made faces at his enemy, rotating his shoulders and neck as if to
release excess tension, then swaggered off, his pride intact. Not so
with his thick-necked opponent. He seemed to come apart at the

seams all at once and had to be restrained by his colleagues, who pulled him away, as he kicked and spitt out curses.

It was over within a few minutes. The Nordic League, all seven of them, trooped off. Protesters started to migrate toward the church bus or in the opposite direction, toward the Metra station three blocks west of the college. Nancy spotted me as she gathered her hair up and fanned her sweaty neck. "Oh, there you are. Want to come over to the house for a beer?"

"In a minute. I have to talk to someone first." She wandered off, looking wilted. Jim angled toward her, as if he planned to catch up with her as soon as they were out of the public eye. I watched Huerta finish chatting up some students and then stepped in his path as he turned toward the bus. "Need a word, Daniel."

He gave me a blank look. "Sorry. Got the wrong guy."

"The shooting at Benito Juarez last fall? That was my case. You gave us some valuable information, remember?"

His eyes flickered over to the church bus. "I'm working," he muttered, and stepped past me.

"Not anymore. It's over."

He froze in his tracks. "What's that supposed to mean?"

"I saw what you were doing. Is this your new assignment, working people up so they can get busted?" He rubbed his mouth with his fist, looked away. "I can't believe they pulled you off Narcotics for this bullshit. Look, you're a good cop. I don't want to mess things up for—"

"So don't."

"Why infiltrate a church group? They're not doing anything illegal."

"Then they got nothing to worry about."

"Unless some cop provokes them into breaking the law. You're putting me in a bad position here. You go back to St. Larry's, I'm going to have to let them know who you are."

"You serious? You'll blow my cover over this?"

"Only if I have to."

He started to say something, then just shook his head and started to walk away.

"Hey, Huerta."

He turned, his hands clenched into fists. "What?"

"You're going the wrong way. Train station's over there."

EIGHT

We sat drinking beer in the kitchen, a room so familiar to me, I could find a box of pasta or the carrot peeler with my eyes closed. Nancy had bought the house when Sophie was a toddler and the town still had pockets of affordable housing. Though the value of the property had soared, her kitchen hadn't changed much. It still had the original chipped porcelain sink, the same massive old stove that leaned to one side and always made lopsided birthday cakes. They could afford to renovate the kitchen now, but Nancy never thought it was quite the right time to start a big messy project. Jim didn't want to change a thing.

But I wasn't conscious of the cheery sunlit room; I was still seeing the hard stare Huerta had given me. I was used to those contests of will that cops and gang-bangers like to have, almost physical in their intensity, like wrestling without touching. This time, he'd ended it by giving me a smirk, as if to say, I know everything about you. He'd waved to his comrades on the church bus, pointed a thumb in the other direction, and sauntered away to join a group of cheerful Northwestern students taking the Metra back to Evanston, as if it had been his plan all along. It was a smart move. The people waiting for him on the church bus would assume he'd hooked up with a girl, good cover for the awkward situation I'd put him in. But the encounter had left me feeling bruised.

Jim was giving me a questioning look. I realized I'd picked away the label of my empty bottle with a thumbnail, leaving a pile of shredded paper on the table. Nancy hadn't noticed my preoccupation; she was telling the girls about the demonstration and making it into a funny story with ridiculous characters. Even world-weary Alice betrayed some excitement about seeing her mother on the six o'clock news.

A rush of warm air stirred my pile of torn paper as the front door opened and slammed shut. We heard giggling and whispers; then Sophie came into the kitchen, pulling Lucas by the hand. He was hanging back, but she dragged him into the room and twined her arm in his. "Crazy scene, huh?" Her words poured out in a jumbled flood of excitement. "That weird neo-Nazi guy with his stupid tie making a speech like at a debate contest. He'd get a lousy score, though; he was way too nervous and his voice was all squeaky. This is Lucas, by the way."

"Hello." Nancy smiled at him as if her daughter routinely brought home boys with tangled hair and filthy clothes. Alice just looked up at the ceiling, martyred again.

"My mom, my stepfather, my sisters. The one with the attitude is Alice; the cute one is Lucy. You already know Anni. What are you doing here anyway?"

"Martin was helping me fix a sink at my place; I gave him a ride home. Were you at the demonstration?"

"We watched from the roof of the Fine Arts Center. I'm working in the costume shop this summer, so they gave me a key to the building, which is way cool, since I can go in anytime I want, except late at night, because the guards come through and kick everybody out. God, it's hot outside. I'm dying of thirst." She released Lucas's arm so she could rummage through the refrigerator shelves. "Iced tea sound good? Isn't there a jug of tea in here?"

"Check behind the milk," Nancy said. She exchanged glances with Jim.

"You talk too much. It's giving me a headache," Alice announced, dragging herself to her feet with all the weight of the world on her shoulders. "I'm going to go read."

"She is *such* a pain," Sophie said into the refrigerator. "I don't know what's got into that child. Iced tea, iced tea—ah, there it is."

"Have a seat, Lucas," Jim said, pulling five-year-old Lucy into his lap to make room and nudging the empty chair out with one foot. But instead, the boy sat warily on the chair closest to the door, sliding his backpack off his shoulder and holding it in his lap in case he had to make a run for it.

Sophie didn't notice his discomfort, too caught up in her own galloping mood. "We have mint in the garden; it grows all over the place. You want mint in your tea? Or wait, I bet we have lemon. That's even better. Isn't there a lemon somewhere?"

"Try the top shelf," Nancy said. "By the way, do you know what happened to that leftover chicken?"

Sophie gave her an apologetic grimace. "Um, we had a picnic? Sorry."

"I wish you'd asked first. I was planning to use it in a curry tonight."

"Oops. I'll just make a big salad for everyone, okay? It's too hot to cook anyway. So, are you going to be on TV, Mom? You sounded way intelligent next to that weirdo." She sliced the lemon, dropped thick pieces into two glasses, licked her fingers. "Only after all the speeches and stuff, I thought there was going to be a huge fight. This kid from St. Larry's—he's been arrested before, like six times—he got in their face at the end, all macho." She looked at me and dissolved in laughter. "It looked so funny, the way you got between them and broke it up. I mean, he was twice your size, easy. Only that other one, the skinhead? He got really angry." She handed Lucas a glass of tea, slurped from her own. "Seriously, he kept staring at you afterward, this icky, evil stare. What a creep."

"Which one was this?" Jim asked me. Five-year-old Lucy was getting restless in his lap, so he reached for a box of crayons and a pad of paper on the shelves behind him. He gave them to hers and she opened the box and scrutinized the colors.

"The one with the head smaller than his neck," I said. "Nothing to worry about. They were just showing off."

"Did you read their obnoxious pamphlet?" Sophie went on. "They don't really want those bones; they just want publicity for their stupid racist ideas. What a rotten way to get it, too. It's so disrespectful. Those bones should be returned to the earth by their own people, to rest there until the end of time. Right? Lucas is an Indian; he knows all about it."

"Really," Nancy said politely. He gave a one-shouldered shrug and drank his tea, still hugging his backpack.

"He's Ojibwa, which is what ignorant people call Chippewa. He's a wonderful artist. I mean really, really good. His grandma still lives on the rez, so he's totally connected to his cultural roots. There's incredible symbolism in his work. I think it's sickening the way those bones were on display for decades in that spooky old house, just lying there with a bunch of moth-eaten old stuffed animals and snake skins and junk. What were they thinking? Would they do that to their own relatives, arrange their remains in a glass case and look at them? I don't think so." She reached for the sugar bowl, stirred two spoonfuls into her drink. "I'm *so* glad you're going to help with Rosa's defense, Anni."

"Whoa, who told you that?"

"Mom. Last night."

"I haven't even talked to Rosa's lawyer yet," I said, wondering about the way Sophie hopscotched from one idea to another, a hunch starting to form.

"You have to help her." Sophie leaned forward earnestly, her words tumbling out faster than ever. "She's innocent. Really. There's no way she killed anyone. She's like the most spiritual person I ever met. She just makes you feel so, so—I don't know what to call it. She calls it grace, but I don't know what that means. I just know that when she talks to you, she *understands,* you know? Understands everything. You have to do this, really."

"Slow down, Sophie," her mother murmured.

She threw her spoon down on the table. "Jeez, you're always saying that. This is important."

"Of course it is. I just meant—"

"I know what you *meant.* I care about this, okay? It's so unfair what they're doing to her. It's just . . . it's *wrong.*" She glared at Jim.

"You will talk to Thea today, won't you?" Nancy asked me.

I looked at Jim and he nodded encouragement. "Hey, I want to know what happened as much as anyone he said."

"Yeah, right," Sophie muttered as she poked at the lemon slice in her glass with the spoon. "Is that why you bug everybody's phones? Why you arrest people without cause, search their houses without warrants? I can't believe you still work for those fascists."

"We talked about that," he said patiently.

"You made dumb excuses. That's not talking."

"Sophie—" her mother protested.

"You don't like his job, either! I hear you fighting about it all the time."

Jim's face went still. Nancy said firmly "This is inappropriate, Sophie. We have guests."

As Nancy spoke, Jim stared at an invisible point in front of him for a moment. Then he gently shifted Lucy out of his lap, kissed the top of her head. "I'd better finish the mowing." He gathered up our empty longnecks, dropped them into the case beside the back door, and went out.

Nancy closed her eyes, then rallied. "You're welcome to join us for dinner, Lucas. And Anni, of course. It won't be anything elaborate, but—"

"Thanks, but I need to get back to town," I said. "Want a lift, Lucas?"

"Sure." He brightened and set his half-finished glass of tea on the floor.

"Give me fifteen minutes."

Sophie jumped up and took hold of Lucas's backpack to pull him to his feet. "We'll be in my room. Just let us know when you're ready to go." We heard their footsteps as they raced up the stairs, a peal of her laughter.

"Great," Nancy muttered to herself. "Here we go again."

"She's pretty revved up."

"And I can tell you exactly what's going to happen next." Her voice was flat, matter-of-fact. "I'll try to get her to see her doctor; she'll refuse. We'll row more and more: She'll disappear."

"I'll find her." Nancy looked at me. "If she runs away, I'll find her. Whatever happens with Rosa Saenz's case, that will still be my first priority."

Nancy gave me a thin smile. "Thanks. But sometimes I wish you could bring back my daughter. You know, the real one, the one who was so bright and funny and had a life in front of her." She said it jokingly, but there was a hopelessness in her tone I hadn't heard before.

Lucy looked between us, then picked up her box of crayons and paper, wound her way between the empty chairs, and climbed into her mother's lap. "I'm going to draw a castle," she announced.

"Brilliant." Nancy gave her a tired smile and stroked her hair as Lucy chose her colors deliberately, one by one. I got up and slipped out the back door.

Jim switched off the mower. "There wasn't much left to do." The humid air was perfumed with cut grass. The lilac hedges that surrounded the tiny yard looked droopy from the heat. Somewhere nearby, a lawn sprinkler made a rhythmic ticking sound.

"I need to be sure. You're really okay with this?"

"Yup, definitely." He perched on the edge of the picnic table, wiped his forehead with his arm. "Most of my colleagues would say I'm crazy to care about the defense of a woman who's accused of killing my father. But this feels right, and things haven't felt right for a long time. I'm third-generation law enforcement. Maybe it sounds naïve, but I took an oath to defend the Constitution against all ene- mies. Rosa Saenz deserves a fair trial. Everybody does."

"How would your father feel about it?"

He laughed. "He'd call me a pansy-ass liberal wuss. My dad was a tough old bastard, and conservative to the core. We didn't see eye-to- eye about politics, but he took the same oath I did. The way things are, the system he worked for his whole life might send an innocent woman to prison. He wouldn't want that, any more than I do. When you get right down to it, it's simple. I don't trust Fiske to get it right. I trust you."

"Not that there's any guarantee I'll find out what happened. It was a long time ago."

"Doesn't matter. I just want an honest investigation. I was trying to explain it to Sophie last night. . . ." His words trailed off and he shook his head. "Waste of time. She doesn't want to hear any expla- nations from me. Her stepfather. Did you hear that? She used to call me her dad."

"She's just pushing your buttons, trying to get you to lose your temper. It almost worked. You had your counting-to-ten face on. Re- member how you taught me to do that?"

"Took a while for you to get the hang of it. Punch 'em out first, ask questions later, that was your motto."

When we first moved in with our grandfather, I had to adjust to an unfamiliar social order with different rules. The rough-and-tumble code of honor that I was used to in the Chicago public schools didn't work on the North Shore. Within the first month at school, I was suspended twice for fighting. Golly patiently probed the anger I carried with me like a constant low-grade fever, gradually helping me understand the feelings that made me strike out, but that took time. Meanwhile, it was Jim's practical advice for coping with taunts and provocations that kept me out of trouble.

"I had a lot to learn," I said.

"You figured it out." He smiled to himself. "Those guys today—what did you notice about them?"

We'd played this game for years, Jim testing my powers of observation. It was oddly comforting to do it again.

"At least two of the ones wearing black shirts spent time in the joint."

"You saw their tats."

"White-power symbols, the number eighty-eight, twin lightning bolts, all do-it-yourself tattoos, not professional. They may have met each other in prison; at least one of them is from the southern end of the state. The guy in the tie—what did he call himself? Folkstone? He's from the Chicago area, going by his accent, one of those nerdy kids who can't protect himself, so he gets other people to do it. Convinces them he's a brainy leader instead of a fish, makes up conspiracy theories so they can feel like they belong to something important, have a ready-made excuse for the things that went wrong in their lives."

He nodded as I spoke, agreeing with my analysis. "Sophie had a point, though. Sounds as if you managed to piss off a racist fanatic."

"You suppose he didn't like me calling him a 'redneck loser'?"

"That could have had something to do with it."

"Interesting, the way their press conference turned into a rally for Rosa Saenz."

"Not too surprising. It's easy these days to organize a crowd, what with cell phones and texting. Makes sense they took advantage of an event orchestrated by white supremacists over a claim about Native

American remains. People are seeing the Saenz case as essentially a race issue."

I remembered Dugan's concern about the racial tensions in the city over two police-involved shootings of black youth. It wouldn't help, having a flaky white supremacist organization brought into it. That made me think about the way Daniel Huerta had insinuated himself among Rosa's supporters, and I wondered if Jim was aware of it.

"I suppose they're under surveillance," I said.

"I doubt it. We used to keep tabs on the fringe groups, the militias and neo-Nazis, but since nine eleven, that's been scaled way back."

"I meant the people at St. Larry's."

"Oh. That wouldn't surprise me." He seemed reluctant to discuss it, though. "So, you going to meet with Thea Adelman?" he asked.

"I need to call her, set something up. It's going to be weird. I'll have to ask you questions about your father, just like any other interview."

"I don't mind, but I'm not sure I can be very useful. Like I said, we weren't that close at the end. I wasn't feeling real patriotic after what I saw in Vietnam."

"The house where he was shot—you have any idea what he was doing there?"

"Meeting an informant, maybe? I really have no idea. He didn't bring his work home. Sounds like you're already developing a theory."

"Just questions. I had some time to kill this morning, did a little digging. There are some inconsistencies."

"Like what?"

"Just—stuff in the autopsy report doesn't seem to fit the scenario." It didn't seem right to go into details about the stippling around the entrance wound or the anomalies of the wound path. Whether they had been close or not, it was his father who was the subject of that clinical document.

"How'd you get hold of that so fast?"

"Uh, well . . . I know a guy."

He chuckled dryly at the familiar code words. "Say no more."

It was how things worked in the City That Works. You need a permit, a variance, a job? No problem, if you know a guy. Otherwise, tough luck. The guy I knew at the office of the medical examiner was a file clerk. Three years ago, I had discovered he had a little business on the side, selling souvenir autopsy reports and photos of the dead, gruesome mementos of violence that sick people collect for reasons I'll never understand. I found out about him when a family member of a fourteen-year-old whose homicide I'd investigated saw the lad's picture for sale on the Internet. I could have had the clerk fired, but he was the kind of slime who always knew a guy and wouldn't have trouble getting another job. I'd settled on scaring the shit out of him instead. He still had his business, but he was more subtle about it, working through a select client list and discreet referrals; there was no danger now that he'd catch an unsuspecting victim's family by surprise. Too bad I didn't "know a guy" at CPD headquarters who would do me a favor and pull the original police reports. There were too many questions that couldn't be answered without knowing more about the crime scene.

I looked at my watch. "I better call Thea Adelman."

"Nancy will be pleased. She's been feeling pretty low lately."

"Lucy's drawing a picture to cheer her up."

He gave me a crooked smile. "She always does that, tries to make everyone feel better. Tough job for a five-year-old. You think I should resign?"

The question caught me by surprise, and for a moment I didn't realize he was serious. "Why? You're one of the good guys. Without you, people like Fiske will be running the show."

"They already are."

"Then they need someone there reminding them how it should be done."

"It hasn't done much good so far. And once word gets out I don't have confidence in Fiske's investigation, that I think Saenz is innocent until proven guilty, I'll be even more irrelevant."

"But you can't just leave. Someone has to stand up for what's right."

"You left."

"Only because I put a woman's life at risk. I couldn't get backup when she needed help. She deserved better. Your job is different. You don't have to worry about situations like that."

"It's my marriage I'm worried about." His mouth went tight, as if saying it out loud had made it too real. He looked around the small yard as if he were an amnesia victim struggling to get his bearings. "I don't want to lose this. I can't."

"It's not you. She just doesn't know what to do about Sophie."

"Neither do I. But if it wasn't for my job, maybe we would be dealing with the problem together."

NINE

phoned Thea Adelman from the kitchen, agreed to meet her at her office at one o'clock the next afternoon. When I went upstairs to get Lucas, there was a flurry of whispers behind the door. Sophie finally opened it, just wide enough for them both to slip out before she pulled it closed behind her. She gave Lucas a look full of conspiratorial significance, then abruptly threw her arms around me, squeezing tight. "I love you, Anni." It was typical of her manic moods, indiscriminate outpourings of emotion. I knew better than to take it seriously, but still it made my eyelids feel prickly as I hugged her back.

"Love you, too. But you need to take care of yourself." I pushed her ragged fringe of bangs back with one finger, fixed her eyes with mine. "Seriously. If your mom wants you to see your shrink, do it, okay?"

"I promise—if you promise to take care of Rosa."

"It's a deal." But I suspected however much she meant it at that moment, she'd forget in the giddy rush of energy flooding her synapses. It was one of the problems with her disease; it was hard to strive for normal, when being manic felt so much better.

ucas climbed into the passenger seat and watched me duck down to check the undercarriage. "Transmission problems?" he asked.

"Something like that." It was becoming second nature, this

paranoid wariness. I was pretty sure I hadn't been followed, but I wasn't going to take any chances. I climbed in and coaxed the engine to life, scanning the street. Everything looked quiet, and when I pulled out, no cars followed suit.

"Sorry about yesterday," he said. "Father Sikora didn't want to leave you behind."

"I wasn't too crazy about it, either. That basement is creepy. There're critters living down there."

"Just mice. They're all over the place." He showed me a hole in his shirt. "They eat my clothes."

"Yuck!"

"Not when I'm wearing 'em—they're scared of people." They just get into all my stuff." Lucas seemed relatively relaxed in my beat-up car. The Tilquist's old-fashioned kitchen was comfortably shabby, compared to some, but places like that implied belonging, and he didn't.

"Has Sophie told you about her illness?" I asked him.

"I know she's on meds."

"She has bipolar disorder. It's sometimes called manic depression. It's a serious disease that causes big mood swings. In her case, she does what they call 'rapid cycling'; she goes through these big ups and downs a lot. When she's up, she feels great, doesn't sleep for nights on end, has terrible judgment. She abuses alcohol and drugs, lets men abuse her, does reckless things. Eventually, she gets psychotic, loses all touch with reality."

He looked around uneasily when I didn't turn on the street that led to the expressway. "Like that time at the church when she was talking to angels and stuff?" he asked.

"Like that. Is there a lot of symbolism in your paintings?"

He snorted. "No. I just paint what I feel like."

"Sophie thinks it's full of symbols. The more manic she gets, the more she finds messages in the world around her. Ordinary things seem loaded with significance, and she comes to believe she's at the center of something really important. To her, it all makes perfect sense, and she can be very persuasive. She's starting another manic phase, and she's got you mixed up in things you shouldn't be doing."

"Nah, we're just friends." He pretended to be looking out the window, unconcerned, but I noticed he reached down and hooked his fingers through a strap of his backpack.

"It's going to get a lot worse. Once she gets delusional, it's hard to persuade her the things she's experiencing aren't real. She won't want help, but she'll need it. You ready for that?"

"I guess. Aren't you going to take the expressway?"

"Later. We need to see Rosa first."

"Huh?"

As I slowed for a stop sign, he shifted in his seat and surreptitiously grasped the door handle. "Forget it, Lucas. You see these houses? These people are loaded. They see you walking down their sidewalk, they'll freak out and call the cops. Besides, I need you to show me how to get in without being seen." We were approaching the estate that had been bequeathed to the college, a two-acre property surrounded by a cast-iron fence overgrown with bushes.

"Shit. How'd you know?"

"Didn't they tell you? I'm a brilliant detective." Actually, it was only a guess that they'd hidden Rosa in the old mansion where the bones had been found, but I knew my hunch had paid off as soon as my route made him uneasy. We were passing the entrance now, its gate secured with a chain and padlock. The turret and gables, that showed through an untended thicket of trees had paint that was blistered and peeling. The neighbors would no doubt love to see this house torn down and replaced by a more up-to-date extravagance. "What's the best way in?"

"Go around the back: There's kind of an alley thing there."

"Is there an alarm system?"

"Sophie turned it off. She came here with her mom a couple times: She memorized the code."

I drove a quarter mile past it, just in case, then came around from the back. I was pleased to see the service entrance behind the house, where I parked the car, was well concealed by overgrown hedges, as was the back lawn. We climbed over the decorative fence without any trouble and were able to approach the massive vine-covered house without being observed—except from inside.

The door opened as Lucas reached for it. He started to apologize, but Rosa just shook her head. "It's all right. Come in." She led us down a hallway and into a high-ceilinged room with mullioned windows that were shrouded in dusty velvet and lace. There was almost no light penetrating the gloom, and my eyes hadn't adjusted from the brightness outside. I got an impression of dark woodwork hung with glassy-eyed animal heads, African masks, carved calabashes, and cloudy glass cases holding cobwebbed taxidermy. As Rosa led us through the clutter, my hand brushed a chair with cushions upholstered in some sort of animal hide bristling with mangy, stiff hair. I put my hands in my pockets with a shudder.

She opened a door at the far end and led us into a smaller, less claustrophobic room. It was dark, too, the single vine-covered window letting in only a dim green glow from outside, but at least the walls were lined with books instead of dead things. There were a desk and a couch, and a pair of wing-backed chairs flanked the fireplace, an oddly formal setting for the short, overweight woman who hadn't showered or changed clothes in three days. Strands of hair that had escaped from her long braid fell limply around her face, and her cheeks were flushed from the heat, but her tired eyes were as alert and intelligent as before. She gestured toward a cooler and a couple of plastic jugs of springwater. "Are you hungry? The kids brought me more food than I can possibly eat."

"No thanks. Look, Thea Adelman has hired me to work on your case. I'm not going to waste time arguing with you, but I think you should turn yourself in. I can take you to Thea right now."

"No. I'm grateful for everything you're doing, but . . . no."

"It's not fair to count on Sophie anymore. She's in no shape—"

"I know. I'll be gone soon. We've already said our good-byes."

"I have a meeting with Adelman tomorrow. Want me to pass anything along?"

She gave me a small smile. "You can tell her I didn't kill Arne Tilquist."

"Do you know who did?" It must have been the product of exhaustion, because her usual guardedness slipped and I saw something in her face before she could censor it. "What can you tell me?"

She sank into one of the wing-backed chairs and seemed to give it serious thought. "I don't have proof," she said finally. "And even if I'm right . . . he's not a bad person. He was tormented by nightmares, drinking too much, confused about his loyalties."

"If he killed a man—"

For moment, her voice hardened. "When Arne Tilquist killed, it was in cold blood, a thoroughly planned display of the power of the state. What happened in that basement was different, an impulsive act by a distraught man. It's hardly justice to condemn him for having a moment of clarity."

"What do you mean by that?"

She sighed and folded her hands in her lap, seeming to regret having said too much. Her next words were chosen carefully. "The person who killed Arne Tilquist did it because he recognized him for what he was."

"That's no excuse for murder."

"No. I'm just explaining what happened. It wasn't premeditated. And it didn't do any good; he still has nightmares."

"So, who are we talking about?" She shook her head slightly, a gentle but determined refusal. "This is stupid. It would be a lot easier to prove your innocence if we could tell the court who's guilty."

"As far as the system is concerned, the truth isn't relevant. The authorities want to find me guilty, and they will."

"Not if I can help it." I reached into my bag to pull out one of the disposable cell phones I'd bought at Best Buy. I had purchased two, planning to switch in a few days to avoid surveillance, so I had one to spare. I handed it to her, then collected the packaging and stuck it back in my bag. I had her give me the number so I could test it by calling from my phone. Then I read out my number, instructing her to put it in as a contact. "Thea Adelman's phone is probably tapped. Mine's new; they won't be able to listen in. Call me when you're ready to put an end to this. Do you have any money?"

"A little, but I don't really need—"

"A dollar will do. Is there some paper in that desk?" Puzzled, she took a bill from her wallet, then opened a drawer, where she found paper and a pen. "Write a note to Thea Adelman, retaining her as your lawyer. Don't date it. Fold it up with the money." She followed my instructions and put it into an envelope that she found in the desk. At my direction, she tucked it into my bag. "I'll see she gets it."

We left, but not before Rosa insisted on packing up the cold chicken for Lucas. She was worried he had missed the evening meal at St. Larry's.

Y ou going to tell Sophie's dad about this?" Lucas asked as we drove away.

"No." It would put Jim in a bind. He would feel a duty to act on the information, even though his daughter would be implicated, and any vestiges of trust she might have in him would be destroyed forever. Relieved, Lucas turned his attention to the food. "What was that she said to you as we left?" I asked him after a few minutes.

He finished gnawing a chicken bone, then set it down on the plastic bag. "*Maajaan.* It means 'go,' but it's also like 'good-bye.' Rosa's been teaching me our language."

"What's your connection to her? Are you related to each other?"

"Both Ojibwa, that's all. My grandma lives kind of close to where Rosa's folks come from. She talks Indian. Bet I could surprise her now.'" Lucas picked the rest of the chicken bones clean before he spoke again. "You think she'll be all right? Rosa, I mean."

"Depends on what she decides to do. Do you know what she has planned?"

"No. But she told us she won't be hiding out in that house for long."

I turned by the college to head toward the expressway. As we passed the student union, I noticed a row of freshly stenciled images on the wall, an orange-and-yellow oval with a blue woman in the center. I nodded toward it. "That's your work, isn't it?"

He shrugged innocently. "I didn't put it there."

I could guess who had. Sophie would have needed only three acetate stencils, already cut from his design, three different colors of spray paint, and only as much time as it took the paint to dry. The woman's shape was deceptively simple, only a few lines, but it was recognizably Rosa Saenz in the guise of a much older icon, the Virgin of Guadalupe. Some devout Mexican-American Catholics might find it sacrilegious, but others would see it as a potent message: Any government that picks on a saintly indigenous woman is messing with a higher authority.

"Very effective."

He bundled the bones back into the bag and wiped his hands on his jeans. "Thanks."

When we got to St. Larry's, Lucas headed off to join some friends. I walked up the steps of the church, where the 7:30 Saturday-evening Mass was coming to a close. I listened to the warbling strains of the recessional hymn, the elderly and dwindling Polish-speaking congregation giving it their best. As I waited in the vestibule, I read the notices pinned up on a board. I learned ten good reasons to vaccinate my baby, whom to call for legal aid if I got in trouble with Immigration, and where a multifamily garage sale was being held that weekend to raise money for Rosa's defense fund. I dawdled until the congregants started to drift out, then walked up to the altar and peered into the sacristy, where the priest was hanging up his cassock. "Can I talk to you, Father?"

For a moment, I thought he would make some excuse, but he gestured toward the rear exit. "I have to speak to a confirmation class, but I can give you ten minutes. Let's go outside. I need a smoke."

I followed him through the back door and onto the porch behind the rectory. He leaned against the railing and offered me a crumpled pack. Chesterfield, Golly's brand. I had to stuff my hands into my pockets to keep from reaching for one. "I quit."

"Me, too, many times. Stupid habit." He lit up, then squinted at me through the smoke. "I'm sorry we left you locked up in that place."

"At least you told the cops where to find me. What did you do with that gun you took off Sophie?"

"I don't have it anymore. And for the record, I don't know where Rosa is."

"That's not why I'm here. You need to be careful what you say, who you trust." I paused, feeling as if I was about to burn the last bridge connecting me to my old career. "I have reason to believe the police planted an undercover cop at the center."

"Only one?" He chuckled at my reaction. "The authorities have had their eye on this place for years."

"They suspected Rosa all this time?"

"Nothing to do with Rosa. When I first came here during the Reagan years, we were one of hundreds of churches to offer sanctuary to refugees from the massacres in Guatemala and El Salvador. We've been on some sort of list ever since." He smiled to himself. "Rosa is good at spotting cops. She can see right through them. But they didn't know about her, not until—when was it, early Thursday morning? At least that's when they came for her."

"Do you know who tipped them off?"

"No. She told me someone recognized her a few weeks ago. Someone from her past. She didn't say who. Maybe from the movement. I think she was protecting him."

"Why didn't she leave when she had the chance?" He shrugged. "Did she indicate this person might have been involved in the crime?"

"No, but there wasn't much time to talk."

"Was there time for her to tell you she was accused of murdering an FBI agent?"

"Why are you asking so many questions?"

"Thea Adelman wants to hire me as an investigator for Rosa's defense team. I'm meeting with her tomorrow. It's possible Rosa's innocent, but I need to know what's going on if I'm going to prove it. When did you learn who she was?"

He contemplated the ash on the end of his cigarette. "I've always known. She was a student at the high school at my first parish. Already a rebel—refused to say the Pledge of Allegiance, got in trouble with the nuns. I was usually in trouble with the nuns, too, so we got along well. She dropped out in her junior year, though she was a good student, could have easily gotten a scholarship to college. She just thought there were more important things to do. We worked together in the peace movement, and when I left Chicago in '69, we kept in touch. That was back when people wrote actual letters." He puffed on his cigarette and looked down the alley, seeing something not visible to me. A smile chased across his face, then faded.

"Do you still have them, the letters she wrote you?"

"I burned them. Given the political situation—" He shrugged. "Didn't want to take chances."

"Did she write about Ishkode, the radical group she joined?"

"She never mentioned it by name. But I knew something was happening to her. She was interested in all kinds of causes, civil rights, the antiwar movement, César Chávez, but it was all . . . theoretical. That changed."

"What happened?"

"She met someone. And suddenly she was telling me what it was like growing up on the reservation. Personal experiences that suddenly connected to a pattern of injustice. She was angry." He snorted. "Well, she always sounded angry, but this was deeper, more personal. She heard a man speak, Logan Hall, a Chippewa, like her, and it changed her life. He grew up on the North Shore with adoptive parents, went to U of C for a year or two. He'd gone up to Minneapolis when the American Indian Movement was starting to form, returned to give a speech about the cause, and when he went back to Minneapolis, she went with him. That was the last letter I got from her."

"What did she say about Hall?"

"Not much. But he made an impression. She told me she realized things that had happened to her father, things she'd experienced in school, were part of a larger pattern, tied to the European exploitation of indigenous people over the centuries. As if all that generalized passion for causes had suddenly become focused, personal. Like a

beam of light passing through a magnifying glass. She was smolder-
ing, about to burst into flame."

"You didn't hear from her again for . . . how long?"

"Years. I only knew about her involvement with the radical group
from news accounts. I didn't think I'd ever see her again after all that
violence and her disappearance into the underground—except for her
picture in the post office." He finished his cigarette and dropped it on
the porch, rubbed it out with his heel, then nudged it over the edge to
fall to the pavement below, already littered with spent butts. "All
blurry, like those missing children on milk cartons."

"When did she resurface?"

"Here? Just over a year ago. She showed up one night, started helping out in the soup line. People do that, just wander in and pick up a
ladle or a towel, start to work. She looked so different, but there was
something about her. . . . I was so startled, I almost said her name out
loud, but she introduced herself before I could speak. Rosa Saenz,
new in town. She hoped she could be of service to the community."

"It had to be risky, coming here."

"It's not hard to disappear in a city this size. After all, many of our
homeless regulars don't exist at all, so far as the authorities are concerned. Latin American countries aren't the only ones with *los desa-
parecidos*."

"But why Chicago? Why this parish, especially once she knew the
cops were watching the place?"

"It was her calling." He saw I was puzzled by the word. "You don't
need to join a religious order to have a calling," he added. "Her work
is here, in this community. That's all I mean." He started to extract
another cigarette, but grimaced. "Some example I'm setting for the
kids." He tucked the pack back into his pocket and glanced at his
watch. "Besides, I'm running late for the confirmation class."

"One last question. Did she ever indicate she knew who killed
Arne Tilquist? Did she give any hint who it might have been?"

"We didn't talk about the past." He started to go inside, then paused. "You have to understand. She changed. Changed totally. Verna Basswood was outspoken and angry, always ready for a fight. She was convinced the only way this country would change was through violent action. Rosa Saenz is a different person. There's no anger in her. She has a kind of peace that she's able to pass on to others. It's a gift, like the laying on of hands. Crying babies, boys squaring up for a fight, drunks—she touches them and says a few words, and they grow calm. I don't know where it came from, that gift of peace, and I don't know where her anger went, but she changed."

"I should take a look at where she lived, check with her neighbors. Do you know her address?"

"Same as mine. She rented a room just down the hall. The FBI already went through it, took some things, though I don't know why. Her only possessions were some clothes and few books."

"She likes to travel light."

"Metaphorically speaking. It's called 'voluntary poverty.'"

As he reached for the door, I stopped him. "I'll keep all this confidential. If the feds find out you knew each other in the seventies, they could charge you with harboring a fugitive."

"They already know. I told them." He was amused by my response. "What's the point in lying? I'm terrible at it."

"You should have asked for a lawyer."

"They just get in the way. Attorneys want to protect their clients; they're not interested in speaking truth to power."

"But don't you realize that—"

"Of course I do. I've been arrested before." He tapped his watch. "Confirmation class."

TEN

Sunday morning is always a good time to go for a run; the streets are nearly empty of cars, the birdsong louder than the usual rumble of city noises. I live at a crossroads in this city of nearly two hundred neighborhoods. A four-mile run can take you around one of the most trendy and gentrified parts of the West Side, through the oldest Puerto Rican community in the Midwest, or into areas where 90 percent of the residents are black or Mexican-American. The boundaries are shifting, as they have for decades, the current trend being to push the poor westward to free up chic urban housing for young professionals, who are almost inevitably white. Lately there had been restiveness along the frontier as rents went up and longtime residents were uprooted. My house had already increased its value, but I didn't like the idea of being surrounded by self-congratulatory "urban pioneers." I wondered whether Thea Adelman, in her attractive Bucktown home, ever noticed the irony of that term.

Early in the morning, while it was still relatively cool, I ran the perimeter of Humboldt Park, then east, down an alley behind the businesses on Division, where I saw the blue-and-yellow stencil of Rosa Saenz on a Dumpster, on a wall in triplicate, on a door. From there, I headed into the shady streets of Ukrainian Village and south to Chicago Avenue. Farther down the avenue, police surveillance cameras had been installed on light poles to discourage a thriving open-air drug market, but at this end of the street, there would be no video of whoever had been busy spraying images of Rosa Saenz on every other storefront. Either Lucas had been hard at work all night or people had made copies of his stencils and fanned out to spread them as far as possible before city employees came along to blast them off or paint over them.

Approaching a park, it occurred to me that Tyler sometimes spent the night camped out behind the basketball court. Maybe I could persuade him to tell me where he got the information he sold to the feds, the name of the person who recognized Rosa Saenz. There was no sign of him there, but I mapped the rest of my run to take in places where I'd seen him before. It wasn't the scenic route.

I spotted him, finally, sprawled on an old couch left beside a Dumpster in an overgrown yard behind an apartment building. A scrawny dog was nosing through a bag of spilled garbage, but it ran off as I approached. Tyler was blissfully loaded and slow to react when I picked up the carving knife that lay beside the sofa. "Hey, whatcha— That's for my protection," he complained, struggling to sit up as I threw it out of reach. But as he peered into the yard, trying to see where it had landed, he started to nod off again.

His eyes sprang open when I picked up the syringe that he'd dropped onto the couch beside him. "No, hey."

"Don't worry, I don't share needles." I tossed it over my shoulder, then picked up the cigar box where he kept the rest of his works. I dumped the contents onto the ground: a pipe, a spoon, a lighter, cotton balls, and a glassine packet of heroin. I picked it up and waggled it in front of him. Tyler made a grab for it, but he missed and toppled off the couch. I helped him back up. "Wake up, Tyler. Got a question for you."

"Illegal search. Got my rights . . ." he mumbled, forgetting his words but keeping his drooping eyes fixed on the packet.

"Who told you Rosa was Verna Basswood?" He blinked vaguely.

"You got paid for that information, remember?" It looked as if he'd been celebrating ever since. The little old ladies he liked to con wouldn't have recognized him now, shirtless and gaunt, his eyes red-rimmed. His knuckles were scabbed over, and one of his knees showed through a tear in his jeans, blood crusting around the ragged edges. He'd either been in a fight or fallen down one time too many. He licked his lips and his eyes started to close. I shook his shoulder. "Who told you about Rosa?"

"Much you paying?"

I held up the glassine packet. "Want your junk back?"

"Bitch."

"Just tell me. Who was it?"

"Some old drunk."

"What's his name?"

He squinted, trying to concentrate. "Ah, it's . . . Don't remember."

"What's he look like, then?"

Tyler leaned toward me. I thought he was about to confide something, but he was just examining the rip in his jeans. He picked at the scab on his knee, puzzled when blood welled up. "Fuck."

I waggled the bag again. "Tyler? Focus."

He looked at his knuckles and shook his head. "Man, this ain't right." He slumped back against the cushions. I tried again to get a description, getting no further than "skinny," "drunk," and "loser," the last of which may have been meant for me. "Ghost stories," he finally said, his eyes half-closed.

"What's that?"

"Tells lame ghost stories all the time. Fucking juicehead." He made another fruitless snatch at the bag of smack. "Come on, gimme my shit. S'all I got left."

I dropped the bag into his lap and left him there nodding off. I'd have to talk to him later. His memory might improve when he needed a fix.

A man with short grizzled hair was standing on the sidewalk outside my house, tapping a notebook impatiently against his leg. He had the sagging suit and the broad build of a cop, but I knew he wasn't one. I was planning evasive maneuvers, when he turned and his jowly face lighted up. "Anni!" he called out, as if I were long-lost friend. "Good to see you."

"Wish I could say the same, Az."

"Aw, don't be that way." He lumbered toward me, beaming. Azad Abkerian, a reporter for the *Chicago Tribune,* had been put on the cops and courts beat decades ago. It was typically the job new journalists got assigned to after an apprenticeship in obituaries, because it was easy. You didn't have to go out and find stories; you just listened to the scanner. But Az had never moved on to better things. It wasn't because he wasn't a good reporter; in fact, he was one of the *Trib*'s best writers and had even been nominated for Pulitzer once. He just fell in love with cops and never got over it. He liked nothing better than rubbing elbows with detectives at a crime scene, carrying Vicks in his pocket to dab under his nose if the body was too ripe, going out for a drink with the guys afterward. He was especially delighted whenever one of the women who hung out at the bar, attracted to uniforms and guns, mistook him for a detective. It never occurred to him he was like those women, just another cop groupie.

Now he was putting on the charm. "I was getting worried about you, kid. Couldn't get through on your phone."

"It's broken."

"That explains why you didn't return my messages. I thought

maybe you didn't like me anymore. This Saenz case is a doozy, isn't it? How'd you get mixed up in it?"

"Gotta go. Nice seeing you, Az."

"Come on, you know me." He started to follow me down the gangway to the back of the house, until I turned and froze him with a look. He spread his hands. "I'm fair; I'll tell it straight."

That was true enough. For someone who needed to cultivate police sources to get his stories, and was lovesick besides, he was unusually evenhanded. He'd gone after the details of what happened the day Hank Cravic lost his temper like a crazed terrier digging up a backyard. Getting the cold shoulder at the bar during the trial must have hurt, but getting the story came first. He sensed me weakening and opened his notebook, clicked a pen. "As I understand it, you were with Rosa Saenz when the feds tried to apprehend her."

"No comment."

"That's okay. I already got it from about six dozen witnesses." He glanced up at me. "Fiske tells me they got Saenz dead to rights for killing Arne Tilquist. But people who know her say it's not possible. You figure she's innocent?"

"Ask her lawyer."

"I will. We're meeting this afternoon, which, frankly, I'm not looking forward to. That lady can talk your ear off." He thumbed back a page of his notebook. "Can you at least confirm you're working with her on the defense?"

"Did Fiske tell you that?"

"Just something I heard," he said vaguely. "You're big pals with Jim Tilquist, right? How's he feel about your involvement in this case?"

"Bye, Az."

"Okay, you don't want to talk about Saenz. I got it, fine. But hang on a sec. There's another thing I'm working on. What do you know about this—what do they call themselves? The Viking Patrol, or . . ." He flipped pages in his notebook.

"You're not giving those assholes more publicity, are you?"

"House style won't let me use *assholes* in a story. Got another adjective I could use?"

"It's not newsworthy. They set the whole thing up to get attention."

"Maybe so, but we got a race angle, a fracas with Rosa Saenz's supporters, and they're arguing over some ancient bones, which you gotta admit is a great hook."

"They're ex-con losers, half-wits who idolize a geeky little racist because he invents conspiracy theories to justify the mess they've made of their lives. You run a story in the *Trib,* it'll make them sound important. They're not; they're trivial."

He was scratching out hieroglyphics in his notepad. "Better than *assholes,* anyway. Now, these bones—"

"Ask Thea Adelman about them, too. Her firm is representing the tribal claimants."

He groaned. "God, I'll never get out of her office. You sure you don't want to say anything about Rosa Saenz? Now's the chance to set the record straight."

"Come on, Az. You actually think I'll fall for that?"

"So sue me for doing my job." He snapped his notebook shut, slipped it in his jacket pocket. "Only there's something you need to know. The stuff I been hearing from my contacts . . . You remember what it was like with Cravic, all the shit your fellow officers gave you? This is going to be a lot worse. Watch your back, kid."

showered, ate breakfast, and spent more time than usual deciding what to wear, but I still had more than an hour to kill before my appointment with Thea Adelman. Just enough time to check out the house where Arne Tilquist had met his end, I decided. It was less than three miles from where I lived.

North Lawndale had been a poor black neighborhood back in 1972, and it still was. Every block had grassy, rubble-filled gaps between buildings. Some of it dated to the riots after Martin Luther King, Jr.'s assassination, when the West Side went up in flames. The rest of the vacant lots were due to the city's policy of bulldozing abandoned properties to prevent them from being taken over by dealers. There were a few signs of renewal, but jobs were scarce and most residents had household incomes below the poverty level.

When I was doing my initial research the day before, I had found a photo and description of the property at the Cook County assessor's Web site. The picture was a few years old, but the building hadn't changed much, a small single-story structure with a sagging front porch and a tiny scrap of a front yard. A faded FOR SALE BY OWNER sign was propped in one window. I punched in the phone number scrawled on the sign, but an answering machine kicked on. I left a message, then checked both front and back doors. There were multiple locks on each, better security than at my place. In the back, I crouched down to peer through the small barred windows cut into the foundation, but they were so grimy and the interior so dark, I couldn't make out any details of the basement where Arne Tilquist had been killed.

I would know more once the owner returned my call and I had a chance to get inside. But now I had to meet with Thea Adelman.

arrived a little early for our 1:00 P.M. meeting. Thea showed me to a chair and told me she'd be a few minutes. Since it was Sunday, there was no receptionist at work and no clients in the waiting room. It was quiet except for the murmur of Thea's and Harvey's voices coming from a nearby room. I took the note I'd instructed Rosa to write out of my bag and slid the envelope into place just under the front door, holding it with a Kleenex so it wouldn't have my prints on it. Not that anyone would be likely to check, but lately I was doing all kinds of things I would have classified as paranoid behavior just a few days earlier.

Thea and Harvey Adelman's modest office, part of a collective formed by half a dozen like-minded attorneys, didn't reflect the national reputation they'd earned for their work in tribal law and civil rights cases. Unlike the men's club woodwork and leather typical of most law offices, the furniture in their waiting room was mismatched, shabby, and comfortable—a decor designed to make those intimidated by the justice system feel a little less alienated. It wasn't doing much for me, though.

There was a box of well-worn toys beside my chair. I picked up a train engine with see-through parts and wound it up. It made chugging noises and plastic pistons went back and forth as its wheels spun, the kind of toy Martin would have loved when he was a kid. I watched the parts move, trying to figure out how it worked, and trying not to think about the meeting I was about to have.

Thea and I rubbed each other the wrong way. It didn't help that she worked on the assumption all cops were racist—though I had to admit there was some truth to that. You're sent out to look for trouble and, sure enough, you find it. You find it enough, you stop seeing kids horsing around and see gang members instead. You notice a young man driving a nice car and figure he bought it with drug money. You assume that woman with a pissed-off look on her face means it for you instead of for the driver of that bus she just missed. It's a form of racism that is an odorless, invisible gas that hangs in the air in cop shops. You don't even know it's there.

But that wasn't the kind of racism Thea meant. She had put me in the same camp as the guys who put on the uniform because it gives them a chance to exert power, who enjoy it most when it's over people they feel are, by definition, inferior: cops who feel righteous when they beat up a collar, who brag on it in the locker room, knowing they're safe. Among friends.

I had joined the police force for a different reason, and so had most of the officers I worked with. But in a job where your life is on the line, loyalty is highly valued, and during the last few months at Harrison, it was made amply clear that I had no friends there. I wasn't even safe.

Harvey grinned at me as he came out of an office, carrying a stack of papers. "Having fun?" I put the train back in the toy box, feeling foolish. "Sorry we kept you waiting," he added. "I'm taking over the NAGPRA claim, so Thea had to bring me up to speed."

"There's something—" I pointed to the floor, where the envelope showed under the door. "Might be important."

Harvey propped his files on the receptionist's desk and bent to pick it up. He pulled out the note inside the envelope and a dollar bill fluttered to the floor. He read the note and passed it on to his wife before bending down to scoop up the bill, giving me a sly wink.

"How did—" she started to say, but swallowed the rest of it.

"Someone slipped it under the door," I said, which, strictly speaking, was true.

"Rosa Saenz has retained us for her legal representation," Thea explained dryly. "Attorney-client privilege is more useful when the client is actually present, of course, but this will certainly make it easier to proceed."

"I'll set up her account," Harvey said, waving the dollar bill with a grin.

Thea led me into her office and indicated a chair, then sat behind her desk, where she straightened a file, rearranged a couple of pencils, folded her hands and stared at them. "Nancy Tilquist called me. She was quite unhappy about how our previous meeting had gone. My experience with the CPD has led me to expect the worst, but apparently I was wrong about you. Please accept my apology."

I shrugged, acknowledging her words without comment. Her mouth tightened. I wasn't following the script; I was supposed to agree that cops were fascist thugs and I was the rare exception, but I didn't feel like it.

"I don't know if you brought a contract with—"

"It's pretty standard." I pulled a file out of my bag, handed two sheets of paper across the desk. She read them carefully, niggled about some of the wording, initialed some changes, and signed both copies, passing them back to me for a countersignature. "I'll give you a deposit for your services. Let's set some ground rules." She tore the check out of its binder and passed it to me. "You need to operate on the assumption you are under surveillance. So long as our client is at large, don't attempt to contact her again. It puts her at unnecessary risk and could compromise our case. Instead, concentrate your efforts on learning as much as you can about the circumstances of the crime she's accused of."

"Yes, ma'am." She looked at me narrowly, suspecting sarcasm, but I kept my expression innocent. "What kind of case do they have?"

"There's little in the public record, and it's too soon for the discovery process. But they have at least one significant piece of physical evidence. They recovered the murder weapon near the scene. It can be traced to Verna Basswood. She purchased it from a pawnshop in Iowa two years before the shooting; it's a clearly documented link. And some of the cartridges remaining in the magazine yielded prints that appear to be Basswood's."

"I didn't see that in the newspapers. How did—Oh, you must know a guy."

She frowned at me. "Apart from the weapon, we don't know what other physical evidence they might have or whom they may call as witnesses. The indictment is less than informative. You'll just have to do the best you can."

"They know for sure Rosa is Verna Basswood. The priest at St. Larry's admitted it to the feds when they questioned him."

"Didn't he have a lawyer with him?" she asked, concerned. "They could charge him."

"He knows. Doesn't seem worried. I don't think he has a clue what prison is like."

"Father Sikora? You don't know him very well, do you?" She looked pleased, as if she'd just scored one for her side. "He was working in Guatemala during their civil war, when the military massacred tens of thousands of indigenous people. He was falsely accused of being a Marxist revolutionary and spent six months in a hellhole before his order negotiated his release. The torture he received there was so severe, he spent months in recovery. He still walks with a limp."

I'd assumed it was just the usual aging process, a touch of arthritis. "He never said anything."

"Well, now you know. Have you had any thoughts about how you might proceed?"

"Arne Tilquist was found dead in the basement of this house." I handed her the picture from the Cook County assessor's Web site. "Hard to say why he was in that neighborhood, alone, unless it was for a prearranged meeting with someone. Possibly an informant. It was a close-contact shot. Looks more like a known-acquaintance thing than an assassination. Also, the angle of the wound path is significant. Basswood was a lot shorter than the victim." I stopped myself from saying more. It was one thing for Thea to have connections, but she wouldn't approve of my taking shortcuts, ordering up an illicit copy of the paperwork. She'd just accuse me of jeopardizing her case again. "We need to request the autopsy report," I said. "And have a pathologist look at the wound path."

"I'll see to it tomorrow." She made a note. "But I'd caution you to avoid drawing premature conclusions based on press accounts. They invariably get things wrong. Do you have anything else?"

I thought about what the priest had told me, that Rosa knew someone had recognized her in the past few months. If this was the same person Rosa had talked about, a man who killed Arne Tilquist in an impulsive moment, he was the key to the case. But I didn't have anything concrete to go on yet, and I didn't want to give Thea another chance to belittle my ideas. "I have a few questions for you. What's the deal with Ishkode? Were they really domestic terrorists? The FBI made them sound like the Red Peril."

Her mouth tightened in distaste at my choice of words. "Nowadays, the definition of 'domestic terrorist' has been expanded to cover pretty much any dissident who commits even a minor criminal offense. It's virtually meaningless as a legal term. It's true that Ishkode was suspected of several criminal acts, including placing a pipe bomb outside police headquarters—which, incidentally, didn't detonate. But members of the organization were never indicted for any of them. Still, the authorities will make the most out of public statements that seem incendiary when taken out of context."

I flipped through my notes. "You mean statements like 'elimination of the thuggish agents of state power is a moral imperative'? Logan Hall said that in a speech. He was telling people they should kill cops."

"It's a mistake to take phrases like that so literally. That kind of language is typical of its time period, not extraordinary at all, given the hyperbolic rhetorical gestures commonly employed by both sides. But taken out of context, it could be damaging."

"Not as damaging as what that bullet did to Arne Tilquist's brain."

"That sort of remark is not helpful."

"Sorry. Comes from having been an agent of the state. I'll try to work on my thuggishness. Another question: After the feds raided that farmhouse—"

"So long as we're analyzing word choice, let's be a bit more accurate. You mean, after the FBI slaughtered five men." Her chin went up, as if there was an invisible jury she needed to impress and I was on the stand for cross-examination. "Surrender wasn't an option. It wasn't a raid; it was an execution, clearly a case of agents short-circuiting the justice system so that they could have their revenge. Logan Hall's autopsy record has been conveniently lost, but it's clear from contemporary reports that excessive force was used."

"Right, whatever. What I'm wondering is this. An unnamed woman was quoted by the press afterward, saying there'd be a reprisal. Do they have proof it was Basswood?"

"Not that I'm aware of, but they will argue she was the only woman in the inner circle, and the only one left to speak for them. Making such a statement and carrying out a murder are two different things, of course."

"Good luck trying that on a jury." She looked ready to embark on a defense of the First Amendment, so I jumped in with another question. "Can the feds retroactively classify this as a terrorist investigation?"

"So they can use provisions of the PATRIOT Act to investigate a crime committed thirty years before its passage? There's not much case law yet, but I doubt they'll take that approach. They'd be handing us automatic grounds for appeal." She started flipping back through her notepad. "Besides, they don't need to, since our phones are already tapped, and we've had our home and offices searched without notification." She glanced at me. "I'm not being paranoid. It started back in 2002, when we did some background work for *Rumsfeld versus Padilla.* If you're at all familiar with the case, you'll know the government doesn't believe suspected terrorists, however slim the evidence against them, deserve their day in court."

She found what she was looking for and detached the page from her legal pad. "I took some notes today on angles to pursue. There's a storefront church not far from the house where Tilquist was shot. The pastor's been involved in homeless outreach for decades. He might know people who could have witnessed something the day of the shooting."

I recognized the name written in her neat script. Alonzo Jones, pastor of the New Day Tabernacle, was a civic leader in North Lawndale and had been helpful to the police in negotiating boundaries during gang disputes and providing information when an abusive husband or a habitual thief needed to be taken out of circulation. He knew me and would give me whatever help he could, but I doubted it would be fruitful.

"It was the middle of winter, the day after Christmas, right? The homeless would have been keeping warm somewhere, not hanging out on the street," I said.

"You could be right, but it shouldn't take too much of your valuable time to check it out," she said with exaggerated patience. "By the way, December twenty-sixth isn't just the day after Christmas. It's the anniversary of the largest mass execution in the nation's history. In 1862, officials in Minnesota hanged thirty-eight Dakota Indians for alleged involvement in the Sioux Uprising. Following the mass hanging, the entire Dakota Nation was deported from the state, the men shipped off to prison, the women, children, and elders put on boxcars and sent to a godforsaken part of South Dakota with nothing but burlap sacks to keep themselves warm. I'll bet you don't remember this from history class."

"Must have been absent that day."

"Doesn't matter. It wasn't in your textbook anyway."

"You think it plays?"

"I'm not saying it does, just that it's a culturally significant date, something a person with no knowledge of native culture might miss." She passed the sheet of paper over the desk with a little "I have to do everything" sigh. "In addition to that pastor's name, I made a list of people who we know had some connection to the movement. The first names are the five members of Ishkode who were killed in Wisconsin, the next group are what police would call 'known sympathizers,' not directly affiliated with the movement, but activists aware of the issues. The last set of names are people who were involved in the American Indian Movement in Minneapolis at the time Logan Hall broke away to form his own group; they may be able to give you some useful background. It would be best to hold the interviews in person. We're prepared to cover reasonable expenses for a trip to Minneapolis. Let me provide you with a supply of my cards so people can check your bona fides." She rummaged in a drawer, pulled out a stack of cards, and wrapped a rubber band around them. "You'll need to be to be sensitive to the power relationships involved. The coercive approach police officers are trained to use won't work here."

"Go easy on the brutality and corruption. Got it."

Her eyebrows pinched as if she had a headache. "That's not what I'm talking about. Native Americans experience prejudice every day, and many of them have had bad experiences with law enforcement. If you rush things, if your questions seem too intrusive, it will be counterproductive. If you want to gain their confidence, you'll have to be patient and let them decide how and when to disclose information. Aggressiveness and adversarial behavior are not part of native culture."

So how'd you get so good at it? I wondered, but all I said was, "I think I can handle it. We finished?"

"For now," she said, sounding regretful that "finished" couldn't be more permanent. "Please hold Monday mornings open. Starting tomorrow, we'll be having weekly briefings of the entire defense team, beginning promptly at eight A.M. If anything important comes up between meetings, call and make an appointment. We'll have to meet face-to-face, since our phones are not secure."

"Ten-four."

She touched her forehead with two fingers for a moment, her eyes closed, as if asking a higher power for strength. Then she stood to escort me with icy courtesy to the door. "Look, we got off on the wrong foot, and I take responsibility for that. Given the work I do, my relations with the CPD tend to be contentious. Nancy told me about how

you provided testimony in the civil suit against Hank Cravic. About
what happened after—the death threats, all of it. It took courage to
do what you did."

"I just answered their questions. Isn't that what you're supposed to
do when you're under oath?"

"Depends on which rules you're playing by. What you did sent an
important message."

I couldn't help laughing. Thea was one of those earnest people
who can keep cool in the face of any kind of abuse—except being
laughed at. "What's so amusing?" she demanded.

"I thought you knew how it works. You're always on television, explaining it to everyone. The city settled; Cravic kept his job. The kid
he roughed up has permanent brain damage. What was that message
again?"

Thea glared at me, furious, as if I'd tricked her somehow. "You
could have lied. That's what cops usually do."

"Well, I didn't. I told the truth, and a lot of good it did. Do me a
favor and save the political speeches for someone else, okay?"

was kicking myself as I headed for my car. It was stupid to have let
Adelman get under my skin like that. I would have to learn to ig-
nore her little digs, her competitiveness, just put my head down
and get the job done. It wasn't about sending messages, about prov-
ing a point or scoring a win in some ideological struggle. I wasn't
working this case for her sake, after all.

Jim wanted an honest investigation. If the questions raised by the
autopsy were any indication, that hadn't happened thirty-five years
ago. I'd start with the evidence, talk to any witnesses I could find, and
see where it led me. If there had been a cover-up, it was time to find
out.

I was almost at my car before I noticed the man leaning against it, eating french fries out of a cardboard container. Special Agent Fiske looked up and extended it toward me. "Want some?"

"No thanks."

"You're a difficult woman to catch. Hardly ever home." He waggled a limp fry at the building that housed the law office. "Does Jim Tilquist know you're working for the other side? Oh, I forgot. It's against your principles to answer questions. I'll just ask him myself next time I see him."

"Is there something you want?"

"Cooperation would be nice. Say, did you know Rosa Saenz has high blood pressure? All that weight, plus she's prediabetic. Perfect conditions for a stroke. Of course, it's controllable with the right medication." He poked around in his container. "Only she left her apartment in a big hurry, didn't take her medicine with her. If you think hiding her from us is doing her a favor, think again. Could be putting her health at risk."

I realized he must have found out that Golly had died of a massive stroke, thanks to neglected high blood pressure, and was using it to goad me. But I remembered how flushed Rosa's cheeks had been, how weary she'd looked. If he was telling the truth, she had been without her medication for four days already. How long did she expect to be able to keep this up? But I didn't let any of what I was thinking show on my face. In spite of his casual style, Fiske was conducting an interrogation, noting every detail.

He scooped some fries into his mouth and mumbled through them. "I have to admit"—he swallowed and wiped his mouth—"I have a hard time understanding where you're coming from. You're willing to testify against a cop who makes a mistake, but you won't help when we're trying to apprehend a cop killer."

"Sure I will. I'll even help you find the right person this time."

He gave me a thin smile. "Always ready with a joke. Bet you

thought it was hilarious, putting our tracker on another car. Not so fun for that elderly couple, though, getting stopped by the police on their way out of town. They were pretty shook-up." He ate the last of his fries. "In town to visit their grandson at Children's Memorial. He has a brain tumor." He bundled up his trash and lobbed it into a nearby trash can, then brushed his hands against each other, still leaning against my car, studying me.

"Mind if I go now?" I asked after a minute.

He moved away with a "Be my guest" gesture, but when I climbed in, he held the door to prevent me from closing it. "Just so you know: Your refusal to cooperate won't change a thing. I'm going to use all the resources at my disposal to find and convict Rosa Saenz, whatever it takes. You might want to think about that." He studied me for a moment longer, his eyes roaming my face as if looking for a chink, a crack, some way to get inside, then released the door and strolled away.

called the owner of the house in North Lawndale again, and left a message when I got the answering machine once more. I made a few more calls, none of them successful, until I reached Logan Hall's adoptive mother, who still lived in Winnetka. She was willing to speak to me, so I drove up to her North Shore home, arriving around 4:00 P.M. She was in her seventies now, living alone since her husband's death, and seemed achingly wounded to see her son's name in the news again. She showed me an album filled with photos of a solemn brown boy posed between two smiling blond parents. During the interview, I took conscientious notes, though she had nothing insightful to tell me, being permanently baffled by the political turn her son's life had taken. She had never met Verna Basswood or any other members of Ishkode. Their son had grown distant in his adolescence and then had stopped speaking to his parents altogether after he dropped out of college. They had done their best, but he'd been angry about so many things. She could tell me details about his first birthday party and his role in the sixth-grade play, but she had no information about the man he'd become. It was as if she knew the little boy in the pictures but not the radical who'd made passionate speeches, the man whose life had ended in a violent shoot-out with federal agents.

The conversation left me feeling low, so I stopped at the college to have dinner in the canteen with Martin. There were times when I needed his quiet, solid presence, and he never minded if I didn't feel like talking. Before heading home, I dropped by the Tilquists' house to give Jim a progress report and see how Sophie was doing. For the second day in a row, Jim had gone to the office to catch up on a few things, Nancy told me. He didn't seem to grasp the meaning of the word *weekend*. Though she didn't say so, there was enough crispness in her tone that I suspected they'd been arguing again. Sophie was revved up and talkative, but not exhibiting the euphoria and delusional thinking typical of a manic state.

"I'm going to have to go to Minneapolis soon," I told Sohie as I left.

"Really? That's where Lucas is from. What are you doing up there?"

"I need to talk to people who knew Verna Basswood when she was involved in the American Indian Movement. The thing is, I don't want to have to worry about you while I'm gone."

"I'll take my pills. I promise. And I'll go to that shrink tomorrow, even though he's a complete moron."

"Sophie—"

"Jeez, don't worry so much. It will be all right."

But something was wrong when I got back to my house. I sensed it the minute I opened the door to my flat: a disturbance in the air, the

faint scent of another person's presence. Wrapping my hand around
the bundle of keys, I silently slipped out the one in the lock and posi-
tioned the tongue between two knuckles. I didn't wear a gun on my
hip anymore, but if I had to use my fist, I wanted it to be loaded. I listened intently, then moved silently across the room to check the bathroom and closet. Nobody there. No sign anyone had been.

Fiske had gotten to me, with his expensive clothes, arrogant confidence, and that little smirk. I was already in the habit of looking over
my shoulder, constantly wondering if I was being watched. Now he
had me thinking my own home wasn't safe.

I threw the windows open and turned on a fan to chase away the
stale air that had accumulated during the day. I sat on the porch with
an ice-cold beer, the alcohol diminishing the lingering unpleasantness
of Agent Fiske's visual strip search. It didn't quite chase away the
image of an elderly couple suddenly surrounded by flashing blue lights
as they made their way home to Nebraska after visiting their sick grand-
child. But for all I knew, he'd made that story up, the twerp.

I twisted the top off another Leinenkugel's and sat at my grandfather's desk to organize the next day's work before calling it a night. I
went over my notes, reread the autopsy report, and glanced at the
sheet of names Thea had given me, thinking about how to track these
people down. It wasn't until I pulled over the stack of printouts I'd
made that morning that I noticed something odd about them. Earlier, I had sorted them into categories—information about the murder, the movement, the victim and his career. The stack had looked
untouched, sitting on the table exactly where I had left it, but the
pages were out of order.

Another two hours passed before I finally got to bed. I found a
neighbor, who told me he'd seen FBI agents around that afternoon.
They and the cops had been crawling all over the place, asking questions. He hadn't see anyone go into my apartment, but he hadn't exactly been looking. With all those badges around, he'd been minding

his own business. How long was this going to go on anyway? he asked. I didn't have any answers for him.

I went back to my flat and went through all of my papers and personal files, a search as thorough as if I were processing a crime scene, but without any clear idea what I was looking for. Nothing else in the flat seemed disturbed. In the end, I began to wonder if I'd somehow mixed those pages up myself.

I climbed into bed, read a book for a while, then switched out the light and listened to the night.

ELEVEN

One thing you could say for Thea Adelman: She knew how to keep meetings short. We gathered in a conference room early on Monday morning, four lawyers, a paralegal, and me. I outlined the questions I was looking into; the lawyers shared cryptic thoughts on the legal issues that would need to be researched. Thea had a way of making people express themselves in as few words as possible, staring hard at them and jiggling her pen if they talked too long. It was over before we finished our mugs of coffee.

There was only one sticky moment between us, just as I arrived. "Perhaps I should have been more explicit," Thea said, instead of saying hello. She folded a newspaper and passed it across the conference table. "I assumed you knew better than to speak to the press."

It was an article inside the Metro section bylined Azad Abkerian, a short piece on the Nordic League. "Sorry. That was meant to be off the record." At least he had gotten the perspective right. On the evening news, the white supremacists had seemed more imposing than they were in person. Az made them look small and foolish. "I told him to speak to you, actually."

"We did quite a long interview about Rosa's case. I'm not sure why that hasn't run yet." Maybe that was the real source of her irritation: I was quoted and she wasn't.

As we wrapped things up, Thea spoke briefly about the demonstration held Saturday at Stony Cliff College. It was understandable that Rosa's supporters wanted to speak up on her behalf, she said, but it was unfortunate nevertheless to be linked with fringe-element white supremacists. She had consulted with Father Sikora about coordinating their efforts. A group of activist organizations would be filing for a permit to hold a combined protest outside the Federal Building the following Sunday. Given the importance of projecting the right media message, she would play a major role in any plans that developed. Ideas or concerns should be routed through her. Any questions?

With the meeting concluded, I headed down to police headquarters. CPD uniforms would have been the first to respond to the murder in that North Lawndale basement thirty-five years ago. Their incident report wouldn't be detailed, but with any luck, it would name any witnesses they'd detained at the scene and describe the position of the body. I would need that information to answer the questions raised in the autopsy.

I parked in the public lot beside the elegant steel and glass building that faced a desolate stretch of South Michigan Avenue. It looked more like a corporate headquarters than a cop shop. From the upper floors, CPD command could hold video roll call with any of the department's districts, map current drug and gang activity using sophisticated geographic information systems, even monitor selected street corners through surveillance cameras, all without leaving the building. Dugan must have had an office on one of those floors, maybe one with a view of the lake. No wonder his mother was upset he'd traded this for Harrison. As I stepped inside, a man, studying a sheaf of papers, reached out blindly to push his way out the door beside me. "Terry, hi."

He stepped back, startled. "Anni? What are you doing here?"

"Paperwork, as usual." When I was new to the job, Terry O'Neill and I had dated for nearly two years, as serious a relationship as any I'd ever been in. Not serious enough for him, though. He wanted to settle down, get married, have kids, but I wasn't ready for that, couldn't hear the word *commitment* without thinking about those hospital wards where they keep the doors locked. We'd parted amicably, and within a couple of months he got engaged to someone else; at last count, they had four kids, whose pictures he was ready to pull out and share at the slightest encouragement. I hadn't seen him in over a year. He'd put on a few pounds, but he still looked good, fit and tanned, a man who felt more at home on the street than at a desk. "Haven't seen you in awhile. You might have heard I'm working as a PI these days."

"I heard." His eyes were an intense deep blue against his tan, laugh lines etched permanently around them. But he wasn't smiling now. "People are saying you're working for the woman that shot Arne Tilquist. Is that true?"

"Not quite. I don't think she shot him."

He looked up and beyond me, his gaze focusing somewhere else. He shook his head slightly. "Testifying against Cravic, I could understand that. I even stuck up for you. But this . . . Jesus, Anni. Why?"

"Same work I always did. A man was killed, and I'm trying to find out—"

"Not 'a man.' Arne Tilquist was in law enforcement. He was one of *us*." He cut me off before I could respond, and his mouth tightened, as if he was holding angrier words back. "You shouldn't be doing this," he finally said, then turned and pushed out the door. I turned to head toward the office where inquiries are filed and realized what he'd been looking at as he stared over my shoulder: a wall covered with star-shaped medallions, each one bearing the name of a fallen officer.

The line was long, a mix of officers and public defenders, skip tracers and insurance investigators. Goose bumps prickled my arms. The air conditioning kept the place cool as a morgue, but the looks I was getting from the cops in the room were even colder. I filled out a request for a copy of the official incident report and waited to turn it in at the counter, ignoring the whispers and stares. When I handed in the form, the gray-haired officer glanced at it, looked up at me, and said it might take a few weeks before I got the records, maybe even a month.

A fter leaving HQ, I stopped at a coffee shop, ordered an iced latte, and started combing through my notes. I couldn't afford to wait while the records division deliberately dragged its heels. Luck was running with me; almost immediately, I found what I needed, a detail among the first notes I'd made while reading through old newspaper accounts of Arne Tilquist's murder. A reporter had included a quote from one of the EMTs who had removed the body. It took a dozen phone calls to track the man down. He was retired now, living in Punta Gorda, Florida.

He sounded cautious when I told him what I was working on. "I know about it; I read the papers from home."

"Must be strange, given you were there."

"Want to know something else that's weird? It's hotter up there than down here. Global warming, the weather's all screwed up." He was silent for a moment. "You're working for that radical?" I wasn't sure if he was referring to Rosa or Thea Adelman. Either way, he didn't seem to approve.

"I'm a private investigator now, but I used to be with the police department. In fact, I worked for years with Arne Tilquist's son. He's as interested as anyone in getting this right."

"You think they didn't?"

"There are some things that don't add up. Which is why it would be really helpful to hear what you saw that day."

"There was a heat wave like this ten years ago. Lot of old people died." It almost sounded like an accusation.

"The city's doing a better job now."

"They'd better." He fell silent again, and I held my breath. "So, what do you want to know?"

He had a good memory. I was able to get more detail than I probably would from the police report—and my run of luck held. Before I finished writing up my notes, my cell phone rang. "You left some messages on my answering machine. That house you been asking about? I could show it to you now if you like." A careful voice, southern and polite, belonging to an elderly cousin of the even more elderly owner.

Within half an hour, she met me in front of the house in North Lawndale, a tiny, ancient woman in a shirtwaist dress that had survived many washings. Her summer handbag matched her shoes and hat, and probably had since the 1950s. I was almost surprised she wasn't wearing gloves.

Her cousin, she told me, had purchased the property for back taxes in 1975. It had been vacant for a number of years, but it was a solid little house. She'd fixed it up and lived there until a year ago, when she took a fall and had to move to a nursing home. Unfortunately, what with one thing and another, it wasn't possible for her to live independently any longer. "The house is perfect for a single person, thoroughly renovated but very reasonably priced nevertheless, an excellent starter home." She pronounced the last phrase as if it were in a foreign language she was having to learn to help her cousin pay the nursing home bills. I felt me a twinge of guilt. I hadn't exactly lied to her when she assumed I was interested in buying the house, but I didn't correct her, either.

"It's in great shape," I said, trying to hide my disappointment as I looked at the tidy avocado counters in the kitchen, the thirty-year-old stove. Chances were that the house-proud owner had long ago obliterated any signs of what had happened here before she bought the house. "The county assessor's records indicated there's a basement."

Her nose wrinkled delicately. "There is a cellar, yes. Unfinished, just an earthen floor. I don't think anyone's been down there in years. My cousin had trouble with her knees, and the stairs were difficult for her. But of course, if you'd like to take a look . . ." She opened a narrow door off the kitchen, and I saw a steep and rickety wooden staircase descending into earthy-smelling darkness. "I believe I'll stay up here, if you don't mind."

"Not at all. I'll be a few minutes."

The light switch didn't work; the utilities must have been shut off. I dug out the penlight in my bag and made my way down the steps. With the passage of decades, I wouldn't be finding any of those unexpected clues you find at a crime scene—a flash of insight from the way a hand is curled or a shirt is rumpled. But even from the other side of thirty-five years, as I stepped onto the earthen floor I felt for just a moment as if I was making contact with the past. Like walking through a cobweb in the dark.

The small windows set high in the walls let in barely enough light to make out ceiling joists, stone walls covered with coarse plasterwork, a dirt floor. Rough wooden shelving lined one wall, filled with mason jars that were draped with dust-thick spiderwebs. They looked like preserves put up back in the Depression, undisturbed since the police had investigated a shooting thirty-five years ago. I picked up a jar and tilted it toward the light but couldn't make out the writing on the lid. Whatever was inside moved sluggishly through thick dark liquid, round shapes bumping together. I set it back, dusted off my hands.

According to the retired EMT I had talked to on the phone, Arne Tilquist had been lying on his back in the center of the room, his head angled toward the foot of the steps. He'd been wearing a dark wool coat, a striped scarf, gray suit—nice clothes, clean as a whistle, not torn or rumpled. As if for some strange reason he'd come from a fancy party and decided to take a nap there. He'd been shot once, in the face, the bullet entering through the left eye, no exit wound. There hadn't been much blood, but a couple of jars of preserves had fallen off the shelves and broken. Peaches. He still remembered the smell.

Reaching for that moment, I closed my eyes and breathed in the earthy scent of the damp walls and dirt floor. My imagination supplied other smells, phantom ones: the coppery scent of fresh blood, the bite of cordite drifting in the air. I visualized the shape sprawled across the ground, right arm flung out, a blackened, oozing place where his left eye had been. His black wool coat fanned out around him, double-breasted jacket buttoned neatly. Someone he had trusted standing over him, still feeling the kick from the pistol, still hearing the shot ringing against the stone walls. Backing away, bumping up against the shelves. Maybe not even registering through the fog of unreality the sound of glass breaking, the smell of syrupy fruit.

Tilquist's head had been close to the bottom step, almost touching it, according to the EMT, and his obituary described him as being two inches over six feet. I paced it out, stood where Arne Tilquist would have stood when he turned and saw the barrel of the gun pointed toward him, the weapon blurred by proximity and disbelief, only enough time to think, *What? No, not like this* before the world exploded.

I turned and took a couple of steps back toward the shelves, raised my arm until the muzzle of the imaginary pistol was only inches from the face I visualized in front of me. Bent my knees to shorten myself by four or five inches, aimed again. Checked the angle of my arm.

I walked over to one of the windows and flipped through the pages of my notebook until I found the notes I'd taken on the autopsy, squinting at them in the dim light, wanting to be sure. Overhead, cobwebs stirred, like the flanks of something breathing. I tucked my notebook back in my bag and took one last look around. There was no sign now of what had happened that day, not even a stain darkening the earthen floor. But I had what I needed.

had started to call Thea Adelman on my cell but then realized the number would show up on the records of her tapped phone, so I stopped at a convenience store to use a pay phone instead. "I have something to report," I told her. "The theory I brought up at the meeting this morning? I found a witness and I've been to the scene. It checks out."

"That's good." She sounded distracted, not registering the meaning of my words. "I was just about to contact you, actually, but I don't appear to have a working phone number for you. I received a disturbing call a short while ago. A death threat. It was . . . very unpleasant."

"Report it to the police."

"As if they'll do anything."

"It'll establish a record, though, which would be useful if it happened again. Chances are that it was just someone trying to ruin your day. I'm sure you've had this sort of thing happen before, but you'll want to take the usual precautions."

"I guess I didn't make it clear. The call was meant for you."

"Oh."

"I wasn't sure at first. I get threatening calls from time to time. But never like this. It was extremely explicit."

"Sexually?"

"Violently sexual. This person is obviously disturbed."

"Did the caller assume he was dialing my number, that I had answered? It wasn't, you know, 'Tell that bitch . . . ' "

"No. He started speaking before I could say anything. He must have assumed he was speaking to you. I didn't realize that until he used your name."

"This was on your direct line? Not the general number for the office?"

"Yes, it must have been."

"Which is unlisted."

"It's on my cards, but not in the phone book, no."

"Do you remember his actual words?"

She didn't answer right away. "I'd rather not repeat it. It was disgusting. I'll write down what I can remember. I know that may sound silly, but—"

"No, I understand. I'd appreciate you making a record of it, though. It would help me get a better sense of where this is coming from."

"It could have been a member of that white supremacist group. That article about the Nordic League that came out this morning quoted you by name, and the things you said weren't exactly complimentary."

"Maybe."

"In any case, I'll get it down before I forget the wording. No doubt the authorities have an accurate copy, but it's difficult to subpoena a record that doesn't officially exist."

I racked the phone and headed back to my car. I was pretty sure that call wasn't the work of the Nordic League; they wouldn't have Thea's direct number. But earlier at police headquarters, I had filled out a request for records, and the form called for an address and phone number. I'd put down my home for a mailing address, but I'd used the number on Thea's card. I didn't want the police to have a record of my unlisted cell phone number, in case they started tracking my calls.

Well, Az had warned me, and in his own way so had my ex-
boyfriend, Terry. This was just the start.

The mood at St. Larry's had changed. Where there had once been
a welcoming and lively hum of community activity, there now
was an atmosphere of tension and distrust. The air was fragrant
with boiled cabbage and stewed meat as volunteers cleared away the
remains of the noon meal. A colorful banner hung defiantly across
the stairwell—WE KNOW THE TRUTH!—decorated with paint-dipped
handprints of all sizes, as if it had been a nursery school project, but
as I walked down the hallway, the faces turned toward me were wary
and suspicious.

Father Sikora looked tired, and as we once again went to the back
so he could have a smoke, I noticed that his limp was worse. "I'm not
sure which is more annoying, federal agents or reporters. I can't get a
thing done." He stuck a cigarette in his mouth, made a pretense of
having trouble sheltering his match to light it, so that he could look
all around us, make sure we were alone. "Have you heard from her?"

"Not since Saturday."

"I'm worried."

"She spent all those years on the run; she must know what she's
doing."

"If she was safe, she'd find a way to let me know."

"It's too soon. With all the police presence, she probably doesn't
want to get you any deeper in trouble." He looked down the alley, blowing smoke out in a thin stream. "What are you not telling me?" I asked.

"She's not on the run. She was finished with all that. The lies, the
hiding. Something's wrong."

"Are you saying . . . Did she have something else in mind, some
kind of plan?"

"I think so. I don't know what it was."

"But she asked me to drive her way up north. Sounds to me like she was making a run for it."

"No. It was time for the truth to come out; she just needed a few days. That's what she told me."

"Well, damn. Would have helped if she'd told me the truth."

"If you knew when she came to your door that she was wanted by the FBI for the murder of Arne Tilquist, would you have helped her? She was buying time."

It made a certain amount of sense. If we had made it out of town and managed to evade capture for even a few hours, she would have had the opportunity to assess whether I would be willing to help, whether I could get Jim Tilquist's cooperation in uncovering the truth. But if I wasn't going to help her, all I would be able to tell the authorities was that she was on her way north.

"Something's not right." The priest took an anxious puff on his cigarette. "Her health's not great. What if she's sick?"

"She didn't look sick to me when I saw her," I said, trying to reassure him, though I remembered her flushed cheeks, and what Fiske had told me, that she had left her blood pressure medication behind. "Listen, I need to find the man who recognized her. All I have so far is that he's old, skinny, drinks, and tells lame ghost stories." Father Sikora shrugged, his face a blank. "I got that description from a police informant, a junkie named Tyler. I need to talk to him again. He's white, in his twenties, long hair, blue eyes, downstate accent. Looks kind of like a picture of Jesus."

"Oh, him. Haven't seen him lately."

I sighed and thought for a moment. "You have a homeless outreach program, right? Those people with the canvas carryalls?" I'd seen volunteers carrying the bags over their shoulders, heading out to find the homeless where they were staying, in underpasses and doorways. They gave away toiletries and over-the-counter medications, candy bars, condoms, and socks, as well as referrals to social services, shelters, and clinics.

"Why? You want one of those canvas bags so you can get their confidence?" He flicked ash off the porch.

"Damn, you're jaded. That was exactly what I had in mind."

"What will you do if you find this man, the one who knew Rosa?"

"Get his story. I'm going to find out who killed Arne Tilquist, even if I have to talk to every skinny old drunk in the city."

He stubbed out his cigarette. "Go see Helen, on the second floor."

It turned out Sister Helen, a genuine nun who apparently belonged to the order of the Sisters of Divine Stubbornness, wouldn't give me one of her carryalls until I had been through the training program, and the next one wasn't scheduled for another two weeks. I explained my work had put me in frequent contact with the homeless, that I could start right away. She finally relented and handed me a stack of reading materials and told me I could begin as soon as she was convinced I'd mastered it all, and completed a week's apprenticeship with one of their experienced volunteers. Not quite the cover I was looking for.

But she knew something about the man who told ghost stories. They had a client who was nicknamed Casper, after some cartoon character. He had shown up in the neighborhood about a month ago, confused and malnourished, unshaven, his gray hair in a ponytail. She hadn't heard his stories, but other clients said he talked about hearing ghosts singing. His eyes were blue, she thought, but she couldn't be sure of his height; he was so very stooped. She hadn't seen him for at least a week, but with so many police in the neighborhood lately, she didn't expect to. He was afraid of anyone in a uniform or a suit. She hoped he was all right. He had a lot of problems, but he was a gentle man, a good man.

TWELVE

was heading to my car, thinking about how to find Casper, when my cell phone rang. I had given the number to only a few people: my brother, the Tilquists—and Rosa. Maybe she was finally ready to surrender.

But it was Nancy. She'd just heard something disturbing and thought I should know. The director of Campus Safety and Security had appeared at the physics lab and escorted Martin away. He wouldn't explain what it was about. Nobody knew what was going on. She said she'd try to find out more, but . . .

I tried dialing S and S while starting the Corolla. It wouldn't catch, and I nearly flooded the engine. I took a breath and managed to coax the engine to life as the dispatcher confirmed that Martin was in the director's office. She couldn't give me any details, she said, but she added in a lower tone that maybe I should come out there, just in case. I switched the disposable phone off and tossed it on the passenger seat. It's safer to drive with both hands when you're dodging through traffic well over the speed limit.

I heard voices echoing down the hall as soon as I entered the college building where the Campus Safety and Security office was located. The physics professor who directed the lab, his student Josh, and three other faculty members were gathered in front of the dispatcher's counter. "For some bizarre reason, your brother has been taken into custody," one of them said to me.

"No, he hasn't," the dispatcher said, exasperated. Though used to debating parking fines with faculty, arguments she always won, she seemed unusually flustered. "They're just . . . they're talking, that's all."

"In Cole's office?" I asked her.

"Yes, but you can't—"

I did anyway. Martin was sitting with his hands gripping one another in his lap. His eyes were on the floor, and he was rocking, almost imperceptibly, forward and back, his way of imposing some kind of order on a situation that was frighteningly unpredictable. Cole Janssen, head of S and S, was slumped back in the chair behind his desk, idly tapping the end of a pencil against the side of his head. He straightened up, his chair back snapping to attention. "Listen, Anni, Martin's not in any—"

"What are you doing here?"

Special Agent Fiske was perched casually on a corner of Janssen's desk, dressed in a suit that had a more stylish cut than those most agents wore, one polished shoe swinging lazily. Another agent stood impassively behind Martin's chair. "Just trying to have a word with your brother."

I looked at Janssen, who flipped the pencil onto his desk and raised his hands in an "I give up" gesture. I rounded on Fiske. "You have no right—"

"I have every right." His quiet, assured voice carried a hum of power. "I'm investigating the murder of a federal agent by domestic terrorists. Maybe you weren't paying attention last time we spoke. I told you I won't leave any avenues unexplored."

"This is idiotic. He can't . . . Anyway, what could Martin possibly have to do with a crime committed thirty-five years ago?"

"He spends a lot of time at your residence. Maybe he was there when Saenz asked you for help. As I understand it, he holds down a job; he's able to operate complex machinery. He's not mentally retarded. He might be able to help us out."

"He wasn't there that morning. I already told you all about it."

"You told us a story that was full of holes." Fiske leaned back, his arms folded across his chest. "You were here last night, meeting with your brother. What was that about? Coaching him to make sure you had your stories straight?"

There was a reddish tinge to the air in the room, and my ears filled with a rushing sound, but I forced my anger into a corner at the back of my brain and closed the door on it. "He has never met Rosa Saenz," I said more calmly. "He has nothing to tell you. And we're not going any further with this without a lawyer present."

Fiske feigned surprise. "A lawyer? Why would he need—"

"I was a cop; I don't take my legal advice from television. You want to question him, you'll have to wait until his attorney's here."

"If he's not involved, he has nothing to worry about. Aren't you being a little paranoid? I'm just trying to get the facts. Why do you find that so threatening?" I gave him a stony look, and his gaze shifted to Martin, who rocked and stared at the floor. Silent patience during an interrogation seems to increase the earth's gravitational field. It weighs on a suspect's shoulders, makes the heart work harder, wraps itself around the windpipe. Most people will say anything rather than let it go on, but Martin wasn't like most people.

"Can I have my office back?" Cole Janssen asked finally.

walked with Martin back to the lab, knowing the best thing to do would be to let him return to work. The orderliness of familiar equipment and routine procedures would calm him down, but not if there was a crowd there. The faculty who turned out in support were too excited, too talkative. I was relieved when they went off to discuss the event over a cup of coffee in the student union, its walls recently decorated with stencils of Our Lady of Social Justice.

When I saw Martin was settled, I went back to talk to Janssen.

We'd known each other since my student days, when he was a young security officer and I had a work-study assignment in S and S. While I went off to investigate violent crime in the city, he'd taken a quieter path, getting a job with the Lake Forest PD and working his way up the ranks before coming back to Stony Cliff to run Campus Safety and Security. He was good at his job, able to get along with students while protecting them from their worst impulses. He'd been at the demonstration Saturday, quietly managing from the sidelines, making sure any flare-ups of hostility would be efficiently tamped out. Now he was tilted back in his chair again, twiddling a pencil between his fingers. "How'd this happen?" I asked him.

"I got a call from the president's office. Fiske and his partner were there, asking for Martin. Wouldn't tell anyone what it was about. Just made it sound like a matter of national security."

"So you invited them to use your office for an interrogation."

"Better than letting them take Martin downtown, which is what Fiske wanted to do. I'm not the bad guy here, Anni."

I knew that was true. Janssen got along well with Martin and had more than once soothed concerns about the wisdom of having a silent eccentric living in the basement of a classroom building.

"Sorry. It's just . . . You saw him. He was scared. And what happened at the end—that was deliberate." Fiske had clapped a friendly hand on Martin's shoulder when he left, as if to say, No hard feelings, buddy. But he'd kept his eyes on me. The message clear: See what I can do? Anytime I want. My brother had pulled away from his grip with a low, distressed moan. He had to calm himself by touching his fingertips with his thumbs in sequence for several minutes, his version of Zen meditation.

"The guy's a prick, all right, but no real harm done. You're working for the defense in the Rosa Saenz case, huh?" He held up his palms. "Not making a judgment, just asking."

"She deserves her day in court."

"You're not the only one who thinks so. See the new decorations on the student union?"

"They're all over Chicago, too." I'd seen more of them from the expressway, on embankments and walls. The city had an aggressive antigraffiti program, usually painting it over or blasting it off walls within days, but even so, it would be hard to keep up. Lucas's stencils were being copied and used everywhere.

"How'd Fiske know you were here yesterday? Are they watching you?"

"Maybe. Either that or they have a source here, someone they asked to keep an eye out after that demonstration on Saturday."

He nodded. We could both imagine a staff member feeling important if asked to assist the authorities, particularly if the request came from an agent as good-looking and well dressed as Fiske, flashing the same credentials they'd seen on TV. With a little encouragement, they'd have plenty to say about Martin. Characteristics that are merely unusual can suddenly appear sinister when someone with a badge shows interest.

"This has nothing to do with Martin, does it?" Janssen said.

"No. Fiske doesn't want me on this case. He already harassed my neighbors, threatened my tenants. Now he's trying to get to me through my brother."

"That's what I figured. Considering how important it supposedly was to national security, he actually didn't have much to ask Martin once we got him over here. Though he was sure asking a lot of questions over in Admin."

"Like what?"

"Like were the staff up to speed on the PATRIOT Act provisions relating to student records? Were we certain all of our international students were properly documented? If served with a National Security Letter, were our IT staff in a position to provide authorities with records of network traffic routed through our servers? All very casual, but it was making the silverbacks plenty nervous." He was referring to the senior administrators, all of whom were past middle age and cautious to a fault.

"Is Martin in trouble?"

"Relax. He has a lot of friends here," Janssen said, studying tooth marks in his pencil as if they were forensic evidence, not really answering the question.

I phoned Nancy to fill her in as I left. She was sputteringly indignant that the FBI would pick on Martin, but she calmed down enough to tell me the good news that Sophie had gone to her psychiatrist that morning without putting up a fuss. He'd adjusted her medication, and would see her in another couple of days. Nancy was too cautious to allow herself to be optimistic, but it seemed a good sign.

I t was a dark blue Honda this time, tailing me from the college into town. I stopped on the way home to pick up some dinner at my favorite restaurant in Little India. As I waited for my order, I mulled over what had just happened. When Fiske laid his hand on my brother's shoulder, his expression was smug; he was relishing the power he wielded. "Whatever it takes," he had said. It made me angry that he would pick on my brother just to show me he could, that he'd uproot the lives of my downstairs tenants by threatening to have Joey deported. He was trying to commandeer my own imagination and turn it against me, to inflict damage at random and let anxiety do the rest. When threats can come from anywhere, you begin to feel the danger's pervasive and inescapable. You become the warden in your own prison of fear. It's a strategy well known to both tyrants and terrorists.

But it made me hopeful. If Fiske was spending so much energy interfering with my personal life, it made me think the front-page case that was supposed to be his ticket to the big time was on shaky ground. The best way I could get back at him would be to prove Rosa's innocence. But I knew I'd have to do it quickly. I could handle threats, but it wouldn't take much to turn Martin's life upside down.

I came out of the restaurant with more food than I could possibly eat, so I walked over to the Accord idling at the end of the block, planning to give the vegetable samosas to the two agents sitting inside, but they peeled away in a hurry as I approached.

The sack of food filled my car with spicy fragrance. I was looking forward to my dinner, but as I climbed the steps to my porch, I found a souvenir that killed my appetite: a large and very dead rat.

My hands shaking with shock and anger, I stowed the food in the refrigerator. Then I went back outside to deal with the rat. It was unpleasant to discover it had been nailed to the porch. I had to use a claw hammer to pry it from the wood, and it had ripened just long enough to be bloated and leaking, as disgusting as possible. Though I scrubbed the planks with Lysol after bagging the rat and taking it down to the Dumpster, I still smelled the stench as I sat down to work.

I compiled a list of all of the homeless shelters and outreach programs in the city and marked them on a map, planning to start the search for Casper tomorrow. It would be a slog, but phone calls wouldn't be as effective as talking to people face-to-face. The one exception I made was to call the North Lawndale pastor I had worked with before. Alonzo Jones of the New Day Tabernacle sounded delighted to hear from me, though that could simply have been the well-oiled mechanism of his charm. When I described Casper, a homeless alcoholic who talked about dead men singing, he knew right away the person I was talking about. He promised they would keep an eye out for the gentleman and let me know if he turned up.

I had finally recovered enough of an appetite to snack on some spinach naan, when Jim Tilquist called, wondering if he could stop by on his way home. My house wasn't on his way home, but I said, "yes, sure," then went around picking up the printouts and notes that were spread out all over the place.

His tread was heavy as he came up the back steps, and his tie was lowered to half-mast. "Got anything cold to drink?" He set his brief-case down.

"Water, tea, beer?"

"Beer." He dropped wearily into the nearest chair.

"One of those Mondays, huh? At least yours didn't start with Thea Adelman chewing you out."

"Guess there's always a silver lining. You've done a lot of work. Looks great."

"It's getting there."

"When's the air conditioning going in?"

"Never. The electrical system couldn't handle the load. Besides—"

"I know, you hate being cooped up." It was an attempt at a joke. We'd had this conversation before, when the Tilquists were installing central air at their home and I'd gone overboard arguing against it, describing the benefits of open windows and fresh air. "Just yanking your chain." He took the bottle of beer I handed him, twisted the cap off, and took a long swallow.

"You hear what Fiske pulled today?"

"I heard. Not much I can do, Anni. I tried to get in to talk to my boss about it, but his schedule was too full. It usually is when I want to talk to him. I've said too many things, burned too many bridges."

"I know how it feels."

"I'll bet." He gave me a crooked grin. "Is Martin okay?"

"He was shook-up, but Cole kept things cool. How'd you hear about it? Was Fiske bragging?"

"Nancy gave me a call."

"She told you about Sophie, then?" He visibly steeled himself. "No, it's nothing bad. She kept that doctor's appointment this morning. Nancy didn't think she would, but she did. I'm surprised she didn't tell you."

"It didn't come up."

"The doctor made an adjustment in her medication, switched antidepressants. He thinks the one she was taking was revving her up too much. Sophie's really trying, Jim. Maybe she'll get through this time without a major incident."

He gave an ambivalent shrug. His reaction was like Nancy's; there had been too many setbacks before. They were both too cautious to allow themselves to have expectations. He took another pull on the beer. "The reason I stopped by . . . you see that piece Abkerian did on the Nordic League?"

"Yeah. I tried to talk him out of giving them more publicity. At least he doesn't take those nuts seriously."

"Maybe he should." Jim reached into his briefcase. "I did a little digging. Their beliefs may seem ridiculous, but each one of them has a history of violence." He laid out a photograph of the one who had been dressed like a missionary, but in the photo he was wearing an orange jumpsuit. His hair was disordered and his eyes looked like burning coals. "Jordan Jacobs, aka John Keefer, aka Brian Folkstone. His specialty is manipulating people to do his dirty work. Went down as an accomplice to arson when the guy he persuaded to set fire to a South Side home implicated him in the crime. The home owner had apparently insulted Folkstone. Can't have that." He dealt out six more photographs, giving each a name and listing their convictions. It seemed my guess was right: They'd met one another in prison and formed an alliance based on a mythologized racial identity. "This is the one who worries me the most," he said, dealing out the last photo. The thick-necked man looked dazed in the mug shot, his close-set eyes vacuous. "Alton Brinks. An eighth-grade dropout, developmentally disabled, a hair-trigger temper. Somehow he got hired by a contractor to drive a truck in Iraq, even though his license had been suspended in Illinois. They sent him home after a few months. Too crazy for Iraq, that ought to tell you something." He held up his bottle. "Got another one of these?"

I reached into the refrigerator for another Leinenkugel's. "He had a hard time adjusting when he got home," Jim went on. "Got addicted to the excitement, came back wired for more. Sent down for eighteen months after going nuts in a bar, putting three men in the hospital. The prison psychiatrist thinks it's only a matter of time before he kills someone. Brinks knows who you are now, thanks to that newspaper story."

"I doubt he reads the *Trib*. More of a *National Enquirer* type."

Jim looked at me for a moment, then reached into his briefcase again and riffled through a folder. He hesitated, then pulled out three photos and spread them on the table. They were fuzzier enlargements made from video—extra footage that never made it onto the television news segment. One of standing between Alton Brinks and the angry Latino teenager. Brinks being held back by his friends. A blurry close-up of Brinks, his chin lowered to his chest, his teeth clenched in a snarl. Compared to his mug shot, it looked as if a mad scientist had flipped a switch, animated him with a current of high-voltage rage. "It's not a joke, Anni. He may not have the brains to track you down, but the man he idolizes does, and you dissed his organization. You need to watch your back."

"That's what Az told me yesterday."

"It's good advice."

"Only he was talking about the police. They're giving me the same treatment I got after Cravic." I pulled one of the printouts closer. The steps of Old Main showed behind Brinks. The angle meant the pictures had been taken by someone in back of the crowd. "This isn't from Channel Seven. You were filming the demonstration."

"Not me." He scooped the pictures up as if they were suddenly classified.

"The FBI. You had someone there, conducting surveillance."

"I didn't know, not until I started asking around about the Nordic League. They'd caught some of it on film."

"By accident. They were filming the protestors from St. Larry's."

"It's pretty standard these days, Anni."

"Gathering information about dissidents? Keeping their pictures on file? Standard for J. Edgar Hoover, maybe. Or Joe Stalin. Jesus, how can this be standard?"

He closed his eyes. "Don't, Anni. Don't turn on me, too."

He sounded so lonely and sad, it made my chest ache. It took several seconds before I could speak. "I'm sorry, I just . . . I'm naïve, I guess. The CPD had someone there, too."

"If it makes you feel any better, they pulled me off the Terrorism Task Force, put someone else in charge."

"What? When did this happen?"

"This morning. They said they need someone with a legal background to review a pending corruption case. The files have already been delivered to my office, all the details of how an asphalt contractor greased a few palms in Springfield. Six boxes' worth, thousands of pages to go through. That should keep me from fucking up anything important for a while. It's a relief, in a way. I'm tired of fighting. Do enough of that at home." He tried to smile, but it didn't work.

"Have you told Nancy?"

"She didn't give me a chance. She was pretty worked up about Martin when she called. Fiske must have thought he could get you to back off by picking on your brother. He obviously doesn't know you."

"Or my brother. Fiske tried this tactic, laying all this heavy silence on him. Didn't work at all. Martin just did that rocking thing he does. Could have done it for hours. It was driving Fiske bananas. He couldn't figure out what to do." That brought a faint smile to Jim's face. "Just wait till we blow his case out of the water," I added. "That'll take the smart-ass down a peg."

"You really think you will?"

"Yup."

"Because Rosa's a good person? That would be Sophie's argument for the defense."

"I've known killers who were basically decent people who got into a corner, did something out of character, but I sure wouldn't want to rely on it as a defense. Luckily, we don't have to. She didn't pull that trigger."

"They traced the gun to her. I understand they picked up her prints on the shells."

"So, someone used her gun. If that's all they got, they're in trouble. The scene doesn't make any sense."

"What do you mean?"

"The angle of the wound path is all wrong for an assailant under five feet tall. The shot was delivered up close. And from everything I've read about your father, it's totally impossible. His gun never left its holster. He didn't even have his jacket unbuttoned. No way he would have let her surprise him and take control like that. He was shot by an acquaintance. Someone he trusted."

Jim didn't have to ask it out loud. His expression asked the question for him: Who?

"Rosa told Father Sikora she was recognized by someone from her past. She wouldn't say who it was. Father Sikora she was protecting him, which suggests someone involved in the movement. She also had a good idea who killed your father. According to her, it was impulsive, unpremeditated, done by someone who was confused about his loyalties. What does that sound like to you?"

Jim's face was blank. He shrugged.

"An informant. Thea Adelman gave me the names of some old-time activists familiar with Ishkode. Apparently, there were Ishkode wanna-bes who helped with leafleting and protests; one of them must have been a snitch. I think your father was meeting someone who had gotten close to the group at his direction, who could lead him to Verna Basswood. Only the guy he met that day brought Verna's gun with him and used it. Maybe he was upset about the shootings in Wisconsin, felt guilty about playing a role in betraying the the radicals, I don't know."

Jim gave himself a little shake, as if needing to wake himself up to process it all. "That makes a lot of sense. You know the old saying, A cop's only as good as his informants? My dad was good. We had our differences, but everyone says he had a gift for getting inside people's heads, making them feel they had a key role to play in the fate of the nation. And he believed it, every bit of it. He thought he was holding the line against forces that were trying to destroy the country. Made people feel important, to be a part of that."

"Only it's a strain when you play both sides. Rosa said this guy was drinking, having nightmares. You get a snitch who's that unstable, they can blow up on you."

"Where will you go with this?"

"The feds were tipped off by a junkie named Tyler. He's the one who found out Rosa was the fugitive they were looking for. I tried to find out where he got it from, but he was too strung out at the time to give me much. Just said that the man who recognized Rosa is old, skinny, a drunk. And he tells lame ghost stories. No idea what that's about, but a couple people confirmed it. I have to talk to Tyler again, when he's not so messed up, see if I can get a lead on this guy."

"So we're talking about someone who was at St. Larry's recently."

"Not a regular, but someone who went there at least once within the past month. It may take awhile to run it down." I'd done it often enough for other cases, coaxed information out of people who wore rags and carried their possessions in plastic bags, who would break off

in the middle of an intelligible sentence to mutter delusional ram-
blings. They didn't need ghost stories; their worlds were full of invisible specters that crowded around them, hissing threats in their ears.
It was what I feared most for Sophie, that she would become one of
them someday. I shook the thought away. "If that doesn't work, I
may be able to come at it from the other direction, talk to people in
Minneapolis who knew about Ishkode, get a lead on who might have
been an informant."

"It's not like you have to find him and get a confession; you just
have to create reasonable doubt. You may already have that, if you
can get a forensic pathologist to back you up."

"No, I'm going to find this guy."

"To show Fiske up?"

"So you can know what happened to your father. Like you helped
me find out about my mom."

His mouth went tight and he looked away. "Thanks," he said after
a moment. "Been a real bastard of a day. Good to know at least one
person's still on my side." He turned to me with a little smile. "Oh,
Anni, don't."

"Sorry. Shit." I scrubbed my hot cheeks with the heel of my hands,
got up to find a tissue so I could blow my stopped-up nose. "Goddamn it. Nancy's just having a rough time right now. Don't give up
on her."

"How can I? I need her."

"She needs you, too. So do the kids." I blew my nose again. "Fuck.
Sorry. Are you okay to drive?" He looked puzzled. I pointed at the
empty longnecks.

"Two beers? No problem."

"It's late, nearly ten. You should be at home. How do you expect to
work things out if you're always working?"

"You're right." He looked a little sheepish as I walked him out onto
the porch. "Oh, those Nordic League guys—"

"Watch my back. I got it."

"Seriously. Don't stick your neck out, not until we have a handle on this group. At least I managed to stir up some interest."

"I'll bet. Pretty handy for public relations if the FBI goes after white supremacists for a change instead of leftists and people of color."

"Whatever works. If those guys make a wrong move, we'll be watching. But people like that, it's hard to predict what they'll do. You still have your service weapon, right?"

"Nah, I sold it to one of the guys at Harrison."

"Why? The city's handgun ban has an exception for ex-cops."

"Can't get a carry permit, though. Besides, for ten years I wore that two-pound hunk of metal on my hip, and I never once took it out of its holster."

"Not once?"

"Well, just at the range for practice. You don't draw your gun if you aren't prepared to use it; that's the rule. When it came right down to it, I was always able to come up an alternative to shooting people."

"Still . . . you need to be careful."

"I'm always careful." I gave him a friendly punch on the arm, then leaned on the railing and watched him go. He seemed less weary, less burdened than when he'd arrived, but from this angle, I could see his hair was much grayer than I'd realized, the silver spiraling from his crown.

I'll never turn on you, I thought to myself. Not ever.

THIRTEEN

called Nancy to tell her Jim was running late on my account. She said something flippantly cynical in response, and I burst like a dam. "Don't you know how much he loves you? He's terrified your relationship might be broken beyond repair; he'll do anything to make it work." She was stunned into silence. When she found her voice, she couldn't form full sentences.

"I gave him a bollocking about Martin today, true enough. But I had no idea . . . He's been so distant, lately, I assumed . . ."

"You've got to give him a chance, Nancy. You mean everything to him, you and the girls. Besides, you can't break up. You're the closest thing Martin and I have to a family."

She snuffled, blew her nose. "Stupid git. Why didn't he say how he felt?"

"He's scared."

"And I'm not? Christ, I'm bloody terrified."

"Talk to him, Nancy. Tonight."

"Right, I will. And Anni, listen . . ."

"Yeah?"

I heard her breath come in a jagged gasp before she could get the words out. "You're a good mate. Thanks, eh?"

I was too wound up to sleep, so I went on-line and spent a couple of hours immersing myself in Ishkode, the American Indian Movement, and the FBI response. It was an odd experience, as if I'd entered a parallel universe. The inflammatory rhetoric on both sides was full of archaic Cold War and Marxist slogans, but in other ways it all

seemed as fresh as today's headlines: an unpopular war, the constant
threat of invisible and powerful enemies, a bitterly divided nation.
Strangest of all was reading the Church Committee Report, a 1976
congressional document that led to legislative changes intended to
rein in domestic surveillance. "Informants have provoked and par-
ticipated in violence and other illegal activities . . . Because of the
nature of wiretaps, microphones and other sophisticated electronic
techniques, it has not always been possible to restrict the monitoring of communications to the persons being investigated . . . labels
such as 'national security,' 'domestic security,' 'subversive activities,' and 'foreign intelligence' have led to unjustified use of these
techniques." If you replaced the word *Communist* in the report with
terrorist, it could have been a critique of counterintelligence activities today.

When I finally switched off my computer and went to bed, I had a
strange feeling, as if two layers of time were folding together, now
and thirty years earlier. When sirens started up somewhere far away
during the night, I thought the authorities were on the hunt for radicals and Communist sympathizers, until I surfaced just long enough
to realize they were in the present. But as soon as I drifted back to
sleep, I was back in the past again, making a familiar journey through
the city to the open trench in Homewood where a nameless young
runaway wearing an India-print skirt and blue glass beads was being
laid to rest. Someone scattered earth over the row of plain pine
coffins, murmuring something. Only this time, it didn't sound like a
prayer. I strained to hear the words more clearly, in case they would
tell me something important, something that had been secret all these
years.

I sat up, drenched in sweat, my heart pounding. The air was thick
with humidity and not a breath stirred through the open windows.
The voice that had been muttering in my dream was real, coming
from someone just outside my door. Were they leaving another dead

rat there, or planning a dramatic reenactment of some of the pornographic violence in that phone call Thea couldn't bear to repeat?

I eased off the bed and found the plumber's wrench among my
tools. With it clenched in one hand, I stepped silently over to the door.
The words came again, low and conspiratorial, too quiet to make out. I
had only a wrench to defend myself, but I'd be damned if I'll let them
intimidate me. I mapped the moves in my head, then twisted the bolt
and yanked the door open with my left hand, brandishing the wrench
in my right. Something lithe leaped down the steps, while a larger
shadow cowered back against the railing. "Whoa, don't! It's me!"

Lucas, I realized, and lowered the wrench. It took him a moment
longer to lower his arms, which were raised protectively around his
head. "What the hell are you doing?" I asked in a harsh whisper.

Lucas whispered, too. "Just petting your cat."

"He isn't my cat. He let you pet him?"

"I think he's hungry."

I leaned against the door frame for a moment, feeling limp after
the surge of adrenaline, then went back inside, set the wrench on the
counter, and groped for the bag of Little Friskies. "Here. There's a
bowl near the bottom of the steps."

"What about water?" he whispered.

I stared at him a moment, then went back in to fill a bowl with water. He hitched his backpack up on his shoulder and took the Friskies
and water, went stealthily down the steps, set the water down and
filled the food bowl, squatting beside them until the cat warily slunk
out of the undergrowth to eat. The only light came from distant
streetlights, no predawn glow lightening the eastern edges of the sky.
A few cars swished by, and a dog barked off in the distance, answered
by one even farther away.

Lucas stroked the bony animal, then came back up the steps, grinning. He was about to say something, but I put a finger to my lips
and motioned him inside, then studied the yard before closing the

door. I peered out at the front street and checked the blinds to make sure they were thoroughly closed. Only then did I switch on the bedside lamp. It cast a tall shadow behind Lucas, making his eyes look big and startled. "You sure looked angry," he said before I could ask him what he'd been doing on my porch.

"Earlier today, I found a dead rat right where you were sitting."

"The cat must like you, leaving a present like that."

"Cats don't nail their presents to the porch. Some cops have a black sense of humor. What are you doing here?"

It took him a moment to pull his mind away from someone's idea of a practical joke. "Oh. Sophie said you're going to Minneapolis. I was hoping I could hitch a ride."

"And you're asking this at four in the morning because—"

"I need to get out of town. I got family up there I can stay with." He fiddled with the straps of his backpack and wouldn't look me in the eye.

"You think the police will pick you up because of the graffiti," I guessed. After a moment's hesitation, he nodded.

I sighed. The last time someone had pulled me out of a dream to ask for help, things hadn't turned out too well. But I didn't have much choice but to do what Lucas asked. Up until now, the mayor had executed a delicate dance around the images of Rosa as the Virgin of Guadalupe that were appearing all over the city; he'd decried the vandalism while avoiding inflaming race relations further. But the evening news had reported the image was appearing on police stations around town, the kind of bold insult that crossed the line. The CPD already knew Lucas from previous run-ins over his tags and would put out his description. He'd get picked up, and then the FBI would want a piece of the action. It wouldn't take Fiske long to find out that Lucas and Sophie had helped Rosa escape.

"You know how to make coffee in that kind of pot?" I pointed to the stove.

"Sure." He looked up hopefully.

"Make some while I get ready. It's going to be a long trip."

It was still dark as we headed out. I'd hastily gathered up my notes, my laptop, and some clothes. Lucas brewed a pot of coffee and poured it into a thermos. We shouldered our backpacks and went stealthily down the back stairs. I instructed Lucas to stay out of sight in the gangway between my house and the next while I made sure the coast was clear. No movement on the street, no tracker attached to my car that I could see in the beam of a penlight, no obvious signs of surveillance. Of course, I had no way of knowing if there was be someone parked down the street, watching in the darkness, or if one of my neighbors was be making a phone call right now, but we had to take our chances. I drove to where he was waiting, pausing just long enough for him to sprint over and climb into the backseat. He lay down out of sight, using his backpack as a pillow as I pulled out, all my senses on high alert.

As I paid my first toll, the eastern sky behind us was pearling with a hint of dawn, the skyscrapers of the Loop silhouetted in my rearview mirror. If someone had been following us, they'd been doing a good job. I poured myself some coffee from the thermos and drove on.

Lucas slept until nearly 8:00 A.M., when I pulled off the interstate at a truck stop. While he studied the breakfast menu, I called Nancy to see how things were going. Better, she told me, thanks to my phone call. As she spoke, I learned things had been worse between her and Jim than I realized. In recent months, he had immersed himself in his work, going in on weekends and staying late in the evenings, rarely coming home before Lucy's bedtime. Usually, he'd stay up after Nancy went to bed, having a few drinks to unwind, more often than not sleeping on the couch. He used his insomnia as an excuse, saying he was plagued by a restlessness that wasn't relieved by the sleeping pills a doctor had prescribed. She'd assumed he was detaching himself from a family that was going to pieces, leaving her to cope alone. They'd gotten into the habit of using the politics of his job for their arguments, a stand-in for other issues too close to the bone. But the night before, they'd talked honestly until 3:00 A.M. They had things to work out, a lot of them, but it was a start.

And miracle of miracles, Sophie seemed to be doing well. It would take a couple of weeks before the change in medication took effect, but she was making a real effort this time. Maybe she'd turned some kind of corner. As she spoke, Nancy kept making the verbal equivalents of touching wood, hedging every expression of hope with caution, but I hadn't heard her sound so optimistic in months. As if the child she'd lost was finally showing signs of coming home.

Before hanging up, she told me about someone in the Twin Cities I should talk to, an expert on the American Indian Movement who was on the faculty at Hamline University. Nancy said she'd give him a ring, let him know to expect me. "And come to think of it," she added, "Jim has an aunt who lives up there, in one of the suburbs of the Twin Cities. She's old and deaf and a bit batty, but she might be able to tell you something about her brother Arne." I scribbled down the names and numbers.

Over breakfast, I asked Lucas about his family in Minneapolis. He grew up there, he said, staying with different relatives, until he got in trouble and a judge put him in a group home for a year. After that, he was old enough to be on his own. His grandmother lived up north, not far from the reservation where Rosa grew up. When he was little, before his mom took off, they stayed with his grandma for a while. There was a lake there with frogs, and he had caught fireflies in a jar. He didn't remember much else, except his grandma talking to his mother in Indian so he wouldn't know what they were saying. Only his mom always answered in English, so it didn't work.

"Are you going to eat the rest of your potatoes?" he asked.

I passed my plate over to him and told him about my mother. Lucas nodded and said it was kind of the same for him, only he'd people to stay with, so he never had to look for her. He didn't know where his mother had gone, hardly ever thought about it.

But after he finished, he wiped his hands with a napkin, then unzipped his backpack just enough to burrow into an inner pocket. He took out a grubby envelope full of folded bits of paper and extracted a strip of photo-booth pictures: four shots of a dark-haired girl— smiling, serious, sticking her tongue out, laughing as someone, unseen, stuck a hand past the curtain to give her horns with two fingers. He watched me as I studied the photos, holding the strip carefully by the edges.

"She has your eyes," I said. He shrugged and took the picture back, his face closing like a door. Showing me that photo was an act of trust, but I knew from my own experience that trust didn't come easily when you'd been betrayed at an early age. That was as far as he could go for now. But after holding that treasured picture, I wanted to give him as many opportunities as it would take for him to know he could count on me.

We continued north in heavy traffic that was equal parts semitrailers, RVs, and pickup trucks towing boats. Lucas fell asleep again in the passenger seat, his backpack tucked between his legs and one hand entangled in a strap, his head pillowed against his shoulder, a drool stain forming on his shirt. I drove past orderly fields of young corn that looked like green corduroy, past marshland and strange rock formations. There were a lot of army vehicles on the road, convoys headed in both directions, as if they weren't sure where the war was. Some of the traffic peeled off west onto Interstate 90, while I followed the signs for Minneapolis.

Hours later, we crossed a bridge and passed a sign that welcomed us to Minnesota. The traffic grew heavier as we approached what Lucas called "the Cities," as if they were the only two in the world. I woke him up as we headed into a spaghetti bowl of highway choices. He rubbed a palm over his sleepy face and looked around. "Just stay on Ninety-four for now," he said.

I reached for my bag, rootled blindly inside for the cell phone. "Want to give your relatives a call, let them know we're coming?"

He stared at the phone, then handed it back. "I don't remember the number."

"You're just going to show up at the door?"

"They won't care."

" 'Home is the place where, when you go there, they have to take you in.' " He looked at me. "Robert Frost. It's from a poem."

"Oh," he said, dismissing it.

"Hey, Lucas." I pointed.

He stared, then laughed incredulously. Someone had spray-painted a row of stenciled images along a concrete embankment: Rosa as the Virgin of Guadalupe. It wasn't exactly the same as his stencil, but close enough. For just a moment, he looked proud and excited, and turned to say something, but that door closed again and he settled back into his seat and looked out the window, a small smile flickering on his face and then fading.

We crossed the Mississippi and drove past a cluster of skyscrapers that looked clean and dainty compared to Chicago's. Lucas pointed me to an exit, then directed me to take several more turns, until we ended up in a residential neighborhood with big wooden houses on tree-lined streets. It was only a couple of miles from the prosperous-looking city center, but the screens on their porches were torn, paint was peeling, and cars that looked a lot like my old Corolla crowded the curbs. But it was a real neighborhood, with kids out playing, parents talking to one another as they kept an eye on things—the kind

of summertime that doesn't exist in neighborhoods where everyone
has central air conditioning and the children have a full schedule of
gymnastics and soccer and piano lessons. It felt as if I'd slipped through
that time warp again. "That's it," Lucas said, pointing to a two-story
frame house with a late-sixties muscle car in the drive.

"You sure?"

"That's my cousin's car. Thanks for the ride."

"Say, would you be interested in some work?" I asked impulsively.
"I'm not from here, don't know my way around. I could use an assistant for the next day or two."

"What do I have to do?"

"Navigate. Help me talk to people. Seventy-five bucks a day, and
meals. What do you say?"

"Yeah, sure."

"I'll stop by here at nine tomorrow morning, all right?"

"Okay. See you." He hitched his backpack over one shoulder and
got out. I watched him go up to the door, knock, have a conversation
with the man who answered. They talked for a long time before the
door opened just wide enough for Lucas to pass inside, his head low
between his shoulders, as if he was trying not to take up too much
space.

I found a cheap motel in North Minneapolis, on one of those wide
streets that looks as if it used to be a major highway to somewhere
but hasn't seen much action in the last forty years. The front over-
hang was lined with pink-and-green neon that buzzed and crackled
like a bug zapper. I checked in, switched on the air, called out for a
pizza, and bought a bottle of red wine at the liquor store conveniently
located next door. A little too conveniently located, I decided later,
listening through the thin walls to a drunk who kept calling people
on the phone to tell them his problems.

I was tired from starting the day at 4:00 A.M. I stretched out on the
bed, luxuriously relaxed. For the first time in nearly a week, I didn't

feel as if I was being watched. The pizza came and I ate a couple of slices, then got on the phone and set up appointments for the next day.

My final call was to the Tilquists. Nancy answered, sounding harassed and edgy. She'd gone her office to pick up some files that morning and discovered someone had broken in and stolen the bones that were the subject of the legal challenge. Brian Folkstone denied any involvement, but the police were working on the theory that a member of the Nordic League was responsible. Her office had been tossed, papers and books strewn all over, and a swastika had been carved crudely into her desk. The box that held the bones had been left behind, but a red wool shawl she had draped over a chair was missing. The police surmised the thief had dumped the bones into the shawl so they could be more easily concealed.

She wasn't happy about the mess or the damage done to her desk, but she was even more upset that she hadn't kept the remains in a safer place. She had simply locked the box containing them in the bottom drawer of her filing cabinet. It wouldn't have taken more than a screwdriver to force it open. Thanks to the crude decoration on her desk, the FBI had joined the investigation, treating it as a hate crime. That was another irritant for Nancy. The young agent assigned to the case turned out to be polite, intelligent, and disarmingly honest. He agreed with her that he was there primarily to offset the bad PR generated by the hunt for Rosa Saenz, then set cheerfully about his work. Since the leader of the Nordic League, Brian Folkstone, denied any involvement, the authorities were now speculating that another member, perhaps Alton Brinks, had acted alone.

"When did this happen?" I asked.

"A security guard walked through the building around five P.M. yesterday. It must have been between then and when I went in today, around ten in the morning."

"How would Alton Brinks have know where the bones were being kept?"

Nancy gave an exasperated sigh. "It wasn't exactly secret. Everyone in the department, including the administrative assistant, knew they were in my office, and you know the college—it's as gossipy as a village. I feel like such an idiot."

We chatted awhile longer. Sophie was naturally wound up over the theft, but she was doing as well as could be expected. Martin was fine; nancy'd made a point of checking in with him after getting my call that morning. And Jim had hardly left her side since the break-in. "It's a bit peculiar, having him about the house constantly." But she said this with a smile in her voice, and I had a feeling he was in the room with her. It was good to hear the warmth in her voice, to know they were able to talk to each other again.

I set the alarm and drank another glass of wine as the long day caught up with me. I drifted off to sleep, still feeling the motion of the highway rolling under me.

Lucas was waiting on the curb outside his cousin's house the next morning, wearing a white T-shirt so new, it still had creases from where it had been folded. His hair was clean and tied back with a rubber band, and he wore jeans that were spattered with paint but not torn. He picked up his backpack and climbed in.

"First stop is with a professor who's supposedly the expert on the American Indian Movement. How do we get to Hamline University?" That destination obviously threw him, so I added, "It's in St. Paul, on Snelling Avenue."

"Oh. Go up to the light and take a right."

After creeping our way across town through heavy traffic, we reached the peaceful green campus, which had a familiar sleepy stillness now that classes weren't in session. We found the building and went inside, where it was even quieter. Lucas kept looking back over his shoulder, adjusting his grip on his backpack, reminding me of how out of place I'd felt the first time I set foot on the grounds of Stony Cliff College. Eventually, I came to feel as at home there as any faculty brat, but I could well remember how the Gothic architecture and shady lawns had made me feel like a trespasser at first, someone they'd throw out as soon as they realized their mistake.

"Dr. Pridoux?" I rapped my knuckles on the open doorway.

The tiny office was crowded with overstuffed bookcases, more books were piled on the floor, and the desk was hidden under papers. A lanky man with a weathered face, wire-rim glasses, and a graying ponytail turned from the open filing cabinet. "Call me Jon." He pushed the drawer of the filing cabinet shut, then steadied a stack of loose papers on top with one hand as it threatened to topple. "You must be Anni. From the Iron Range?"

"Sorry?"

"The Finnish name. Thought you might be from northern Minnesota."

"Not that I know of. This is my assistant, Lucas. . . ." I realized I had no idea what his last name was, but that didn't faze the professor.

"Anishinaabeg?" he asked, extending his hand for a shake. Lucas nodded. "Me, too. Pembina Band."

"Bois Forte on my mother's side," Lucas told him. I didn't know what any of it meant, but Jon Pridoux nodded as if everything was settled now. He waved vaguely in front of his desk as he sat and pushed some papers around uselessly. "Have a seat, guys." It took me a moment to find a chair hidden under a stack of journals. "Just put those anywhere. There's another chair around here somewhere." He peered around the room over his glasses.

"I'm fine," Lucas said quickly, planting himself in the doorway, as if preparing for an earthquake of books.

"So, you're a friend of Nancy Tilquist?"

"We've known each other for years." I fished out my license and

passed it across the desk, along with one of Thea's cards. "As I mentioned last night, I'm an investigator working on Rosa Saenz's defense. Feel free to call Thea Adelman if you want to check it out."

He glanced at my license before handing it back. "Nancy's word is
good enough for me." He tucked Thea's card under his blotter.
"That's some crazy NAGPRA case she's got on her hands."

"It would have been straightforward, only a flaky white supremacist group filed a counterclaim."

"I have a former student working on a dissertation on pagan white
supremacist organizations. He would love to talk to you about this
group. Any chance you could make time to meet him while you're in
the area?"

"I don't know much, but sure. You have his number? I'll give him
a call."

He jotted a name and number on a scrap of paper and handed it
to me. Bartering over, it was time for business. "What can I do for
you?"

"I understand you're working on a definitive history of the American Indian Movement. I was hoping to get some background on how
AIM got started. Why Ishkode was formed. Anything you can tell me
about Rosa Saenz's situation back then."

"All I know about Saenz is what I've read in the papers, but I met
Verna Basswood a few times."

"What was she like?"

He leaned back in his chair, tenting his hands, one leg crossed over
his knee. He was wearing cowboy boots, scuffed and worn, under
frayed jeans. "Nothing like Rosa Saenz," he finally said. "When I saw
her picture on the evening news—man, I never would have made the
connection."

"I know what you mean. Rosa doesn't look much like the woman
on the Most Wanted posters."

"Verna didn't, either." Pridoux turned to riffle through some files stacked on a shelf behind him, then handed me an eight-by-ten photo. "Can you tell which one she is?"

A crowd of young people stood in a room decorated with shabby furniture, posters on the wall: Che Guevara, Jimi Hendrix, Sitting Bull, all rendered in psychedelic colors. I put my finger on a girl, shorter than the others, in a miniskirt, combat boots, and an olive green army jacket that swamped her hands even with its sleeves turned up. Long black hair fell straight around a face that was thin, sharp, and serious. He nodded. "How'd you know?"

"Her height, mostly."

"Recognize anyone else?"

"Russell Means?" I ventured, and he nodded. "Clyde Bellecourt. The one next to Verna is Logan Hall. Don't know any of the others."

"That's me," he said, pointing at a shaggy-haired, rail-thin teenager slouching at the edge of the group.

"You were in the movement?"

"Nah, not really. I was still in high school. I just hung out, bummed cigarettes, hit on girls, tried to look older than I was. Those revolutionary days had a strange effect on me. I couldn't strike a balance between political commitment and the sex and drugs thing." He glanced at Lucas, gave him a "Boys will be boys" grin. "Sex and drugs generally won out."

"When did you meet Verna?"

"Would have been . . . let's see, the spring of '70." His eyes took on a distant look as he stared at the bookshelves above my head, remembering. "She came up to the Cities with Logan Hall after she heard him give a speech in Chicago. A little whirlwind of focused rage. New to the movement, so she came to things with fresh energy. A lot of the others were getting discouraged, worn-out by the bickering, the suspicion, embittered by all the setbacks. Logan had really pushed her buttons."

"What was he like?"

"Intense, angry, committed. He was involved from the early days, in at the beginning of the Alcatraz occupation. By the time I met him, he had come to believe violent action was the only way to go. He wanted to lead the movement in that direction."

"But?"

"Nobody wanted to follow. They didn't want to be led anywhere by him. He alienated people. Too abrupt, too quick with his tongue. Too white."

"How do you mean?"

"Pushy, arrogant. Anyone who disagreed with him was just backward and dense. He grew up in a wealthy suburb of Chicago, went to a big-name private university, thought he was better than the rest of us. He wasn't deferential to anybody, had no patience with traditionals—which was a big mistake, since their support was essential to the movement—and he sure as hell had no time for the kind of kid I was in those days. To be honest? I don't think he was real comfortable around us. He was adopted as a baby by a wealthy white couple. All he knew about Indians was what he'd read in books."

I thought about those pictures Hall's adoptive mother had shown me, and her bewilderment at his rejection of everything she and her husband had tried to give him, including their love. "What about Verna? How did people respond to her?"

"She wasn't anything like him. She spent her early years on the rez, so she knew poverty and racism firsthand. And while she agreed with Hall that it was time to switch tactics, to fight violence, with violence since nothing else had worked, she didn't treat any of us with disrespect."

I looked at the photograph again. "Were Verna and Logan Hall romantically involved?"

He frowned. "What does that have to do with anything?"

"We need to anticipate how the prosecution will build its case. They'll claim it goes to motive."

"They were sleeping together," he said reluctantly. "Which wasn't a big deal back then. Post-Pill, pre-AIDS, things were pretty free and easy. I doubt Hall loved anyone but himself, but Verna really fell for him. Nobody could figure out the attraction. In fact, a lot of people assumed he was working for the FBI. He kept saying we should blow things up, kill some pigs. That made people back off him real fast."

"You think he might have been a plant?"

"No. If he had been, he would have stayed in Minneapolis, done more to break up the organization. Instead, he stormed off to form his own movement, and hardly anyone went with him. Though at least one of those must have been a rat. Somebody told federal agents about a meeting they were having in Chicago, and that led directly to the massacre in Wisconsin."

"Any idea who that informant was?"

"No. Could have been more than one, for all I know. That's how the feds operated."

"Thea Adelman seems to think the FBI used unnecessary force when they raided that farmhouse."

He gave a bitter chuckle. "That's one way of putting it."

"The claim is that Rosa—Verna, I mean—killed Arne Tilquist in reprisal. He was found dead in a basement, shot at close range. Does that make any sense to you?"

"What are you asking? Was Verna brave enough to do it? No question about it."

"No, I meant could she have arranged a meeting with an FBI agent and shot him in the face at close range without him putting up any resistance?"

"That's how it was done?" His fingers searched his shirt pocket blindly for a pen.

"There was no sign of struggle. The barrel was less than a foot from his left eye. Tilquist never drew his weapon."

Pridoux pulled over a yellow pad and jotted some notes. "One bullet?" It wasn't a rhetorical question. He waited for my answer.

"Right. Twenty-two-caliber. All it takes, when you're that close."

"Interesting." He sat back, tapping his pen against his teeth. I wondered if he had picked up on the same inconsistencies I had, but he raised something I hadn't even thought of. "If you were really pissed off at someone, wanted to show the world how you felt—"

"You'd probably pull the trigger more than once."

"You know how many times Logan Hall was hit? Twenty-seven. When he was already down with multiple wounds, more than one of them serious enough to be fatal, someone stood over him, pointed a forty-five at his head, and emptied the clip."

"Where did you get this? I haven't seen that information anywhere."

"It was in the medical examiner's report. Good thing they had fingerprints to identify Hall; dental records would have been useless."

"You've seen Hall's autopsy report? Thea Adelman told me it had been lost."

He bounced his pen against his yellow pad for a moment, thinking, then glanced at Lucas and seemed to make up his mind about something. He pulled a key ring from his pocket, unlocked his desk drawer, and, after a brief search, pulled out a stapled bundle of papers. He went through another moment of hesitation before he handed it to me.

The pages were grainy photocopies of photocopies. Even with the formal medical terminology and generic body diagrams, the document made for grim reading. Though the narrative was a dry recital of facts, the sheer excess conveyed a sense of shock. No wonder the report had been "lost."

"Where'd you get this?" I asked.

"Never mind." He reached across the desk and took the report from me, looking as if he regretted letting it out of his drawer. "Look,

I'm not excusing anybody, just trying to put Tilquist's murder in context."

"That's exactly what I'm looking for, context. I need to understand what was going on back then. What motivated this group that Logan Hall started? Why did Verna Basswood think violence was the only option?"

He tipped his chair back, balancing on two legs, and looked at me for a moment. "Let's get some coffee," he finally said. "This'll take awhile."

FOURTEEN

W e went to a café called Ginko a few blocks up Snelling. It had the usual potted plants, a cluster of shabby lounge furniture, mismatched tables and chairs, and a long menu of elaborate coffee concoctions. Aside from the barista, a student Pridoux knew by name, we had the place to ourselves.

Once we got our coffee, the professor got down to business. He started with some background on the social and economic status of Native Americans in 1968, the year the American Indian Movement was founded—high rates of poverty, joblessness, and suicide, low rates of decent health care, educational attainment, and hope. "Hasn't changed a hell of a lot," he commented dryly. He sketched out AIM's growth from a local Twin Cities–based organization to a national movement after the dramatic takeover of Alcatraz Island and the occupation of the Bureau of Indian Affairs in Washington, D. C. He outlined the FBI's counterintelligence practices of the time, including its assault on the movement and its leaders. I had a feeling we were getting a lecture he'd given semester after semester, but it was interesting, and Lucas was following Pridoux's words intently, totally absorbed.

Logan Hall's break with the organization came soon after Rosa followed him to Minneapolis. The movement was already riddled with FBI informants and provocateurs. When Hall goaded members to take a more militant stance, he was ostracized. With half a dozen supporters—including Basswood—he returned to Chicago and founded Ishkode. "It's an Anishinaabe word," Pridoux said.

"Means 'fire,' " Lucas said, embarrassed when the professor nodded approvingly at him.

"Like a prairie fire. A necessity of the ecosystem. The fire that destroys in order to restore." He had brought a file of documents with him, mostly official records of one kind or another that he'd obtained over the years through the Freedom of Information Act. I scanned through them as the student brought us refills and stopped to chat with Pridoux about a course she'd taken from him. "What do you make of it?" he asked me, nodding at the papers.

"Reading between the lines—"

"Don't have much choice," Pridoux pointed out. At least half the sentences were hidden under thick black marker.

"Looks as if the feds weren't in any hurry to shut Logan Hall's movement down, not until the shooting in Chicago. Which is odd, because they had an informant in place for two years." Not surprisingly, any identifying information about the snitch had been blacked out.

"Makes sense, though. Remember, while Logan Hall was doing his radical thing in Chicago, the FBI was trying to portray AIM as a sufficiently dangerous threat that they could destroy it totally, by force if need be. Logan Hall was useful to them."

"Useful?"

"Even if he wasn't competent enough to build a pipe bomb that actually worked, he issued regular communiqués, calling on people to kill police, blow up courtrooms, overthrow the government by violent means. He wasn't much of a threat to public safety, but he sure liked to sound like one. It gave them a great excuse to go after radical Indians."

"So what prompted the raid on their meeting? Why not let him keep issuing his manifestos?"

"Good question." He sipped his coffee. "I can think of two possibilities. One, the FBI needed positive publicity. They like to time a major bust to hit the news whenever the public is questioning their competence. They might have needed a headline announcing the foiling of a major threat at that particular time for public relations purposes. And when it failed . . ."

"All the more reason to take a hard line in Wisconsin. If the members of Ishkode escaped, the FBI would look even more incompetent." Lucas had nudged one of the pages closer and was reading it with an anxious frown on his face. An account of the farmhouse raid, most of the action covered up with thick black lines. "What's the other possibility?"

"Something personal. Tilquist angling for a promotion or competing for resources, wanting the glory."

Like Fiske, I thought, determined to get a conviction by any means necessary because it would boost his career. I picked up one of Pridoux's documents. Apparently, Verna Basswood had escaped the farmhouse slaughter because she was in Madison at the time, trying to raise funds. The organization hadn't even had enough cash on hand to buy paper for their next manifesto, much less for guns or high explosives. "Can I get copies of these?"

"Sure, if you'll provide me Arne Tilquist's autopsy report."

"You got it. That other report, the one that officially was 'lost'—"

His face was suddenly guarded. "I shouldn't have shown it to you. I told the source who provided it that I wouldn't make it public until after his death."

"Look, I'm not asking you to break a confidence. But it would be incredibly helpful if I could talk to the man who gave it to you." He'd been there at that farmhouse raid; I was convinced of that. Pridoux had used words and images that weren't found in that clinical document.

"Forget it. It was hard for him to give me that report; it felt like he was committing treason. He's old, he's sick, and he just wants to be left alone. I promised."

"Just let him decide whether he wants to talk to me or not. On his own terms."

"He won't."

"Thea Adelman's phones are probably tapped, but I have a cell phone they don't know about. I'll give you the number. Pass it along if you can."

He shook his head, but he took the number.

L ucas and I spent the rest of the day running down contacts and tracing leads. The biggest challenge was finding a man named Andy Two Dogs, who not only had been active in AIM But had been born on the same reservation as Verna and had gone to her elementary school. He had been homeless off and on for the past five years; his homelessness was on at the moment, so I let Lucas take the lead, showing me a side of Minneapolis tourists don't see, a different Mall of America, one that featured pawnshops, liquor stores, and crack dealers text-messaging their clients. I had always pictured Minnesota as being filled with blond, blue-eyed Scandinavians, but in this part of town at least, they were outnumbered by Latinos, Asians, and regal-looking Somali women in head scarves and traditional robes. While giving Lucas space to talk to a man who didn't seem to want his company, let alone mine, I pretended to wait for a bus at a crowded stop and called Jon Pridoux's graduate student, the one who was interested in the Nordic League. He said he'd love to talk to me and suggested we have breakfast the next day. I jotted down the directions he gave me to a café near the University of Minnesota.

Since Lucas seemed to fare better without me, I kept my distance, loitering across the street from where he was working. Every now and then, he'd catch my eye and we'd meet around the next corner, where he'd fill me in. At one point, I was amused to see him fall in with one of the rare white people on the street, a young woman who reminded me of Sophie, dressed in a collection of secondhand rags that looked stylish on her slim figure. She had a canvas bag slung over her shoulder that looked like the ones the volunteers at St. Larry's used, only hers said StreetWorks on it. A program for homeless youth, Lucas told me at our next rendezvous.

We found Andy Two Dogs finally, eating a peanut butter sandwich outside a tarp-and-cardboard encampment on a bluff over the Mississippi River. He'd found a good spot with enough breeze to discourage the million or so mosquitoes that had swarmed around us as we scrambled through the woods looking for him. He was happy to share his peanut butter with us. He wasn't so eager to share his memories of Verna, but I let Lucas do all the talking, and in time the man's wariness diminished and he started telling stories. I didn't write any of it down, since the one time I had reached into my bag for my notebook, he fell silent and watchful. I put it back and just listened. Afterward, we stopped at a Mexican restaurant on Lake Street for a late supper and Lucas helped fill in the blanks as I wrote down everything I could recall. Then I flipped back through all of my notes, making sure I hadn't missed anything.

"Is this going to help Rosa, you think?" Lucas asked.

"I hope so." In fact, we had exhausted all the names Thea Adelman and Jon Pridoux had given me and still had no ID for a skinny old man who told ghost stories, or a link to any other informant who might have been having conflicted loyalties the day Arne Tilquist met his death. But we'd passed out a lot of Thea's cards. I hoped someone with useful information would eventually call her.

"What are we doing tomorrow?"

"Actually, I think we're done, Lucas."

"I was thinking maybe we should go up to the rez tomorrow, talk to people there. Be easier having me along."

"I wasn't planning to. Rosa left there long before she got involved in the movement, and she doesn't have family there anymore."

"But she asked you to take her to someplace near Bemidji. She must have friends she was trying to reach."

"If she did, they're better off if I leave them alone." Lucas moodily pushed the last of his rice and beans around on his plate. "Look, you worked really hard, easily two days' work today. I'll pay you—"

"It's not that. It's just . . . my grandma lives near there," he muttered.

"You even know the address? You haven't been there since you were little."

"My cousin gave me her number. I called her, got directions. I thought maybe you could take me up there, but . . . it's okay, I'll just hitch."

"How far is it?"

"Couple hundred miles."

"Let's do it," I said, surprising myself. "Might be useful to get reactions from people living in the town where Rosa grew up. We can leave right after I talk to Jon Pridoux's graduate student. We're getting together for breakfast at a place called the Seward Café."

"I know where that is. I can meet you there."

"Okay. Say nine o'clock?" I glanced at my watch. "Finish up. We have to get you back to your relatives before they start worrying about you."

"Um, actually, that didn't work out. Can you drop me somewhere else instead?"

I started to ask him about it, but his face was blank, as if whatever had happened, it had to be protected under a shell of indifference.

The address he gave me was for a youth shelter, a pleasant-looking house on a shady street in St. Paul that the girl with the Street-Works bag had told him about, but Lucas seemed reluctant to get out of the car. "We're on an expense account," I said. "We can get you a room in the motel where I'm staying, though, I got to be honest, it's crummier than this place."

"Nah, I'll stay here." But still he sat, hugging his backpack to his chest. "I didn't know about any of that stuff," he finally said. "How the government went after people. What happened out at Pine Ridge. You think it's all true?"

"Yeah, that's probably how it happened."

He opened the door to get out, but something was still bothering him. "You know, when we were looking for Andy Two Dogs? Nobody said 'Oh yeah, he's the guy that went to Washington and occupied the Bureau of Indian Affairs, stood up to the FBI and U.S. marshals at Wounded Knee. They think he's just some homeless bum, but he was part of history."

With that off his chest, he slung his backpack over one shoulder and said good night. I waited at the curb until he spoke to someone at the door, threw me a loose wave, and went inside.

When I got to my motel, I poured some wine and switched on the local news. Rosa Saenz was the lead story. The hunt for her was apparently ruffling as many feathers in Minnesota as in Chicago. Earlier in the day, a group of protestors had picketed the federal courthouse to protest the gestapo tactics of the FBI and their unauthorized presence on sovereign land. A spokeswoman from the Minneapolis Field Office denied any improprieties and said they were working closely with local Native American leaders and tribal authorities as they followed up leads on the fugitive's whereabouts. She made it clear that anyone who sheltered Rosa would be prosecuted to the full extent of the law.

And the next story made clear what that meant. Father Sikora had been arrested; if convicted of harboring a fugitive, he could face up to ten years in prison. There was a brief clip of Thea Adelman looking and sounding indignant, footage of agents removing boxes of evidence from St. Larry's Community Center, police holding back a crowd of angry protestors. Fiske was there, directing the work. He turned and looked directly at the camera, giving me the weird sensation he was sharing the moment with me.

When they moved on to the weather, I switched the television off and sat thinking. Rosa had been in the wind for nearly a week a now. She'd told Father Sikora she was finished running, that it was time for the truth to come out. The memory of that gloomy mansion came back to me, dusty cases full of relics, glassy eyes staring from the animal heads mounted on the walls.

I pulled out my cell, found the number of the phone I'd given her, and, after a moment's hesitation, punched it in.

"Rosa?" A breathless voice, tight with anxiety. It was familiar but so unexpected, it took me a moment to identify it.

"Sophie? Where'd you get this phone?"

"She left it for me. I've been waiting and waiting for her to call."

"What do you mean, 'she left it'?"

"I went back to that old house on Sunday with extra food, just in case, but she was gone, just like she said. But she left the phone there, in that little room with all the books. She wanted me to have it."

"How do you know? Did she leave you a note?"

"Duh, that would be stupid. If the FBI got there first, that would get me in trouble. She wouldn't put me at risk like that. No, she hid the phone underneath a chair."

Either that, I thought, or she left in a hurry, dropped it in her haste, and it got kicked under some furniture. "Did she leave anything else?"

"No, you couldn't tell she'd been there at all. But it's Wednesday already. I was sure she'd call by now. Did you hear about Father Sikora? They could send him to prison for years."

"That's not going to happen," I said firmly. "Rosa didn't kill your grandfather, and I'm going to prove it. But you need to hold it together, okay?"

"I am. I even went to that dumb shrink again today."

"Good. Lucas is with me, by the way."

"Ooh, are you going to take him to see his grandmother?"

"Yes, as it happens."

"He always talks about her. That'll make him really happy. Don't worry about me, okay? I'll be fine. But I better hang up now. I want to keep this line open in case Rosa's trying to call me."

I set my phone on the bedside table, feeling uneasy. Sophie's belief that Rosa had left that phone for her was typical bipolar logic, finding significance where there wasn't any, but it made no sense. Given the massive dragnet, how had Rosa been able to avoid capture for nearly a week? Either the skills she had acquired over the past thirty-five years of living underground had given her an uncanny ability to vanish without a trace or the plan she had hinted at had gone terribly wrong.

FIFTEEN

t was just past midnight when my cell phone woke me. I fumbled for it, thinking it would be Sophie, but it was a male voice, a muffled, hoarse whisper, grating, like sandpaper. "Koskinen?"

"Who is this?" I demanded, expecting pornographic snuff talk—until I remembered my former workmates didn't have this number. I sat up. "Forget it. I don't need to know."

"That's right, you don't." He dragged in a breath, as if he'd just run up a flight of stairs. "You been asking questions about Logan Hall's group."

Jon Pridoux had passed my number along after all. "Can we talk?"

I listened to his strained breathing for a moment. "Corner of Lake and Bloomington. Face east. There's a building being rehabbed half a block down on the north side. Around the back."

"You want to meet there now?" I started to ask, but he hung up before I finished the question.

parked in the lot of a Mexican *supermercado,* closed for the night, and headed down Lake toward the gutted building. The bars on the street were still open and doing a lively business. A pair of hookers shared a smoke on the corner, keeping an eye out for customers and cops. Three men wearing tooled boots and pearl-buttoned shirts strolled by, arguing in Spanish, which was interspersed with flat midwestern words. "Twins" and "Metrodome" kept popping up like lumps in a pudding. I walked past the two-story structure, built of brick the color of clotted blood. All of the windows were gone, covered over with torn plastic, which made a whispering flutter. I continued for a couple of blocks to make sure I wasn't being followed, then went up the alley at the rear, mentally marking exits and fallback positions just in case.

A security light on a pole glowed over the building, its back torn open, a gaping cavity shrouded in sheets of cloudy plastic that stirred like a big creature breathing. Whoever had started the renovation must have run out of money or ambition. A fence had been erected around the construction site, but it was a halfhearted effort and it leaned drunkenly, leaving a gap that was wide enough for access. Food wrappers were trapped against the chain link, and cigarette butts and condoms littered the ground. It was a warm night, but as I stepped through the curtains of plastic, the air inside felt cool and dank. Voices and traffic sounds from the street were distorted, echoing oddly against the exposed brick. I sensed movement in one corner, a shape drawing back deeper into the shadows. "That's far enough," a voice rasped from the darkness. "Stay there, where I can see you."

I heard a labored intake of breath. A car with a loud stereo system passed by on Lake Street, its bass line like the heartbeat of something big and dangerous prowling by. "You're working for Basswood." A raspy voice, half growl, half whisper. Upper midwestern, white.

"Her lawyer hired me as an investigator."

That labored breathing again. I couldn't see him, but I guessed he would be past middle age, overweight, out of shape. Suffering from emphysema or a heart condition that stole his breath. "You testified against a cop." Flat, uninflected statement of fact.

"He beat up a kid for no reason."

"Most cops don't rat each other out."

"Most cops don't give kids permanent brain damage."

"And now you're defending a cop killer."

"She didn't kill him. I'm trying to find out who did."

"So you can get her off?"

"So the guy who really did it doesn't go free."

"Lift your shirt."

It wasn't a Mardi Gras moment; he wanted to make sure I wasn't wired. I bared my midriff and turned so he could see there was no cord concealed under my clothing, front or back.

The silence was total for a while. I couldn't even hear him breathing. A long minute dragged by before he spoke. "Look for a guy named Pete Spellman."

"Where would I find him?"

"Fuck knows. Could be dead, for all I know. Used to hang out on Wacker."

That must have been at least seven years ago, then, I thought. Lower Wacker Drive was a maze of streets and underground loading docks under the Loop. Since the Great Depression, the homeless had kept frostbite away by sleeping on grates that leaked warm air from the office buildings and department stores on the Magnificent Mile. In 1999, owners of the most expensive real estate in Chicago had persuaded the city to fence off the subterranean places where the cold and hungry congregated, not the thousands that bedded down there during the thirties, but still a hundred or more on cold nights. Some went to shelters; other went into subsidized housing and job training. A lot of them just disappeared. A major renovation project since then had erased all signs of what was once the largest homeless shelter in the city.

"Got a description?"

"Mixed-blood Dakota. Brown skin, blue eyes, six two, but you wouldn't know, way he hunches over. Weighs maybe one forty. Long gray hair that's as dirty as the rest of him. When he's on the juice, he talks about the Sioux Uprising like it's still going on."

"He was involved in Tilquist's murder?"

A humorless chuckle came out of the darkness on a waft of bourbon. "Tilquist called the meeting, but Pete was the one who walked
out of that basement alive."

"How do you know this?"

"Pete told me."

"Why didn't you report it to the authorities?"

"I *was* the fucking authorities." I heard that intake of breath again,
rasping, as if something in his chest was blocking it and he had to use
all his strength to fight for air. "Don't try to trip me up. I don't have
to tell you any of this." His panting was loud, as if I were sharing the
darkness with a hurt animal.

"I won't bother you after this," I said. "Nobody will know we had
this conversation. But you worked with Tilquist. What let up to his
murder?"

Street noises came to us, distorted and remote. The silence went on
so long, I began to think he'd slipped away, but then he started speaking again, softly, as if he was talking to himself. "It was supposed to
be simple. We had a no-knock, just pop the door and grab 'em. We
would find detonators, literature, guns. If we didn't—fuck it, we had
throw-downs. But it all went wrong. They knew; they were expecting
us. While we were outside the door, waiting for the signal to use the
battering ram, they opened fire down the stairwell from the next
landing up. Looked like strobe lights in the dark. One of us, Katsourinis, he got hit. I remember him jerking around in the muzzle
flashes. Looked like he'd grabbed hold of a live current and couldn't
let go. He fell against me and we both went down. I thought I'd
pissed myself, but it was from when his bladder went. And his blood.
He lost a lot of blood."

I heard that labored breathing again, in and out, dragged past
some barrier into his lungs. "Few days later, we surrounded that
farmhouse where they'd holed up."

Another long silence. He swallowed and choked on something in his chest, coughed. He took a deep breath. "We all went a little crazy that day. But Tilquist, he was the worst. He kept saying we could do whatever we wanted but Logan Hall was his. And when he found him lying there, still alive, oh man, Arne was so happy." He gasped for breath and thick phlegm rattled in his chest. "The guy's guts were spilling out of his side; he was all twisted up with the pain and screaming. Christ, I still hear it, those screams. Tilquist crouched over him and took his chin and looked him in the eye, waited until he understood. And then he straightened up and . . . *bang, bang, bang,* over and over. Emptied his clip. Later, outside, I saw Arne had brain tissue all over his pants from standing so close when he blew Itali's head apart. And . . ." A strange chuckle, thick with congestion. "I laughed. I laughed so hard, I threw up. You wouldn't understand that."

"I've had friends shot on the job. I've been angry, too."

"You have no idea. In those days, we were alone. We fought for a country that didn't want us to exist. The only people that understood anything were other cops. These so-called peaceniks were trying to blow up the country, burn it down, destroy everything, but we were the ones got spat on, jeered at, got rocks thrown at us. We were doing it for *them*. My own kids—" He cut his words short, made a noise like a growl. "It doesn't matter. Who gives a fuck anyway? Basswood has that hotshot lawyer. She'll get off. The rest of it . . . you don't know what you're getting into. I'm serious. You should leave it buried, where it belongs."

"I can't do that. Tilquist's son is with the FBI himself. He's a good agent, a good man, and he deserves the truth. If there was a cover-up, it was a betrayal of everything he believes in."

The man in dark laughed again, a weird despairing sound, the kind you hear from jumpers as they look down from a ledge, but he choked on phlegm and had to fight for breath, gasping and wheezing desperately. This time it went on so long, I took a step toward him. "No! Stay back." He coughed and spat. "Oh, man," he muttered exhaustedly.

"You okay?"

"Not dead yet." A minute passed, two minutes, and I smelled the bourbon again. "Some pair, huh? You and me, we know all about it." His tune was almost fond, as if we were strangers sitting at the same bar night after night.

"About what really happened to Tilquist?"

"About betrayal. Ah, fuck it. Find Pete Spellman, if he hasn't killed himself by now. If somebody else hasn't shut him up."

" 'Somebody else'? Like who?"

"Better get to him first, that's all. Maybe he'll tell you how it happened. Christ knows, it's weighed on him long enough." I had a feeling he was talking about the weight he was carrying himself, the screams he still heard, the images he tried to drown in whiskey.

"Supposing I can find this guy, he may not want to talk to me. He knows you. Is there a name I could—"

That raspy chuckle again. "I'm not that drunk. Get out of here. And don't stick around to tail me, 'cause you won't see me leave."

SIXTEEN

woke early, too wired to sleep, so I went running while it was still relatively cool, then showered and checked out of the motel. I thought I'd get to my meeting with the graduate student early, but the city's streets crossed each other at confusing angles and I ended up on the wrong side of a tangle of interstates before I found the Seward Café.

It wasn't far from the part of town where Lucas and I had combed the streets looking for Andy Two Dogs, but it was closer to the University of Minnesota, and the ragged clientele inside were mostly young and white, chowing down on huge platters of eggs and beans, whole-wheat pancakes, and various vegetarian and vegan options. A muscled skinhead leaned against the counter, wearing steel-toed work boots and a faded Grain Belt T-shirt, a barbed-wire tattoo encircling one arm. He looked like a recruit for the Nordic League, or maybe a vice cop, but he was chatting easily with a willowy girl whose dirty bare toes peeked out from under a floor-length wraparound skirt. It was red and orange and had flowers and parrots and block-printed elephants marching around it, tail to trunk. The man looked over at me. "Are you Anni?"

"Travis? Good to meet you." The girl headed over to join friends at a table.

"Someone you know?" he asked, and I realized I'd been staring at her.

"No." But her skirt looked just like the one I remembered my mother wearing, and for just a moment, I smelled its spicy scent. I pushed the memory aside and shook his hand. "This is my treat. I can put it down as expenses." He didn't look much like a grad student, but he probably didn't have a lot of cash to spare, and a frame as big as his took feeding. Besides, I owed his former professor for putting me in touch with his source. We ordered, got mugs of coffee, and found a corner table in view of the front door and with room for Lucas whenever he arrived. "So, you're doing a dissertation on white supremacist organizations?"

"Pagan groups in particular. This Nordic League—never heard of them until I got wind of their NAGPRA challenge a couple of weeks ago. What do you know about them?"

I gave him a quick rundown of what little I knew, describing the black shirts with the Dungeons and Dragons motif, the prison tattoos, the effective way their leader had set up a confrontation for the cameras. "They hooked up in prison, all of them serving time for violent crimes. The leader, Brian Folkstone—which is an alias, by the way—got someone to burn down a house for him, which seems to be his style. He's a weedy-looking guy, the kind you'd expect to get picked on in school, or made into someone's punch his first day in the joint. But he's good at manipulating people, and he's got a lot of theories. He's definitely the one in charge."

"I checked out their Web site. It has the usual *Bell Curve* claims about race and intelligence, the standard conspiracy talk about how the scientifically proven truth is being suppressed."

"And a bizarre idea that Europeans were the original Americans."

"That's not so unusual, actually. Back in the seventeenth and eighteenth centuries, a lot of people insisted one of the native languages—Mandan, I think—was a dialect of Welsh, which they took as proof there were westward travelers before Columbus. And, of course, there really were Norse settlements in North America. Just not as early as this Nordic League claims."

My name was called out and we got up to fetch our platters of food. "What's with the pagan angle?" I asked when we were settled again. "I always thought of white supremacists as being Christian—in a loose sense of the word."

"Most of these groups are a repackaging of neo-Nazi militias. Some adopted one brand or other of fundamentalist beliefs, like the Christian Identity Movement. They're the ones who have gotten the most attention, but lots of racist groups embrace pagan traditions, wanting to get in touch with their rape-and-pillage roots. Odinism is big."

I caught sight of Lucas coming in the front door, blinking around. He wasn't dressed neatly for work this time. His hair was tangled and his once-white T-shirt was streaked with dirt. I waved him over, introduced to him to Travis, then took our mugs to get refills so I could talk to him privately. "You look like shit," I muttered to him. "Didn't you get any sleep at that place?"

"They kicked me out."

"Why?"

"This girl kept trying to get into my stuff. It pissed me off."

I figured there was more to the story than that, but it would have to wait. I slipped him a ten-dollar bill to buy his breakfast and carried coffee back to our table. "These groups you're studying," I asked Travis. "Do they pose a threat, generally?"

"Depends on what you mean by 'threat.' Without another Waco, a Ruby Ridge, they're not likely to form a cohesive movement, the way the militias were trying to do twenty years ago. People who join groups like these have problems with authority, so organizations usually don't last long. They're always fighting over leadership. But that doesn't mean they're not dangerous. Didn't take many people to load a truck with fertilizer and fuel oil and blow up a federal building in Oklahoma City. In fact, I'd say the risk is greater now than it is been in years."

"Why?"

"Since nine/eleven, the Justice Department's focus has been on Islamic fundamentalists and left-wing movements, especially antiwar and environmentalist organizations, not on good ol' boy terrorists." Lucas drifted over, took a chair, and hunched over his mug of coffee. "Also, there's the whole immigration debate heating up the race rhetoric. And the prison situation."

"Meaning . . ."

"A lot of people who pulled long jolts under mandatory sentencing have been rejoining society in recent years. They get introduced to these 'faith traditions' in the joint. Being a religion, it's a form of association that's protected." He took a bite, mumbled through his food, "Once they get out, they can't vote, can't get jobs; they're at the bottom of the socioeconomic heap. The social organization inside is defined by race, so when these guys get out, it's like they just got a graduate degree in racism. They're angry, and they stick together, since all they have left that's positive in their lives is loyalty to one another."

"Makes sense. How'd you decide on this topic for your research?"

Travis waggled a fork, signaling he'd answer as soon as he finished another mouthful of food. "Grew up in Idaho, had an uncle involved in an offshoot of Christian Identity. He was a good guy, actually wanted to understand what motivated him to join an outfit like that. But I ended up going with pagans, since there's not a lot of research on them yet. Pridoux told me these Nordic Leaguers stole the native remains from that college the other night."

"They vandalized the place, too. A faculty member's office. One of them carved a swastika into her desk."

"Huh?" Lucas set his mug down suddenly, coffee splashing onto the table.

"Yeah, they made a real mess. Tossed books and files all over the place."

"A swastika?" Travis said. "Weird. Like leaving a signed confession."

"Brian Folkstone, the group's leader, denies involvement, and he's probably telling the truth. He might have wanted to steal the bones, but he wouldn't have left a Nazi symbol behind. The police think one of one of the group members acted alone. There's one in particular with impulse-control problems. The FBI is looking for him. They're considering it a hate crime."

"The theft is a strange twist," Travis said. "Don't remember that happening before. Though of course this isn't the first time that a pagan group has challenged a NAGPRA claim—there's Kennewick Man." When he saw I didn't have a clue, he added, "That nine-thousand-year-old skeleton found in eastern Washington State a few years ago? Four different tribes filed repatriation claims. A white neo-pagan group called Asatru countersued because one of the first scientists to examine the remains said the skull looked European."

"Sounds familiar. The Nordic League found some old publication that said these bones were Caucasian. What happened in the Washington case?"

"Asatru ran out of money for filing fees, eventually dropped the whole thing. Then it came down to the tribes versus the scientists who wanted to study the bones. Last I heard, the scientists were winning." He scraped the last of the food from his plate and patted his belly with a contented sigh. "Thanks for the meal. Say, what's going on with Rosa Saenz? Incredible they haven't caught her yet. I'm thinking about heading down to Chicago for that demonstration. Lot of my friends are going. It's going to be huge." He grinned. "Sixty-eight all over again."

What did he mean?" Lucas asked me as we drove away from the café. " 'Sixty-eight'?"

"He was talking about a riot in Chicago during the Vietnam War. Antiwar demonstrators got into it with police during the Democratic National Convention. Hundreds of people were arrested, and a lot of heads were busted."

"Whoa, wrong direction," Lucas objected as I swung onto a ramp for the interstate.

"I have to stop by Hamline again, just for a minute. What happened at the shelter last night?"

"Like I said, this girl kept trying to get into my stuff." Lucas had his backpack in his lap, his arms wrapped around it, as if still on guard against her.

"What did you do?"

"Told her to knock it off."

"Then what?"

"They said I had to leave." I waited. He shifted resentfully in his seat. "I got mad, okay?" he finally burst out. "She just wouldn't quit, kept grabbing my backpack and laughing at me. I barely pushed her, but she made a big deal out of it."

"What are you carrying in there, the crown jewels?" He glowered out the window. "She figured out how to get you in trouble, and you walked right into it. You have to learn ways to avoid losing your temper like that. When we first moved in with my grandfather, the kids at school gave us a hard time, which was nothing new. But we finally had a good place to live and I didn't want to screw it up. And it put me in a tough spot, because the only way I knew how to respond was physical. You know, hitting people, biting, scratching, pushing their heads into toilets."

That got his attention. "You really did that?"

"The toilet thing, only to girls. I wasn't allowed in the boys' rest room. It worked all right in the city, but you can't get away with that shit on the North Shore. My grandfather was smart. He got me to talk about things so I could figure out why I got so mad. And Sophie's dad taught me techniques for controlling my temper. It's something he had to learn himself. You take a lot of crap from people when you're a cop, but you have to stay cool, keep in control."

"They don't always. Sometimes they bust people's heads."

I thought about that demonstration coming up. When I'd come across an official report about the fighting at the '68 convention the other night a few nights earlier, one that concluded it was a police riot, I'd skimmed it with mixed feelings. I couldn't help but picture Hank Cravic's big angry face as he whipped his baton across the back of a kid's head with a *crack* I could still hear all too clearly. But I also remembered how much I'd hated being assigned to crowd control when I was in uniform. It didn't matter whether it was a parade or a concert or a political demonstration, it always felt as if violence was lurking there, hiding in the spaces between people, just waiting for its moment to turn the whole crowd against us.

I pulled up in a loading zone and left Lucas in the car. Jon Pridoux was pulling the door of his office closed when he saw me. "Oh, hi. I'm on my way to a meeting, but—"

"I just have a quick question for you." It was one I had to ask in person. It wasn't likely Pridoux's phone was being monitored, but I couldn't take chances. I glanced around the empty hallway. It must have been contagious, because he looked over his shoulder suspiciously. "Pete Spellman," I said, keeping my voice low. "Mixed-blood Dakota. I've never seen that name in anything I've read, and nobody's mentioned it. Did it turn up in your research at all?"

He gave it some thought. "Could be in some official document under black ink. I don't recognize it." It sounded as if he was telling the truth.

"All right. Don't mention it to anyone, okay? Oh, and if you talk to that guy again, tell him thanks."

"I don't know what you're talking about." This time, it sounded like a lie.

SEVENTEEN

Lucas slept soundly as I drove north, first on the interstate, then on two-lane roads that went through gently rolling countryside. I could have made better time, but I stuck to the posted speed limit, made sure I signaled at every turn, and if a light turned amber, I put on the brakes. I didn't want to give the guys in the tan Taurus that was following us any excuse to pull us over. Soon after a sign welcomed us to the White Earth Reservation, I pulled into a gas station. Lucas sat up in a panic, clutching his bag. "What's going on?"

"Getting gas. Welcome to the rez. You don't have anything illegal in there, do you?"

He hugged it even tighter to his chest. "Like what?"

"Like that gun Father Sikora took from Sophie?"

"No."

"Drugs?"

"No! Why you asking?"

"Just checking." I got out and filled the tank, then I racked the pump handle, walked over to the Taurus pulled up in a slot in front of the station, and tapped on the driver's window. "How you doing?" I asked the men inside when the window powered down. "Listen, if you need to use the john or anything, I'll wait."

"Excuse me?"

"You been following me for the past two hundred miles. Sure you don't need a bathroom break?" The driver gave me a stony look, but his partner stared straight ahead, having trouble suppressing a grin.

"Who were you talking to?" Lucas asked me when I climbed back in the car, peering back at the Taurus.

"They're FBI. Been following us since we left Minneapolis."

His head snapped around to stare out the front windshield. "Shit," he whispered.

"It's nothing to worry about. They've been following me around for days." He didn't seem reassured. "Lucas, they aren't exactly being subtle. They want us to know we're being watched. It's a form of intimidation, that's all."

"Yeah, but . . ."

I looked at him. "What's going on, Lucas?"

"I don't want them bothering my grandma, that's all. She's old; she'd be scared. Just drop me off somewhere. I can get there by myself."

"No. I'll let them follow us for now, but when the time comes, I'll shake them off. Good enough?" He thought about it and nodded, but he didn't relax.

The Taurus stayed with us like a shadow all the way to Grassy Creek, the town where Rosa was born and spent her first years. *Town* was an exaggeration. It was unincorporated, no more than a water tower, a bar, a gas station that had closed twenty years earlier, and a handful of run-down houses. It could have been a ghost town, except for the twitch of a curtain and the sound of a door slamming as we approached. We bought cold drinks at the bar, a tiny place that smelled of stale cigarettes and mildew, but the glum bartender was tired of talking to reporters and lawmen. He'd never met Rosa, didn't know anything about her. Just wished people would leave folks alone.

The county seat was where all the action was. Camera crews, law enforcement, and activists had all set up camp outside the courthouse. The mood was a strange mix of county fair and political rally, laced with an undercurrent of tension. Speakers took turns at a microphone, while reporters milled through the crowd in search of local color and usable quotes. There were petitions being circulated on everything from land recovery to banning genetically altered wild rice. Vendors sold cold drinks, hot dogs, fry bread, and mini-donuts. One stand manned by a student group from Bemidji State University had T-shirts for sale, all proceeds to go to Rosa's defense fund. Lucas raised his eyebrows at me when we saw they were using his graffiti image of Rosa, but he wasn't about to claim credit, given all the watchful eyes on us. He glanced nervously over his shoulder as I bought a dozen shirts in different sizes, including a child-size one for Lucy, the Tilquists' five-year-old. Everyone we talked to had opinions about Rosa, but we couldn't find anyone who had actually met her in person.

When we started strolling back to the Corolla, our FBI shadows hurried to their vehicle. They had shed their suit coats and looked wilted from the heat. The older one's face was bright pink from too much sun; the younger one was brushing crumbs off his front from the fry bread he'd bought at a stand.

"You have the directions to your grandma's house?" I asked Lucas. He handed me a folded piece of notebook paper. I compared his sketch to the state map. "Okay, here's what I want to do." I showed him, running my finger along back roads. "Time to lose these guys. Keep an eye on the map so you can help me find the turns. If this doesn't work, you'll have to help me come up with another route."

But it wasn't necessary. They got held up when a slow-moving farm machine pulled in front of them; a couple of crossroads and a wooded ravine later, we were on our own.

Within twenty minutes, we were at his grandmother's house. It looked like one of Lucy's drawings, a tiny cabin with a window on each side of the front door, a pointy roof, a chimney. The paint had been scoured away by the weather over the years, leaving the planks a silvery color, and the roof tiles were green with moss. It was surrounded by birch trees and pines and outbuildings in various stages of decay, one of them no more than a hummock of broken bricks and lumber. The lake Lucas remembered was behind the house, only you couldn't see it for all the reeds. It looked as if the unmowed grass in the yard continued into the water, growing taller and darker, whispering with a secret sound. A small and wizened dog ran to meet the car, barking and trotting back and forth busily as I parked. A woman who looked a lot like Rosa, short and plump and brown, with long graying hair in a ponytail, came out onto the porch. The little dog ran to her side, making indignant woofing noises at us.

"You mind if I talk to her by myself?" Lucas asked me.

"Go ahead. I can wait a little while, in case it doesn't work out."

"I'm not staying here." He seemed shocked by the idea. "I'm going back to Chicago with you."

"I thought you had to leave town."

"No, I just . . . I have to give her something. You'll wait for me, won't you?"

"Sure, if that's what you want."

"This won't take long." He climbed out and reached for his backpack. He started toward the porch, lifting a hand tentatively, not raising it above his waist, the kind of wave you use when you aren't sure if the person who just waved to you is actually greeting someone else. "*Boozhoo, Nokomis,*" he said.

"*Aaniin, Noozhis.*" There was no dramatic long-lost-relative scene, not even a hug. She simply opened the screen door and they went inside.

I got out to stretch my legs and think. The air smelled of water and moss and resin from the pines. A chipmunk rose up on its hind legs to look at me, made an irritated chirping sound, and disappeared into the grass. I sat on a fallen tree trunk and listened to the reeds rustle and the scolding of jays. Every now and then, the upper branches of the pines stirred overhead and made a low roaring sound like traffic on a distant highway. I closed my eyes and played the day backward, from Lucas's reaction to being followed to his being kicked out of the shelter because a girl was too inquisitive about the contents of his backpack. By the time Lucas came out of the house, grinning and relaxed, as if a burden had been lifted from his shoulders, I had guessed what it was he had to give his grandma.

"Okay, we can go now. You see how surprised she was when she heard me talking in our language?" he added as we walked together toward the car.

She hadn't shown any emotion that I could see, but I didn't say so. Instead, I reached into the backseat for a T-shirt. "We should give her one of these. Sit still; I'll do it."

Ignoring his protest, I went over to the screen door, knocked on the doorjamb, and walked inside without waiting for an invitation. "Some students from Bemidji State were selling these shirts." She moved a newspaper on the table behind her, then shifted some other things, as if tidying up. "We thought you should have one. Lucas made the design. He's a talented artist."

She took it from me. "He was always a good drawer when he was little."

"He's a great kid. Took quite a risk bringing those bones here." I nodded toward a bundle wrapped in a red shawl, which she had tried to hide under the newspaper.

"You going to tell?"

"I don't know. They're the subject of a federal lawsuit, but I don't want Lucas to get in trouble. What will you do with them?"

"Make sure they get back to their people. I got Shawnee friends in Oklahoma. I don't care what the government says; that's where they belong."

"How do you know they're Shawnee?"

"I looked it up on the Internet." She didn't exactly smile at my reaction, but her cheeks dimpled. "What, you think we still live in te-pees? I was going to give Lucas my e-mail address, but he says he don't know how to do it."

"I can show him."

"Okay. Let me give you my IM account, too." She wrote them in my notebook. "I said he could stay here if he wants, but they ain't any jobs around here. He likes Chicago anyway. Says he got friends there." She looked at me, her eyes like hard, bright stones.

"Yes, he has friends."

"Good." She handed my notebook back and nodded, as if we had just signed some kind of contract.

EIGHTEEN

t was Sophie's idea, Lucas told me as we drove away. She'd hatched the plan as soon as she heard I was going to Minneapolis. Took her mother's office keys, found the bones, wrapped them up in the shawl, and then set it up to look like the racist group was responsible. She had asked Lucas to take them, figuring he would be able to get them back to their own people. His relatives in Minneapolis didn't want anything to do with it, so he called his grandma. She knew what to do.

"You realize how dangerous that was?"

"I know, but . . . You going to turn us in?"

"No." I was furious with Sophie for being so thoughtless, taking such a crazy risk and dragging Lucas and his family into it. But Fiske would use the incident to sidetrack and discredit me, and I didn't have time for that. I had to find Pete Spellman.

ithout an FBI escort, I made better time back to the outskirts of the Twin Cities. I took a couple of rooms in a motel, then called Jim's aunt, who was willing to talk to me that evening, even though she clearly thought that 8:00 P.M. was scandalously late for a social call.

The elderly and somewhat deaf woman had a picture of her brother Arne on her wall—the same square-jawed formal portrait that had run in the paper—flanked by framed commendations and a letter of condolence from the director of the FBI, as if it was some sort of shrine. She talked about how brave he was, how dedicated, but apart from superlatives, I didn't get much sense of him as an individual. He'd passed into a martyr's heaven, which rubs away most of the details that make a person human. I sat beside her on a floral couch as she reminisced and turned the pages of a photo album, which contained the usual family pictures of weddings, baptisms, graduations, vacations. Three images in particular struck me.

The first showed a burly, blond, preteen Arne Tilquist, who was the spitting image of his father. Both of them were dressed in camo, smiling as they stood beside a gutted deer suspended upside down from a tree limb. "How they loved to hunt," his sister murmured. "Arne was so disappointed Jim didn't care for it. It's something fathers and sons should do together, don't you think?"

The next was a formal studio portrait of Jim wearing an army uniform and standing in front of a flag. He look skinny and resolute and impossibly young. "He had just turned twenty, his aunt explained, and was about to ship out to Vietnam," his aunt said. With his buzz-cut hair and formal pose, it looked like the pictures of the youngest casualties from Iraq running on the evening news.

The third photo was one of Jim after his return. He appeared at the edge of a group photo, some family gathering. He was standing apart from the others, holding a bottle of beer, a cigarette clamped between two fingers as he stared beyond the camera. He had grown a beard and his hair reached his shoulders, but he was still skinny, still young—except for his eyes, which were hollow and haunted.

"It was the war," his aunt told me. "When he came home, he jumped at every sound, lost his temper at the littlest things. Couldn't sit still, couldn't sleep, even if he drank enough to fell an ox. And oh, how they fought, the two of them. About the war, about civil rights, about everything. But that was how it was in those days. Children didn't get on with their parents. 'The generation gap,' it was called.

Seemed all the young people rebelled, challenged authority, ran away to live in communes and such. The sad thing was, for all the arguments, Jim adored his father. When Arne was killed, he was so devastated, he went to pieces, spent weeks in a clinic."

She clapped a hand over her mouth, her parchment cheeks reddening. "We went to such lengths to keep it quiet. Not that there was anything to be ashamed of—so many boys coming home from that war had difficulties—but if it had turned up in a background check, he would never have gotten a job in law enforcement. They even took up a collection to pay for it, Arne's colleagues in the Bureau. It was a private clinic and terribly expensive, but Arne's friends were good to the family; they took care of his boy."

Jim had turned out fine, of course. He pulled himself together, finished college, went to the Academy, even got a law degree. Now he was in the Bureau, just like his dad. There had been an article about the two of them in a local paper a year or so ago. She had an extra copy she could give me, she said, if she could just remember where she had put it. It wasn't a paper she normally read, she added she as unearthed it from a closet and handed it to me, a *Village Voice*-style tabloid called *City Pages,* with music reviews, ads for acupuncture and aromatherapy, and personals that would have turned her hair even whiter had she could been able to decode the acronyms. "Isn't that a good picture of Arne?"

I agreed, thinking she must be too blind to read the blurry newsprint. It was a savage profile. Arne Tilquist was portrayed as a mean-spirited fascist with sociopathic tendencies, doing his job with a brutal enthusiasm that presaged the post-9/11 conflict between security and civil liberties. In contrast, Jim came across as intelligent and cautious, and the author of the article made the most of the irony. Unidentified sources said Jim was one of the rare voices in the Bureau who raised concerns about the PATRIOT Act and its constitutionally questionable provisions. Jim had given the journalist only a few carefully worded direct quotes. He'd refused to pass judgment on the radical accused of Arne Tilquist's murder. He'd stated bluntly that the counterintelligence programs of the time were illegal. He'd declined to say anything at all about his father. The conclusion drawn was that there was nothing good to say, and even his own son knew it.

Before I left, she asked me not say anything about Jim's stay in the clinic. Her nephew was a proud man, she said, and he would hate for anyone to know. And she worried it might harm his career. I reassured her I wouldn't tell.

But after I went back to the motel, I lay awake in bed, seeing that photograph of the lean young man with haunted eyes, and I couldn't help wondering about the things he'd never told me.

We left at dawn. Lucas was groggy. He had never stayed in a motel before and had been so mesmerized by the cable choices, he'd apparently stayed up most of the night channel-surfing in his room. At any rate, he fell asleep as soon as we got onto the interstate.

By midmorning, I pulled into a gas station to fill the tank and get some coffee. I called the Tilquists. Jim answered. Since Nancy's office had been vandalized, he was staying close to home, using up some of the vacation time he'd never gotten around to taking. Alton Brinks, the dim-witted Nordic Leaguer who was being sought for the break-in, had managed to evade capture so far. Given Brinks's s record of violence, Jim wanted to make sure his family was safe. He'd been putting in such crazy hours the last few months he practically had to get to know Lucy all over again. And Alice, too, though she barely spoke to any of them these days, always had her nose in a book. As for Sophie . . . well, it was too soon for the change in medication to have had much effect yet.

"She's not doing well?"

"Just gets wound up about things. She's mad that we won't let her go to that demonstration planned for Sunday. It's going to be big, and it could get nasty. It's the last thing she needs, but she thinks I'm being a fascist. She was upset that Father Sikora was arrested, even though the judge has already released him on his own recognizance. And then, when the agent who's working on the break-in asked her a few questions—well, you know how dramatic she gets. You'd think it was the Spanish Inquisition."

"Don't let him question her without a lawyer, Jim."

"It was nothing. She has a part-time job on campus; he just needed to know if she saw anything, that's all."

I didn't want to put him on the spot by telling him Sophie was responsible for the theft, but he had to know enough to take precautions. "The Nordic League isn't the only group with a claim to those bones," I said carefully. "If this agent is any good at his job, he'll have to consider every possibility, and Sophie is pretty outspoken about whose claim is the right one."

"If he drags my daughter into this—"

"He doesn't have much choice. Think about it. Technically, Sophie had access to Nancy's office; she had motive. Unless Alton Brinks is caught and confesses, this agent has to follow up, and there's no telling what she might say. Insist on a lawyer." Jim was silent for a moment before he cursed under his breath. We both knew that becoming the focus of an investigation would feed Sophie's self-absorbed excitement, and she couldn't afford it right now.

He was surprised to hear I'd visited his aunt. He said, "I should get up to see her one of these days. How did she seem?" I gave him an innocuous account. She hadn't been able to tell me anything useful for the investigation, but I saw a lot of family photos. Jim groaned when I mentioned the *City Pages* article. He seemed relieved when I told him his aunt liked the pictures but hadn't been able to make out the small print.

"There was a picture of you in uniform, when you joined the army. You looked really young."

"Young and stupid. What did my aunt say?"

"She didn't think it was stupid. She's proud of you."

I heard a piping voice in the background. He had to go; Lucy was kicking his butt at checkers. But before hanging up, he remembered something. A detective from Area 4 was trying to reach me. Not Dugan, some guy named Martinez. He wouldn't say what it was about, just left his name and number and a request for me to get in touch when I was back in town. Whatever it was, it didn't seem to be urgent.

had one more stop to make before we headed back to Chicago. Lucas helped me navigate through an alphabet soup of lettered county trunk roads in southeastern Wisconsin, until we found the gravel drive that led to Nick Katsourinis's isolated home.

It looked as if nothing about the small farmhouse had been changed in a hundred years, except a ramp had been added to the front porch. I hadn't called ahead, but the disabled ex-FBI agent had his own early-warning system. As I parked in the shade of a huge cottonwood, the car was surrounded by a pack of baying animals that looked like wolves and were doing their best to sound like them.

"You get along with dogs?" I asked Lucas, but his wide eyes were enough of an answer. One of the beasts threw himself against my window, yellow fangs displayed, and Lucas shrank deeper into his seat.

There was a sharp whistle and the pack raced off to the porch, where a man had come through the screen door. He was stocky, with a thick beard, a barrel chest, and arms bulging with muscles that he used to propel his wheelchair. He watched me with a closed expression

as I climbed out of the car. One of the dogs was pulling back his lip
to show me his sharp teeth. Another one specialized in glowering at
me with insane yellow eyes.

"They won't attack unless I say so," the man called from the
porch. "Which, if you're a reporter, is going to happen real soon."

"I'm not a reporter," I said quickly, then added cautiously, "How
do you feel about private investigators?"

"Don't get so many of those. Who's your pal?"

Lucas was pretending to be absorbed in the road map and was
mostly hidden behind its folds. "Just a kid who needed a ride back to
Chicago."

"Chicago, huh?" Katsourinis studied me as I took a few steps toward the porch. The sun was high in the sky now, a disk of white heat
that baked my shoulders. The grass under my feet was brittle. The
dog with the crazed eyes started growling low in his throat, his head
sunk low between his shoulders. As he crept forward, Katsourinis
reached out and grabbed the bristling ruff of his neck. We looked at
each other as the dog quivered under his hand like a tightened spring.
"You're working for Basswood."

"I have some questions I'd like to ask you."

"I'll bet you do." He flashed a smile that was no friendlier than his
dog's snarl, but he abruptly turned his chair and opened the screen
door. Unsure whether it was an invitation or some kind of challenge,
I climbed up the porch steps warily. The dogs all took a sniff at my
jeans before plopping down on the porch, tongues hanging out of
their big doggy smiles. No hard feelings, just doing our job.

Katsourinis pointed me into an old-fashioned kitchen. There was
no air conditioning, but a hay-scented breeze teased the curtains at
the window, and the room felt cool after the baking sun outside. He
wheeled over to the refrigerator and got out a couple of beers. "What
about your friend?"

"He's fine." I got my license out and traded it for one of the bottles.

He squinted at it. "Kind of name is that?"

"Finnish."

"Don't look like a Finn." He flipped it over, examining it.

"I just got that license a few weeks ago. I was with the CPD for ten years. In fact, first time I laid eyes on our client, I was canvassing the neighborhood after a shooting and stopped by St. Larry's. They have a community center—"

"I know. I grew up on the West Side."

The scent of now-mown hay and cowpats drifted through the screened windows. A couple of ponies cropped grass along a fence. It was hard to place this suspicious old fed in a setting like this. Even harder to figure out how to get him to talk to me. "Makes a change, living out in the country like this." I gave him a smile, but his eyes remained cold.

"Lot of things changed when I got shot."

"Rosa has worked at St. Larry's for the past year," I said, trying again. "She's become sort of a grandmother to the neighborhood kids. Everyone who knows her says she couldn't have killed anyone."

"But there's no doubt she's Verna Basswood."

"Right."

"An active member of Logan Hall's group."

"That's true."

"Which advocated violence."

"So I understand."

"Planted a bomb in front of police headquarters. Called for the violent overthrow of the government. Told people killing pigs was justifiable homicide."

"They said a lot of stupid things."

"So this grandmother type that wouldn't hurt a fly—what's your question again?"

"I think I'm wasting your time." I set the bottle down and got up to leave. "I'm sorry to have bothered you."

"Hey, take it easy. I'm just messing with you." He patted the air to coax me back into my chair. "Siddown and drink your goddamn beer." He ran his fingers through his thick graying hair. "Sorry, I don't get many visitors. I'm an antisocial asshole. Just ask the neighbors."

"That's okay; I'll take your word for it."

He snorted. "I suppose you want to know how Arne Tilquist ended up dead in that basement, but I'm not going be able to help you. I was in the hospital when it happened and, frankly, I had other things on my mind." He upended his longneck and emptied it.

"How long did you work together as partners?"

"Three years. We worked together, but 'partners' is stretching it."

"You were both investigating Ishkode."

"He got his start at the Minneapolis Field Office; he knew the key players in the American Indian Movement. I knew my way around other radical groups in Chicago. Made sense for us to pool our resources."

"Except . . ."

"He did his thing; I did mine. He liked to cultivate sources; I liked to bust heads. Different strokes."

"Ishkode was small and insular, but there were some individuals who hung around its fringes, wanting to be part of it. Were you able to flip any of them?"

"Arne might have. That was his style, and he was good at it."

"Did he ever indicate who was giving him his information?"

"Not Arne. He kept his cards close to his chest. Why are you so interested in his informants?"

"I'm just trying to get a handle on this thing."

"Good luck. I never did."

"What do you mean?"

He sighed, looked over his shoulder, gave one wheel of his chair a nudge, and rolled back to hook another beer out of the fridge. "Look, what made you want to be a cop? Family connections? Your dad on the job?"

"Not that I know of. Never met him."

He gave me a crooked grin. "I withdraw the question. Was it some moral imperative to serve and protect?"

"Not really. I got to know a cop. Looked like interesting work, and I thought I'd be good at it."

"Same with me. I probably would have gone to work in the restaurant. My family served the best food in Greektown. Still does, in fact. But we were at war and I scored in the draft lottery. I had no idea what we were doing there. I just followed orders and tried to keep my ass off the front lines. Got assigned to some intelligence work and turned out to be pretty good at it. By the time I got home, I was hooked on the adrenaline kick. Civilian life just didn't have enough edge to it, so I signed on with the FBI. Never occurred to me to question whether what we were doing was right or not, any more than it did in Nam. I wasn't into politics. I just needed that buzz." He swallowed some beer, shook his head. "Saving the country from anti-American conspirators? Not me. That's what Tilquist was up to. Now, he was a man of principle." He held the bottle up, made a silent toast.

"Tilquist's son was in Vietnam."

"I remember that. Arne complained his kid had turned into a Communist. Only I guess not, since I read in the papers he's working for the Bureau now. Ol' Arne would be proud."

"The night of that raid. The night you got shot. Can we talk about that?"

He looked at the label on his bottle, rubbed a thumb against it, gave me a one-shoulder shrug.

"You expected a fairly simple bust, but somehow they got wind of your arrival and put up a fight."

"Right. We had information they were meeting in an apartment on the second floor. We were getting ready to bust down the door when they opened fire from the next floor up. That's pretty much all I know about it. I was out of the picture after that—permanently."

"How'd they know you were coming?"

He shrugged. "Somebody fucked up."

"Where'd the information about the meeting come from?"

"I assume Arne got it from one of his little helpers."

"Was he having problems with any of them?"

"Who knows? He guarded them like state secrets."

"The day of the raid, who else was there with you?"

"Forget it. They won't talk to you."

"They might."

"Didn't you learn anything when you were on the job? Rule one: You don't talk, ever."

"We're talking."

"Yeah, well." He finished off his beer, belched behind his fist. "I was always kind of a fuckup when it came to rules. Arne had a different approach to the job than I had. He really believed in what he was doing. It was his religion."

"And you?"

"I didn't give a damn about politics. I didn't even want to hear about it. Used to piss him off, my attitude."

"But he got pretty worked up when you took that bullet. Sounds to me as if he took some serious anger with him when they raided that farmhouse in Wisconsin."

"I couldn't say. I wasn't there." He yanked another beer out of the refrigerator. The move was practiced. He didn't even have to look to find the longneck.

"The agent leading the Basswood investigation now is a guy named Fiske. You know him?"

"We've met. Another man of principle, just like Arne. Come to think of it, Fiske didn't like my attitude, either."

The dogs started to bark as a car crunched on the gravel outside. I pictured them savaging a reporter. Katsourinis chuckled at my reaction. "Take it easy. They sound happy."

"They sounded happy about tearing me apart, too."

"Different kind of happiness. I know these mutts."

The screen door banged open and a boy of about four came running across the room, throwing himself against Katsourinis so hard, it pushed the wheelchair back against the counter. "Hi, Grandpa!" he yelled happily, hugging his legs.

"Hey, punkin." He pulled the boy up into his lap.

"You smell like beer," the little boy muttered affectionately, twining his fingers in the burly man's beard.

"My daughter, Elena," he said as a young woman came in with a grocery sack. She nodded at me warily, then frowned pointedly at the bottles lined up on the kitchen table. "Don't give me a hard time, sweetie. I don't have too many pleasures in life and I wasn't expecting two of 'em to walk in the door."

That coaxed a small smile out of her. "Sweet talker. I was out shopping and picked up a few things for you. Nicky wanted to visit the ponies."

"I thought you wanted to visit me." He frowned fiercely down at the little boy, who just giggled as he slid down his grandpa's legs. "This is Anni . . . something Finnish. Up from Chicago to talk about old times."

Her face darkened. "Why can't you people leave him alone?"

"She's not a fed. She's not even a reporter. She's part of Verna Basswood's defense team." His daughter looked between us, confused. "Take Nicky out back, why don't you. We're almost finished."

She set the bag of groceries on the counter and followed the boy, who went whooping out the back door.

"Nice kid."

"Both of 'em." He reached behind him automatically for the

refrigerator, then stopped. "Better not, with the boy around. She hates it when I drink."

"I didn't know you had a daughter."

"I met her mom in Madison when I was a confused son of a bitch, taking a few classes, trying to figure out what to do with my life after landing in this chair. Atoning for my sins." He pulled a wallet out, found a photograph, and smiled to himself before he passed it over. She was striking, with high cheekbones and a wide bucktoothed smile, but there was a hint of sadness in her huge dark eyes. "We had three kids together. Don't look so surprised. My legs may not work, but what's between 'em does."

I gave the photo back and he stared at it a moment, her sadness finding a reflection in his eyes before he slipped it back into his wallet. "We split up years ago. I'm not an easy guy to get along with. I'm moody and sarcastic and I don't sleep good at night. She put up with me as long as she could. Now she sends Elena out to check on me, make sure I'm not turning into a complete recluse." He gathered the bottles up, hooking his fingers in the necks, and wheeled over to drop them into a case of empties. "Look, where were we anyway? You were asking about Fiske." He looked tired suddenly, his face drained and gray.

"Right. He's pretty driven."

"Don't know about Fiske, but Tilquist sure was a man on a mission. He was out to kill some Indians, and when they raided that farmhouse, he missed one. That really pissed him off."

"Excuse me?"

He snorted at my response. "Arne Tilquist grew up in some god-forsaken small town in Minnesota. His dad was a sheriff's deputy who brought hate home with him every day of his life. Tilquist thought Indians were dirt, and Indians with attitude were worse than dirt. He wasn't crazy about jigs either, or Jews, or beaners, or Chinks, you name it. He wasn't too sure about Greeks." He gave me a grin that reminded me of the dog's snarl. "You said he took some serious anger to that raid, making it sound righteous. A cop gets shot? Hit the streets and take no prisoners. The fact of the matter is, Arne Tilquist took serious anger with him everywhere. He took it to the office, he took it on the street, he slept with it at night. I don't know if he was born that way or if he learned it at his father's knee, only it was always there and it didn't have anything to do with what happened to me." He reached blindly for the refrigerator behind him. "You want to know the truth? Arne Tilquist was the biggest asshole I ever worked with. And given where I worked, that's saying something."

NINETEEN

M y phone began to chirp just as I was putting my seat belt back on. "Ms. Koskinen? This is Alonzo Jones. Pastor of the New Day Tabernacle?" he added when his name didn't seem to register. "You had asked me to keep an eye out for the gentleman who goes by the name of Casper."

"Oh, right." Casper, the homeless alcoholic who told ghost stories, whose name I now knew was actually Pete Spellman. "Have you heard anything?"

"He's here."

"He's at your church? Now?"

"But I'm afraid he can't speak to you at the moment. He arrived here quite intoxicated."

I glanced at my watch. It would take at least three hours to get back to the city, add another hour or two to get through rush-hour traffic. "I'm out of town, probably won't get there until six or seven tonight. Can you hang on to him that long?"

He chuckled. "Loud as he's snoring, he should be here for a while, so don't you worry."

I said good-bye, asked Lucas to start looking for the quickest route to the interstate, and called the Tilquists. Sophie snatched up the phone on the first ring. "Where are you?" she demanded.

"In Wisconsin. We're on our way home."

"She still hasn't called," she said, dropping her voice to a whisper. "I'm getting really worried."

"Rosa managed to stay underground for over thirty years, Sophie. She knows what she's doing." I managed to sound far more confident than I was.

"You wouldn't believe what's been going on here. This FBI agent was grilling me yesterday. They've been practically occupying the city. Everybody's really mad about it. There's this huge demonstration being planned for Rosa on Sunday, the 'Vigil for Truth,' they're calling it, only my parents say I can't even go, which is so totally unfair. I mean, I'm old enough—"

"We made a deal, remember? I'm taking care of my end of it. You need to take care of yours, which means you have to listen to your parents."

"Like I have a choice. This sucks. Why can't you be on my side?"

"I am. We all are."

"I'm doing what they say, but it's so lame. Like going to the doctor all the time. He's so annoying. He asks the same questions every time. Just like that FBI guy, trying to trip me up. I really hate it."

"Just hang in there, okay? I need to talk to your dad. Is he there?"

"He's always here. Feels like I'm under house arrest."

Jim came on the phone so quickly, I was sure her last dig was for his benefit. "What's up?"

"The guy I told you about Monday night when you stopped by my place? He's the one, Jim. I got confirmation from a source while we were in Minneapolis. Even better, I know where he is. It'll take five or six hours before I can get there, but everything's falling into place."

"That's great."

"You sound a little . . . Are you okay?"

"Yeah. Hang on a sec, I'm taking this into another room." I waited, feeling vaguely unsettled. "You didn't tell us you were getting death threats."

"Just one."

"Four, so far. Thea Adelman has been taping them, ever since the

first. You didn't give her a working phone number; she had no way of
warning you."

"Her phones are tapped. I don't want them to know this number."

"Well, anyway, she finally got worried enough that she asked me
what to do. I listened to the tapes. They're bad, Anni. Really sick."

"Just angry cops blowing off steam."

"I don't think so. I'm afraid I stirred up a hornet's nest with this
investigation into the Nordic League, and it looks as if Alton Brinks
is blaming you."

"You sure he's the one making those calls?"

"A couple of agents questioned Brian Folkstone. No big thing, but
ever since, he's been on radio talk shows, saying the federal government set them up by faking the theft of the bones. Brinks is still on
the loose. A couple of cops spotted him on Damen Avenue yesterday,
less than a mile from your house. When he saw the cops, he ran into
a store. The owner kept a pistol under the counter. It took Brinks
about three seconds to fracture his skull, break his collarbone, rupture
his spleen—and take the gun. This guy's dangerous."

"Good thing this suspect I'm going to talk to is sleeping it off at the
New Day Tabernacle, then. Hard for a lunatic white supremacist to
sneak up on me in a neighborhood that's ninety-nine percent black."

"Don't joke about it, Anni. This is serious."

"I know, but I need to get this man to talk to me. He's the key to
everything, Jim. And I can't afford to let Fiske find him first."

But as it turned out, I didn't make it to the church. Around 5:30,
just as I was pulling out of the Elgin toll plaza, my phone rang.
It was Jim. He didn't want to alarm me, he said, but it looked as
if Martin was missing. He'd notified Stony Cliff security; they were
organizing a search.

I called Martin's cell number. His phone was turned off, or the battery was dead. I left a message, my voice so calm, it sounded as if someone else was speaking the words, then pushed my anxiety away so I could focus on figuring out the quickest route to Stony Cliff.

Martin's apartment in the basement of the science building looked the same as always—the neatly made bed, pots of cactus on the windowsills, the shelf under the television that held a plastic tyrannosaurus and a Transformer toy that he'd had ever since I could remember. The toys served as bookends for a small set of textbooks: *Introduction to Quantum Mechanics, Heat and Thermodynamics,* and *The Physics of Solids*—Complimentary copies his boss had given him. The words were too hard for him to read, but he liked having them anyway.

"What's the situation?" I asked Cole Janssen, head of Campus Safety and Security, who had arranged to meet me there.

"Josh Cohen, the student working in the lab, says Martin left at five o'clock, as usual. Looks like he stopped by here to change. The clothes he was wearing are in the hamper. Jim Tilquist came by at quarter past. He and Nancy have been checking in on Martin while you've been out of town. But he wasn't here."

"It's Friday. Martin goes to the gym on Fridays," I said.

"That's where Jim looked next. But the kid who works the desk says he never showed up."

I thought about the path Martin would have taken. "That wooded area, right before you get to the gym. It's close to the road."

"We checked. Didn't see anything that would indicate a struggle."

"It's near the loading dock behind the art building. Someone pulled in there and waited until Martin got to the part of the path that's hidden behind the trees. That's where it happened."

"We don't know if anything happened."

"*Something* happened." I swallowed my anger, told myself to breathe slowly, stay calm.

"He might have just gone somewhere on his own." But Janssen said it without much conviction. He knew as well as I did that Martin was obsessive about his routine.

"Do you have Fiske's number?" Janssen looked away. "Come on, he must have given you his card. Maybe he decided to question Martin again."

"And abducted him to do it? That's crazy." But Janssen got out his wallet and poked through it until he found the card. A cell number had been written on the back. I pulled my phone out of my bag and punched the numbers in.

"Fiske." He sounded brisk and in control.

"Where's my brother?"

"Excuse me?"

"Downtown? In a holding cell somewhere? Where is he?"

"Is this Koskinen? I have no idea where your brother is."

"You're lying."

"Why would I be lying?"

"Because it's what you do. If you hurt him—"

"I don't know what the problem is, but if your brother's wandered off—"

"He didn't wander off. Somebody took him."

"I suggest you check with the local police instead of yelling at me."

"I swear to God, Fiske, if you people hurt him, I'll rip your head off. If you so much as *touch* him again, I'll kill you. *I'll fucking kill you.*"

"Jesus, Anni." Janssen had pried the phone out of my hand and was now holding it to his chest, staring at me. "You just threatened a federal agent. Want to get yourself arrested?"

My throat felt scraped from shouting. "He didn't hear; he'd already hung up." I waited for a wave of dizziness to pass. Then I went into Martin's bathroom and threw up.

im had organized a search party, which was already making a sweep of the campus and the town, from the lake to the railroad tracks. I filed a missing person's report with the CPD and gave Martin's description to the state police, neither of which would do anything with it. I bought another disposable phone and gave the number to everyone to use so the other line would be free if Martin tried to call. I checked the hospitals and called the jails. I drove into the city and checked my flat, talked to my neighbors, and asked at the corner store, where Martin occasionally bought a bottle of pop or a candy bar. Then I drove between my house and the train station, scouring the streets for any sign of him, just to be doing something. When Sophie was missing, it sometimes took hours, even days, to find her, but at least I could always guess where she might have gone. I knew Martin wouldn't go anywhere, not voluntarily.

That burst of anger had short-circuited something in my emotions. I hadn't lost my temper like that in a long time. Now I watched myself go through the motions, numbed. Except my throat still hurt.

It was after ten o'clock when my phone rang. I stupidly picked up the wrong one, then realized my mistake and pulled up along the nearest curb and found the other one. The call was coming from his cell phone. "Martin?"

No answer. "Martin, talk to me. I want to come and get you, but I don't know where you are." All I heard was his breathing, shallow and fast, as if he'd just been running. "It's okay. Just take it easy. I'm going to come get you." I listened for any sound in the background that would give me a clue. I could hear traffic sounds, voices. Some public place. He gave a funny little moan, like the rusty hinge of a door closing. "Hang on, okay? Don't turn off the phone." I picked up the other phone, scrabbled through my wallet to find the card I needed.

"Yo, Dugan here."

"It's Anni. My brother's in trouble. Can you get the location of his cell phone?"

"Ah, well, if he calls nine one one, they can—"

"He couldn't tell them what's wrong; they'd think it was a prank. I need it traced. If I give you the number—"

"Ho boy, I don't know. . . . Is it on?"

"It's on. I've been talking to him. I don't know how long the battery will last."

"Give me the number. I'll see what I can do."

I gave him Martin's number and the number of my new phone. Then I picked up the other phone and focused on my brother. "Listen, I know you're scared. But if you could tell me anything about where you are, anything at all—"

"Anni." Two syllables, loud and pleading. Fix things. Make it all right.

"You have to stay calm, Martin. I'm trying to find you, okay? But you have to be cool till we figure out where you are." I heard sirens in the distance, voices calling out. "Martin? You still there?"

He made that creaky hinge sound.

"I know you're frightened. But I need you to concentrate. I'm going to ask you some questions, okay? It sounds like you're outside. Are there buildings where you are?"

"No."

"No buildings?"

"No. Yes . . . no."

"Are there trees?"

But he'd used up all his words. He started humming, an anxious, ragged sound that had a rhythm to it. He was rocking, trying to keep it together.

My other phone rang. It was Dugan. "Are you anywhere near Millennium Park?"

"Christ, let me think. A mile, maybe. That's where his phone signal's coming from?"

"I don't know yet. But there's some situation with an EDP there, and the description sounds like it could be your brother. Hey, careful!" I had pulled away from the curb too fast. He could hear the angry horn that blared at me. "Won't do him any good if you're in a wreck."

"I know. Thanks."

EDP was police shorthand for "emotionally disturbed person." They usually attracted official attention only when they were seen as a threat, a disturbance that required action. I switched phones, forcing my voice to sound calmer than I felt. "Hey, Martin, guess what? I think I know where you are. Is it a park? Tall buildings all around, and a . . . a silver thing that looks like a giant jelly bean?" He hummed uncertainly. "Two lit-up walls with big faces on them?"

"Ah!"

"Sit still. I'll be there soon."

I dropped the phone into my lap and dodged cars and red lights until I got to Michigan Avenue, where a uniformed officer with a flashlight was trying to redirect traffic. Her whistle shrieked as I ignored her gestures and plowed past her, crossing the avenue to pull up beside a cluster of cruisers. Their light bars made frantic neon zigzags across the reflective surface of the silver sculpture shaped like a bean. People were being herded by police toward the northern end of the park. Their excited voices sounded like the buzz of a party or an audience waiting for the show to begin.

"Whoa, lady!" Someone grabbed my arm. "Can't go over there."

"That EDP's my brother."

"Oh, yeah? Well—"

"Let me through. He's not dangerous. I can calm him down."

I tried to pull away, but he kept my arm in a tight grip. "Just hold on a minute while I check—ow, fuck!" I stomped on his instep hard enough to make him lose his grip, then ran.

Martin was sitting on the grass in a pool of light under a street-lamp, bobbing back and forth. His humming had turned into a kind of keening howl, a stress reaction I hadn't seen from him in years. Police were sheltering behind one of the three squad cars that had been pulled up onto the grass. Two cops had guns trained on him over the roof of the cruisers. "Can't tell for sure," a cop was saying into the radio on his shoulder. "He's holding something."

"It's a goddamn cell phone," I said as I passed him. I slowed to a walk and went up to sit beside Martin on the grass. He reeked of alcohol and his shirt was torn, but I couldn't see any blood or bruises. I gently detached the phone from his hands, held it up so the police could see it, and tossed it on the grass. He rocked and wailed as I talked to him quietly, hoping that sooner or later my presence would penetrate through the terror that was scrambling his perceptions of the world around him. The enormous faces projected on the fifty-foot-high glass sculpture nearby raised their giant eyebrows and smiled as police radios crackled around us.

H ow's he doing?" Jim whispered from the doorway.

"Sleeping."

"Something *you* should be doing."

"I'll sack out on his couch pretty soon." It had taken hours to get Martin home. I'd had to talk to the police, to medics, to doctors who wanted to put my brother on a seventy-two-hour hold in a locked ward. Fatigue was stuffing my brain with cotton, but my nerves were still buzzing from the strain of keeping my temper.

Jim showed me a pizza box. "Hungry?"

"Starved." I joined him in the hall, leaving the door to Martin's apartment half-open. There was a shabby lounge in this corner of the building, with a cast-off love seat and armchair, a coffee table holding tattered issues of *Physics Today* and *New Scientist*. "How'd you find a pizzeria open this late?"

"It's leftovers from the search." Jim set a six-pack of ginger ale beside the pizza box. He looked ready to drop himself, his face lined and weary.

"Mmm, it's delicious," I mumbled through a mouthful, suddenly ravenous. "Help yourself."

"Already had plenty. Search parties always consume more calories than they burn."

"Thanks for organizing it. You know what's weird? I was so careful to plan everything out in case something happened to me. Never even thought about how I'd handle it if something happened to Martin." I popped open a can of ginger ale. "Not well, if tonight's anything to go on."

"I heard you chewed Fiske out."

"I tried, only the bastard hung up on me."

"You think Martin will ever be able to explain what happened?"

"No, and I don't want to press him on it. You remember when we first moved in with our grandfather, and everyone was telling Golly he should be institutionalized? He was like that tonight, really hard to reach. It would just upset him again, asking questions."

"He's never gotten drunk before, has he?"

"He wasn't drunk. That booze was on his clothes, not on his breath." I had a sudden vivid vision of men laughing as they splashed Martin with whiskey. "Part of their plan. Nobody wants to help a derelict who's acting strange. But they could have gotten him killed." I pictured the tension in the stance of the officers who'd had their weapons drawn, watching intently for one wrong move.

"Who's 'they'?"

"Some pissed-off cops who wanted to play a stupid prank."

"Alton Brinks is still at large. Could have been him."

"If he's as violent as you say, things would have turned out even worse."

"Maybe that was his intention, but your brother managed to escape. His shirt was torn."

"Probably tore it himself. He pulls at his clothes when he's upset." I picked up another slice of pizza, let fatigue lap around me like gentle waves. I closed my eyes for a minute. When I opened them, Jim was studying me, a strange expression on his face. "What?"

"How do you do it? It can't be easy, taking care of someone like your brother year after year."

"You kidding? Martin's the easiest person in the world. He doesn't tell lies, doesn't play mind games. You never have worry you'll hurt his feelings or wonder what he really meant by something he said. Other people are hard to deal with, not him. Except when he gets upset, like tonight. Then . . . you just have to be patient."

"You're a better person than I am."

There was a level of discouragement in his tone that told me things must not be going well with Sophie, but he looked so tired, it didn't seem the right time to ask about it. "Say, whatever happened to Lucas?" I asked instead. I hadn't thought about him for hours.

"He's staying at our place tonight. Worked hard on the search. Nice kid."

"Yeah, he is." I yawned. "Can't believe I forgot all about that suspect I was so hot to interview. The pastor at the New Day Tabernacle said he'd hang on to him for me, but not for this long. I'll check first thing in the morning, but chances are the guy's gone by now." I picked up another slice, wondering if I could stay awake long enough to eat it.

"Anni, I know I encouraged you to take this case, but you already have enough to get Rosa off the hook. Maybe you should back off for now."

"But she's—"

"Thea Adelman can take the issues you've raised about the crime scene to the U.S. attorney right now. It will tear a huge hole in Fiske's investigation, which is becoming a political liability anyway. I still have friends in that office. With the right information in their hands, with a nudge from me, I'm hoping they'll push to drop the charges against Rosa."

"For their own political reasons."

"Nobody wants to prosecute a losing case."

"But I'm so close. Don't you want to know?"

He rubbed his face. "I thought I did. But it's not worth it, not if it puts you at risk. I was so worried we'd find Martin's body tonight."

"You and me both."

"The only reason you and Martin are involved in any of this is because you've been trying to help me find out what happened to my father. But you want to know something? You're the one who taught me what a family should be. Eleven years old, and you'd take on the whole world for your brother." His gaze focused on something far away; then he shook his head. "I was a good son, followed in the old man's footsteps. Even now, those ridiculous hours I was putting in on the CTTF? Still trying to prove something to him. But I could never be the kind of person he was, and it's taken all these years to realize I don't even want to."

"But . . . everything's coming together. You want me to drop it now?"

"Rosa Saenz shouldn't be convicted of a crime she didn't commit, but if my father was shot by one of his informants, someone who was drunk and mixed up and has spent the rest of his life paying for his mistakes . . . I don't know, what kind of justice is served by locking him up now? Besides, this case is getting Sophie all worked up. It's as if she has some receiver in her head that picks up all the energy around it and amplifies it, feeding her mania. It's time I stopped trying to be a good son and tried being a good father instead."

osh Cohen came by in the morning to see how Martin was doing and volunteered to stick around. I had dozed off and on for a couple of hours on the couch, but I was tired enough to take him up on his offer. As I walked to the car, looking forward to my own bed, I phoned the pastor of the New Day Tabernacle. As I'd predicted, my suspect was gone, but not for the reasons I'd expected. An FBI agent had showed up at the door the previous evening, demanding to see him; in spite of his inebriation, Spellman had overheard and escaped out the back.

I drove home, foggy with exhaustion, wondering how Fiske had found out where he was, all of my thoughts fading out before I could finish them. As I started to climb the steps to my flat, the three-legged cat startled me, rocketing down the stairs and brushing past my ankles. He'd been inside my flat, apparently helping himself to the cat food spilled on the floor. Either that or he had been lapping at the puddle of milk.

The front door was open, hanging crookedly on one hinge, the wood splintered and raw. Books and papers were tossed around like giant confetti and the couch had been slashed, stuffing pulled out and sprinkled around the room. The cupboards were open, most of their contents swept out onto the floor, as was the food in the refrigerator. A jar of salsa had been thrown so hard against the wall, it had left a jagged gash, the red sauce dripping from it like a wound. Someone had dipped a towel into the puddle it left on the floor and used it to paint a word across the wall: *traitor*. Under the scrawl, a photograph was pegged to the wall with a kitchen knife—one of me standing proudly in my new CPD uniform between my brother and grandfather. The knife point was stuck through my face.

I searched through the mess in a daze, pausing to wrap a kitchen towel around my left hand when I cut it on some glass. Then I called 911. On impulse, I also called the *Tribune*'s city desk, then went out on the porch to sit on the top step and wait.

Az Abkerian arrived first. He looked up at me as I sat hunched on the top step, my arms wrapped tight around my chest. "You okay?"

"Take a look."

He huffed his way up the steps and poked his head into my flat. "Holy shit," he said reverently, then took a digital camera out of his pocket. He was still taking pictures and asking questions I didn't feel like answering when two uniformed officers arrived, obviously unhappy to find a reporter there. One stayed at the bottom of the steps, muttering apprehensively into his radio, while the other one climbed the stairs. "Sir, you need to leave. We have to preserve the evidence."

Az slipped the camera back into his pocket and patted it. "No problem, I got what I need. But let me ask you a question."

"You need to go, sir." The cop was brawny but young and nervous, his eyes flickering to his partner, who was still on the radio.

Az squinted at his name tag, jotted it down in his notebook. "No comment from Officer Walsh. Got it." He started down the stairs but turned to say, "Sorry about the mess in there, kid." Then he raised his bushy eyebrows. "How long you been on the job, Walsh? So concerned about preserving the crime scene that you don't even check the welfare of the victim?" Az waggled a triumphant finger at me. "Look at that. Blood."

I burrowed my hands farther under my arms to hide the stained kitchen towel. "I cut it on some glass. It's nothing."

"Ma'am, you'd better let us—" The older cop stumped up the stairs, reached out a hand.

"Don't you touch me!"

In the silence that followed, a car door slammed on the street out front and Dugan came loping around the bottom of the steps. "Anni? What happened?"

"Cut her hand," one of the cops told him tersely. "Refusing treatment."

Dugan fixed Az with a look and gestured over his shoulder with his thumb. Emboldened, the two cops hustled the reporter out of the yard. Dugan looked inside my flat, whistled, then sat beside me. "Jerks."

"Tough luck you caught it. Going to be a political headache."

"Not my headache, though. I was just in my car, heard your address come across the radio. You get any sleep last night?"

"Not really."

"How's your brother doing?"

"He'll be okay."

"How bad's the hand? Can I take a look?"

I thought about it, then unfolded my arms from around my chest. "I was looking for this." I showed him the picture of my mother, stained along one edge with some of the liquid spilled on the floor, the faded colors starting to bleed together. I'd been holding it so tightly, it was crumpled.

The detective assigned to the break-in arrived. He asked a few questions, confirmed I didn't want medical attention, and let me go. I was stumbling with exhaustion, so I didn't protest when Dugan picked up my backpack and said he'd drive. I climbed into his Jeep and he set the backpack on the floor by my feet. "What's in there, bricks?"

"Just a laptop and some clothes. I've been out of town."

"Where to?"

I didn't know how to answer, since I was having trouble sorting through a sluggish muddle of thoughts. Martin needed to get back to his routine, I couldn't show up at his apartment like this, and the Tilquists had their hands full with Sophie. As Dugan waited patiently for an answer, a car pulled up beside the CPD cruiser and double-parked. Like clowns at the circus, four men in suits climbed out. Fiske spotted me and came over to the Jeep. Dugan showed him his teeth in something that wasn't really a smile. "What brings the feds here?"

"Someone we're keeping tabs on might be involved, a violent of-fender who's got a thing about Ms. Koskinen. We on for tomorrow?"

"That's up to my boss."

Fiske leaned down to peer past Dugan at me. "You don't look so good. Up all night with your brother, I suppose."

"In fact, we're just leaving," Dugan said.

Fiske gave us a knowing smile, patted the window frame, stepped away from the car, and Dugan pulled out. I couldn't tell if his coming within an inch of clipping Fiske's car was intentional or not. He almost clipped another one when he turned a corner.

"What's tomorrow?" I asked.

"I got assigned to some bullshit task force, preparing for the demonstration tomorrow night. I think my mom set me up. She has connections everywhere."

We were crossing the Ship Canal before I thought to ask Dugan where we going. He had a spare room, he told me. Nothing fancy, but at least I could get some sleep. That sounded like such a good idea, I dozed off.

I jerked awake when he pulled into a garage behind his aunt's Hyde Park house. He ushered me out of the garage and onto a flagged path that wound through masses of flowers filling the fenced yard. With morning sunlight catching in the blossoms and the drowsy buzz of insects, it felt like a sanctuary. "Your aunt's some gardener."

"Not her. She hates getting dirt under her fingernails. She lets me mess around back here."

"You did this? It's like something from a magazine."

"Yeah, *Weeds Weekly*. Turning into a jungle out here."

There was an Adirondack chair in the shade of a small tree that had delicate red leaves, the branches reaching down to create a sheltered spot. I could see Dugan sitting there, drinking a cold beer after work, relaxing in a place where things were growing instead of dying. "I wonder if I could do something with my backyard. Not like this, just some flowers."

"Sure you could. Put in a raised bed along the fence, some perennials. With that big walnut, you have a lot of shade, but there's stuff that would work."

"A walnut tree. Is that what it is?"

He glanced back at me, making a shocked and appalled face at my ignorance. We went down some stone steps and into his basement flat, which was dim and cool and green. He had me sit in an easy chair while he hastily scooped up some dishes and empty glasses. Then he came back with antiseptic wipes and bandages. "You could take that to a restorer," he said as he cleaned the cut on my hand, nodding toward the picture I still clutched in my right hand. "My aunt had some family photos redone. Amazing what they were able to do."

I set the photo on the table beside the chair. "It's not important. I don't even know why I wanted to find it so badly. Wasn't thinking straight."

"Is that your mom? She looks young."

"She was only eighteen when she left us." He examined the cut as I spoke, wiped it again. "Literally. Sat us down on a bench in Union Station with a box of powdered doughnuts and a Coke, told us to be

good, and walked away. We were so good, it took hours before someone finally began to wonder what the hell two little kids were doing at
a train station in the middle of the night."

He pressed cotton against the seeping blood. "That must have
been scary. Hold this." He unwrapped a Band-Aid.

"I was too young to know what was going on. Martin's the one
who remembers." I lifted the cotton and he covered the cut with the
bandage. "Always remembered to be good, too. Not me. I was worried they'd send him away to wherever they put kids like him, so I'd
make trouble to get them to pay attention to me instead."

"Did it work?"

"Sort of. We didn't get separated, but we moved a lot, until we went
to live with my grandfather. I mean, the man we called our grandfather." I wondered if that photo with a knife stuck through it could be
restored. I didn't have many pictures of the three of us together.

"He must have been quite a guy."

"He was." I drifted away for a moment, thinking about the com-
fort of his tweedy, tobacco-scented hugs. "You don't smoke, do you?"
I asked Dugan suddenly.

"No."

I sighed. "Neither do I."

"Spare room is through there." He pointed. "Bathroom's down the
hall. I'll be out back if you need anything. Get some rest."

When I woke, I was confused about where I was until I took in
the bookcases and the cluttered desk and remembered it was
Dugan's guest room, the one that doubled as his study. I
checked my watch. Nearly six hours had passed. For a few minutes, I
lay there, watching sunlight dapple the leaves outside the window,
thinking.

It couldn't be a coincidence that just as I was about to connect with Spellman, my brother went missing. How had Fiske intercepted that phone call from the pastor telling me where the homeless man was? I thought I'd been so careful. Somehow, though, he'd found out and set up a distraction to keep me occupied, using cops all too happy to give me trouble. Apparently, after they left my brother off downtown, confused and disoriented, they'd gone to my house to have some more fun. The CPD brass would be eager to embrace the theory that a hotheaded white supremacist was responsible, but the evidence was against it. At least three different sets of shoes had tracked through the sticky mess on the floor. Besides, Alton Brinks might have called me a lot of things, but not traitor.

I thought about the papers that had been tossed around the flat, wondering if Fiske had made anything of them. Luckily, I had the most complete set of notes with me, on my laptop. I sat up and reached for the backpack I'd set beside the bed.

It was gone.

There were voices coming from outside. Dugan was yanking up weeds and tossing them in a pile while a man who was unmistakably a cop lounged in the Adirondack chair with a can of beer. "Hey, Anni. You remember—" Dugan started to say.

"Where's my stuff?"

He stared, taken aback by my abruptness. "I heard your phone ringing. I was afraid it would wake you up, so I moved your bags into the living room. Sorry if—"

"It's okay, but . . . I better check my messages."

"It's all on the couch."

I went inside, dug both phones out of my bag. No messages on the older phone, whose number was known to only a small handful of people. I switched it off. Only one message on the new one—from Sophie, her voice anxious and rambling. Rosa hadn't called; she was so worried. Her words tumbled together, nearly incoherent. I couldn't deal with it now. Instead, I made a couple of quick phone calls, then slipped the phone back into my bag.

I'd slept for six hours. Dugan would have had plenty of time to prowl through my computer files, download my notes, even copy the whole hard drive, browser cache and all. I unzipped the backpack, slipped my palm against the laptop to see if it was still warm.

He stood in the doorway watching me, his lanky shape dark against the sun outside. "Everything all right?"

"I don't know." I drew my hand out. His face was in shadow; I couldn't make out his expression. "I have to get going."

"Okay, I'll just wash my hands—"

"I called for a cab."

"Call them back and cancel it."

"I already put you out enough. Besides, you have a friend—"

"Martinez? He's here to see you."

"Me?"

"About one of his cases."

I hoisted the backpack, slung my purse over my shoulder, and went out into the yard. The man raised his can in a salute. "Paul Martinez. Remember me? You used to date Terry O'Neill, right? We met at a party once."

"I have a cab coming in a few minutes. What do you need?"

"You ready for another beer?" Dugan asked Martinez.

"Sure, what the hell." Dugan disappeared inside. Martinez tapped his empty can against the broad arm of the Adirondack chair, studying me. "This won't take long. Got a stiff on my hands. Homeless guy."

Shit. I sank down on one of the folding chairs Dugan had set out. "A skinny old alcoholic?"

"A skinny young heroin addict." Martinez looked so relaxed in his chair, he appeared half-asleep, but through those drowsy eyes he was watching me closely.

"Tyler."

"Looks like your typical overdose, but his father's making a stink. He's a Baptist preacher downstate, made enough campaign contributions, he thinks he has pull in Springfield. Been demanding a thorough investigation. He was under the impression his kid was working for the police."

"Tyler was a C.I. Not mine, though." I felt a pang of regret. I didn't like Tyler, but dying on the street with a needle in your arm was a sad way to go.

"What I'm wondering is how your prints got all over his gear."

So that was it. "Last Sunday, around eight in the morning, I tried to talk to him, took his stash to get his attention. Didn't work, though. He was too strung out to be coherent."

"How strung out?"

"Not enough to OD. He had maybe half an ounce in his possession when I talked to him, said it was all he had left."

"White?"

"Brown. Not tar, though. Powder."

"Why did you want to talk to him?"

"I'm sure you know what case I'm working. I thought the guy might know something. When did he die?"

Martinez tapped his can against the armrest again, sending himself a message in Morse code. "Tuesday," he said at last. "With about a hundred bucks' worth of skag still in his pocket. China white, twenty-five percent pure, laced with fentanyl. Guess he got a little carried away when he had another payday. Wonder who he's been selling his information to lately?"

I felt a slow fuse of anger sizzling inside. "I'd check with Special Agent Fiske at the FBI field office."

Martinez rubbed his mouth. "Whoa," he murmured to himself.

Dugan came out, handed a beer to Martinez, pulled a ring of keys from his pocket. "Your cab's here. I'll let you out the front." I followed him around the side of the house, waited as he unlocked a wrought-iron gate. "Look, moving your stuff while you were asleep, I'm sorry if . . ."

"Don't worry about it."

He followed me to the cab, stood awkwardly beside it. "Can I call you sometime?"

I couldn't trust him. There were too many things he didn't tell me, too many unanswered questions prickling under my skin, warning me to be careful. I slung my bags in the cab and turned to look at him. "You have my number."

I thought there might be a trace of guilt on his face; either that or the smug satisfaction that he'd gotten away with it, some sign of what was going on with him. But all I got as he pushed the door shut was his usual cockeyed grin, as if it was all one big joke.

collected my Corolla and drove to Thea Adelman's house in Bucktown to outline everything I had so far. If my informants were going to start dying on me, I wanted to be sure everything I'd learned so far was on record. Harvey took notes as Thea quizzed me, going over every detail until she had reduced it to its elements. Like Jim, she advised me to forget about finding Spellman while she negotiated with the U.S. attorney's office. She had received promising signals from a source in the office that a faction would press to drop the charges against her client. It wasn't a sure thing, and discussions were at a delicate stage. She didn't want anything jeopardizing it.

I understood. Her client was her only concern. But I had other worries. Whatever was going on with the prosecutors, someone inside the FBI had gone looking for Spellman, the only man who knew what really had happened in that basement thirty-five years ago. Spellman had managed to slip away, but after Tyler's convenient overdose, I couldn't help feeling the man who told ghost stories was the next one who might be silenced.

After leaving the Adelman's house, I took a brief break to drive up to Stony Cliff and eat dinner with Martin. He was still so tense, he had to put his fork down to go through a series of repetitive movements twice while we ate, but he'd come a long way from the state he'd been in the previous night. I walked him to his apartment, where he and Josh were planning a marathon viewing of some bootleg copies of *Dr. Who*. Then I headed back to the city.

I needed to find Spellman. But first I had to disappear.

I parked the Corolla in the lot of a big drugstore off Milwaukee and bought supplies, then crossed the street to a coffee shop, where I ordered a triple espresso and used their toilet to trim my hair short and dye it a rusty henna color. I worked what was left of it into punky spikes with gel. It looked awful, but at least it didn't look like me. Then I slipped out the back, used a circuitous route to the Damen El station, rode out to O'Hare, and rented a small nondescript car. For the next four hours, I connected with old informants while watching over my shoulder for police.

The call finally came. A hooker named Atlanta, who had sometimes been reliable in the past, said she knew where Casper was, could take me to him. We rendezvoused at an underpass under the Green Line tracks of the El, where she greeted me like a long-lost friend, not surprising, given how much I had promised to pay for her information. "What you do to your hair, girl?"

"The package said it would wash out."

"You better hope."

I sent her into a nearby corner store to buy a bottle of fortified wine and cigarettes. Then she led me across a wasteland of vacant land between the El and the fenced-off railway lines. It was dark, remote from the nearest streetlight. Atlanta picked her way carefully, tottering on her stacked heels and cursing under her breath. We were angling toward a crumbling maze of knee-high walls showing through weeds and brush, the remains of an apartment building that had burned to its foundations some time ago. As we approached, cats sprang out of the undergrowth and scurried away, slinking low to the ground. She looked over a wall at a sack of garbage and a pile of rags. "Yo, Casper. Got you some wine, baby."

The rags stirred, then scrabbled away from us, making a startled cry, a hand reaching out to snatch at the plastic bags sitting nearby. Atlanta chanted comforting words in molasses tones. "No, no, no, it's okay, sugar. She ain't the police; she's a friend of mine. She just want to hear them crazy stories you tell. Now don't go running off, baby, 'cause I promised, all right?"

He fetched up against a corner, wedged in, as if he wanted to dissolve into the rubble and disappear. I stepped over a wall into the maze, squatted down to be at his level, and held out the pack of cigarettes along with a book of matches. After a moment's hesitation, he reached out, snatched them out of my hand. "She got wine for you, too, but you got to tell your stories first." Atlanta sounded bored all of a sudden. "Crazy old fucker. We done? 'Cause I gotta go see somebody." She took folded bills from me and tucked them demurely into her top before making her way across the wasteland back to the street, muttering complaints about the uneven ground as she sashayed away. Silence settled around us. "They say you see ghosts," I said.

He didn't respond. A block away, an El train came rattling down the elevated tracks, sparks spitting down from the rails. I waited, forcing my breathing to relax, my pulse to slow. He was as feral as those cats; I didn't want to frighten him. But finally I heard the familiar rustle of a cigarette package being opened. "Don't see 'em," he said finally, his voice rusty. "I hear 'em." He scratched a match to life. Shadows carved deep hollows in his cheeks as he pulled on the cigarette, his pale eyes closing in pleasure, thin gray hair falling around his gaunt face. Then he flicked the match away and we were in darkness again, only the ember of his cigarette glowing orange to mark his place. "Hear 'em singing, nights like this."

"What does it sound like?"

He made a humming sound, a single warbling note that faded away. "It's the death song. They're going to the scaffold."

It triggered the memory of something I'd heard in the dark in a ruined building in another city. "The Sioux Uprising. You know all about it."

"Little Crow's war. The people were starving, see, so they had to fight back. Army came, and thirty-eight were hanged, all on one scaffold." The ember flared as he drew again. "Day after Christmas."

"There was another man who died the day after Christmas. Lying in a basement."

"They cut them down and buried them in the riverbank," he said, as if I hadn't spoken, his voice almost a chant, a story worn smooth with use. "And the doctors came in the night, dug them up, and laid their bodies out on the tallest roofs of the town for the crows to pick clean. That's what happened. That's real history."

"Why did they do that?"

He chuckled. "Wanted them bones. String them together with wire, hang them in their offices. Men of science. They'd say to their patients, 'Let me show you, here, on my skeleton. It's all right. Don't be afraid. We call him John.' " He hummed to himself again, a note that rose and fell, then faded away, his head bowed as if he was asleep or in a trance. "Why I don't go to no doctors," he muttered to himself.

"The other dead man, lying on a dirt floor. Some jars fell off the shelf and broke, remember?"

"Peaches. When you gonna give me that wine?"

"Soon. You went there that night to meet him, didn't you?"

"They put them in boxcars," he said, his voice rising again, dreamy. "Sent the women and children out on the prairie, nothing to keep them warm. The men, they were sent off to prison. Where I'd go, if I told. That's what they said."

"Who said?"

"You know who." He said it without rancor, just secret knowledge we shared. "Them preserves smelled sweet, but the air was burned, like this." He raised his face and sniffed. For a moment, I thought

I smelled cordite, then realized it was rising from the soil, the acrid smell of ashes left from the fire that had razed this building to its bare foundations long ago.

"You tell people about the thirty-eight Indians who were hanged."

"I have to. Nobody knows about it. Like it never happened."

"You're the only one who knows the truth about what happened in that basement the day after Christmas. They think Verna did it."

"They do not, the lying bastards." He shifted in the dark, growing agitated. "I told 'em what happened. But they went after her instead, and she had to run away. Gone all those years, and then she came back. People said she could cure you with her touch. Only I got drunk and told that boy, and now he's dead. She won't never forgive me now."

"Tell me what happened, so we can make it right."

"You can't make it right. I got them all killed, and that boy, too. Nobody can forgive me now. 'Cept maybe a priest."

"I know a priest."

We sat in the weedy foundations for another hour, hearing nothing except occasional voices calling from the street, the rumble of freight trains on the far side of the embankment, the rattle of the El, sometimes a siren in the distance. When I saw someone moving toward us, I tensed and rehearsed escape routes, until I recognized the peculiar rhythm, rising and falling, lopsided from his limp. He paused, a lonely shape in the gloom. "Over here," I hissed. Pete had wandered to the far corner of the ruin, where he crouched against a wall, mumbling to himself.

"Sorry it took so long," Father Sikora said, his voice grating with pain. "Didn't want to take the car in case I was followed."

"He was getting the shakes. I let him have some wine."

"How drunk is he?"

"Not drunk. Just . . . confused. He says he grew up Catholic, wants to make his confession."

"It's called 'reconciliation' now." The priest reached into his pocket and unrolled a stole, put it around his neck. "You understand, I won't be able to tell you—"

"I know. It doesn't matter, I just . . . He's upset, convinced he'll go to hell if he isn't forgiven."

"Where is he?"

I pointed and he waved me away, limped over to the huddled shape to sit on one of the crumbled walls close by. "I don't remember what I'm supposed to say," I heard Pete wail, but the priest murmured reassuringly. I went to the opposite end of the ruin and sat with my back against one of the walls, where I could watch approaches from three sides. The El had shut down for the night, no more trains rumbling overhead. The murmur of their voices was peaceful, making me think for a moment we could be in the ruins of an ancient abbey. The sky overhead had a reddish tinge to it. If there were stars up there, they were hidden.

But then I heard a helicopter approaching. I called out a warning. It came quickly, the sound of rotors chopping the air, a powerful beam of light probing from overhead, sweeping across the ground until it found me. An unmarked sedan roared up the street and jumped the curb, followed by cruisers, their light bars flashing. Cops jumped out to chase me as I zigzagged away, hoping to draw their attention as red and blue lights pulsed across the wasteland. One of my pursuers fell heavily with a curse; another got close enough to slam my shoulder with his baton. A hand grabbed my shirt; an arm circled my neck. The helicopter's searchlight scorched the ground, turning everything white as I fought and kicked. Something ripped open inside, letting loose the fear and fury of an angry child. "Jesus Christ! She bit me, the bitch!" A blow from a fist left my head ringing.

The priest called out over the clamor. "I absolve you in the name of the Father—" But his voice was cut off as he was surrounded by a scrum of uniforms. They tumbled to the ground in a struggling mass, and I was down, too, a knee pressed into my back, dirt grating between my teeth as my arms were wrenched back, cuffs clicked over my wrists.

T his is exactly what I was afraid of." Thea Adelman looked me up and down, her calm tone a reproach. "Any hope we had of reaching an agreement is over."

Harvey shrugged. "Though to be honest . . ."

"There never was much hope. Reason is in short supply in the prosecutor's office these days. Still, getting charged with—how many offenses was it?"

"Aggravated assault, obstruction, resisting arrest, trespassing . . ." Harvey counted them off on his fingers, sounding almost proud of me. "Pretty much everything they could come up with." I'd spent hours being questioned by Fiske and other agents, then a few hours more trying to sleep on a bench in the federal lockup before Harvey Adelman came to take me through a bond hearing, pulled off on a Sunday afternoon only because someone influential called in favors with a judge. My guess was that Jim'd had a hand in it. I was out on bail, but Father Sikora's release had been revoked, a situation Thea clearly blamed on me. As for Pete Spellman, he somehow had managed to slip away, vanishing as thoroughly as one of his ghosts.

"Someone will take you to a doctor," Thea announced. She looked around the hallway to select a volunteer from among the half a dozen lawyers and activists who were involved with Father Sikora's case and preparing for the demonstration later in the evening.

My arm was scraped, one cheek was turning purple with bruises, and a molar felt loose when I probed it with my tongue. But I had been in too many small rooms lately; I couldn't do it anymore. "That's okay. It looks worse than it feels."

"How it feels is irrelevant," she snapped. "Documentation of police misconduct could be useful at the prelim."

"There wasn't any misconduct. I gave as good as I got."

She sighed. "We don't have time for this," she said to Harvey.

One of the lawyers broke in. "There's a crowd of reporters outside. Think we should make a statement?"

Another one, thumbing a BlackBerry, made a whoop. "Fox just went with the conspiracy theory." I'd picked up enough fragments while waiting for the bond hearing to guess what he was talking about. Someone official but unnamed had leaked a cynical rumor that Father Sikora was being questioned about his involvement in Latin American radical movements that were hostile to the United States. "They'll be linking him to Al Qaeda next."

"Already did." Another young technophile held out his phone. "Check out this blog. All part of the global terrorist movement trying to destroy Western values."

"We need to say something," Harvey said to his wife.

"But we have to frame it carefully." She frowned, outlining it in her head. "Our key points should be that we aren't the only ones who are challenging Fiske's investigation. Officials within the U.S. attorney's office are raising questions. Tilquist's own son is even opposed to the direction it's going. We need to tell people that Father Sikora was arrested in the midst of administering a sacrament. And we have evidence that will exonerate Rosa Saenz. There's been a cover-up for the past thirty-five years—only we need another word. *Cover-up* is too much of a cliché."

"You're not going mention Spellman by name, are you?" I asked.

Thea turned and gave me a clinical look, reminding me of Fiske's expression when he'd suggested I be given a psych evaluation: You're delusional, Koskinen, inventing conspiracies, behaving aggressively. You've gone over the edge. You should get some help. "It appears your theory was wrong," Thea said. "The sanctity of the confessional doesn't extend to what wasn't said. Whatever Spellman confessed to, Father Sikora tells me it didn't include murdering Arne Tilquist."

She returned to the more important business of crafting a message, and I drifted to a bench along the wall, feeling suddenly as disoriented as when I'd taken the blow to the side of my head. If Spellman was a witness, not the killer, the FBI wanted him silenced because he knew Rosa was innocent. And because he knew who was really guilty. The autopsy report told me the shot was close-up, from someone Arne knew and trusted. But maybe it hadn't been an impulsive act. Maybe it had been a cold-blooded execution, covered up by the people who'd done it. The nameless ex-FBI agent in Minneapolis had told me I didn't know what I was getting into, that I should leave it buried. Had he given me any clues about what had really happened? I wanted to look at the notes I had taken after our meeting that night, see if I could tell where I'd gone wrong, but they were on my computer in the trunk of a rental car parked on the West Side, no doubt impounded by now. I leaned my head back against the wall and closed my eyes, realizing what that meant. They had access to everything. They'd retrace all my steps, harass and intimidate every witness. . . .

"You okay?" Harvey peered down at me, concerned.

"I think I made a huge mistake."

"They weren't going to dismiss those charges anyway. You should go home, get some rest."

"I can't go home."

Harvey gave me a puzzled half smile, as if I'd made an obscure literary reference that didn't fit the situation, then drifted back to the strategizing session. I took out my phone, returned to me a few minutes ago in a bag, along with my keys, wallet, and some spare change.

I ignored the messages winking at me and punched in the Tilquists' number. It was the closest place to home I could think of.

"Anni? Where've you been?" Nancy's voice was taut as a wire about to snap. "I must have left ten messages."

"I got arrested last night."

My words apparently didn't register. "Jim's not answering his phone, either. I finally called the police. They're here now, but they say they can't do anything."

"The police? What's going on?"

"It's Sophie." Whatever grip Nancy had on herself was slipping. "I don't know what to do. Can you come? Right now?"

"I'm on my way," I told her.

TWENTY-TWO

S
he's gone." Nancy said it dully, as if she had cracked and her emotions had leaked out, leaving her empty inside. Lucy snuggled up against her on the couch, pleating the cloth of her mother's shirttail with deep concentration, as if it was important to get it just right. It had taken me nearly an hour to fight my way through a scrum of curious reporters, ride the El to the Damen station to retrieve my car, and drive up to Stony Cliff. "What happened to you?" she added as my bruised face registered.

"It's a long story."

Alice sat at the other end of the couch, her arms wrapped around her legs, chin on her knees. "Your hair looks awful."

"I know. It's supposed to wash out. Nancy, can I get you something?" Her face was pale, her eyes blank. Maybe a shot of whiskey would help.

"I'd kill for a cup of tea."

"I'll put the kettle on." Alice unfolded her legs and stood up. "Don't know if I can find a cup, though. Sophie broke everything she could get her hands on."

"She got violent?" I asked Nancy after Alice stalked out. I was used to Sophie being verbally abusive, reckless, delusional—but not physically aggressive.

"After the police left. She was furious I'd called them, though they didn't do anything. They said she hadn't violated any laws, and they couldn't take her to a hospital against her will. It's so stupid. It was perfectly obvious she needed help."

Nancy was frustrated, but we both knew from past experience that it was legally impossible to force treatment on a person who was merely psychotic and delusional. The police could act only if someone had broken a law or seemed to pose an immediate threat to herself or others. Driving parents insane with worry didn't count.

I peeked into the kitchen. It looked like mine, full of broken crockery and overturned chairs. Alice was filling the kettle at the sink, smudging tears away with the heel of her hand. "See what she did?"

"Must shave been really scary."

Alice thumped the kettle on the stove without answering.

I went back to the living room and walked Nancy through it. Sophie had been growing more manic over the past two days, talking nonstop and staying awake all night, but whenever the possibility of seeing her doctor was raised, she wouldn't consider it. There was nothing wrong with her, she insisted. And though obviously something was very wrong, she was lucid enough, just running on a faster speed than the rest of the world.

"But that changed. After Jim left for an emergency meeting, all of Sophie's energy morphed into full-blown delusional paranoia. Her father's departure was a sign that things were on the move. Portents began to link together, revealing a pattern that put her in the center of a web of conspiracy, her parents in league with the government, and all of them against her. And as her anxiety rose, so did her sense of her own importance. She was the only one who knew what was going on, the only one who could put an end to it, so long as she evaded capture to do what she had to do. What exactly that might be seemed as unclear to Sophie as to everyone else. Alice, who had managed to find mugs for all of us, joined the conversation, adding dry details from time to time, like Sophie insisting the television be tuned to CNN because Wolf Blitzer was giving out encoded messages. Or that Rosa Saenz was sending her instructions on a disposable cell phone with a dead battery.

Nancy snatched up the phone beside her when it rang, and after a anxious greeting her temper boiled over. "Where the *hell* have you been? She's gone right off the rails, and you won't even answer your bloody mobile, you selfish bastard!" She dissolved into jagged, hic-cupping sobs. I took the phone from her and explained to Jim what had been going on. Nancy struggled to recover her composure and shamefacedly comforted Lucy, who was upset by all the shouting. Alice just glowered, fed up with everything and everyone.

Jim rushed in twenty minutes later and looked helplessly at his wife. "I should have been here."

Tears started to roll down Nancy's cheeks and she waved a hand, signaling her inability to speak. Then she got up and went to him and he folded her in his arms, murmuring broken apologies. "I'm so sorry. I didn't mean . . . We'll find her. I promise."

Alice watched them with her face scrunched up, her mouth tight and trembling. Jim reached out to include her in his embrace, but she slapped his arm away. "I don't want you to find her. I hate her. I wish she was dead."

She turned and ran into the kitchen. Nancy followed. We heard her murmuring, Alice's voice interrupting, raging with tearful fury, dissolving into a wail of guilt. "I didn't mean it!"

Jim closed his eyes. He looked as if something was being gouged and twisted deep inside his chest, but he steeled himself, took a breath, and sat down to pull Lucy into his lap so he could explain in simple terms something none of them could ever really understand.

Nancy briskly recruited the girls to help clean up the mess in the kitchen while Jim and I planned the search. He phoned in a missing person's report, even though it wouldn't get any attention now, with police on double shifts to cover the demonstration. We started mak-ing a list of places to look, squats and cemeteries and parks where I'd found her before. Then I told him how Sophie had helped Rosa hide out, first in the warehouse on Bubbly Creek, then the old mansion.

"And you didn't you tell me?"

"Jim, I couldn't. You would have had to take Rosa into custody, and Sophie would never have forgiven either of us. I thought I could handle—"

He cut me off with a wave of his hand. "I get it. Where else?"

We finished the list. He said he would check them out, acting merely as a spotter, given the sinister role he played in Sophie's conspiracy fantasies. If he saw her, he would call me to handle the delicate work of talking her into going to the hospital.

While he did that, I would go to the Vigil for Truth demonstration, where she was most likely headed. Afterward, I would make the rounds of coffeehouses, universities, activist organizations, and anywhere else where she might be plugging into the political scene, feeding off the excitement. Those places were all off-limits to Jim; he was a representative of the government that was persecuting Rosa Saenz and Father Sikora. His presence would only legitimize his daughter's fear and encourage others to help her hide from us.

"Though technically I'm not a government agent anymore," he said as an afterthought. I handed in my badge and gun a couple of hours ago. It's not official yet, the special agent in charge has to sign off on it. But I'm done."

"Oh, Jim . . . why?"

He gave me a humorless grin. "What's that phrase people use when they're in disgrace? I want to spend more time with my family."

"That's bullshit. You're not in disgrace."

"Want to bet? It's true anyway—I need to be with my family until we figure out how to deal with Sophie. It's tearing us apart."

left my car in the Wicker Park neighborhood and rode the Blue Line to the Loop. The train was unusually crowded for a Sunday evening, an uneasy mixture of blacks and Latinos in their Sunday best and trendy youngsters wearing ragged clothes, even though they could afford to pay fifteen hundred a month to rent lofts as they colonized the West Side. The sidewalks downtown were choked with people carrying banners and signs and huge papier-mâché puppets. Though the city had denied a permit to march, insisting traffic must not be disrupted, motorists were being directed away from the city center as squad cars, emergency vehicles, and vans ready to transport arrestees filled the streets.

I was swept toward Federal Plaza in an elbow-to-elbow crowd moving like a slow but strong current. It will be impossible to find Sophie in this crush, I thought, and I had to suppress a rising sense of panic as the crowd grew denser, fed by tributary side streets, all heading toward the Federal Building. The press of humanity and its potential for chaos made me want to turn and fight my way out. But I couldn't give in to the impulse. I had to find Sophie, and there was no doubt in my mind she was somewhere in the crowd.

I tried to imagine how she would react to the protest in her current state of mind. There was something compelling about being part of a mass of people, all committed to the same cause, all fueled by the same anger. She would be buoyed up, exhilarated by the almost spiritual sense of solidarity and fervor, every delusional thought she'd had in the past hours confirmed and fed by the enthusiasm in the air. The grim ranks of helmeted riot police, their duty belts loaded with batons and pepper spray, Tasers and guns, would only confirm her conviction that there were dark forces arrayed against her in some vast Manichaean struggle. I wasn't suffering from her biochemical imbalance, but even I couldn't help wondering if the cops who'd tormented my brother and trashed my flat weren't watching me from behind those visors.

Because the flow moving toward the plaza was constricted by barriers, the rally was under way before we got there. A political preacher was leading the faithful in call and response. I couldn't make out the words; they were distorted, echoing against the surrounding sky-scrapers. As I got closer, peering through gaps in the line of police surrounding the square, I caught a glimpse of faces illuminated by candles, rapt and intense, and felt the surge of unity among them as protesters chanted together. There was a kind of reckless joy in the air, mingled with impassioned seriousness.

I pulled myself up onto the trim of a building and climbed precariously onto a window ledge so I could scan the crowd for Sophie, but it was hopeless. Too many people, thousands of them, surrounded by hundreds of police in riot gear.

High over the crowd, an elaborate puppet of J. Edgar Hoover in a floral dress waved pudgy papier-mâché hands over the crowd, the bald dome and jowls an unmistakable likeness, even though a Hitler mustache had been added. Nearby, an bedspread-size appliquéd banner depicting Rosa as the Virgin of Guadalupe was held up high, making the plaza look like a Chicago *zócalo* hosting a religious festival. Thousands of candles were reflected in the obsidian glass of the Federal Building, which loomed above, a gleaming black monolith of power. Calder's *Flamingo* seemed incongruous beside it, like a gigantic water bird on skinny legs sheltering the mass of protesters that crowded under its legs. I wondered if any of the humming energy of the crowd reached the floor of the Dirksen Building, where Father Sikora was locked up.

More speeches were made, including a measured yet impassioned address by Thea Adelman. She hit on all the strategic talking points, skillfully evoking the plight of indigenous peoples worldwide, the sordid past of FBI misconduct, and the Orwellian implications of current policies, managing to get across the idea there was a cover-up going on without actually saying so. The mother of one of the black teens who had been killed in a police-involved shooting a few weeks earlier made a tearful tribute to her son, pleading for peace and justice. An immigrant rights activist spoke of Father Sikora's gift for serving both an aging Polish community and an influx of Latino res-

idents in a hardscrabble West Side parish. Before the speeches came
to an end, I climbed down from my perch and started to work my
way to the edge of the crowd. My best guess was that Sophie would
head to St. Larry's, though she might simply be carried wherever the
crowd went, like a twig in a torrent.

As the official program ended, people began to flow out of the
plaza. The stairs to El stations were blocked with too many bodies
trying to squeeze onto the cast-iron steps at once. Uniformed police
were trying to keep the streets open, but the weight of the crowd
pushed wooden barricades aside. In spite of warnings delivered over a
bullhorn, the energy of the crowd was giddy and triumphant as it
surged into the street, banners and gesticulating puppets wobbling
over protestors' heads.

I headed toward the river on foot. Public transportation was
jammed, and traffic was gridlocked. I figured that maybe once I got
away from the Loop, I'd be able to flag down a cab, but it was beginning to look as if I would have to walk the three or four miles to St.
Larry's. The mood began to sour as the news spread through the
crowd that the police were making mass arrests. Cruisers filled the
streets as helicopters hovered overhead. They belonged to news oper-
ations, not law enforcement, but the warlike sound of rotors beating
in the sky added to the crowd's sense of being under attack. As I
crossed the Randolph Street bridge, word passed from one person to
another that an impromptu and unauthorized protest was forming up
at the Haymarket Memorial. I assumed Sophie might head there if
she heard the rumor. But I couldn't afford to be arrested again, not
while she was still loose in the city in a psychotic state. I called Jim
and told him I was heading to St. Larry's. He told me a contact of his
would be watching out for Sophie's name as arrests were processed,
but over two hundred protestors had already been taken into custody,
and more arrests were likely. It would be sometime Monday before
they were all entered into the system.

Lucas was in the kitchen at St. Larry's, apparently recruited to make sandwiches for anyone who needed a snack between street battles. He hadn't seen Sophie, and neither had anyone else there. A television was tuned to a news channel, where overheated pundits analyzed the significance of the scrimmaging between police and young protesters at the site of the Haymarket Riot. Scenes from Federal Plaza were intercut with archival footage of the violence at the Democratic Convention of 1968. I stared at the television, looking for Sophie, until I realized I was watching the same clips played over and over. Someone called out that police were coming up the front steps. As a woman loudly recited the rules of passive resistance as if reviewing a catechism lesson, I slipped out the back.

The next few hours were a blur. I trekked to coffeehouses and college hangouts and places where activists gathered to discuss their next move, giving my number out to anyone who would take it. The purple bruise on my cheek helped; people assumed I'd earned it in a scuffle with police, who were out in force. At one point, as I was talking to a crowd of Loyola students, bandannas around their necks, peace symbols and anarchist slogans sewn onto their clothes, a police officer down the block pointed, identifying me by name to three burly comrades. The students closed ranks to distract them while one led me down an alley, up a wooden staircase, and through an apartment with a fire escape that let out on another street. He treated it as a kind of hide-and-seek game, but I hoped nobody was getting beaten up or detained for helping me.

At 3:00 A.M., I was driving aimlessly, out of leads, when I spotted a cluster of people gathered on the steps of the Field Museum, the J. Edgar Hoover puppet on the top step, his giant disembodied head looking bizarre under the floodlit classical pillars of the museum. As I drove toward them, Jim called. Sophie still hadn't been logged in among those arrested, and he'd exhausted the list we'd made of places to check out. It sounded as if he was exhausted, too. He told me he'd start retracing his steps, just in case.

"Did you try that warehouse on Bubbly Creek?" I asked.

"I went by there earlier, didn't see anything."

"It's only a mile or two from where I am right now. After I have a word with J. Edgar and his friends, I'll head over there."

"A word with . . . You're talking to the FBI?"

"No, these people have a huge puppet. . . . Never mind. I'll call you once I check out the warehouse."

The pr-dawn sky was a sullen pewter color as I pulled into the gravel drive beside the old brick building. Jim's Acura was already there, nosed up against Nancy's old green Volvo. We'd found her. I closed my eyes for a moment, drained and relieved.

I climbed out of the car, slipped through the opening in the chain-link fence, and walked alongside the murky olive water that was still as a mirror except for the bubbles that broke the surface here and there. It smelled much worse than last time, as if the carcasses that had been dumped in the creek a century ago were filling the air with their slaughterhouse stench. "Sophie?" I called out as I walked through the waist-high weeds toward the dark, gaping door. "Jim?"

"She's here." The smell was stronger inside. I pushed against the half-opened door. Lucas's makeshift furniture was piled in a heap against it, as if Sophie had tried to barricade herself inside. Jim was sitting against the painted wall, his shirt stained with blood, knees drawn up. His face was gray and drawn in the light that seeped through the gap in the roof. Sophie cowered in the opposite corner, darting us anxious glances as she mumbled a slurry of secret words to herself. Her arms were a gory mess, blood seeping from her shoulders to her wrists.

"She thought we had implanted chips under her skin," Jim said. "She was trying to cut them out."

"Are you hurt?" I asked him.

"Me?"

"Your shirt."

He pulled it out to look at it. "Must be her blood. I had to take the knife away from her. And this." He lifted a hand from his lap to show me a familiar snub-nosed .38. "She took a shot at me."

"That smell."

"It's coming from the cellar." I stepped over to the door, opened it. Fat flies looped out, buzzing past my ears. The metal staircase that had been loosely bolted to the wall had fallen away into the darkness.

"Is it Rosa Saenz?"

Jim closed his eyes and nodded. "It's not Sophie's fault. She didn't know what she was doing."

As sirens began to howl in the distance, his daughter slid to the floor and pulled at her hair, whimpering in terror. I shut the basement door and went over to sit beside her. At first, she cowered away from me, but as the sirens drew closer she crept into to my arms and let me stroke her hair and rock her the way I had when she was a child, a little girl always wanting one more story.

TWENTY-THREE

The next days passed in a strange, still backwater of calm and domesticity. The outside world didn't exist, except when it appeared on the front doorstep every morning, smelling of newsprint and ink. Jim asked me to stay at the house in Stony Cliff so someone could be with the girls while Nancy was at the hospital and he tied up loose ends at work. The SAC had refused to accept Jim's resignation, urging him to retire at the end of the following month instead. It was a compromise both could live with. The Bureau would avoid the black eye of having a senior agent resign over the handling of the investigation into his father's death; Jim would go quietly in exchange for the health benefits and pension his family needed.

Nancy went to the hospital every day to be with Sophie. Though "with Sophie" was a stretch, she told me. When her daughter was in a manic state, she was demanding and contentious, seeking attention and constantly putting herself at risk through reckless behavior. What inevitably followed was less exhausting for her family, but worse for Sophie, the part of the cycle when the risk of suicide was highest. Now she was unresponsive and withdrawn and would spend the entire day in bed if the nurses didn't insist on making her get up and sit in the dayroom with the other patients. Nancy made an effort to speak to her daughter, telling her what her sisters were doing or about an interesting story she'd seen in the paper, but it was like talking to someone in a coma, no telling if any of it was getting through. "Of course," Nancy said, "Sophie is heavily sedated, taking painkillers, along with large doses of psychotropic drugs. The cuts on her arms aren't deep, but she cut away large patches of skin. A plastic surgeon has discussed procedures to deal with the scars, but . . ." Nancy's voice trailed away, as it always did when talking about the future. She wasn't ready to think about it yet, needing to stay in this small, placid bubble of daily routine for as long as possible.

Jim worried that reporters might find their way to their home in Stony Cliff, prying for information at a time when the family's emotions were too raw to share. But so far, investigators had kept a tight lid on Sophie's involvement. News reports were sketchy, limited to the official word that Rosa Saenz's body had been discovered in an abandoned building; the ME had determined the cause of death was a massive stroke, with blunt-force trauma as a possible contributing factor. A juvenile had been questioned at the scene, but no charges had been filed. The exact circumstances were still being pieced together by police. The mayor gathered community leaders and held a press conference. In his typically impatient and ungrammatical way the mayor pleaded with the city to remain calm and avoid irresponsible rumormongering while the police did their job. There would be no cover-up; he gave his word on it.

Wednesday evening, after the girls were in bed, the three of us sat talking over a bottle of wine. It was good to see Nancy curled against Jim on the couch, his arm casually draped around her shoulders, occasionally stroking her arm. After a meandering conversation, Jim mentioned he'd talked to a friend about representing Sophie if charges were brought against her. He murmured a name and Nancy nodded. "Nice bloke. He'll do a good job."

"He's sure a plea can be worked out. Given her age and history, the court will go for treatment, not a prison sentence."

"Court-ordered treatment—it's a kind of commitment, then?" Nancy asked.

"It certainly isn't voluntary."

"Hold on," I said. "There's no reason to assume Sophie was responsible for Rosa's death."

"She told me—"

"Sophie was psychotic at the time; you can't trust what she said."

"Guess we should hire Anni for the defense," Jim joked.

Nancy wasn't amused. She set her wineglass down so hard, I thought the stem would snap. "She may not be legally responsible for what happened, but if her actions led to a woman's death, there have to be consequences. We can't let things go on like this."

"But listen. Rosa was missing for over a week before her body was found. Sophie was doing fine at that time. A little manic, but not delusional. Not violent."

"You sound like Sophie. You'd prefer to blame everything on some elaborate conspiracy," Nancy said. "That would be convenient, wouldn't it? The fact is, she's been utterly unpredictable for years, capable of anything. You have no idea what it's been like." She snatched up her empty wineglass and went into the kitchen.

"Sorry. This is tough for her," Jim said in a low voice.

"I know. But Jim, the timing doesn't make any sense. Sophie wasn't delusional until the day of the demonstration. That body had already been there for days."

"You can't be sure, in this heat. And anyway, Nancy's right. Sophie's good at fooling people when she's manic, and she's unpredictable."

"All I'm saying is, don't let this lawyer cut a deal too quickly. She could end up in a facility for years because of something she didn't do."

Nancy came back in with a bottle of wine. "At least she'd be getting some help," she said firmly, putting an end to the discussion. "Anyone want to try this Shiraz?"

o official statement had been made about the murder indictment pending against Rosa Saenz, but an unnamed high-ranking source at the Justice Department told a *Tribune* reporter that the case was being reevaluated. Apparently, a battle was going on between two factions, one that favored taking a firm law-and-order stance and one that wanted to avoid a political disaster before the next election. Letters to the editor and op-ed columns were also divided, with Rosa depicted as a saint or a terrorist mastermind, a heroine or a throwback to a turbulent and dangerous era.

But in the Tilquist household, we had an unspoken agreement to leave the radio and television turned off, except when the girls watched old videos. Nancy had no interest in anything beyond her family's immediate needs. Lucy was too young to read the papers, and Alice only looked at the comics, pointedly avoiding the front page. She had shed her pose of adolescent cynicism and spent a lot of time playing Let's Pretend with her little sister, as if retreating to an earlier, less complicated age.

"She's being far too sweet and even-tempered," Nancy mused one afternoon as Alice and Lucy watched a video of *Beauty and the Beast,* the two of them so mesmerized, they almost looked drugged. "It isn't normal." But she didn't want to force Alice to talk about her feelings, not yet. She said maybe she would make an appointment with a therapist for her, but not until later, when things were more settled. . . .

I kept my phone switched off but checked my messages each morning. The police had found my rental car with the front window smashed and the trunk jimmied open. The cop I spoke to said he hoped there wasn't anything valuable in there, because there wasn't much chance I'd recover it, not in that neighborhood. The rental company wanted to talk to me about my insurance. Harvey reported he had been able to defer the prelim and was hopeful the prosecution would drop the complaints against me altogether. Dugan told my voice mail that he and some friends had cleaned up the spilled food in my apartment and fixed the broken door. Az Abkerian's story, complete with photos of the destruction and the word *traitor* scrawled across my wall, came out the day after the demonstration and was causing a big stink. The official line was that some angry white supremacist was behind the incident, but Internal Affairs was investigating. Dugan promised he would feed my cat and keep an eye on things until . . . whenever. There was a brief silence before he said good-bye, just enough room for an unspoken question.

I slept on a foldout couch in the Tilquists' study, usually reading late into the night, sipping a glass of wine as I tried to adjust to the muffled stillness of central air conditioning. It was hard to sleep without the usual hum of city noises. One night, I was awakened by a cry, cut off before I could be sure I hadn't dreamed it. When I went upstairs to check, I could hear the murmur of voices in Nancy and Jim's room. Alice came out of her bedroom. Just her dad, she told me, sleepily padding toward the bathroom. He had bad dreams sometimes.

I asked Nancy about it the next morning. "The war," she said vaguely. "Sometimes he's in a burning village, or motoring up a river full of floating bodies. That one was a favorite after Katrina; he had it night after night. This time, he was crossing a rice paddy with his platoon while a sniper shot at them. Rather dull stuff, as his dreams go." I wondered if he'd told her Sophie had tried to shoot him and whether that had entwined itself with his dreams, but I didn't ask.

On Friday, I called Dugan to arrange to get into my flat. Dugan offered to meet me there Saturday morning with the keys to the new door he and his friends had installed. Since Jim would be home all weekend and could watch the girls while Nancy was at the hospital, it seemed a good time to get started on the cleanup.

As I was getting ready to go, Jim told me he had something for me. I followed him into the garage. He opened the trunk of his Acura, lifted out a Kevlar vest. "On loan from the Bureau. Hope it fits. It's the smallest one I could find."

"What's this for?"

"It's just precautionary. Don't mention this to Nancy, but I'm not spending all my time at work emptying my desk. I got the investigation into the Nordic League started, and I want to see it through. Brian Folkstone is getting squirrelly, and we still don't have a line on the crazy one, Alton Brinks."

"You actually expect me to wear this thing?" I lifted the heavy vest. "It's ninety-five degrees in the shade."

"Jesus, Anni. He's made threats against your life. You're about to return to an apartment he tore to—"

"He's not the one who trashed my flat. I don't even think he made those calls."

"So, fine, some pissed-off cop did it. Who cares? Just humor me and wear the damn vest, would you?"

Dugan was leaning against his Jeep outside my house. He made a pained face when he caught sight of me. "I know," I said. "It was supposed to wash out." Some of it had; what was left was a strange purplish color.

"Not your hair, that bruise. Looks sore."

"Looks like an oil slick, but it doesn't hurt anymore."

"What happened?"

"According to the official record, I resisted arrest."

"Huh. Wonder what the other guy looks like." He handed me a set of keys, picked up a sack from a Polish bakery from the hood of his car, and followed me down the gangway to the back of the house. "Your cat doesn't like me. He always hides when I'm around."

"He doesn't like anybody." Dugan followed me upstairs, watched me fit the shiny key into the new lock. "Thanks for doing all this. How much do I owe you?"

"Forget it."

"No, really."

"Some asshole cops did the damage. Let some cops who aren't assholes take care of it. Seems fair to me."

I steeled myself as I opened the door, but it wasn't as bad as I'd expected. "You guys did a lot of work." The floor was clean, the broken glass and couch stuffing had been disposed of, and all the papers that had been scattered around were in a neat stack on my desk. I went over to the wall, ran my hand across it. The angry word was painted over, the gash in the wall repaired. But even though the surface was so smooth that I couldn't feel the place where the drywall had been patched, it felt as if there was an unhealed scar there.

"Hope you don't mind, but I found the name of your insurance company in your files. They sent an adjustor out. His card's on your desk."

"Thanks."

"Most of your dishes got broken. Some of your books were ruined. Your grandfather's desk has a big scratch on it, but it's not real deep. A little sanding and refinishing, it should be good as new."

Something Martin could do, I figured. "Listen, there was a photo stuck to the wall. . . ."

"I took it to the place my aunt used to get her pictures restored, one I told you about? The guy there said he'd see what he could do. Coffee?" He held up his bag.

"Let's drink it on the porch. It's too stuffy in here." Especially with a bulletproof vest under my blouse. I knew Dugan couldn't miss it, but he didn't comment. Instead, as we sat on the top step, drinking coffee and eating pastries he redesigned my backyard, pointing out where the brick patio should go, the raised flower bed, the kind of ground cover that would work in shade. "Going to the service tonight?" he asked as he put his empty coffee cup back into the paper bag.

"I don't think so. I don't like crowds." Father Sikora had accepted a rapidly negotiated plea a few days earlier and had been released on probation. I hadn't talked to him since the night he heard Pete Spellman's confession, but though he had avoided speaking to the media, he was quoted in Rosa's obituary. It was only one line, a few simple words, but they carried more heartfelt loss than all the statements of outrage and grief being reported in the press. He was among several priests who were going to lead memorial Mass for Rosa that had been moved to Humboldt Park when it became clear the number of people who wanted to attend was far too large for St. Larry's. "You assigned to it?"

"Yeah, everybody's on OT. Low-key presence, though, no riot gear. We have to be on our best behavior. Hizzoner's going to be there." Stung by the bad publicity generated by the number of arrests made at the demonstration the previous Sunday, and the flurry of lawsuits that followed, the mayor had announced he was going to attend, as if to say neither police nor citizens would dare cause trouble, not in his presence. He was also saying to Rosa's supporters and to the faction at the Justice Department that wanted the case shelved that he was taking their side.

Dugan brushed crumbs off his clothes. "It's weird, how Rosa Saenz ended up in the same place we found you. In a basement, just like the man she was accused of killing all those years ago."

"Except she didn't."

"You've made that perfectly clear. It was good work."

"Only I still don't know who killed him."

"One of his informants. That seems to be the working theory anyway."

"What's the theory about Rosa?"

"Hard to say. Only thing anyone seems to know for sure is that it wasn't suicide."

"The paper said she died of a stroke."

"Technically, that's what killed her. But she had a blow to the head, too."

"So they're looking at a homicide?"

"Not necessarily. That staircase that was so shaky? If the bolts failed and it came apart from the wall, it might have caused her to fall and bang her head. The body was lying there for a week in this heat; it's not so easy to be sure of the sequence of events. Finished with that?" He took my empty cup from me, dropped it into the bag.

"Thanks for the breakfast. And everything."

"If there's anything more I can do—"

"No, I just need to figure out what's broken, what I need to do next."

After he left, I went back inside, opened the windows wide, made a list of things I had to replace or repair, going through my cupboards and drawers, trying not to feel the presence of those angry men. Even with the wall painted over, they'd left a lingering threat in the room, a coiled promise: You'll never be safe. You'll never know when it could happen again, or where. . . .

"Fuck you," I said out loud, then went into the bathroom, where my rainbow-hued cheek was reflected in the maze of the shattered mirror over the sink. I stripped off my blouse, the Kevlar vest, and the cotton undershirt that was drenched with itchy sweat. I showered off, dressed in fresh clothes, and dropped the vest beside the door so I wouldn't forget it. They weren't going to intimidate me, not in my own house. I added "bathroom mirror" to my list.

Then I sat at my grandfather's desk and read through the stack of papers, trying to fit in what I could remember from the notes that were on my missing computer. I set the files aside and sat back, rubbing a finger along the gouge in the polished wood, trying to put together the pieces of this case so they made sense.

TWENTY-FOUR

Early Monday morning, federal agents executed a search warrant at Brian Folkstone's apartment and seized eight illegal handguns, two shotguns, a high-powered rifle, and a box of armor-piercing ammunition. Folkstone and two other members of the Nordic League were taken into custody. A press conference was held in one of the briefing rooms of the Dirksen Building late in the afternoon, just in time for the evening news. The authorities apparently hoped it might ameliorate some of the bad press generated by the violence following the Vigil for Truth demonstration and the discovery of Rosa Saenz's body—particularly since the U.S. attorney making the announcement could point to Arne Tilquist's son as the agent who had doggedly pursued these violent white supremacists, the crowning achievement of a long and distinguished career in criminal justice. See? We can be good guys when we try.

Access to the media event was tightly controlled. I didn't want to see the performance anyway. Instead, I waited outside the Federal Building as office workers flooded out with the press. More agents and officials left. And finally Jim emerged, tugging at the knot in his tie as he stepped out into the heat.

"Anni? What are you doing here? Are the girls—"

"Nancy took them to a friend's house for the afternoon."

"She's not too happy about all this dog and pony show. Were you in there?"

"No."

"It was stupid. People who didn't give a shit, trying to make it sound important. But it's my last case. I want to see this through."

"I need to talk to you about something."

"You got that vest on?" I nodded. "Okay, then. Let's walk to the park."

We headed down Adams toward the lake. In front of the Art Institute, tourists carrying bags from the museum store staggered like zombies, stunned with the heat. We headed up the sidewalk toward Millennium Park.

"I've been thinking about this case. Your father's murder," I finally said. "For thirty-five years, there was an easy explanation. But the evidence didn't stack up. I found a few pieces that fit together, and they seemed to point to a man who had hung around the fringes of the group, trying to fit in while selling intelligence to the feds."

"Pete Spellman. He hasn't been found yet."

"I was wrong about him. Turned out he had other things on his conscience, like ratting out his friends and getting them killed. He didn't shoot your father." I paused by the fountain, where a fine, cool spray drifted toward us. Kids in bathing suits splashed in the wading pool between the two tall glass pillars, their shrieks rising whenever the giant animated faces projected on the glass pursed their digitally generated lips to spit out fire-hose sprays. "No, it had to be bigger than Pete Spellman, something so big that the woman they originally accused had to die so it wouldn't be exposed at trial. So important that the priest who had given her shelter had to be locked up, and even the junkie who talked to a witness had to be silenced."

Jim frowned at the kids splashing in the fountain, as if he was thinking of something else. "Let's keep moving," he said, and started strolling toward the gardens, which were bristling with prairie grasses and flowers.

"Most murders are so small," I said, "they barely make it into the paper. A family dispute, a drunken argument. A pointless burst of anger that ends in a death for one and a lifetime of regret for the other. Nearly all of the homicides I worked were like that. But this one, this was different, part of a conspiracy that has lasted for decades. And even while Fiske made me feel powerless, always looking over my shoulder, making me think my movements were being traced, my calls tapped, I felt as if I was at the center of something huge and meaningful, trying to figure it out. And the weird thing is, it felt kind of good. Like Sophie when she's manic. All those interlocking patterns, just about to snap into place. Life usually isn't like that."

"So did you figure it out?" Jim asked.

"I'm not sure. It suited Fiske to make this crime seem big and important, just like it suited your father's colleagues to pin it on a known radical, to give everyone the impression your father died for the cause. It suited me and Thea and all those people in Federal Plaza holding candles and chanting slogans to think the government was engaged in a big conspiracy to cover up the truth, because it fit so well with other things that made us angry. But what it if was an ordinary crime? A small, sad family dispute, like most of them? I was looking for someone who was drinking heavily, suffered from nightmares, who was confused about his loyalties. Which pretty much describes you thirty-five years ago."

I couldn't bring myself to look at him, see how he was reacting. I took a breath, feeling sick. "The thing is, I can see you killing your father in an impulsive moment. I can see your father's friends wanting to pin it on a known radical. But that you would kill Rosa and blame it on your daughter, that's the part I'm having trouble with." *Tell me I'm crazy, Jim. Tell me I have it all wrong . . .*

"I didn't kill Rosa," Jim said at last. A tour group started up a garden path toward us. We headed away from them, walking toward the wide-open lawn under the pavilion trellis.

"She called," he said. "Asked me to meet at that mansion where

Sophie had taken her to hide. Spellman had told her he saw me leave that basement with the gun still in my hand. The Bureau told him to keep it quiet, and he had for years, until he recognized her a few weeks ago. She wasn't sure how to approach me and waited too long. They got a tip and she had to run. She wanted it to end; she wanted me to tell the world what really happened. Only I couldn't. What would happen to the girls, to Nancy, if I went to prison? When Rosa reached out and put her hand on my arm, I thought . . . I don't know, she seemed so . . . so *powerful* suddenly. I pushed her away and—" He stared, as if it was happening right in front of him.

"She hit her head," I said softly.

"No. I didn't push her that hard. Something weird happened. She sat down suddenly with this strange look on her face and said something that didn't make any sense. It took me awhile to realize she was having a stroke. I started to drive her to the hospital, but she had another stroke and died while we were still in the car. So I thought—no, I didn't think; I just acted. Took her body to that warehouse, pulled the staircase away from the wall so it would look like an accident. It felt as if someone else was making all the decisions, fixing the problem, like after I took that gun from my father and shot him. I just tossed it away and went home, and I never told anyone about it."

"What about Sophie?"

"I didn't plan it that way. But the state she was in, cutting the skin off her arms? It just seemed . . . I knew she wouldn't be sent to prison. She'd get the help she needs."

"And you could keep lying to all of us."

"Anni—"

"You were my friend, the one who listened to me, who helped me find out what happened to my mother."

"We never found out what happened; we only found her grave— and a safe place for you and your brother to live. Wasn't that enough? Isn't that what really matters?"

"It was a lie, all of it. I don't even know who you are anymore."

He looked around to see if we were alone, then turned to me suddenly. I felt a blow in the center of my chest; then something hot seared my shoulder. We fell together, his weight pinning me down. I tried to push him away, but he gripped me tightly as the pain drilled through me, hot blood soaking my clothes. I heard screams and police announcing and, under the shrill howl of sirens, the echoing memory of gunshots.

But it wasn't until I struggled out from under Jim's weight that I saw the two holes torn in his back, saw the scarlet pool seeping out from under him into the grass. His hand twitched and his eyes locked on mine as he tried to say something, but only blood came out.

high school linebacker and a construction worker from Honduras tackled Alton Brinks as he took aim at me for another shot. He was arraigned on two counts of attempted murder and several lesser offenses. The state's attorney stood ready to upgrade the charges if Jim's condition didn't improve.

He lay in a room full of machinery, nearly hidden by all the tubes and pumps and monitors. As soon as he was moved out of the ICU, I dragged my IV stand into his room and found a place in a corner to plug it in. At first, the medical staff objected, but they eventually let me stay. My wound was uncomplicated. Unlike Jim, I hadn't even lost that much blood.

Nancy sat in the chair beside him during the day, holding his hand. Her parents flew in from England to look after the girls and provide their daughter with support that mostly consisted of pats on the shoulder, murmurings about the weather, and thermoses of tea. When they stopped by, they would glance at me nervously, even after I was discharged and wearing real clothes instead of a hospital gown.

Dozens of cops and agents who knew him from work stopped by and said well-meaning things. When Nancy left for home at night, I would take her seat beside him and listen to the mechanical whoosh of air that inflated his lungs, the gurgle as excess fluid was suctioned from his chest cavity. Sometimes I'd have one-sided conversations with him in my head. *What should I do?* Or *I didn't mean what I said.* Or just *Don't go.*

But he did, three weeks later. Without ever regaining consciousness.

TWENTY-FIVE

s this where we do it? Just sitting in chairs like this?"

"If that's all right."

"I thought . . . I don't know, I thought there was special furniture or something."

"You've been watching too many old movies."

Three months had passed since Jim's funeral. There had been speeches and funny, tearful stories and bagpipes; more food than would fit in Nancy's refrigerator; too many reporters and television cameras. But eventually the clamor died down, the grandparents returned home to the UK, and Nancy and her daughters settled into a new routine—one with a big hole in it the size of Jim.

The police investigation concluded that Sophie had played no role in Rosa Saenz's death, which was ruled to be of natural causes. A spokesman told reporters she'd suffered a fatal stroke that might have occurred as she attempted to use a staircase that was not securely bolted to the wall; the resulting fall would account for the head trauma. Sophie was released from the hospital as soon as the medications had done their work and her depression lifted enough for her to manage. Nancy and Alice and even little Lucy were seeing a therapist to deal with their grief. It helped, Nancy told me. Hint, hint.

But I didn't want to talk about my feelings. I couldn't, not yet. Instead, I filled my day with tasks that could be checked off a list. I shopped for mismatched dishes at a St. Vincent de Paul shop, restocked my cupboards, and ordered a new laptop. I wrote my report for Thea Adelman while sitting on the couch that Father Sikora had

had a couple of parishioners haul up the back stairs, supposedly a do-
nation that none of their needy families wanted, but it was too nice
for me to believe that. I couldn't work at Golly's desk, because as
soon as Martin saw the scratch, he had to refinish it. It wasn't just a
flaw; it was a disturbance of the time-space continuum, at least in
Martin's universe. He had stripped off the old finish and was slowly
sanding the surface smooth, using finer and finer grades of sandpaper
wrapped around a block, enjoying the repetitive rhythm of it, making it right, taking his time.

I wished I could fix my problems like that, just rubbing back and
forth until it was all smooth again. Instead, I did some routine investigative work that the Adelmans put my way and the occasional job
for one of Nancy's acquaintances. My specialty of tracking down disturbed teens was apparently in demand.

"So what's the trouble?" He brought me back to the present with a
gentle prompt.

"I need to talk to someone, but it's . . . What we say in here, it's
privileged, right?"

"Yes."

"Because that's the problem. I don't know if I should tell anyone
this. Or if I shouldn't keep it quiet. I don't know the right thing to
do."

"Why don't you tell me for starters. Then you can decide if it goes
any further."

"Okay. It's the case I was working on, right? Rosa Saenz was on
the run for over thirty years, accused of murdering Arne Tilquist on
the day after Christmas in 1972. About a year and half ago, a profile
of him ran in a Minneapolis alternative paper; the article drew paral-
lels between the dirty tricks that Arne was part of and today's climate
of surveillance and political repression. It quoted Arne's son, Jim. He
sounded reasonable, a champion of civil liberties, even. I don't know
where Rosa was all that time, but I'm guessing she read that story and

thought maybe, just maybe, she could talk him into reopening the case, setting things right.

"But when she came back to Chicago, she found out she knew only half of the story. The informant she thought was responsible for the murder wasn't. Pete Spellman was a snitch, a man who played both sides back in the seventies, a man who knew the authorities had gone way too far when they massacred a radical group in a farmhouse in Wisconsin. Arne called him to a meeting and brought a gun he'd seized earlier, a weapon that could be linked to Rosa. Not only did they have a sales record that she'd bought it at a pawnshop; she'd left her prints on the shells when she loaded it. He planned to use that gun to get rid of his informant, who knew too much, and Rosa would take the fall. Nice and tidy. Only his son followed him. His son, Jim, who was probably drunk at the time, angry about the situation in Wisconsin, about everything his father stood for. His nerves were in tatters after his tour in Vietnam. They'd been arguing a lot."

I could picture his father taunting him: You don't even have the stomach to hunt deer. What made you think you could be a warrior? Jesus, how did I end up with a longhaired Communist pansy for a son?

"They had a confrontation down there. Jim got the gun away from his father and—*bang*—shot him in the head."

It all happened so fast, so forever. Backing away, the jars of peaches rocking on the shelves and smashing on the floor. His powerful, handsome father lying with his coat fanned out around him, looking up at the ceiling with an "I'll be damned" look on his dead face.

"Spellman saw Jim leave. He knew what had happened. And he was told to keep it quiet."

"Because the authorities had someone better to blame?"

"Right. They wanted to take Verna Basswood down, and besides, they were cops. They'd look after their own. They got Arne's messed-up kid into some kind of treatment, and he straightened up. Went on the job. Became a detective, the one who listened to an eleven-year-old girl who needed help. My best friend. They protected him. And I'm the one who got him killed."

"Let's back up a minute. Why did you need help, and what did he do?"

"My mother abandoned us when my brother was four and I was two. We were in foster care, but my brother was having a lot of problems. We really needed a different living situation, or he was going to end up in some horrible institution. Jim helped me find a place to live and taught me how to handle my anger. Showed me how to act so my feelings didn't show. Guess he was good at that."

"You sound angry now."

"I am. I'm *so* pissed off, the way he . . . Oh shit."

"Take your time." He waited.

"Thing is, he's a hero, right? He took those bullets for me. Hold the presses. He saved my life. But the only reason that guy was taking shots at us was because Jim stirred him and his stupid little gang of racists up as a distraction. Or penance, or whatever."

"Penance?"

"He didn't like the way things were going with the Bureau. Neither did his wife; she nagged him about it all the time. Maybe he thought if he went after dangerous white supremacists, it would balance things out. Only they weren't dangerous; they were just a pathetic little bunch of losers, until they thought they were under attack. He made me wear a bulletproof vest. But even though it turned out he'd been getting death threats from them himself, he didn't wear one." I unconsciously rubbed the place where the first bullet had hit my chest, just above my heart. The bruise had faded long ago, but I knew exactly where it was.

"What does that tell you?"

"That he wanted out. That he didn't want to face the truth. He wanted his family to remember him as a good man, not a killer who let someone else take the heat. But it pisses me off, because he left me here with this, this *knowledge,* and I don't know what to do with it."

"You can't save Rosa with it."

"No, but . . ."

"The Justice Department is all but admitting the case against her was fabricated. They aren't pursuing any other leads at this time."

"But he set me up."

"You think he knew Alton Brinks was looking for you that day?"

"Looking for both of us. Jim kept watching over his shoulder, moving us away from where kids were. They'd just had a press conference; he had to have known it was possible."

"So why was it your fault? I'm not sure I understand that part. You had a job to do—"

"That's another thing that pisses me off. Why did he tell me to take that job in the first place?"

"What do you think?"

"At first, I said I wouldn't take the job because, you know, it was his dad. And he told me it was the only way he'd know what was going on, that Fiske wouldn't tell him anything. And he wanted the truth. Which was a big lie."

"Maybe he wanted you to know the truth."

"No. I think he just felt bad about Rosa taking the fall. Soon as I had enough evidence to create reasonable doubt, he tried to get me to back off. He might have even used my brother. When I finally had a lead on Pete Spellman, when I was going to pick him up, I told Jim where I was headed. And next thing I know, some guy with FBI credentials turns up asking for Spellman, and then my brother goes missing. I'm not sure it was Jim's doing, but if it was, that was pretty low."

"So that's why you're angry?"

"No! Jesus."

"Because he lied to you?"

"I'm angry because I need him and he's *gone*."

"It's not the first time someone's left you."

"My mom? That's totally different. She was only eighteen. She'd been on the street since she was fourteen. She used drugs and she turned tricks, and she knew she couldn't take care of us. I didn't always understand that; I was angry with her for years. But now I've seen enough teenaged mothers to know how hard that must have been, for her, to walk away from the only people in the world who looked up to her, who loved her no matter what. But she knew she had to do it, and it must have hurt like hell."

"Maybe Jim had to do it, too. Or maybe he just saw a man aiming a gun at you and did what came naturally. Could be as simple as that."

"Nothing about this is simple."

"Somebody important in your life kept a secret from you." He sneaked a look at his watch. "And now he's gone and you miss him like crazy. Not all that complicated."

"It is to me. Looks like our time's up, huh?"

"I have another appointment, but we can talk again. If it helps."

"Listen, I probably should have told you this up front, but I'm not really Catholic. I mean, this foster mother had us baptized and made us go to Mass, but at the next place, they were Baptists, so I don't actually know how this absolution thing works."

"First, you tell me your sins."

"Weren't you listening? I got my best friend killed."

"Bullshit. Alton Brinks is the one who killed him, not you. But if it makes you feel any better, say three Hail Marys and three Our Fathers."

"Do you have those written down somewhere, because I don't think I remember all the words."

"Let's go for alternative sentencing. Talk to Sister Helen, find out when the next training for her homeless outreach program is. She'll put you through your paces." Father Sikora pushed himself up from his chair, suppressing a small sigh of pain. He pulled the stole off from around his neck, tossed it on his desk, winced at his watch and felt for his cigarettes. "The budget committee will have to wait. I need a smoke."

I t was one of those blustery mornings in March, with a Canadian cold front duking it out with spring. The wind was acting like a juvenile delinquent, looking up women's skirts, snatching hats off old men's heads and rolling them down the street. There was a cutting edge to it, stinging my cheeks and numbing my fingers, the kind of day when Chicago lives up to its nickname. I'd been up all night and was looking for a cup of coffee when I ran into Dugan on Division Street. He looked as exhausted as I felt and was headed for the same place: Leo's Lunchroom.

It had gone upscale, like the rest of the neighborhood, since I had first started going there years ago. Roast duck and salmon had been added to their offerings, but they still made the best Reuben sandwich in the known universe, and you could get breakfast all day, or until they ran out of potatoes. That's what it said on the menu anyway; I'd never known them to actually run out. We sat at the counter and got mugs of coffee. "I'm buying," I said, and he started to object. "I still owe you a meal, remember?"

"Oh, right." I'd called him when a UPS truck brought the package: two tattered and stained photographs, two restored ones in frames, looking as if they'd belonged to someone who took much better care of her valuables than I did. We'd set a date to share a meal, but something came up and he'd had to cancel. We'd tried three more times, but if it wasn't his job interfering, it was mine. "We have to start meeting like this," he joked, but his smile didn't last long.

"You look tired," I said

"Didn't sleep too well last night."

"A case you're working?"

"One of those where you walk in the door and you know what happened. Hospital reports a suspicious death. Mama says the baby fell out of his crib, but guess what?"

"The boyfriend?"

"He can't figure out what's the big deal. It was an accident, and besides, he said he was sorry. He's sixteen." Dugan traced a scratch in the countertop with a fingertip. "What kept you up last night?"

I burrowed into my leather bag, pulled out a snapshot. "Ever see this kid around?"

"He's missing?"

"Not at the moment. I found him a few hours ago having a conversation with an angel in Calvary Cemetery. Time before that, he was trying to hop a freight train to Argentina. He's schizophrenic. The meds work most of the time, but every few months his voices tell him it's time to get in trouble. His parents pay me a retainer to chase after him. You ever see him doing something idiotic, give me a call." I gave him one of the million or so cards I'd had printed up. I'd never get rid of them all.

"Whoa, looks official."

"I'm not hard up for work. You'd be surprised how many people with money have screwed-up kids."

"I used to work out of Belmont, remember? Doesn't surprise me at all." He tucked it into his jacket pocket and scratched his crooked nose.

Our food came. We ate in silence for a while—or rather, I ate; Dugan pushed food around his plate. "You should come by sometime," I said. "You know the wall you and your friends fixed? I got the hottest young artist in town to decorate it for me."

"White latex wasn't good enough for you?"

"It was fine, but this stencil is really cool. Edgy street art, to quote the catalog. This guy used to beautify the city at no charge, but now he's got a dealer who sells his stuff at a gallery in Lincoln Park." Lucas was nervous about the gushing praise and figured it was all some kind of scam—a pretty accurate description of the art business, actually. But it provided enough money to buy supplies and pay his share of the rent on a flat over a pawnshop on Chicago Avenue that he shared with young friends whose housekeeping style was a good match for the squats he was used to. He probably felt right at home in that mess. And while he missed choosing his own canvases, he didn't have to worry about getting arrested.

As I rounded up the last of my scrambled eggs, Dugan was picking at his food, probably mulling over the mystery of a sixteen-year-old boy and a dead child. I pointed my fork at him. "Breakfast is the most important meal of the day. Clean your plate."

"How come you always sound like my mom?" But he made an effort and got through most of it before wiping his chin with a napkin. "That body you found last fall? Got a lead she came up from East Saint Louis, but it didn't pan out. Still haven't identified her."

I had been carrying one of Sister Helen's canvas bags around on a crisp autumn evening, sharing a thermos of coffee with a couple of geezers who were warming themselves around an oil-can fire, when they looked at each other and one told me there was a bad smell coming from an abandoned car two blocks over. I checked it out and called the police. A week or two later, I mentioned it to Dugan when we were on the phone. She was in her mid-twenties, undernourished, eight weeks pregnant, and loaded on fentanyl-laced skag, like Tyler and at least three dozen fatal overdoses in the past year.

"Probably never will," I said.

"I hate not even having a name for her, though. Feels wrong."

"You can go to her service anyway."

"What service?"

"At the Chicago Temple. They hold a memorial service toward the end of May for everyone buried by the county. I'll be there. I always go."

He looked at me, remembering my mother, then stared down into his coffee as if the steam rising off it might spell out something insightful he could say. I spread jelly on my last piece of toast, feeling drowsy. But when I glanced out the front windows, I was jolted awake. "*Shit!* I don't believe it."

"What?" Dugan looked around.

"It's snowing again."

"Don't worry, this late in the season it won't stick, and we could use the moisture. Which reminds me." He patted his pockets, came out with an envelope and a stub of a pencil. "We have work to do."

"We do?"

"It's almost April. We have to start planning your garden."